The Bo(

A Hollywood Tale

By J. Michael Willard

VIDALIA HOUSE PUBLISHERS
Orlando, Kyiv, Istanbul

NONFICTION BY: J. MICHAEL WILLARD

My Time to Shine (biography of lead singers in the
Platters, Temptations and the Drifters)
The Flack: A PR Journey
Dancing With the Bear: Crisis Management in Eastern
Europe
The Optimistic Alien
The Accidental Headline
The Portfolio Bubble
The Silverback Diaries
Conquer Your Fears: Own the Room

FICTION BY: J. MICHAEL WILLARD

Extra Wives
The Legacy of Moon Pie Jefferson
Urania: A Fable
A Thief Wears a Burning Hat
A Mean Old Man
Killing Friends
Sweet Sofia and the Serial Killer
The Book of Fairleigh: A Hollywood Tale

Contact: J. Michael Willard mike.Willard@twg.com.ua
Cover Design: Valya Willard

DEDICATION

To my children:
Kelly, Rob, Maria, Mia, and Valya

May you always realize as George Eliot (Mary Ann Evans) wrote: It's never too late to be who you might have been.

CONTENTS

CHAPTER 1
AN ITINERANT COUPLE

Ruth Johns wanted a baby. That's how it all began.

Her husband Joshua either shot blanks, or his sperm count was less than his IQ, the number of which could — most likely— be counted on his seven toes. In a whiskey-inspired moment, he had shot three appendages off to claim disability payments.

It didn't work. Johns found he couldn't fill out the paperwork without having proper identification, such as a birth certificate, driver's license, or even a Social Security number.

He had none of those. Neither Joshua nor Ruth, for any official purposes, existed. They originally had come from so far up an East Tennessee hollow that birds didn't even venture. As far as officialdom was concerned, they were ghosts.

The Johns had been seen around the Mall of

Millenia in West Orlando for the last two weeks. They were easily identifiable. They appeared eccentric but harmless. The mall was upscale, not the sort of place a vagabond couple would typically frequent. Joshua carried a large duffle bag over his shoulder. It appeared to be empty.

If this were England, the Johns' would be associated with the Travelers, a wandering tribe of Romani ethnic journeyers. In the US, the descriptor probably would be the Johnsons', meaning a group that did shoddy home repair work, fleecing hard-working people out of their hard-earned money. In Romania, they would be called gypsies, or Roma.

They were none of these. Instead, the Johns were mountain people, the sort of folks often ridiculed in television shows by actors whose tender feet had never felt the dew or hands that grappled for catfish along the banks of a muddy river. They were far removed from civilization, not necessary in distance, but certainly from the mores of white tablecloth society.

Joshua was tall, very tall at 6'5", and he wore a floppy, misshapen hat with a Mickey Mouse patch atop his frazzled mop of dirty gray hair. He sported an unkempt salt and pepper beard laced with tobacco stains. His bib-overalls were two inches too short and had numerous holes that revealed his long, red underwear. He looked a lot like the cowboy sidekick Gabby Hays, only scruffier.

Joshua Johns also had a constant smile on his face, which made him distinctive in this crowd of people who went about their Christmas shopping like water bugs scurrying around at the edge of a pond. He tipped his hat to the ladies and had a gracious "mornin'" and 'evening'" for the gents. He patted little kids on the head, which caused parents to pull their charges a little closer and give the "don't talk to strangers" admonishment. Unfortunately, he was missing two teeth that otherwise would have been prominent, giving his mouth the look of a Jack-O-Lantern. This affected his speech, causing him to hiss each greeting.

In one hand, he clutched a Gideon Bible, which he had taken from the Highway 441 Motel, a cheap, mostly trucker stop away from tourist destinations. The Bible seemed more a prop than any religious affectation. He toted it like a loaf of bread and wasn't into converting sinners. It was a curious statement; and, in a way, lent credibility to the couple's general appearance. He had paid in advance for the room with a Visa card pilfered from a college student's backpack at the Greyhound Bus station. This was the way the Johns lived—by their half-wits and a primordial survival instinct. Practice had made them rather good at it.

His wife Ruth appeared a good quarter-century younger than her husband, mainly because Joshua could have passed for 40 or 70 in age. She completed a bizarre paradox, an image, and dress most conveniently conveyed by women folk in Amish settlements. Ruth wore her jet black hair in a severe bun and, strangely, a 1960s-style choker collar around her neck. She was a foot and inches shorter than her husband and measured to just below his expansive chest. She wore a frown, a natural downward curl of her mouth, and it seemed tattooed on her bony, milky white face. Her dress was a plain, A-line dark mustard skirt that came almost to the top of her old-fashioned, lace-up, and severely pointed black shoes. She looked like somebody's great-great-grandmother from a Civil War-era tintype photo. She was only 25.

For the first couple of days, the mall's security had followed them around. They mostly loitered in the food court, purchasing copious amounts of burgers and fries. They dodged in and out of shops, never making a purchase. Often they could be seen in the center of the mall at an elaborate Santa Claus throne. It was here a line of fresh-faced children waited impatiently to offer utterly selfish wishes for Christmas Day. The couple took pleasure in the reaction of kids sitting in Santa's lap. It was only then that Ruth's perpetual gloom gave way to a slight smile.

When they first made an appearance, the mall's security team closely followed their movements on the CCTV cameras. The guards were particularly interested in the green canvas duffle bag that the tall man hoisted about effortlessly. They eventually determined that it was simply a bag that two street people used to collect whatever loot they amassed for everyday living. They were not shoplifters, for not once were they seen shoving an item into the bag or their pockets. After a while, Joshua and Ruth were simply part of the crazy quilt of characters that makes up the American mall scene. However, the Johns were decidedly different.

"It doesn't have to be a baby," Ruth said in a sing-song voice as she tugged at Joshua's sleeve in front of the Santa display. "That little girl there is so cute."

"If that's what you want, Ruthie," Joshua said as if she were referring to a Suzy No Tears doll and not a living being. "She's tiny. Shouldn't be difficult."

The girl to whom she pointed was a pixie-looking kid who had been struggling to climb on Santa's knee as the merry man wrapped up a previous discussion about a GI Joe rifle, roller blades, and a gee-whizz computer game. She had golden hair and green eyes, and her skin was fair. Once successfully in Santa's lap, the girl told Santa her name was Fairleigh. She said she was four.

"That's a fascinating name. And what would you like Santa to bring you for Christmas, Fairleigh?" asked the jolly man in a monotone. She was the 150th child he had seen during his afternoon shift, and he was anxious for a bathroom break.

"All I want…" she started haltingly, but with a severe expression on a face that seemed to convey a sober, determined intent. "All I want…"

"Yes, yes?" Santa was becoming impatient. His bladder was screaming.

"All I want is for my daddy's novel to be sold in a bookstore," she finally blurted. "He's worked so hard on it. It's about me, his little girl."

For a moment, the mall Santa had a puzzled, confused look underneath his white beard. He was accustomed to the little tykes asking for the moon and more.

"Uh, well, I think that's a possibility."

His words trailed off as he reached for the red and white sign, which notified all that Santa was on a 20-minute break.

"Yes, that one," Ruth whispered in her husband's ear. "The little girl with the green eyes."

CHAPTER 2
PRESENT DAY AT PINK'S HOTDOG
EMPORIUM LOS ANGELES, SPRING, 2020

Something troubled the young actress Natalie Courant, though she knew not what and certainly not why.

The screenplay was like a whiff of fading but still lingering perfume. The young lady wore a blue and red Atlanta Braves baseball cap pulled down over her eyes, shadowing frown wrinkles.

She was bothered, though not necessarily troubled. She had stayed up most of the night with a sick and aging cat named Fluffy. The cat was a stray, a variation of calico, but Natalie couldn't tell when first taken in. A mutt had mangled her.

She read over the 110-page treatment slowly, occasionally taking a sip from a vanilla-flavored cola. There was a sense of foreboding whatever the script contained— and the clues were stacked like translucent logs. Yet, at the same time, it was an enticing, compelling read, just as her addiction to lemon drops she acquired as a child growing up. Where? Who the hell knows? She wasn't sure herself.

It had to be, of course, West Virginia, but she had absolutely no memory before the age of four, and even that digit was the number of years people believed to be her age. She had no official birth certificate. Her supposed parents were an itinerant couple heavy on gospel verse but shiftless as an aging but well-fed stray cat.

All she knew was what had been related to her by the couple who raised her and the stories she heard later hanging out at Charlie Jones' bar, the Purple Onion, in Charleston's East End. It could be said she grew up in that honky-tonk, and was, from the beginning of time, its talented mascot. Occasionally, she would perform Patsy Cline's "Crazy" while parading among beer bottles atop the bar. Charlie would tone down the lights and point a bandstand spot on her. Charlie sold a lot of beer on those nights. Her auburn hair glistened and her green eyes — an unusual combination—were like emerald lanterns.

Natalie's story was contradictory, as most mysteries tend to be. It was a riddle akin to the Turkish princess ring given by an ex-boyfriend who pawned it off as the genuine article. But the script before her did feel uncommonly authentic, conjuring memories behind a muslin veil of shambolic thoughts.

That particular boyfriend, Billy Ray Summer, had lasted fewer months than the season his name implied. He went the way of other boyfriends, gently cast aside, though not with prejudice. She loved them all at the moment.

Though they tended to round first base, they were stopped short, panting and sweating, galloping toward an elusive home plate that was not to be. Nevertheless, it never hurt her popularity. In her senior year, she was the homecoming queen at George Washington High School and a steady in the cast of the Charleston Light Opera player. She had a voice that lilted and dipped and caused spines to tingle. She was more Linda Ronstadt than Dolly Parton. Her voice had a smoky texture, like an expensive single malt scotch.

Oddly, the script she was reading conjured home smells, like simmering-popping meatloaf in the oven, white school paste slapped on poster board, and the sweet, soda fountain bouquet of the Five and Dime. For sure, Charleston's Woolworth on Capitol Street had disappeared eons ago, but the facade remained. One could still smell the peanut aroma of the nut shop next door. Maybe that was it.

But this was odd. She had never experienced those smells to the her knowledge, though she seemed to know them as a dream previewing at the mind's Rialto. The gold velvety curtains, though, were pulled tight. Whatever it was, whatever went before, it was no longer her life. It simply teased her memory, failing to trigger a hint. It was not something to which she wished to devote time. She was, after all, merely a teenager, edging into her 20s with ambition and dreams. She didn't want to be a throw-away starlit. She wanted to be a star.

Natalie's 's mind wandered like a wild Mustang over a yellowish-brown western tumbleweed plain. She was a typical young lady in many ways, but in others, she had lived a lifetime, and a fragment of that lifetime, she couldn't

9

recall. So where does one turn when there is no there, there?

Her early remembrances were of her dad, who wasn't her natural father, but someone she became acquainted with under unusual circumstances. Charlie was the man who enrolled her in and walked her daily to Sacred Heart Elementary School on Quarrier Street. That's what she called him, Charlie.

Charlie was not Catholic. He was more a member of the church of what's happing now, which has daily, often hourly, services within the minds of its vast membership of everyday blokes who drink, cuss, and, on occasion, fool around a little. His name was of the good-time variety, not Charles but Charlie. He had fought like hell to keep her when child welfare said a thrice-divorced saloon keeper ands ex-con had no business adopting a small child.

Besides, she was such a mystery. The local dairy, United Inc., promised to put her face on a milk carton, but it was to no avail. Even after years of being so billboarded in West Virginia and, indeed, throughout much of the nation, no one claimed the little girl.

In the meantime, however, as the bureaucratic machinations slowly marched on, Charlie and his most recent ex-wife, Beverly, gained community support for adoption not just from Purple Onion patrons but even from a few church people, including the minister of the First Baptist Church.

Charlie and the girl bonded over the strangest of

circumstances. She had simply appeared one busy night at his lounge in Charleston's East End. She had been deposited in a booth. Her name, at that time, was understood to be Mary, or at least, so she thought.

For sure, the girl's name in the screenplay's title was rather run-of-the-mill, Frances Leigh. The title of the script, in itself, wasn't predictive of any commercial success. It stirred hardly any excitement. It was simply prostrated tombstone-like on the first page in 24-point type. Other than Natalie and the girl in the script having green eyes, an occurrence with only two percent of the population, there was nothing in common between the script's character and the young star. The first pages of the script, however, piqued Natalie's interest. Always a reader, she liked a good yarn. This was a curl up on a rainy night with a glass of wine story.

Frances Leigh was also the name of the proposed movie, a simple story about a young girl and a reclusive old man. Each year, the man worked 45 days as a department store Santa Claus at Macy's in an Orlando, Florida mall, the one named Millennium, a short hop from the various Disney attractions that drew millions each year.

Natalie had never been to Disney World, and the park was not something that would necessarily draw her interest. Though, for sure, given a normal childhood, she quite possibly would be one of the millions of kids with a pair of plastic mouse ears making the pilgrimage to Central Florida. Unfortunately, however, she never had a fairytale childhood.

To Cletus Reed, her agent sitting across from her at Pinks, she had often told that Charlie Jones — despite serving time in prison for manslaughter and the stigma of running a sometimes raucous honky-tonk — was the kindest man she had ever met. He treated her as if she were a little princess. He was her Daddy Warbucks, and she his Little Orphan Annie, though Charlie was far from being wealthy.

Charlie and Cletus were the two men who had the most influence on her young life. There was also Charlie's wife, Beverly Jones, who became Charlie's fourth marriage. She was a two-fer for Charlie. He re-hitched with Bev to pass muster with the West Virginia Child Welfare Department, forming the facade of a stable family, a ruse they managed to pull off. Over time, they made the show marriage a real one.

The girl's first hazy memories were of shivering, not because she was frightened, but because she was in a canvas sack, being bounced around in the back of a truck. It was summer, but the air conditioning was on in the van, and a vent poured frosty air. The odd couple in the front seat avoided the major highways and traveled over mountains with serpentine curves. The girl wobbled from one side of the vehicle to the other, picking up bruises and cuts from the jostling journey of what turned into several months.

There seemed to be no destination, merely following the broken white lines, stopping at isolated roadside parks for pee breaks in nearby woods. On those occasions, they let her out, but far from anyone who could ask questions.

By this time, she looked like a refugee from some forgotten country, an aborigine with matted hair and dark circles under her eyes. Her bumps had bumps. She was beyond being scared. After rebelling as any child would at first, over time, she began to accept this status. She was a captured animal tamed into submission.

The couple insisted she call them momma and papa, and when she complained or whimpered, she felt the slap of a hand through the sack she was required to occupy. A "damnit kid" accompanied it. "I told you to call Ruthie mommy." This confused her. She knew she already had a mommy, but that memory was fading by the hour.

It went on like this throughout the journey. All slept in the van, generally in Wal-Mart parking lots, until they came to a stop in front of a bar in Charleston one evening. The girl could see the flashing neon through the bag. She didn't know it at the time, but it was the Purple Onion Lounge. This stopping point was to be the beginning of Mary Jones's new life. The previous one became, over the years, a blur. It wasn't that she didn't want to remember; it was simply such a dark forest, she was afraid to enter.

—

"Well, what do you think?" asked the actresses' agent as he took a furtive sip from a mid-day high ball, his first of generally three or four during a day. Sometimes his nostalgic nighttime sipping became more serious.

Unlike the Charlie of old, Reed was a gentleman drinker. The libation was more regimen than habit. It was fuel. He liked the taste but could never recall having a hangover, even a headache. It was odd that Reed should be sampling booze at a famous hotdog stand as the California sun radiated through the picture window. Reed, though, cared nothing of cultural niceties or convention. He poured the drink from a silver flask into a Coca-Cola branded paper cup. In every way, the agent lived within his world.

Natalie didn't immediately answer. Instead, she peered over the top of the script at her agent, smiled thinly, and then went back to reading the last two pages. He had sent it to her by courier the previous night. She had read most of it, but not all. Instead, she was more attentive to her Fluffy, the kitten suffering from an overindulgence of hairballs.

"Hold your horses, Cletus," she said absently, a moment or two later.

Reed had requested the tete-a-tete at Pinks. They met there on occasion to discuss business and life. It was often crowded with tourists and, therefore, an unlikely setting for a movie star in the making. However, no one recognized her and didn't know the dapper elderly gent, who, in Hollywood circles, was even more prominent.

Reed had become a father figure to her, a role he had accepted reluctantly at first but now guarded it with a natural and slightly possessive passion. He had become comfortable with the relationship. He loved her as he would love a daughter.

She had told him the story of Charlie Jones, the

saloon owner who took her in nearly 16 years earlier and guided her through childhood and her teen years. It was Charlie who comforted her through her first period, which frightened her. He had watched her go off to her high school prom. He had walked her to her first talent show, and the big fellow had cried salty tears when she performed "Somewhere Over the Rainbow."

Charlie had seen her through her first breakup with a boyfriend, a fellow who had been captain of the George Washington High football team. Carl Stoner had broken her heart, and Charlie's first inclination was to break him. Instead, though, he held his daughter close and salty tears escaped from his own eyes. Charlie never insisted or even asked to be called papa or daddy. For a fellow who wasn't at all into kids, he had been the near-perfect father for her.

Mary would awake after a frightful nightmare at night, and both Charlie and Beverly would rush to her room at the first whimpering sounds. The mystery was that she couldn't put the fragments of her past life together. Humpty Dumpty had taken a great fall, and there was no way they could help the child recollect the pieces.

They tried. Along with state authorities and Kanawha County Sheriff Danny Jenkins's assistance, they attempted to match fingerprints taken off a whiskey glass at the Purple Onion, but every database came up blank. It was as if the odd couple never existed. Officially, they probably never did.

Then one day, Charlie up and died due to clogged arteries and perhaps too many pepperoni rolls at the Purple

Onion. His daughter had warned him to no avail to lose weight, but Charlie insisted a 240-pound frame was merely an adjunct of his bar-owning personality. He couldn't rule over his small kingdom as a featherweight. He never really had to toss anyone out. They cowered before him and left peacefully. However, he called his bulk an essential part of his image.

He might have been right. Everyone best knows his or her own mojo. The whole damn town, it seemed, attended his funeral, even his few enemies to make sure he was actually dead.

CHAPTER 3
CLETUS REED: AGENT EXTRAORDINARY

Cletus Reed was no Charlie Jones and didn't pretend to be.

In truth, a hair away from his 85th birthday, Reed could be Natalie's great grandfather. They made for an odd pairing in this community of oddities.

The agent remembered celebrating the end of the Korean War. Her recollection was of a black President named Obama, who she admired, which made her unusual in her conservative community.

Though the ice blue spring day was warm with only a hint of a breeze and a mustard dollop sun hung lazily in the sky, Reed was dressed in his usual dark, pinstriped and vested suit. The ensemble was completed with pocket watch and silver chain, a gift from his late wife in the long-gone 1960s. It was more than an affectation but less than a necessary adjunct. In a nod to modernity, he possessed an iPhone and did his best to become acquainted with its functions. He depended on it for telling time, though, at his age, it seemed almost irrelevant. Time was what it was, nothing more, nothing less.

Reed had taken off his 1950s style Fedora, something his doctor had urged him to wear when splotches of skin cancer appeared two decades earlier. He looked a lot like Gregory Peck in To Kill a Mocking Bird without the hat, though thinner and gaunt-faced with sunken cheeks. His blue eyes, however, sparkled.

Reed seemed a character from another age, a gilded, golden Hollywood that died long ago, most likely with disaster-themed movies backed by mega budgets. He, though, looked comfortable, nary a bead of sweat on his California tan. He was a young-looking octogenarian and could pass for 65. For an old guy, the garden club's blue-haired ladies would consider him handsome and quite a find; that is if he were a gardener and knew a petunia from a potato plant. Since his wife died years earlier, his only full-time companion was a succession of people-friendly dogs, the latest Sammy.

The agent had always been more at home with drawing room dramas and scripts so tightly written they squeaked. He preferred narratives that honored dialogue, plots that seemed to have more to them than simply blowing up people and buildings. Action heroes were just so much bang, bang, and chop, chop. His spirit was more poetic, though certainly not in a syrupy way. He feasted on Tennessee Williams' plays.

Long ago, he had worked with Williams and the

novelist/screenwriter William Faulkner. He could name and place drop with the best of them, and he—it could easily be said—waded in the brackish backwaters of cinematic history. He had been poker buddies with the famed director Howard Hawks, and Peck sought his advice on whether The Man in the Gray Flannel Suit would help or hinder his career. It was a controversial movie for its time.

When still in his 20s, he had advised a young Charlton Heston to take the lead role in Ben Hur, which propelled the actor's career in the 1960s. He was, especially in his early days, a go-to sort of industry shaman, though he wore that mantel, even power, as if it were merely a paper tissue cape. He lorded over no one and everyone. It all had to do with demeanor, character and grace.

These days, due to her surging fame, his teen client received dozens of scripts each week, most unsolicited. Reed thumbed through all, generally spending no more than a gulp of coffee on each. Usually, if the first 20 lines didn't provoke interest, the script was chucked into a nearby trash can. However, he dreaded the thought of missing a cinematic jewel. So, he kept up the charade of looking at every one. Unlike many in the business, he never ridiculed the writer, no matter how amateurish or laughable. He realized the sweat and the sacrifice that went into any creative product. He loved the written word, sometimes even imperfect words.

Reed had a practiced eye for a good script. His name was attached as co-producer and writer on several high grossing movies and one Broadway musical collaboration that ran five years. While not a professional musician, he loved his guitar and had hundreds of song fragments in his desk drawer. His name had been attached as a co-writer on several pop hits, though he insisted songwriting wasn't his forte. These days his fingers were gnarled, and arthritis plagued the more difficult fretting, but he still loved to play for himself and his dog, who didn't complain and seemed to enjoy it.

At this stage of life, Reed didn't need Tinseltown, nor did he need the 10 to 20 percent agent's cut, which was a full five or 10 percent above the norm for his line of work. He could be living in a mini-mansion, playing golf every day, and sipping cocktails at his leisure. However, Reed didn't play golf. He didn't know a putter from a hockey stick. Forty years back, he purchased a plot of prime Malibu beachfront. He lived there in a 50-foot trailer with his books, vintage Martin Dreadnaught guitar, Sammy the Airedale, and memories. He was in the agent business for the love of it and not the hustle. He grew tired of the phony game in his forties, and once he did, he became even more successful as the Hollywood wise man, though he certainly didn't publicize himself that way. It just happened.

This Francis Leigh script, though, was different from most, mainly because he had, in essence, made it his own. He had read the book on which it was based; and, being quite the entrepreneur, had purchased the movie rights for pocket change from the author. It was a mere $5,000. The fellow seemed desperate for cash, and Reed saw a precious bauble where others might see a plain old rock. By this time, the book had already been consigned to the two-dollar bin at Barnes and Noble, and that's where Reed discovered it, a happenstance meeting of eyes on a rather nondescript, nothing book with a dull cover. The author jumped at Reed's offer. He probably would have taken a dinner discount coupon to the Red Lobster restaurant.

However, it was a good book, if not a great book. It spoke to Reed in ways few stories had. These days finding a publisher was like winning the trifecta at the ponies on three consecutive days. Still, the author had somehow managed to convince a regional imprint, Vision Press of Atlanta, Ga., to take his effort. However, distribution had been minimal and sales dismal.

The agent took the book back to his trailer and pulled an all-nighter. The purchase of it was an afterthought. The title teased him, and it was, after all, a mere couple of bucks. The Book of Francis Leigh almost seemed like an operative phrase and not the finished title.

While listening to the Pacific waves, partaking a little Gentleman Jack and with the warm breath of Sammy on his face, he devoured the manuscript. It was not a page-turner, merely a warm, believable story of an eccentric old gent and a teenager. It was not a romance for sure, but it was companionship. Before morning, he knew it would be an excellent vehicle for his favorite and, at this point in life, only client, Natalie Courant.

There was something about the story that nagged at him. Perhaps he saw himself as the old Santa and his young actress as the teen who befriended him. After turning the last page, and as the sun was coming up, he visited his wife's grave at Hollywood Memorial Park. He felt compelled to discuss it with Abigail and his late daughter,

Caroline.

Reed commissioned a screenplay by one of the best wordsmiths in the business, Jock Lane. The fellow had a string of award-winning movies to his credit, including one that was up against Natalie Currant's "Outer Worldly" sci-fi film. However, the agent rejected the final product and re-wrote it himself, paying Lane handsomely for his efforts. "Jock, your script is brilliant—it just doesn't ring true for me. It's not about you—it's me." Lane was a professional. He was not disappointed and wished the agent luck.

It took 20 laborious drafts before Reed felt he had done the book justice and was ready to show it to his client. He was nervous about the meeting and had twice canceled to review it once again. He had even visited the author simply to get a feel for the backstory. It was not a pleasant experience. Why this book? Why this plot? Was it a real-life tale—something the author experienced? Reed had to know.

He flew from Los Angeles to New York for a dinner with friends, and then dog-legged it to Florida. The first meeting with the author had been an awkward negotiation for script rights and the handing over of a cashier's check. The second trip, taken more out of curiosity, was rebuffed outright by the author. At first, William Wendell had been marginally polite. But when Reed pressed for details, the author showed him to the door of the East Orlando home. He seemed nervous, downright antagonistic.

"Hey, old man, I sold you the rights. Do what you will with the goddamn thing. I hardly made a dime from it," he said as Reed attempted to converse through a screen door. "I made up the story, simple as that. I have an imagination."

The trip was 24-hours, but the meeting was less than ten minutes. It was a good thing Reed had asked the taxi driver to wait. He thought to himself how foolish he was. A telephone call would have yielded the same results without the two grand first-class tickets. However, Cletus's curiosity gene was doing the jitterbug. He felt driven to visit the author, and he knew there had to be more to the story than meets the eye.

Reed was not deterred. He was more determined, and he had a compelling reason: The heart doctor at UCLA Health said the posterior vein to his left ventricle looked like a soggy noodle, and he might want to get his affairs in order. That had been two years and a couple of medical stints ago. Arranging his affairs took only a week. There were no living relatives to whom he was close. He already knew where he would like to lie, within a foot of his late wife, Abigail, and his child. The doctor didn't misdiagnose. He simply didn't comprehend Reed's tenacity to occupy vertical space on the planet and leave on his own terms.

As for Reed's will, he signed papers bequeathing everything to the St. Jude's Children's Hospital in Memphis, established by the entertainer Danny Thomas. If one were to think this was a generous gesture, Reed dismissed such nonsense. He said the sole reason was he was smitten by actress Marlo Thomas, daughter of Danny, his friend. He also would acknowledge that Abigail was pleased with her husband's fantasies of watching Marlo on the old "That

Girl" TV series. She humored him.

"I think the script has promise. It would be a change of pace coming off that lost in space movie," the actress replied, studiously, as if she had given it much thought. She hadn't. She had absolute trust in her agent's wisdom. Her time on the silver screen would have to be shared with a child actress, someone to play Francis Leigh at a younger age. Natalie didn't mind.

Reed had picked a science-fiction epic for Natalie's debut and had relentlessly lobbied Panther Studios to take a chance on his unknown discovery. "We'll do it for union scale and a small percentage on the take, say five," he said.

While the project was low budget, he chose the film because it put Natalie on the big screen for a full hour and a half. He wanted the world to see what he saw, the flash of her green eyes, the mischievous smile, the playful laugh, and an absolute cardiac seriousness when she curled her lips and raised her brows. He had also fallen in love with her lush Susan Pleshette-low voice.

The movie had become the sleeper of the Oscar season, though few figured her for the golden statue. After all, it was a sci-fi movie. However, It had already grossed $300 million and climbing. Toy manufacturers were knocking on his door, bidding for licenses to manufacture Natalie Currant figurines and a bobblehead doll. The studio, which initially wanted little to do with the space project, was in discussions with scriptwriters over a sequel.

Reed hated this part of it. The thought that Natalie would need an entourage of accountants, schedulers, and personal assistants was, to him, everything that was wrong with the business. He wanted it kept simple. A star in infancy is beautiful. One in full bloom can be ugly and petulant. He had seen it before so many times over his long career. Early in his career, he had mentored a very young Sandra Dee and was in weekly tit-for-tat combat with her controlling mother. It was a depressing thought.

"Don't knock the 'Outer Worldly" project. It has you up for an Oscar for that 120 minutes of celluloid. The word on people's lips is 'Natalie Currant, the next Meryl Streep."

"It was digital, you Goofus," Natalie laughed. "Besides, comparing me to Meryl is like comparing Van Gogh to a sign painter. Cletus, never kid a kidder."

Few people in the business could talk to Reed, as did his young star. She was brash but in a respectful manner. While the agent might be considered an apparatchik, he was not an anachronism. He freely advised young agents, writers, and directors who often knocked timidly on the door of his beachside trailer. He always invited them in for coffee laced with a nip of sour mash.

Natalie Currant had a lot going for her, including modesty. She had a vanilla ice cream beauty that turned heads, and a come hither look that on-screen cause male hormones to explode and teen girls to envy, even copy by the multitudes. Yet, in her plain scarf, simple blue dress, and thick glasses, she looked the stereotype of a young librarian. She was not incognito to avoid notice at Pinks. It was her regular appearance. She was hopelessly nearsighted and wore contacts on the set. Her white scarf hid a waterfall of locks that, if allowed free, would traverse her entire, slender back.

Natalie looked nothing like Streep, more like a Faye Dunaway in her prime. In stature, she was tiny but appeared much taller on screen. Her voice was whiskey flavored, and it reminded the old agent not just of smoky-toned Pleshette but of Bette Davis. It was the voice and those piercing eyes that gave Natalie star power. It didn't hurt that she could also act on cue, turn a simple tear into a dramatic flood, or show a kinetic fury as if she had multiple personalities.

Natalie wasn't her name. It was Mary, a garden variety calling, a name in a soup bowl of familiar, largely forgettable characters. Currant was not her last name either, merely an invention of her agent. Natalie, one would suspect, came from the late actress Natalie Wood, a Reed contemporary. The name Currant was a puzzle, though the agent loved fermented grapes from a particular hillside in Normandy as a second choice to Gentleman Jack.

Mary had been plucked from obscurity by Reed, who just happened to catch her in a musical production of Annie Get Your Gun at a small playhouse in Charleston, West Virginia. She played the title role of the sharpshooting Annie Oakley. Reed, who once saw the late actress Lee Remick in the part, went away that evening convince he had found his new star. This came home to him when she belted out her rendition of "You Can't Get a Man With a

Gun," and he saw the explosive range of facial expressions that the girl projected in the three-minute Irving Berlin song. It brought the house down.

Reed had been coaxed to Charleston by the West Virginia Film Commission director, an old friend. The agent was to be the featured speaker at a symposium at the State's cultural center. It was his first visit to West Virginia, his home state, in many years and the last place he expected to find the green-eyed talent, a woman so captivating it was as if a fiery meteor had shot from the heavens and landed on stage. She dazzled.

After the performance, the agent made it backstage and gave Mary Jones his card. It simply read: Cletus Reed, Talent Agent, Hollywood, Ca. He had added his mobile number in ink with the notation, "Please call. Might have something for you."

At the time, Reed was sure the surprise finding of the young lady would be, in essence, his last hooray. After all, the hourglass was emptying, and his old dog Sammy needed more of his attention. Financially, he was more than secure, and he had no one else who depended on him. He figured she would look him up on Google and discover his bonafides.

But then, after two weeks, Mary Jones had not called. He had to take the initiative, chasing her down through a number he found for the Charleston Light Opera Guild for whom she had been performing. Within a week, he had set this 19-year-old up in a small efficiency and had enrolled her in acting classes with a long-time confidant.

He encouraged her to take night classes at UCLA and provided an "investment stipend" for living expenses. At first, she was wary, and then she wasn't. She just wanted to make this old guy proud of her.

"So, you want me to do this Francis Leigh thing," she said as she took a bite from her chili-loaded, foot-long hotdog and wiped a smear of dark juice from her mouth. "You going to make any money off this one, Cletus Reed?"

"Hell, who knows. I've got enough saved to keep Sammy in quality Alpo and me an occasional liquid indulgence," said Reed. "Who needs more?"

Her's was an earnest question. She had not yet in life, or her budding career come to the "what's in it for me" stage. She was genuinely concerned about her mentor. As for the script, if Reed had said he wanted her to do a remake of the original "Texas Chainsaw Massacre," she would have signed on. Such was her devotion to the old guy. It was not unlike the relationship between the character and the old man in the Francis Leigh script.

Natalie had no idea that Panther Studio had nixed the Francis Leigh proposal with hardly a moment's consideration. They saw dollar figures from an "Outer Worldly" sequel and didn't want to consider the agent's re-written work. Reed didn't care and didn't negotiate. He wanted total control of the project. He also wanted the filming to go before the "Outer Worldly" sequel, which was undoubtedly bankable. He felt it was strategically wrong so soon for Natalie. Sure, it would make money, but to Reed, it would be crap with hair in it. Rarely do sequels match the original, and it would simply be a dumbing down of the previous flick, which, in the agent's view, was only passable because it had Natalie as the star. Reed was also aware the studio would go around him to get to his client.

The actress also had no clue Reed had written the Francis Leigh script or that he had refinanced his Malibu beachfront. He also sold his Apple stock and invested much of his entire savings to sponsor the project.

"You know Natalie. If this movie makes money, it's because I made the right decision. If moviegoers stay away from it, that's life and their loss," he said. "I'm following my gut, and the tell-tell ache in my little toe on my left foot. It's never led me astray."

Included in the papers his lawyer had drawn up was a $5 million guarantee for Natalie Currant should, as the insurance companies so cleverly put it, "he be removed from the picture" while the film was in progress. She also would receive the sum as salary if the movie were a total bust.

To complete the jerry-rigged project, Reed had put together an independent, union film crew, one that included old acquaintances with whom he knew he could work and who would understand the importance of the film to him. Among the crew was an aging director whose big moment in show business was serving as stage manager for comedian Bob Hope's USO shows in various war zones. Johnny Swift had also directed a couple of "B" horror movies of little note, including "Here Comes Bloody Santa Claus."

The agent had worked with him 40 years ago on several projects unrelated to the movie business. Reed had produced television commercials, and they had teamed together on the Crisco account. They had kept in touch through the decades, and Reed bet on people and ideas. He had always felt Swift had directorial capabilities, but in Hollywood—though a big guy —he was like a butterfly among buzzards.

"So Natalie, you in?"

The early afternoon crowd at Pinks had thinned. She reached over to him and grabbed his hand. Natalie could see he was shaking. The doctor had called it a benign tremor. His left hand occasionally held the other to calm it. His blue eyes looked like two pools of quivering ponds. They seemed to plead.

"Cletus, what the hell you say?" She flashed an impish, playful frown. "You know good and well that if you asked me to star in a publicly filmed porno flick at the corner of Hollywood and Vine, I'd be there naked as a jaybird."

The comment was more than he expected. He was from an old Victorian school. He blushed while he laughed to himself that his Abigail would approve of this uninhibited ingenue, a teenager who was both hopelessly naive and streetwise worldly.

Reed didn't believe in fate. One's hard work determined the future;   but, whatever it was, he was thankful that their planets had met in Tinseltown.

——-

On the morning the agent finished reading William Wendell's book, he drove his1955 white Caddy convertible, a car driven by Paul Newman in the movie Hud, to Hollywood Memorial Park cemetery. There, he parked on a curve and walked up the hill to Abigail's gravestone, which also had his name on it. Next to it was Caroline's.

He was so impressed by the proposed film's possibilities, he wanted to talk it over with his long-dead wife, too, perhaps, get the final approval from the beyond. He knew beforehand she would heartily endorse it.

With the sun filtering through the palms and the ground moist with daybreak dew, he removed his Fedora and folded his arms in front of him. He was not a religious man. It was not a prayer, but it was a dialogue.

"Abigail, this Natalie is so much like our darling Caroline. This movie will be my last," he whispered. "I am tired, as I am sure you can see. But it has been a good life, but less of a life without you and our daughter."

Then, with a salty tear plopping to his stiff white shirt, he delivered his message:

"I want to tell this story classically and the way stories were once told. I want it to be memorable—no, I want it to be more. I want it to be heroic."

History, of course, will never record whether Abigail replied or even gave a sign. We do not know if there were rustling leaves or if a single drop of rain fell. Abigail had died four decades earlier, mostly of a broken heart, though the doctors called it pancreatic cancer.

Two weeks before she died, their green-eyed 18-year-old daughter, Caroline, was killed by a hit-and-run driver a short block from Pinks hotdog emporium.

CHAPTER 4
THE BLISSFUL THREE

Jeremy Britnell had a perfect life, except for unfulfilled literary ambitions. He had married his childhood sweetheart, Sarah, and they had a beautiful little girl. Her name was Fairleigh.

He had a good job, though it didn't pay a fortune. However, it kept food on the table, a late model Ford Taurus in the garage, and a neat three-bedroom, two-bath home in Hawks Estates. Their suburban community was just beyond the Disney attractions, a short distance from Interstate 4.

But Jeremy had pictured much more for himself by age 30. He figured he would be working for the New York Times and would have successful novels under his belt. As a writer, Jeremy didn't fancy himself either a Hemingway or a Steinbeck but was confident he was sufficiently talented to pen fiction that could be commercially viable and have a modicum of literary merit. He felt himself more in the mold of a Sinclair Lewis, for the thoughts he strung together attacked the ironies and conventions of the time. In the end, though, they were often cloaked in happily-ever-after parables but absent sentimentality. His literary rambling tended toward sweet and sour, like a tart gumdrop.

When he was still in high school, Britnell had seen an old movie based on Ernest Hemingway's book, "Farewell to Arms," and was determined to be both a journalist and a successful author. He achieved the former. He was a general assignment staff writer for the Orlando Sentinel, not precisely the Times but a credible, medium-sized market newspaper with a history of civic goodness and a conservative bent. Britnell leaned more to progressive liberal, though without any tendencies toward burn-the-building-down social change.

Because he was a talented wordsmith, the powers that be at the Sentinel held out the possibility of his having a twice-weekly column—someday. He could turn a phrase. He was witty. That ultimately, though, seemed rather far off. He had been at the newspaper for eight years, from the moment he graduated from the University of Florida. He had started on the copy desk, eventually gravitating to the paper's heartbeat, the city desk, before being given a roaming general assignment task. He liked the freedom.

Britnell didn't want to be like Herman Thomson, the white-haired gent in the back of the newsroom. He was nearly 60 and had been at the newspaper for thirty of those years. Thomson was once again about to dress up as a clown to offer a first-person perspective on Disney's Magic Kingdom Festival for the fifth year running. While the senior reporter enjoyed his status as a seasonal clown personality, it was a designation Britnell would rather forgo should some editor decide they needed a younger fellow in the outfit.

Jeremy continued to have this compulsion to put his fictional accounts on paper. He had a vivid imagination that lent itself to surprising resolves. As a writer, he had this jujitsu talent to incorporate literary twists that kept his stories interesting. He wrote early in the morning, generally for two hours before leaving for work and then late at night. His goal was 1,000 words a day, more on weekends. It pained him not to reach his goal, and even though Sarah would urge him to come to bed, the light would stay on until he reached the 1,000th word. Like a persistent and avid runner, writing for someone who loves the craft was an addiction.

Sarah, the former Sarah Farnsworth, encouraged him to keep up his efforts even in the face of rejection slips which he ceremoniously tacked to the kitchen wall with a single thumbtack. The tiny tack eventually yielded to a small nail which a larger one later replaced. It wasn't long before he had three unpublished novels to his credit and was working on a fourth. This one, he promised himself, would be his masterpiece. Forget the Pulitzer Prize; he was aiming for a Nobel. Such are the whimsical dreams of writers. He was writing the story for his daughter, Fairleigh, and the life he dreamed for her.

"You're a great writer Jeremy. Everyone says so. You just need that one break which is right around the corner," said Sarah, bucking up the young reporter. She didn't want him to accept failure, ever.

In a market of minimal readers and instant storyline gratification, hope and a prayer weren't good enough. Book publishers published personalities, not writers. A presidential mistress or a starlet could make a bestseller's list, but not an ordinary, everyday scribe. He had a better chance of winning the Florida Powerball Lottery, which Jeremy played weekly.

"Look, Jeremy, Steven King had hundreds of rejection slips before someone picked up on Carrie," she told him, though she wasn't sure of her facts. "You've got more talent in your pinky than King has in his entire being."

That was, of course, an exaggeration. Sarah was a fan and a wife devoted to only two planetary beings, Jeremy and their daughter, Fairleigh. Nevertheless, she was protective to an extraordinary degree, losing her parents at an early age when a tornado swept through their East Orlando trailer park. The trailer was found a block away, and Sarah was the only survivor. She had been visiting her playmates three trailers down when the storm zeroed in on their green and cream abode, lifted it to the sky, and then hopscotched to a nearby shopping center which it left in piles of concrete blocks.

Sarah was raised in a series of foster homes around Central Florida, never feeling that any temporary parent would last more than a few months. She had the luck of the draw, and it was a rotten draw. She grew up a painfully shy, withdrawn woman with a colossal inferiority complex that, for this slender woman, cast a giant shadow over her entire outlook on life.

That changed when she met Jeremy Britnell. He was a fellow with brash, outsized ambition that dwarfed his physical presence. They dated through junior and senior high school and married their fourth year at the University of Florida, where they studied journalism. She was the one who excelled in grades, but he was the one who had a talent with words and a curiosity that made him the brand of journalist to whom others in the profession looked up.

Jeremy wanted to take on the world. Sarah simply wanted peace in her corner of it. She was content to be the cheerleader on the sidelines, sharing real estate on terra firma that approximated his. Yet, in every way, they were so different than they were alike. They fed off one another's weaknesses, but in a healthy way. She lost her shyness, becoming a spokesperson for various Central Florida charity causes. Of particular interest to Sarah was mental health, mainly because she knew it was her secret demon.

The couple made the word soulmate a cliche. They were so deeply in love that there was no oxygen remaining for those extracurricular activities that make for everyday social life. They had a few close friends, mostly other Sentinel reporters, and they rarely ventured outside of Jeremy's work circle.

In the beginning, it was an uneasy pairing. Sarah was never one hundred percent sure the two halves made a whole. She was a delicate flower; he a sturdy shrub. The fact that she felt their situation fleeting made the marriage constantly a ship adrift near rocky shoals. She could not shake the tenuous feeling of her transient childhood. It smothered her and visited her often in nightmares.

Then, Fairleigh came along, and for the next four years, their life was at a comfortable dead calm. The daughter was the anchor Sarah needed to feel they constituted a real home and that her marriage wasn't merely a 15-minute coffee break from reality. She was radiantly happy.

During this period, the after-burner of Jeremy's creativity kicked in. First, of course, it helped that he had gained some attention with a self-generated series he wrote for his newspaper on the city's slum housing and the miserly landlords who collected rent by the week. The stories played out on the front page, and his colleagues assured him he was sure to win the Florida Press Association Award for investigative reporting.

A little encouragement went a long way. Jeremy completed the novel he was working on, based on the couple's trips to The Mall at Millenia. and roughly on the person he envisioned his daughter Fairleigh one day becoming. While waiting for a better title to strike his fancy, he typed The Book of Fairleigh on the initial page as a working title. He finished the novel in six months and began the arduous process of pitching it to publishers. He had now decided it would be called Bright Eyes.

Not unlike the serendipity of the tornado that struck when Sarah was a child, a seismic happening, however, was to drastically alter the couple's world. It would trample asunder the papier--mâché enclosure in which they had wrapped themselves.

Nothing would be the same again.

It wasn't unusual for the couple, with Fairleigh in tow, to cruise the mall. They often went there simply to window-shop, stop by Panda Express for fried rice and orange-flavored shrimp, and, on occasion, take in a Disney movie at the cineplex. On this particular day, a Saturday, they both had read good reviews about a flick that wasn't suitable for a four-year-old. They were discerning parents, and this particular shoot-em-up had a high body count. It was rated parental guidance recommended.

The mall had a commercial nursery on the premises, which offered story-time and games for children while their parents shopped. The price was reasonable. It seemed a logical, safe, and good parenting solution. They dropped Fairleigh off in the care of a matronly appearing employee who looked like the child's grandmother. The woman had a Sunday school perfume smell and a laugh that caused her tummy to roll.

It was the worst mistake they could make.

CHAPTER 5
PURVIS PERIWINKLE

"Please, Madam, settle down. I am sure we will find your daughter. What's her name? Her age? What does she look like? What was she wearing?"

In the beginning, the Mall at Millenia security guard spoke calmly, recalling the training lesson catechism. He knew his grandmother would be disappointed if he lost another job, even one such as this that required few talents other than the ability to stand for much of an eight-hour shift.

Purvis Periwinkle was fired from Taco Bell a week earlier for mixing up orders, causing a massive traffic backup and a symphony of angry blaring horns. His nervous system melted like microwaved ice cream, and he sat down behind the cash register counter and whimpered, just short of an outright cry. He wouldn't come out until his grandma arrived and consoled him. He was 30 years old.

"Purvis, now you come out from under there, boy,"

she summoned in her Sunday School teacher falsetto. She had on a dress with splashes of green and yellow flowers and a wide-brimmed bonnet of prehistoric fashion.

Purvis had looked up at her and wiped the tears from his eyes. He spoke with hesitation. "Gladys, I'm a Hogan," the boy insisted. "Momma was a Hogan, and that makes me a Hogan, doesn't it? You're a Hogan."

"I told you, boy, I named you after a famous personage. Be proud of the Periwinkle name. Harry Hogan, your long-dead grandfather, was a lowdown grifter. I gave you a respectable name when your mama took off for God knows where."

Purvis was considered dim-appearing but was no dummy. He had a unique brand of autism. The clinical name was Asperger Syndrome, though the street name was simply "slightly weird." Purvis had scoured the internet for the name Periwinkle. Unfortunately, the only reference he found was for a plant by that name used for treating diarrhea, vaginal discharge, and, on occasion, toothaches. He was not impressed, but then he rarely, if ever, contradicted his grandma.

In an earlier life, Gladys Hogan had risen to the rank of major in the Soviet military. Before she became a Hogan, she was an Andropov. She had been a Beaucoup after Hogan, but that union was brief and not memorable.

Purvis was named after a vaudeville comedian of yesteryear with whom his grandmother was infatuated. Periwinkle, the performer, not the Taco Bell employee turned rent-a-cop, won Gladys' heart when showcased in Milton Berle's Texaco Star Theater in the post-war 50s. She was certain Periwinkle had wooed her via the magic of television and electronic beams. Moreover, she had managed to score a signed autographed picture of the funny man with what her grandson felt was a sissy non-de-plume. By the way, Gladys kept volumes of scrapbooks documenting Periwinkle's marginal career, so her imagining a love story seemed almost plausible. Alternate realities for grandma and grandson were, in essence, reality re-imagined.

It made little difference that her grandson was, by all rights, legally a Hogan and not a Periwinkle. She wanted him to be a Periwinkle, and that was that. The boy's mother, Helena, was unmarried when the bastard boy was born; and, the story later related to the youngster was that she fled the household shortly after the at-home midwife issuance of the child. It seems another gentleman caller with Brill Cream slick hair, a toothy grin, and white buck shoes swept her off her feet.

It helped that Helena's new fellow owned a new Pontiac GTO, which was vermillion red and complimented her dyed rose-tinted hair. He also had a full wallet, the origin of which could have been an armed robbery, pickpocketing, or the luck of a golden lottery ticket. It was doubtful he had earned it. For this narrative, his name or alias is unimportant because the newborn never met his mother outside his temporary stay in her belly. Neither she nor this Smiling Jack—a suitable appropriation for the no-name boyfriend—were ever to be seen again by child or grandmother. This was probably for the best. Current events didn't portend a promising future for Helena and her momentary guy.

Contrary to birth certificates and common sense, batshit crazy ruled the day in this nuclear unit. Eventually, our Mall militia man accepted the old lady's wishes. He referred to himself as Purvis Periwinkle, despite the teasing heaped on him through adolescence and the schoolyard punishment he endured, especially from girls. Purvis was far from handsome and looked much like the Alfred E. Neuman character, the mascot of a humor magazine. However, he was tall and probably could do more damage in fisticuffs than one would imagine. He, however, was a peaceful sort.

Even as a young man with the appropriate appendages for making an everyday living, such as healthy arms, legs, and a baby-making apparatus, he lived in the household of the woman he called Gladys, never referring to her as his grandmother. She did offer an option: "Call me either Major Hogan or Gladys, either will do," she told Purvis when she packed him off to the first grade.

Of course, he was curious about girls. He liked how they smelled but was too timid to explore his options as he grew older and watched his classmates, operating apparently with ease. His insular thoughts of Gladys were constantly doing battle. At times, he figured since she smoked three packs of unfiltered Camel cigarettes a day, she would eventually die of some horrible disease. That would be a good time, he thought, to change his name to something more manly. He favored Gus and felt it fit nicely with Hogan.

However, it was a fact Purvis loved Gladys, and if she were to go on to whatever heavenly reward she did or didn't deserve, he would more than miss her. She was, in essence, what a service dog is to the blind, a comfort animal to the neurotic. Though she didn't know it at the time, her grandson was simply a slow starter, but with potential.

Purvis had an actual name on his birth certificate. It was Leslie Hogan and marginally more appealing to him. Still, before being issued a Social Security card, Gladys saw to it that Purvis Periwinkle would officially be his handle in the here and now and in the ever after.

In his early 20s, Purvis grew a whisper-thin mustache that looked as if it were applied with a woman's eyeliner. He wanted to look like a cool Doc Holiday character in the movie "Tombstone", but the affectation gave the impression of someone's goofy sidekick instead. In other words, he didn't inspire confidence, even though he practiced Val Kilmer's classic line in his bedroom mirror: "Why, Johnny Ringo, you look like somebody just walked over your grave."

His attempt at growing a full beard was a disaster. The growth never quite connected with its hoped-for destination, leaving large areas of defoliated white space with red freckles. With this start in life, one might suggest Purvis cash in what chips he had and seek the lowest common denominator of a job, a Beetle Bailey position cleaning latrines or, perhaps, working at the toll collecting station on the Florida Sunshine State Parkway. After all, he was somewhat proficient with numbers, even higher denominations.

But that was not Purvis. After the Taco Bell debacle, he felt the mall security guard post was the ground rung on his repressed desire to become a law officer. In such a position, he could command respect, even if he were neither allowed a sidearm or a real badge. He was issued a billy club which he kept holstered.

———

We left the Britnell's in an agitated state. Young Fairleigh had disappeared, and a novice security guard was confronting his first challenge on the job. After the initial series of perfunctory but adequate questions, Purvis felt that old familiar Taco Bell panic creeping into his voice. He could hear his tummy gurgling like a dishwasher and felt the urge to seek the men's room. His first thought was to call Gladys. She would know—as she had throughout his life-exactly what to do.

But this was the day of Purvis Periwinkle's transformation. Pushed to the brink for a lifetime, it was now or never. He had reached the caboose of the humiliation train. He could either pull the emergency cord or buck himself up. He pictured Gladys in her ridiculous bonnet and pocketbook so large it dragged the floor, lecturing him for not just this but multiple failures. He envisioned a crowd gathered around witnessing a barrage of put-downs.

On this day, Purvis was reborn. No, not as some Dirty Harry-style mall cop with a stick, but as a detective with powers of observation. Also, a modicum of diplomatic sense swept over him. His voice didn't squeak when he spoke but had more of a Bing Crosby lower gear.

"Mr. Britnell, don't worry. We will find your daughter. For the last two days, I had been suspicious of a straggly-looking couple, even followed them around. They carried a huge sack and seemed interested in the children around the Mall's Santa Claus display. They looked as if they were from some religious cult. On the first day I saw them, I followed them outside as they got into an old Volkswagen van."

As Purvis talked, he called in a possible kidnapping to the Orlando police, relaying the license plate number he had dutifully put in a notebook. Within a matter of moments, the description of the van and the license number was broadcast to Florida's Highway Patrol. Perhaps Purvis had found his calling.

It was this unfortunate happenstance that brought Periwinkle and the Britnell family together. Neither knew that their mall meeting would, as luck would have it, cast characters together in a ship of errant souls. The Jeremy and Sarah were lost until they found each other. Purvis was only in the orbit of his grandmother until freed by circumstances. Together, however, they were silver cylinders in a pinball machine, randomly in motion.

Purvis was rail thin, and his security slacks were held up by a belt sizes larger than his 29-inch waist, the tail of which slapped back and forth when he walked. Despite his awkward mannerisms, Periwinkle attempted to play the competent, even efficient mall cop. While the couple, by no means, were put at ease, they felt the guard's compassion and sincerity in the middle of white heat fear and the out-of-body feeling that this couldn't be happening to them.

But yet it was happening and to Jeremy and Sarah Britnell of Hawks Nest subdivision, a relatively normal couple of modest means with hope and technicolor dreams. They were about to become the central characters in a nightmare that would define their future in the bleakest of terms. Along the way, they had collected the future fortunes of a security guard misfit.

A chill tap-danced up Jeremy's spine, and then a cloud of blue gloom. He had felt this way one time before, but only through the rushed words and frightened eyes of a father who helplessly watched divers search the murky bottom of a Florida lake for a missing teenager. At the time, he was anguished as he knew this father must be, and now—this very moment—the image of the man came back to him. It had only been last year, and he was chronicling events as a news reporter. Now, he was the man in the bullseye of tragedy.

Usually, a quick search of the mall's exciting enticements for a four-year-old would discover Fairleigh captivated by the sights and sounds stores embraced during the holiday season. She would be sitting wide-eyed watching a display, maybe a toy train traversing tunnels and a miniature city. It would be a nervous moment, but there would eventually be an audible sigh of relief, a finger-wagging admonishment, ending with hugs and smiles. It would simply be another anxious moment in parenting.

But now, it had been 45 minutes since the child was discovered missing, and the windows of opportunity were fast closing. Three other guards who patrolled the massive commercial structure arrived, and the search party divided, going in different directions of a mall that covered 1.1 million square meters. By now, a contingent of Orlando police and several detectives had big-footed Purvis and were taking charge, asking the same questions as had Purvis. Not as sensitive as Periwinkle, this primary officer made the mistake of telling Sarah and Jeremy about a previous incident he recalled from a television drama. In that case, the child disappeared forever. Sarah, who had regained her composure with Periwinkle's calm and comforting demeanor, was flooding tears again.

The couple had, indeed, lost their only child. She disappeared from the most common of places, a child's nursery in the center of an upscale mall where millions of dollars bought Christmas knick-knacks, what-nots, and clothing items certain to be returned. The grumpy Santa Claus was still on his holiday throne, making promises he could not keep and pretending to be jolly when he would rather be at the pub sucking on a long neck beer and watching a Saturday football game. Santa, and everyone, were oblivious of the drama taking place a few storefronts away.

Sarah was on the verge of panicking. Jeremy, generally snow cone cool, was fighting to keep his wits for Sarah's sake. The woman in charge of the PlayTime nursery protested she had only left the playroom for a mere moment, and besides, she was just coming on duty.

"We changed shifts," she said. "I was only in the ladies' room a moment or two putting on my PlayTime outfit. Alice had to leave before I emerged. The last I saw her, the little girl was in the corner playing with her doll. Wait! I remember this strange couple with their faces pressed against the window looking in. Do you think..?"

The Britnell's had casually returned from the cineplex, which was not more than 50 yards away and on the same floor as the PlayTime Nursery. On the way, they discussed that the movie was overrated and certainly didn't deserve the Four Stars given it by the Orlando Sentinel reviewer. They carried a half bucket of cheese-flavored popcorn, having saved it for Fairleigh. It was her favorite.

Within only five minutes, with Ruth creating a simple diversion at Santa's throne by pretending to be blind, lost, and hysterical while drawing the crowd's attention, Joshua walked into the nursery. He scooped up the child without being noticed. Snuggled in the large sack, Fairleigh wasn't sure what was happening but thought it must be some sort of game organized for her amusement.

The escalator just a few steps away, Joshua — who by now was a common sight at the mall—slipped out to the parking lot and the waiting 1962 Volkswagen van. He tossed the child in the back like a sack of laundry, hitting her head hard against the wheel well. She was conscious but confused. It was only then that she cried out, "Where's mommy? Where's mommy?"

It took a few nervous moments for Joshua to hot-wire the van that had been recently dead-of-night acquired from a used car lot on US 441 called "No Money Down Don's." The sign in the vehicle's window had a price tag on the junker of $459.99, but it was hardly worth that amount even as scape medal. The van sputtered a half dozen times before finally catching, groaning and moaning,

Ruthie, meanwhile, had a miraculous transformation. She shyly thanked the group in a hoarse whisper for their concern or, perhaps, curiosity. In keeping with the aesthetic motif of her dress and severe demeanor, the kidnapping accomplice complained that the devil had momentarily engulfed her with evil spirits. She was now, however, perfectly fine. She was anxious to visit her newfound child and walked zombie-like, the same route Joshua had taken escaping the mall.

Mall crowds are, in general, more concerned about last-minute Christmas shopping than genuine human frailties. So onlookers were content to gaze after her, mumbling to one another about the strange occurrence, as Ruthie navigated her way to the escalator. They were once again a happy family-- a common-law husband's promise had been fulfilled.

By sunset, they approached the Florida-Georgia line on Interstate 95, stopping long enough at the welcome station to score free coffee, a complimentary bag of Georgia peanuts, and to have an up-close and personal inspection of the child they would name Mary. Joshua also rifled through a collection of current but swiped license plates he carried for apparent purposes and chose one because it was colorful and had a catchy slogan: "Wild, Wonderful West Virginia."

Other than a red bump at the crown of her head, the couple's first up-close inspection of Fairleigh, who had fallen asleep in the canvas sack, was of a healthy child. She opened her eyes and repeated a refrain they were to hear often: "Where's mama? Where's daddy?" To which, Ruthie replied, "I'm your mommy now. Joshua here is your daddy."

Ruthie turned to Joshua, "Where are we headed now?"

He replied, "Our license plate says West Virginia. That's as good a place as any to raise a young'un. They got hills like back home."

"What do you think her name is, Daddy Joshua?"

"Don't make much difference, does it, Mommy Ruthie? I sort of like Mary since she came to us at Christmas time, and, you could say, she is a gift from the Virgin Mary."

"Joshua, you are so smart and so Godly. We're a good, Christian family to raise a child. I like the name, Mary."

CHAPTER 6
A LOST CHILD

These events all occurred 15 years ago, and, as the saying goes, a lot of water has gone under the bridge; and, in fact, swept that old bridge far away. Not even wood splinters remained.

Oddly enough, lousy fortune for the Britnell's turned into good luck for security guard Purvis Periwinkle. He gained his independence from Gladys Hogan and recaptured a soul he never knew or thought he would encounter again—even by accident just walking down the main street of casual existence.

His life became intertwined with the shredded remnants of the Britnell couple, which, at this point, couldn't be considered a couple in the usual sense of the word. The baling wire was frayed.

Sarah never recovered the trauma of her missing child, and, given her previous insecurities, the blue fog of mental confusion revisited like Banquo's ghost. She wasn't catatonic, merely a serene version of her former self. It was as if she had been gutted of emotional brainwaves, and what was left were her basic survival instincts on a long, winding road with absolutely no end.

She was a zombie without an attitude. There was no fight left, only an occasional faint smile of undetermined cause and grey-green eyes that often searched out points over a horizon. While she had never seen them, visions of the odd couple described by Purvis and other witnesses came to Sarah nightly. She was curious about them, but, for a strange reason, her thoughts were absent of anger.

Sarah's prospects were for her to grow to middle-age at The Hanover Center, a pleasant enough place in a tranquil countryside setting a few miles southeast of Orlando outside a town called St. Cloud. She was admitted under a unique Florida disability program, and the $125,000 a year residence care fee was paid for by an anonymous family foundation. Jeremy couldn't begin to support her treatment at Hanover, but when he requested the name of the generous family, he was stonewalled. While it was indeed a fortunate happenstance, no luck could suppress Jeremy's despair over losing his daughter and wife in that one collective moment.

Through it all, Jeremy visited Sarah daily. He was there for her when she awoke, taking her for breakfast at the facility's small cafeteria, and then for a stroll around the gardens. Jeremy held her hand, but it was clammy. It was the hand of someone he once knew, but now she had journeyed far from him. Sarah was in her world with no doors or windows to escape. Not even the gentle breeze could flow through.

On occasion, she called Jeremy Dr. Casey, a soap opera character she watched every afternoon. Other times, she would ask him his name and then promptly forget it a moment later. Unfortunately, he was not prepared for this. The doctors had told him there was always a possibility she would recover, but he should face the fact that normalcy— whatever that meant in Britnell's world—might never return.

Jeremy was as patient as a faithful hound dog. Every moment he held on to the slender reed that when he awoke, Fairleigh would walk into the room laughing, and he would turn his head and see the wakeup eyes of his Sarah and her mussed up hair flowing over on his pillow. Each afternoon, he returned to the center and again in the early evening. She had been his everything and, after the disappearance of Fairleigh, was his only thing. The doctors informed him he would be taking an enormous risk if he removed her from Hanover to live with him.

"Jeremy, she doesn't know who in the hell you are," said Dr. Clarence Gardner, the chief psychiatrist. He prescribed her medicine and held one-way therapy sessions where Sarah, while appearing attentive, was a civilization away. "Son, twice she has attempted to walk away from here, saying she was headed home to Dallas. From what you told me, she's never even been to Dallas. She just watches reruns of that old TV show."

To be near the center, Jeremy sold the couple's suburban home and found a houseboat located on a lake a stone's throw from Hanover. It was a modest abode, room enough for a trundle bed and a bachelor kitchen. He had electricity powered by a used Onan generator to charge his computer and watch occasional television.

For the most practical reasons, he abandoned his newspaper career. Instead, he dedicated his life to finding Fairleigh and — after a while—locating other children who were inexplicably separated from their parents. This became, in the aggregate, no less than a holy mission. Given his lot in life, it was a purpose. It was enough for him and too much at the same time. He did some freelance writing, which helped pay his meager upkeep. He paid cash for the boat with proceeds from his house and named it with his crude artistry on the stern, "Fairleigh." He traded his Ford Taurus he had recently purchased with Sarah for a 20-year-old pickup truck and pocketed a few grand in the process. He wouldn't starve.

Jeremy visited the Orlando Police Department so often some of the newer officers thought he was a plain-clothed cop they simply had not met yet. Each time, the answer was the same. We are doing everything possible, Mr. Britnell, to find your daughter. The case seems to have grown cold, but we're following every possible clue. It wasn't as if it were a needle in a haystack. The leads were billboarded in neon: An odd-looking hillbilly couple and a small girl—an old Volkswagen van. For heaven's sake, in the beginning, they had the number of the Florida license plate. It haunted him that his daughter might be within earshot of him, and he not know it. Perhaps the abductors had changed Fairleigh's appearance and theirs. The van's license plate had been lifted from an old Buick for sale at

Al's Used Cars and was one of several Joshua used to mix and match at frequent intervals.

Such thoughts messed continuously with Jeremy's mind. Also, at the police station, he had overheard an unsettling comment: "Someone should tell that poor fellow it has been months. We're now looking for a body, not an alive girl. They were comments meant not to be heard. Everyone at the station sympathized with Jeremy, and many had encountered him as a reporter for the local newspaper.

The Fairleigh case had garnered national interest and was featured on the national news. Britnell was interviewed on multiple occasions on television, radio, and in various publications. He felt by being a megaphone for his daughter's disappearance someone could offer a relevant clue. He even published his cell phone number, hoping that whoever had his daughter would call and ask for a ransom. He wouldn't have had the money to pay it, but at least there would be progress. He had not anticipated the deluge of crackpot calls. However, the public's memory is shorter than that of a gnat, and the Fairleigh disappearance was a snapshot in time, forgotten with next week's headlines.

While not finding either Fairleigh or what might be left of her, Jeremy's efforts at putting lost children with desperate parents together garnered a modicum of notoriety. This was true particularly after he located the Jimmy Johnson kid.

Jimmy, who was Fairleigh's age, was last seen in front of his house where he was playing hide-and-seek with an imaginary friend who the youngster called Mr. Bojangles, a fellow who danced a funny jig on cue with only him hearing the melodic tune that juiced his feet to action. It was sort of a mountain man clog with a silent orchestra.

Mr. Bojangles, of course, was not at all invisible. He just told little Jimmy he was. Having taught to be respectful of elders—even weird ones—Jimmy took Mr. Bojangles at his word and obeyed when told to hide in a house at the end of the street, which most everyone assumed was vacant. It wasn't. It belonged to Mr. Bojangles, who no one had ever seen enter or leave the modest red brick home. The grass had not been cut in nearly a year, and the approach to it looked like a jungle. It was a neighborhood eyesore.

For the most part, Bojangles was a nocturnal character, though, on weekends, he had been seen in Orlando's Eola Park dancing music-less by the lake. He was considered harmless, even funny, by the police who patrolled the area. He was different from the other street denizens who panhandled for booze because he didn't offer his cap for change.

In the red brick house at the end of the street, Mr. Bojangles fed Jimmy an assortment of sweets, mostly Reese's Peanut Butter Cups, to which the kid became addicted. Bojangles cared for him and danced on cue as the boy laughed and gnawed his way through a mountain of candy. The child felt it was Halloween 24-7. He didn't seem to have the slightest inclination to return to his home, which was only a long block down the street.

After Jimmy had been entertained by the dancing

Mr. Bojangles for several days, the lad was discovered by a former reporter named Britnell, though not through any super sleuthing on Jeremy's part. The tow-head child had not been harmed in any way, though he was hyped up on a sugar high and didn't want to abandon Mr. Bojangles for his ordinary, kid life. Who could blame him? The tyke felt he had fallen into the lap of buttercup luxury. Bojangles played with him as if the two were playmates the same age and enjoyed the same child-like games, hide and seek a favorite.

Jeremy had appeared on various local television programs to talk about his missing daughter, hoping against hope that someone could offer a clue. During this particular morning broadcast on the program FrontPage Detective program on WOLF-TV, he just happened to mention the story of the hour about the missing Jimmy Johnson child. Britnell said he could feel the pain of Jimmy's mom and dad. Prefacing it by saying he was not an expert on such matters, Jeremy explained to the television audience how important it was to find Jimmy within 48 hours, a figure that the FBI had given him in the early moments of Fairleigh's disappearance. The channel was kind enough to list his cell phone number on the bottom of the screen.

Almost immediately after the program, Jeremy received a call from a frightened Mr. Bojangles. It was the name he adopted for himself in the month following his wife and child's tragic accident for which he was responsible. He was a journeyman civil service employee working for the city and had celebrated with a couple of beers at last year's office Christmas party before picking up his wife, who was shopping for presents.

Though not charged in the accident, Bojangles wore his guilt like a shroud. He had escaped miraculously without a scratch while his wife and son were killed instantly in the railroad crossing collision. His late-model Ford was no match for the 18,000-ton freight train that barreled into him, pushing his car a football field length down the track. Impatient to get home to watch a bowl game, he had foolishly attempted to race the train to the other side of the track. The police found he was not legally drunk, way under the legal alcohol limit.

"Mr. Britnell, I saw you on television tonight," said Mr. Bojangles, who had formerly referred to himself as Sammy Snead, a shy government clerk who rarely ever drank more than egg nog at Christmas and a sip of communion wine at church. His voice sounded strange as if it were coming from the bottom of a well.

"How can I help you, sir?"

"You're the fellow who hunts for missing kids, right? Your daughter was kidnapped, right? I can't help you with finding your daughter, but I know where little Jimmy is. He's here with me now, and we're just playing together. He's laughing. I'm laughing. I never meant any harm?"

Mr. Bojangles was taken into custody. The psychiatric evaluation suggested he was traumatized after the death of his wife and child and, though thoroughly unsettled and delusional, was probably not dangerous. Nevertheless, Jeremy, whose wife resided full-time at an extended care facility for folks with scrambled minds, could sympathize with Sneed/Bojangles. He almost envied his escapism.

Jeremy didn't immediately call in the authorities, as he should have. Instead, he drove to Bojangles home, saw Jimmy was neither harmed nor even frightened. Britnell sat down with the deluded fellow, and they talked for nearly an hour, with Bojangles telling the story of his family misfortune. It was the first time he had spoken of it in detail following the accident.

Only after promising Bojangles he would accompany him to return the boy to his parents did he notify the police and relate what he was doing. He attempted to explain why he was handling the situation in this way. They were puzzled and wanted to advance, metaphorically, with guns blazing, but his relationship with the cop shop was such they backed off. They respected his wishes as if he were a fellow officer.

This incident gained Britnell statewide notoriety. That's when a deliciously weird Cherokee Bleu came aboard his boat and into his life, completely interrupting its trajectory.

She was a producer for the local television series FrontPage Detective, the program on which he had appeared.

CHAPTER 7
I'M GOING TO MAKE YOU A STAR

When the lady with the floppy hat and dangly earrings approached his rust-bucket of a boat, Jeremy protested he wasn't dressed for company. He was attired in his usual Tom Sawyer get-up while puttering around.

Britnell had shed himself of everything but Levi cutoffs and a Florida Gator's cap in the face of a searing mid-day sun. He looked and sounded like a cracker, a name sometimes given in place of the more familiar redneck in other southern climes.

He was neither cracker nor redneck, though he was an incompetent nautical captain. The sound of his 60-horsepower Mercury engine frightened him. The boat rarely left the dock.

The previous boat owner had propped a rarely used cane pole on the metal railing that encircled the boat. The remains of a long-dead eviscerated worm waved in the wind. Jeremy had never had a use for the cane pole. He had never gigged a frog, clubbed an alligator, or grappled along a muddy river bank for catfish. He was neither a fisherman nor hunter and felt the deer that roamed the fields around the lake should be issued flak jackets during hunting season.

On the boat, his only protection was a pair of shish kabob sticks, though the fellow who sold him the craft suggested he at least have a .22 caliber rifle to scare off the occasional bobcat that could make ferocious noises. But that simply wasn't Jeremy.

The voice approaching his boat interrupted his daydream about how he could be of service to a community he cared little or nothing about and to which he only tangentially was a member. He was primarily driven by the possibility his efforts would, in some way, provide clues to finding his missing daughter. Also, would his talents as a curiosity-seeking reporter be of value in finding children who disappeared?

"Permission to come aboard, Captain?" The woman, who was probably a little older but appeared to be edging out of her late teens, shouted from the makeshift dock as she grabbed a splinter-laced railing that required some dexterity to maneuver.

"I assume so," replied Jeremy. "Who the hell are you? And, tell me, ma'am, is that the proper boat etiquette? I honestly don't know— and, besides, I'm really not a captain. I'm an imposter."

"Hell if I know Jeremy Butler Britnell," she replied

with the name that came on his birth certificate and the court summons he ignored for not paying dozens of parking tickets in downtown Orlando. "I might not look the part, but I am just as much a bona fide television reporter as you once were a newspaper guy. I work for WOLF-TV. Have you heard of it?"

"Yeah, of course, I have. The station runs commercials for the Florida Powerball Lottery. As you can probably tell, I've never been fortunate enough to win."

Jeremy had run into reporters from the station at various times, covering the police beat. He wasn't impressed with the lot, but this possibly had something to do with the pre-ordained prejudice against the broadcast media. Folks of Britnell's tribe generally held TV people in contempt if not up to outright ridicule. They joked that the electronic media was a passing fad, even after the internet exploded with content and social media drivel.

"Nah, Jeremy, on maritime niceties, I'm clueless. I always heard the anthem of guys: That if it floats, flies, or fucks, it's always best to rent it," she said as she climbed awkwardly over the gunwale. "Damn, I used the F-word. Does that embarrass you, Jeremy Butler Britnell?"

"I've heard it before," he said. "You apparently know me, but I don't have a clue who you are, except you are with a television channel I hardly ever watch."

"I'm Cherokee Bleu. I'm a producer-slash-reporter-slash-Girl Friday for FrontPage Detective, the program on which you appeared recently; then, by golly, you immediately went out and located that Jimmy Johnson kid, On occasion, I'm on-air talent."

"That's nice. You might ask your boss if he needs a strong fellow to take out the station's trash. I'm unemployed but available. But I guess you have that covered as well. By the way, you won me over as a multi-talented lady," said Britnell. "I welcome you on the good ship, Fairleigh, home of the mostly free but rarely brave."

Britnell had summed her up. She was excessively cute, though not beauty queen beautiful. She was raven-haired with a streak of peroxide dividing a front bang. She didn't immediately impress as a serious journalist or anyone who would go beyond the berg markets in television world. Her name seemed an affectation over the moon, and, indeed, it was. If she were a Cherokee, then he was Buffalo Bob. She did look a little like a movie-land Pocahontas. Her light brown skin seemed more than just a beach suntan.

From her eyes, she felt Jeremy's natural almost naked look was colorful and exactly what her show needed, a soulful swamp aborigine moaning over his lost family — and to wit, one who searched for other missing children. She was right on each count. But the characterization was only partly true.

In real life, before his family tragedy, Jeremy was mostly a button-down chap who was heart-attack serious much of the time. He was a responsible family fellow who drank a thimble of whiskey each night as if he were a proper church deacon. But Britnell, who wrote fiction and lived for the most part in a make-believe world, wondered at times if a more colorful motif, and publicity just might aid him in finding Fairleigh. So, he did the expected for Cherokee—put on the dog a little. He could be a swamp man for this lady.

Cherokee was sufficiently wily about what popped the public's cork. She had this idea of changing the program's name to the more ephemeral "Finding Little Jimmy," even though Little Jimmy had already been found and Mr. Bojangles hustled off for intense examination. Bojangles was awarded an extended stay at a mental facility, during which time he remained an active computer pen pal with Britnell. To Cherokee, the imagined show's title was evergreen and could be a metaphor for any child lost or taken from their parents. Later, it morphed entirely to the more encompassing, What's Happening Now.

"Jeremy, I'm going to make you famous, not just in this town--this monument to a rodent--but throughout WOLF's signal range and beyond," she declared, sitting down without asking on the side of his unkempt bed.

"Little lumpy," she said, characterizing her comfort.

"I like it that way—lumpy life. Lumpy bed and, by the way, I never said I wanted to be famous, Ms. Bleu," responded the laconic scribe. "I only want to find Fairleigh, and perhaps publicity can help. If I'm successful, maybe my wife will be well again. She's left me in spirit, but I will never abandon her."

He immediately felt his declaration sounded more

like a boast and apologized.

"That's so sweet, Jeremy. You are obviously the class of the male genre. I haven't met many men like you," she said, with a frown and a smile that came simultaneously from the curvatures of her full mouth. "In fact, I've NEVER met such a guy. Most, when I come on to them, like—if you are paying attention—I'm doing to you right now, react differently than you. They want to jump my bones and shout 'Powder River, let her buck'. But, you should know from the outset that this is just my approach to hide those deep-seated insecurities. I'm really just being polite because I'm country southern. Jeremy, can't you see I want to help you?"

Jeremy blushed in his half-nakedness as gleaming sweat beaded on his chest, and a puzzled look swept his face. Cherokee batted her eyes and smiled demurely. "Really, we can do this together, but you have to want it, and you're going to have to take some direction from me."

"What do you mean? Direction? If I am rather lame on the pickup, blame it on the sun."

"Jeremy, you strike me as a very literary fellow. I am told you like to write—that you like to tell stories. Isn't that true?"

"Well, yes, ma'am," he replied warily, "I'm a would-be, wan-a-bee but never have been."

He was unsure where the line of conversation was going and not sure he wanted to go there. But, Cherokee had captured his attention. He always considered himself an inventive but wholly ethical reporter. He never put a line in his copy he couldn't back up with a tape recorder or his notes. He wondered if Cherokee Bleu was heading in the opposite direction. If so, it didn't interest him.

Cherokee reached out and put her hand on his knee at the end of his cutoffs, stroking his bare skin absently. Her face melted into the solemnness of a funeral home reception. It was impossible to discern whether this was real or fake or a prelude to some gigantic, emotional eruption. She seemed such a volatile soul. It was frightening.

"It's nothing like you're thinking, Jeremy. I merely want you to romance the product a little. Be the character I know you can be—the Florida cracker with a heart of gold that has suffered a life catastrophe and still finds it in your heart to help others. That's what the Jimmy Johnson story is all about. That's what you are all about."

"I'm listening, but I am not connecting the dots. Romancing the product is an advertising term—like selling a headache cure for cancer. Help me out here. I'm confused. You want me to be a different personality, and then what—I'm not a phony," he said.

Instead of a gentle knee caress, she slapped him a good one on the side of his leg.

"Of course you're not, Jeremy. You're as real as they come. For us to pull this off and make it into must-watch television, you are just going to have to be a little more of who you already are. Listen, new friend; I'm flying blind here. I'm just a young—what? — a couple of years younger than you—television reporter/producer on the make. Do you know how hard it is for a girl like me, one who didn't go to any fancy journalism school and who has this Daisy Mae personality and no real connections to break into this business without fucking for success? I'll tell you, Bubba. Damn hard. And, for your information, I don't do that."

"Don't do what?"

"You know, what I just said. I might not be a classic virgin, but I don't do that unless I'm almost in love, certainly very seriously in like," she added. "And today— and I think I used it twice— was the first time I had used the F-word since Alabama beat Ole Miss in a close game in Oxford town."

Jeremy had started his journalism career at the University of Florida covering the Gators for the Orlando Sentinel, dictating a practice story five days a week, and writing a locker room sidebar on game day. He was orange and blue through and through. He well understood the drama and heartbreak of a big game loss. He smiled limply at her explanation.

"Are you real Cherokee Bleu? Or am I imagining someone showed up on my boat unannounced and is seducing me into becoming a television freak?"

"Freak? No, a genuine star. A local hero with the potential to go national. And to be honest. My name's not Cherokee. I've never met a Cherokee Indian except at the movies. My real moniker is Mary Blige, and I'm from Biloxi, Mississippi. However, that name, Blige, was already taken by some singer," she said in a rush of truthfulness. "Oh, hell, even that's a lie. Fact is, my real mama was a Seminole who did the dirty with my papa, a Blige, and I'm the unholy result of that hushed-up coupling."

"Interesting yarn," said Britnell. "Which part should I believe?"

"All of it, Swamp Daddy," she said with some assurance.

The name Blige was familiar to him. He was sure he had seen the name prominently mentioned in the pages of the Sentinel. Then, he recalled. The big boss, the major banana at the newspaper, the one whose name appeared on his paychecks, the one who dictated that a palm tree be inserted in a photo to replace a fellow he didn't much care about, the man who, more than anyone, had convinced the Disney folks to plant theme parks in Central Florida, yes, it was that William Blige. He was a minor legend. He also owned television stations, including WOLF.

There was no denying Cherokee Bleu's ambitions were already lit fireworks. In truth, she wanted to use Britnell and his accompanying tragedy as a stepping stone to improve her station's ratings and to, most likely, get a network position and nationwide viewers. She saw a well-themed and produced local show as her ticket, and she had sufficient moxie and tease to pull it off. She also appeared attracted to this married fellow whose wife was just over the hill in a mental institution. She had no rhyme nor reason for her feelings. It bothered her conscience—but not too much.

"Well, what do you think, Jeremy boy?" she finally queried. Her expression and saucer-eyes looked to Britnell like the cocker spaniel he had as a child. The pooch begged for treats on his hind legs. Cherokee was sitting so close on the bed Jeremy could feel static between them.

Britnell didn't respond to her obvious entreaties. He nervously got up and went about making a third cup of coffee, looking for a shirt to cover his sun-browned skin. It wasn't that he was obsessively shy; he just hadn't been this close to a woman, much less one as attractive as Cherokee, since Sarah departed for la-la land three winters back. He felt he was betraying her.

Finally, he said, "You know ma'am, Fairleigh would be seven years old this week. Not knowing where she is has left a black hole in my gut. It is an early morning sadness and a late evening misery. I sometimes medicate that hurt with a bottle of hooch—the brand of poison is interchangeable. Then, I see imaginary witches. They never go away. So, lady, I don't need a comforting pillow of a job. I need a solution to that hurt."

"Jeremy, I'm offering you one. I'm sure my boss will go along with it when I flutter my eyes, sashay my fanny, and tell him the station's coffers will be filled with gold— that last move, of course, sealing the deal."

"Be serious, Cherokee. Do you really think this will help me find Fairleigh, or is it just your basic red herring with polka dots pulled out of a magician's hat?" he said.

She shrugged her shoulders. "What do you have to lose, Swamp Daddy? The ticket to this dance is free. All you have to do is show up, look seriously anguished and apply your God-given talents to reconnecting little tykes with mommies and daddies. I'll do everything else."

"Oh, is that all?"

Jeremy was sarcastic. He had the humor of a poker player with a dead man's hand. He had chased multiple leads over the months, and those months were turning into years. A spooky medium had told him to look West. He had paid her $59.99 for that sage advice, and he, wondering if there were more to her soothsaying, begged her to cough up more hints. West could be anywhere from the outskirts of Orlando to San Francisco and beyond. The medium added he should also consider North and South and, for good measure, along the Eastern Seaboard. In other words, she had managed to cover a people mass of about three hundred million souls. She had covered all the bases for his penny short of sixty bucks. The spiritualist had been early days of blue sky musing when he was more than desperate. Time, though, had tamed his desperation. Reality had sunk in.

"Cherokee, having a television program is not my life's ambition. In the first place, I'm a print guy, a scribe, and television to me is Alice and Wonderland," he said, preparing a rationalized reason before giving up an outright no way refusal. "I think you need to find a glamour boy with perfect teeth and a wide-as-the-ocean smile…and.."

He stopped short of a never-ever declaration.

"Having second thoughts, Jeremy?" she asked.

"Yes," he replied, turning on a dime. "I'll do it. Just a couple of promises I want from you? Never ask me to do something Sarah would be ashamed to show or tell Fairleigh— however far that day is into the future. And, working with you because —believe it or not, I trust you, crazy me—no one tells me what stories or leads to pursue. I will, though, consult with you."

"Now we're talking, Ke-mo sah-bee," she said and stuck out a dainty paw to finalize the deal. He took it. It was warm and, to him, spoke truth behind Cherokee's difficult to figure out veil.

"Oh, and one other thing," he said, as if an afterthought, though it was not nearly. "I've recently started working with someone as an assistant—kind of a leg man. I've found him very helpful in solving cases. I don't mean to bust the budget, but, for lack of a better term, let's call him a sort of Sancho Panza, or, if you prefer his actual name—which he detests— it's Purvis Periwinkle."

"Does he ride a donkey named Dapple?" she responded, in keeping with the Don Quixote story. "Yes, Mr. Swamp fellow, I might look like a dumb brunette, but Mr. Cervantes was drummed into me in my Spanish class at Ole Miss. I had to translate the whole thing into Spanish, which seemed rather silly since it was written in Spanish. But, to answer your question: Sure, of course, I might have to wiggle and walk a mile for the moneyman, but we can swing it if it's reasonable."

"If I know Sancho, he'll work for Big Macs, party favors, and bling you might have leftover from your station's Christmas party," replied Britnell. "Really, I need him, and I have a special attachment since he has been active in helping me locate Fairleigh. Think of what you would pay for a security guard, and I will make up the difference."

"Okay, money bags. It's a deal. Thanks for the coffee. I have to go now and figure out how I can close the deal with my office. You obviously read that Donnie Trump guy's book 'Art of the Deal'. You even get dinner out of this one. You're not vegetarian, are you?"

"Not a chance," he laughed, an unusual exercise of facial muscles these days.

Jeremy walked her off the dock and to her car. It was a late model Porsche, the type of wheels about which Britnell could only dream.

"Nice car. I was under the distinct impression you were a poor girl from Mississippi. You know, just off the farm. Probably a cheerleader and damn popular because you are..well.. Cherokee Bleu. This is the type of car I would have to knock over 7-11 stores every night for the rest of my life just to pay for the tires."

"Jeremy, poor is relative," she started in a monotone, looking at the ground. I should have told you that my uncle owns the television station where I work, WLOF, and a bunch of others out West. He also owns the newspaper for which you so recently worked."

"That Blige?" Britnell tried not to act too surprised.

"So, technically, strictly speaking, I'm not poor. My given name wasn't Cherokee, and I probably can afford to buy you dinner at Disney Springs some night if you care to join me, partner. Or, we can fly to New York on my plane. It's a nifty twin-engine Beechcraft Baron. I'm in training to fly small jets, but I haven't sufficient hours yet to solo. I know this terrific place just off-Broadway. So, Jeremy, yes, I think I lied to you big time. I'm sure you have done that yourself on occasion in pursuit of something other than the door prize. But I do want to help you become what I know you can be...and also to find Fairleigh."

Jeremy had the obvious question. "But why me? I have a sad story, that's all."

"Oh, Mr. Britnell, I'm a sad story-eater. My coming here today is no accident. I have followed your wanderings and musings for the last two years. I read your writing in the Sentinel before that."

Jeremy scratched the back of his head and squinted at her, a look that shouted forever doubt but then again, just maybe. "So, you're a rich stalker slumming in the low-rent district. Doesn't that beat all? You had me going for a while, Cherokee. In that case, I want a raise for my faithful Sancho, Purvis Periwinkle."

"Don't press your luck, Swampy," she laughed.

By this time, Britnell simply didn't know what to think of Ms. Cherokee Bleu, who was neither Cherokee but was from the Blige linage. She was a blue ribbon baby who was sure to live in a fancy manor in the rich-flavored section of town, most likely Winter Park. Jeremy was well-acquainted with personality facades because he was, in fact, hiding behind one himself. She intrigued him, and that curiosity, in itself, haunted him.

In this short span, he had reserved a room for her in his consciousness. He felt, however, that getting too close was cheating Sarah. His heart and soul belonged to Sarah, whether it was the old Sarah he married or the withering ghost she had become.

Jeremy's eyes followed the red Porsche as it traversed a rutted orange grove road of sand and rock and disappeared. He continued to watch the horizon for several minutes.

The sun was eye-level but fast sinking. The cocktail that was his life had just been shaken, none to gently.

CHAPTER 8
LOST LOVE

It was the shank of the day, time for Jeremy to forget this Cherokee lady and walk to the mental health home that was extinguishing his hope, the flimsy thought that Sarah would return to him.

He enjoyed the nearly two-mile walk each day, though his arrival was not something graciously anticipated by the patient in Room 249. She dreaded his coming. To her, he was Dr. Ben Casey, a young man without the usual white frock and dangling stethoscope. She was hesitant around him, even scared.

Dr. Casey didn't seem to have a purpose, and he could be so touchy-feely with her that Sarah thought about reporting him to the hospital nurses. In Dallas, there wouldn't be a Dr. Casey. Everyone would be professional.

The doctors were less than optimistic about her chances of recovery. They had spoken to Jeremy in whispered tones as if Sarah were in the same room, which she wasn't. They had seen such cases before and in a mid-evil period—really just a half-century ago— would have tried electric shocks and even, perhaps, a discredited operation.

Sarah was, figuratively, already lobotomized. Hence, they did what they could, gentle talk, tough talk, an inspirational sermonette, and, of course, a colorful array of pills. The blue ones for Sarah had a particular fatal attraction. So, she collected them, one each day of the two given, building a sizable stash over time.

As Jeremy walked on, the roof of the Hanover Clinic in his sight, thoughts crowded his head, almost as they did when he wrote a novel, characters yapped in his ear like Australian magpies. He had lost Fairleigh, but there was a reed of hope that by the slimmest of chances, a clue would break daylight.

He held on to that thought, a lifeline with which he took to sleep each night. Miracles had happened before. He had read about it, and had seen television footage of the joyful reunion. It was packaged in gauzy images with a melodic soundtrack. Even if everyone else lost hope, it was up to him to remain steadfast.

As he approached the crest of the hill, he could see in the distance patients of the Hanover facility on the expansive lawn. He had been thinking of Fairleigh, picturing her in the various stages of her evolving life. She would be seven, fast heading into the third grade at Park Edge Elementary school in their middle-class Hawk's Nest neighborhood. She would be playing on a swing set, and he would gently shove her back and forth. He then pictured her as a perky teenager, with all the problems of a developing girl, and then as a young woman, perhaps following in his footsteps as a journalist. In each of these mind frames, Sarah was part of the photograph. Jeremy traced the metamorphic changes in detail over the 25-minute walk. He pictured grandchildren he and Sarah would dote over in old age.

As Fairleigh developed right before his life in cinemascope, however, the image of a Sarah began to fade, fragmented into ever-increasing numbers of pixels. The juxtaposition was jarring. It was not the way it was supposed to be. They had planned a future, and while it would never be perfect, it would be satisfactory, even at dead calm, and that would be sufficient. Now, at the moment, absolutely everything had to be looked at in the forever past tense, hidden behind memory clouds.

As he approached the Hanover facility, a nurse saw him coming from a distance. He saw her frantically hurry back inside to retrieve the hospital administrator and Sarah's doctor. They were prepared for him as he walked through the double glass doors. The doctor had a surprised look as if Jeremy didn't visit every single day at this precise hour. Some of the patients could set their daily pill lineup outside the pharmacy door by his arrival. Britnell, who often thought in headlines large and small, saw this one as a billboard on Times Square. Both the doctor and nurse telegraphed the news. His Sarah had left for Dallas, checking out of the Hanover facility.

It was always difficult to tell a loved one that a wife,

husband, or child had died. In Sarah's case, her ending was a matter of her choice. She did it on her terms and in her own time. The doctor said, simply, "I'm sorry, Jeremy. She's gone."

"Gone where?" Though he asked, he knew.

"She expired," the doctor said.

"Expired? Expired?" said Jeremy, his voice rising. "A credit card expires. You mean she died."

It was an odd rejoinder, but grief impacts people in varying ways. Jeremy Britnell was angry. Angry at the Hanover Clinic. Angry at the doctor and angry with Sarah. He was also mad at himself.

After collecting sky blue sleeping pills saved for the planned exit, she was not prepared to meet this Dr. Casey, who called himself Jeremy and who seemed to be constantly smiling. It was the mask he wore to show a brave face.

Sarah laughed at her deception. She had pulled off the ultimate joke on her Dr. Casey and that she could now journey westward to her Dallas whenever she pleased, using whatever transportation she could imagine.

The doctor said her journey was painless, that she simply floated away.

"Yes, obviously," said the bitter husband, then a minor, sarcastic laugh, "I guess she took the last train to

Dallas."

CHAPTER 9
GONE TO DALLAS

Of course, Jeremy had heard the ring of his mobile phone, and, from time to time, he would glance at it, see the caller's name, and then ignore it.

The text messages would be the same, often from people with whom he worked at the newspaper. He did not want or appreciate condolences or cheer-up bon mots.

He wanted misery. He wanted to wallow in it.

However, he did take a call from oddball Purvis Periwinkle, who ironically had become his pal, and would drop by occasionally to check on him. It wasn't an extended conversation.

"Can I bring you anything, chief?"

"Nah, I'm doing fine, Purvis.

Cherokee Bleu-Blige called him numerous times over

the following days and left messages on his phone. The St. Cloud Home for Funerals telephoned, wanting to discuss the necessary arrangements.

Did he want the deluxe casket or the standard in which Sarah would lie? Did he want a decorative liner that would also prevent leakage from groundwater? Never a detail person, except as a rather precise reporter, Britnell ignored them all.

Jeremy was not available. He wasn't home for anyone, including himself. Besides, he had company in his loneliness. He was holding a seance with bottles of Jack Daniels, his Martin D-28 guitar, and a wood-framed, double picture of Sarah and Fairleigh, which he cradled on his stomach.

In a prone position and managing to bring glasses of whiskey to his lips, he only occasionally spilled gulps on his shirt. After all, the liquor was expensive, and he didn't have a real job. He also had something else: A .45 caliber Beretta described in catalogs as a tactical weapon. Nowhere in the Beretta sales pitch was it called a swell gun for suicides. Having purchased it at a gun show at the city's municipal auditorium, he tried the barrel fit to his temple, then to his mouth, and then he fell asleep. When he awoke, the gun was at his side, cocked.

Jeremy did show up two days later for Sarah's burial, courtesy of Purvis, who had cleaned the empty Coca-Cola cans and chocolate wrappers from his own Ford pickup. As they drove to the cemetery, neither said a word, though Periwinkle did note with a grunt the dreary weather.

"Suppose to get better tomorrow, Jeremy. What do you think?"

There was silence.

The event was held without a formal service at the gravesite under the direction of the institution's chaplain. He offered up a string of well-worn cliches he read from a folded paper. It was apparent he hadn't spent a lot of time in preparation. Sarah wasn't the religious sort. The litany, though, was sufficiently accurate to portray it as an official, bona fide send-off.

Though was so drunk, he could hardly stand. He wavered over the mound of earth. The chaplain Rev. Mortimer Hoggs and Purvis —the only other attendees— steadied him. As fitting the occasion, the skies were devil dark without the decency to spit a cool rain. Sarah was in a fine carbon metal coffin. They charged Britnell for the Deluxe version since he had not responded to the sales pitch, and Purvis had posted a downpayment on the entire shebang, which, in total, would set him back four grand, a princely sum for the former Taco Bell screwup.

Sarah wouldn't have cared if she were buried in a cardboard box. Instead, though, the casket had a cloudy pink hue mixed with shiny gray, and the trimmings, picked out by the funeral home director, were white lace with purple bows. Judy Garland's "Somewhere Over the Rainbow" was provided by a boom box set up on a portable podium. There was an extra charge for this, itemized under musical interlude.

If Jeremy were aware on this solemn occasion, he would wonder, though probably not aloud, whether Sarah had finally made it to Dallas and whether she had come in contact with the antagonist, the infamous J.R. Once, he had written a story about death and funerals. This topic had little interest to him but was assigned by his city editor.

Once he researched—and this is what he recalled at this particular moment—he learned that with death, cell structure breaks down, causing the body's tissue to become a watery mush. After about a year, the corpse's clothes decompose due to chemicals the body has produced. And, just like that, his lovely, shy Sarah would change from being a sleeping beauty to naked mush. The macabre thought terrified and sickened him. That's no way to arrive in Dallas.

Purvis grabbed him by the arm, gently pulling him away from the grave and away from the cemetery. He hesitated just a moment but obliged. The service had lasted less than 20-minutes, obviously the express version. The Rev. Hoggs had expected an extra gratuity at the end, and Purvis obliged him.

As they reached the parking lot, Cherokee was sitting in her Porsche. She had a yellow scarf over her head and was absent the dancing eyes and teasing sass. She dropped her hands from the steering wheel she was holding so tightly her fingers were pinched pink. She gave him a warm, sympathetic smile, proper post-funeral continence.

"Hi Cherokee," Jeremy said absently; with Purvis

holding him up less, he fell over into her car. He had the blurry-eyed look of someone who had journeyed to hell and had stayed for breakfast and an eye-opener. He still managed a cagey grin. "What are you doing here, sweetheart? Long time, no see."

The sound, for sure, wasn't really Britnell speaking. It was an out-of-body reflection of the cinematography of yesteryear. It was a drunk Bogie in Casablanca. It was Jeremy being his other self, the unpublished writer of neither note nor notoriety. It was the make-believe fellow who had been comfortable being Sarah's husband and Fairleigh's dad. The everyman man who was striving to stand out in the crowd of faceless strugglers and pitiful strivers waiting in line for that one elusive chance that always seemed a blip over the next horizon. It all now seemed somewhat distant, faded, and unimportant. Certainly not in the Top 20 on the dance chart. Okay, lyrics perhaps, but you couldn't stroll, sashay, twist or bop to the beat.

"Hi Jeremy, pretty rotten to hell, fucked up day, isn't it partner," she said. "I tried to call you. I left messages. I'm so sorry about Sarah. She's no longer in pain."

Cherokee was not happy with her words. She spoke as if Sarah were a friend, but they had never met, unless perchance in the Wal-Mart, and it was doubtful Cherokee ever shopped where they shouted "Everyday Low Prices." She felt her condolences represented a soulless and inadequate soliloquy and started again after searching for thoughts. She sucked up a deep breath, and her chest heaved.

"Oh Jeremy, Jeremy, let me be with you for a while. Don't push me away, friend. I don't know why, but I think you need me right now. I can help you, trust me. It's part of my job as your manager."

"Uh, manager? Don't need a manager but could use an afternoon toddy," he slurred.

Standing to the side, Purvis nodded goofily at Cherokee taking charge. He was afraid to have the responsibility. It was a challenge beyond his talents, but he wanted his friend to be whole again and was glad she had mercifully intervened.

"I'll check in with you later, buddy," he said, and to Cherokee, who he had just met, "You take care of Jeremy, please. His hurt is powerful, and he's my friend."

She needn't have implored him. Cherokee had shed all her pretensions, her sorority sister fake-ness, her rich girl faux European lilt that she could turn on and off like a light switch. She was all in, not as a girlfriend or wife, for she was undoubtedly neither, but as someone who magnetically felt the survival of Jeremy Britnell was simply up to her. One simply doesn't turn down a holy commission.

"Come with me, Jeremy. I'll take you to your boat, and from there, mister, I'm just going to play it by ear because, on this day, you are like one of those thousand-word puzzles jumbled up in a box, and we need to find at least two pieces that fit together."

Jeremy surrendered.

"Okay, manager, but do you mind stopping at the ABC Liquor store? I have a toothache and need it needs medication."

"In your dreams," she replied, but under her breath.

He steadied himself on the Porsche as he swayed back and forth until he found the opposite door and flopped himself on the seat beside her. He managed a mere few words before he nodded off.

"This is not me," he muttered. "Is it?"

"No, Sleeping Beauty, it's not you."

By the time they arrived at the boat dock, Jeremy had begun to open his eyes. It was a slow process, and then they darted this way and that way like he was watching a ping-pong match. It was as if he were viewing an awake world for the first time. Jeremy didn't realize where he was or how he had managed to get there. It took a moment for familiarity to ring true. He glanced over at Cherokee. She was waiting for him to regain a semblance of the here and now.

"How you feeling, Swamp Daddy? Are you seeing one of me or three? Whatever you do, don't upchuck in the car. Puke is hard to get out of leather upholstery. Just lean over the side and projectile blow."

"Damn, you have a lot of demands, Miss Geronimo," he mumbled, but as he did, he indeed heaved overboard, taking care not to hit the freshly polished red paint.

"Damn, and on our first date," she laughed at her exaggeration, and handed him a handkerchief.

Jeremy still was not focusing, but instinctively realized he was violating all the probity he inherited from the poor but morally upright Britnell clan. The proper verities re-enforced by his wife on the few occasions he stepped out of line with colorful verbiage after one beer over his limit of two. He wondered how in the world this false ingenue parachuted into his pathetic state.

"Trust me, novice drunk. You're going to feel better almost immediately. I'll get you to that tub of yours, and I just bet I can put together a concoction that will perk you right up. I carry a small bottle of Tabasco sauce, milkweed, and Calico Cat piss in my purse for just such an occasion."

"You're joking, I hope," he said weakly.

"Yeah, partner, milkweed is toxic, and I don't have a Calico Cat, but If you have a Dr. Pepper and carbonated soda, you'll be good as new. You do have Dr. Pepper, right? In Mississippi, it's the drink of champions mixed, of course, with a bag of Tom's peanuts. I doubt you have peanuts."

He vaguely followed what she was saying. He was having trouble maneuvering his noggin back to sanity.

Jeremy managed the rickety gangway with some difficulty. His equilibrium teetered and tottered, and he took baby steps as if he were avoiding crunching eggs. Once inside the boat cabin, he veered toward the sofa bed, flopping down, he exhaled as if managing an extraordinary feat. He placed his hands in his face and stared at the floor. He wondered if the creaking movement was a symptom of his current depravity or caused by the gentle waves lapping against his boat. It really didn't matter. Just another life mystery visiting him on the worst goddamn day of his whole goddamn life.

"Look at me, partner. This is the first day of the rest of your existence. We're going to get through this," she assured him as she forced him to look up. She cradled his face in her hands.

"Why me, Cherokee?" Jeremy whispered. "You're not kin. You know absolutely nothing about me. Are you a Florence Nightingale specializing in washed-up journalists and drunks? Who was your tough case last week, some poor sap sitting on the curb on Church Street?"

"Well, my pathetic friend, you asked the big 'why' question. It's the dough, the big bucks. It's as simple as that," she told him. "I'm a gold digger, and you're my hapless mark. Fact is, we have the possibility of putting together a good gig—one that helps skyrocket my ratings, extend your Warhol fifteen minutes of fame for a few more clicks, while, at the same time, actually helping a few people. Plus, my uncle's bank account gets fuel injections of cash, and I remain his favorite niece. Simple as that Swamp Daddy."

Jeremy eyed her while she caught her breath for another extended salvo. He had been raised in a 39-foot trailer, back before they were double-wides and called mobile homes. He had sold donuts door-to-door as a 12-year-old to bring extra money into the household. His family home after the trailer was on Reaves Terrace, a jumble of public housing units near downtown Orlando, located across from a graveyard and a community baseball field. His dad was a good and honest man but never made it out of 9th grade. He drove a milk truck for T.G. Lee Dairy and held cookware dinner parties in the evenings where he sold stainless steel pots and pans to mostly country folk who couldn't afford it. His mom babysat for whomever she could and labored as a cashier at the Winn-Dixie. Life was hardscrabble, and the once-a-week lottery ticket his old man bought was both a joke and a lifeline. He never won. He never really came close, though he faithfully watched the televised drawing on Friday night, provided he didn't have a cookware gig.

"Oh, thought you might have given up on the idea that I was small screen material, that I, perhaps, could entertain with stale Groucho jokes while magically finding missing children and putting them with parents. And at the end of the program, everyone joins in, the parents, the children and, of course, me your host, in singing 'Kumbaya, my Lord'. What's your role, Cherokee, master of ceremonies. Keeping the tigers on the stools with a whip. That's cool."

Jeremy usually wasn't this sarcastic, but his id and his ego were galloping at heartbreak speed to the edge of a cliff on this particular day. That hidden gene kicked in, and he had this undefinable desire to push back at a woman who was kind to him. She was the Good Samaritan, but here he was using artillery he didn't know he even had to tear her down to size. He didn't want anyone's kindness, whatever the motive. But, she just smiled at him, a China plate, placid look, easily interpreted as not giving a donkey's dong about his inebriated opinion. His selfish thoughts were just so much confetti swirling in the wind. Where they lit, she would study them, and make sense of a situation that defied logic in a world where children had birthday parties at McDonald's, blew up colorful balloons, and laughed as if all was right in their neighborhood and tiny homes.

Cherokee grabbed his shoulders, maneuvered him up straight, and lectured away, but in a soft voice, not that of an impatient shrew but someone wise beyond her age. The words had the impact of exploding grenades.

"Listen, asshole. You think this is the worst day of your life, and you might be right. I'm fucking sorry about that, but my deal —which you actually shook hands-on— was not selfish collusion on my part. It's one of those win-win situations," she said. "And, believe me, buster, you need a win."

"A strict business deal, huh," Britnell burped.

"Why, Jeremy, did you think there was something more to it, like those eyes of yours caused my hormones to jitterbug and my heart to palpitate? You have to be kidding. That only happens when I listen to old Frank Sinatra recordings. I might be a hopeless romantic in the abstract, but Swamp Daddy, you ain't no Frankie blue eyes—not even close."

"I'm not?" It was a query to which he knew the answer. He had never been a babe magnet, and everyone in his world knew he and Sarah had been inseparable.

"No, in your current situation, you're more a Frankenstein than Frank," she laughed. The moment broke the tension he had manufactured.

"I checked upon you," said Jeremy, pursing his mouth and squinting his eyes. "Your uncle is one of the richest men in the south. My guess is your trust funds have trust funds. Am I a special project for the rich kid in town?"

"Is that a big problem? Should I disavow it? Give up my Porsche for a Volkswagen? Start buying my clothes at the bargain counter of Sears Roebuck, next to where they sell the tools and the Maytag washing machines. Nah, I don't think so. There are, my friend, advantages to being a silver-spooned refugee from the Gulf Coast of Mississippi whose uncle got incredibly lucky and whose daddy checked out long ago because he had a love affair with the bottle. Actually, the same brand as I see on your counter."

"Ahh, so now it all begins to make sense. At first, I thought it was an Oedipus complex, but now it's clear it's more a savior fascination. You want to rescue this whiskey-soaked fellow who's on a superhighway to your daddy's destination. Well, I am sorry about your daddy," said

Jeremy, who thought he had it all figured out. "But I'm not your daddy, or even your third cousin, twice removed. "

Cherokee put her hands on her hips, then lifted them in the air in frustration, as if she were calling on a higher power to intervene.

"First off, Swamp Boy, as a psychologist, you'd make a fairly good auto mechanic. You've obviously never contemplated Carl Jung, or you would have known the difference between the Oedipus complex and the Electra complex. Why can't you just be satisfied? You are a product, a brand, and I want to promote and sell you like Colgate toothpaste. You know, five different ingredients to make the girls go wild. New and improved. Buy the economy size, and you get a free toothbrush. That's me, buddy. I'm a marketer lady with a small screen talent and run-away ambition."

Britnell had missed the various clues. She was kidnapping his mind from the thoughts he should be having. The day had been a rung of Dante's hell which he could have never imagined. What would Sarah think? Then, it occurred to him she probably had no particular thoughts other than what's the weather like in Dallas, and do I have the proper shoes to introduce myself to that J.R. fellow on the oldies but goodies television reruns.

Jeremy surrendered, propping himself against the cushions that lined the trundle bed. Clarity had returned but in all of its deep purple and rather depressing glory.

"Cherokee, I'm not prepared for this conversation. I

just buried my wife today. My daughter has been missing for two years, and I haven't a solid clue as to what might've happened to her. Good fortune is not something that stalks me," he said. "I'm the fellow who without bad luck would have no luck at all."

"Yeah, I know, it's hopelessly sad, especially when you quote cliches from country songs. You know something, feller, you're so damn lucky I came along. Maybe I'll stay. Maybe...no, I will stay tonight to see you through to sunrise. If you awake and want breakfast, I'll fix it for you—or maybe you for me. Do you have an extra toothbrush? I'm not picky. I make a Mississippi Mud Omelette to die for. You do have eggs, don't you?"

She went over to the fridge and reconnoitered. "Hmm, a little ham, milk that's not sour, and some mystery sauce. Yeah, I can make do with that."

"What do you mean, stay, Cherokee?" He eyed her warily.

Sense and sensibility returned slowly. Given the circumstances of the day, he wasn't in the mood for an extra outside adventure that was forbidden just a few days earlier when Sarah was a zombie but still warm with an occasional hint of clarity. He had only partaken of such once during a fraternity challenge, and then the lady, Lulu, he recalled, was a hefty slam ma'am and he had what they called in the parlance of the time sloppy seconds, or maybe thirds or fourths. He wasn't even positive he had completed the deal, but Miss Lulu had let out a Rebel yell, so something must have happened that evening. He didn't remember.

While not married, he and Sarah were a couple at the time, and it bore on his conscience such that he confessed his sins—first to a doctor when he felt he had caught something awful and then to his girlfriend. She said she was disappointed but forgave him. That almost made his transgression worse. It mattered not to him that most guys his age with hormones popping like fried bacon wouldn't give it a moment's thought. The doctor had told him he confessed his sins for nothing. He had so much beer his prostate was squealing.

Cherokee was patient as he surveyed his none-to-dramatic journey in pleasure. She saw that his booze-soaked brain was still in the recovery stage.

"Stay, my friend, is a four-letter word of common usage. It should be rather obvious. I'm not going to leave you tonight on this the worse day of your goddamn life—as you put it—one where you're feeling so depressed you might take a deep dive and become a large morsel for those gigantic catfish rumored in Lake Last Chance."

"I'm not the type," protested Britnell. "I'm fine by myself. Besides, I have my buddy Jack Daniels, and I feel the after-party is about to begin. I have a special invitation to attend. Would you like to join me for a nightcap, a hair of the dog tipple?"

Cherokee walked over to the counter where his whiskey lived in lonely seclusion, waiting for its servant to return. She poured the remnants into an ice tea glass, actually a Mason jar, and waved it in front of Jeremy's nose. He reached out for it, caught air, and she pulled it back. He nearly fell from the bed to the floor. Then, she sashayed out the sliding glass doors and tossed his last fortifications over the side, but not in one big move, but slowly. Through the door, he could see every drop going into the lake.

"What the hell you do that for?"

He wavered between nuclear meltdown pissed-off and desperation. He was in training to be an alcoholic, a beginner's course he took up after Fairleigh's disappearance, but he had not mastered the finer points of rage at this point.

"Jeremy, forget about that poison. I'm your poison tonight, and, I promise, it won't kill you." She nudged him back on the bed, and he fell into the soft cushions as easily as a stuffed animal. Still, he protested.

"Forgive me, Cherokee, but I don't know what the hell you have in mind."

'You probably don't, Swamp Boy, but do you like surprises?"

"In a word, no," he said. "I'm only 30, and I have already had too many 'Pop Goes the Weasel' experiences. My days are punctuated by Freddy Kruger visits, my nights by Jason, and sometimes every moment seems like Friday the 13th. I don't need surprises, pleasant or otherwise."

Without further ceremony, Cherokee pulled herself up on the bed beside him. She had this contemplative look, this bronze complexion, accented by faintly rose cheeks. Her depthless eyes seemed to have no end. Jeremy wondered if she was simply bewitching or whether she was the witch.

"You're mine for tonight. But just don't get too excited when I pull my jeans off. I promise not to seduce you—not that you are even capable of shagging a pillow, and believe me, in the sack, I ain't no pillow. I'm a Mustang bronco who yells and bites. Are you getting just a little excited?"

With that, Cherokee stuck her legs in the air, unbuttoned her jeans, and executed in a fluid motion a removal, extracting her body from the most confining piece of clothing, and revealing a white bikini patch that covered almost nothing.

"By the way, Jeremy, I honestly don't want you to fuck me tonight. I have a feeling your Southern Baptist conscience would severely haunt you as we grow old together, have two-point-five little crumb-snatchers, and live in a double-wide off your $2.50 in author royalties a week. This, of course, after my uncle has cut off my trust funds because I didn't produce the super-duper Jeremy Britnell show about missing kids and add substantially to moneybags' bottom line. By the way, you've been pre-advertised and sold. My uncle thinks I might have some gift as a talent scout."

"Why do I feel I was just insulted, Cherokee?"

"Oh man," she pouted, "I'm sorry if I torpedoed your psychic, Mr. Britnell. I am sure you will survive. Hey, where is the remote control? Are you going to get naked, or am I just going to be embarrassed by being outrageously forward?"

"Anything else?"

"Yeah, do you like baseball? Tampa Bay is the game of the week. You wouldn't happen to have any popcorn here, would you? I'm famished."

CHAPTER 10
THE SEVENTH INNING STRETCH

It was just before the seventh-inning stretch and the refrain "take me out to the ball game" of a Tampa Bay-Kansas City Royals contest when Cherokee nibbled Jeremy's ear, rolling her tongue inside.

His first impulse was to push her away, but he got over it.

On the battlefield, it's called initiating the match, an aggressive action to soften defenses. The same is true, one assumes, in romance, unless, of course, the attention is more Machiavellian and the motive is economically driven. That was exactly Britnell's first thought. He was a paycheck, but then, this lady was richer than a Rockefeller.

At this point, though, it was difficult for Jeremy to tell with Cherokee, who he had only met a few weeks earlier. Since that initial meeting, she visited him nightly, swooping onto his boat ghost-like, but only in his imagination. He couldn't, no matter how he tried, erase her from his consciousness. He chased away sleep, summoning her until the apparition crawled under covers beside him. The fact that she was, in living color, on his bed now, mostly undressed, and within hours of him having buried his wife, was monumentally confusing but not sufficiently disturbing to will her away.

"That tickles," Jeremy said. It was neither complaint nor irritation but more an understated passive comment.

The fact was, the tableau of early Christian upbringing was playing tug-of-war with his instinctive id on one side and his moralistic superego on the other. His id had the advantage by a long shot, which was pretty typical in such situations. He felt he was in control, though, and could call a halt at any time. He often fooled himself that way as a newsman and on such weighty topics as choosing plastic, boxes, or paper sacks at the Winn-Dixie market.

Cherokee had kept on her white briefs and a blue Polo shirt with a WOLF-TV logo. All in all, it was a fetching presentation for a guy celibate for nearly three years. He was lying nervous but comfortable in his olive-brown skivvies, and old Rumpelstiltskin — Sarah's pet name for his southern direction—was preening for glory. It was a blatant, uncontrolled show of the flag.

"Are you complaining?" She wiggled so close to him they were mating spoons. "Forgive me, Swamp Boy, but I want you. And not as a thirst quencher, but as an I want to wake up in the morning to sour whiskey breath and sweet sweat after the world's greatest shag. And then I want the same for dessert."

Jeremy was the type of fellow who allowed porno ads on the internet to tease but was sure if he were even to take a peek, the computer camera lens would light up like a klieg, klaxons would go off, and someone, somewhere would register him like a horny soul and, most likely, sex-crazed. A sex offender sign would be put next to his pickup in the sandy space under an orange tree.

"I know, you want to make money for your uncle off me," said Britnell, abstractly, keeping away from the main topic. He did what people often do in such embarrassing situations. He coughed in his hand and looked out through the sliding glass door to some distant object across the lake. He thought he saw a pelican, but it could just have easily been a vulture in the moonlit distance.

The truth was Jeremy was in a teenage wet dream zone, and though now mostly sober, was not quite within his wits. His retort to Cherokee bordered on an insult. It lacked any normal male intuitiveness. An average person might scream obscenities and flee the scene. This Ms. Blige was anything but ordinary.

"Believe me, Cherokee, I understand that, and I'm beginning to accept the idea, even if I never saw myself as a pitchman, even if it is for a good cause. I'm more of a behind-the-scenes type."

"Don't be obtuse," she feigned exasperation. "Did you hear me right, Jeremy? I said I wanted you. I know that makes me a horrible person, particularly on this particular day, but the clock has slipped past midnight, and this is, in essence, your birthday of sorts. You are now investigative reporter Jeremy Britnell, out to defeat evil and right wrongs. You have a new job, a new semi-girlfriend though you haven't realized it yet, as well as the aforementioned personal manager. You, my fellow, were struck with pixie dust this evening. Don't blow it."

She had rarely called him by his actual name, merely by a collection of random proper nouns that paraded through her head and, in some way, reminded her of a silly appellation that never came close to the mark. He knew this as the gospel according to the Britnell history of exploded egos. He was just plain old Jeremy, nothing special, not a swamp creature, and, by the way—he would later say—"there's no swamp Cherokee within thirty miles of this lake."

"So Jeremy, are you going to give me a long, wet kiss and seduce me this early a.m., or are you going to waste that terrific boner, which, if it expires, could cause you to break out in hives and have serious mental complications,"

Jeremy looked into her eyes, and they exploded in the moonlight into golden amber shards. They were slightly recessed, and he, no student of great art for sure, imagined a face painted by a 17th Century master, Vermeer. But Cherokee was no babydoll with porcelain skin. She had ragamuffin edges even though she was on the periphery of blue blood pretensions. At times, she could be that truck-stop harlot, but one who had a soft heart. Jeremy was the prime example of that. He had been tapped and trapped and was on a superhighway to being smitten.

Cherokee was, of course, right. He sighed as if realizing that the grass is green and the sky is blue for the first time. His breath came from the pit of his lungs. He was no longer confused or conflicted with his lovely Sarah in a cemetery a half-hour away, a place he would never visit for a convenient reason: She was not there. Sarah was in Dallas.

"Well, Cherokee, when you put it that way..my options are apparent and limited.

—

They ended up having a lifetime of nose bleed highs and sweet chariot lows, of catfights and mongrel dog dust-ups. It was apparent to others—if not them-- they were like peanut butter and jelly with a ripe half banana mushed in between. It was a damn near-perfect mixture of total opposites.

What she saw in him from the get-go was an unadulterated mystery of the scary kind. At first, it was intriguing, then damn near compulsion. Being brought up by the black sheep of the Blige family, the incredibly miscast Roy Blige, there were diminished expectations for her as the progeny of a ne'er do well. Roy could tackle at least a quart of vodka a day and still stand in line to collect winnings at the ponies.

When Roy's throat exploded from drink and his liver was eviscerated like mash potatoes, a 14-year-old Cherokee — still Mary Blige at the time —paid her last respects to her daddy at the Gulf Coast Veterans Health Care System.

Roy had been a combat veteran in Vietnam and had Post Traumatic Stress Disorder, something awful. He had managed, perhaps through accident or happenstance, to save the lives of most of his platoon in a Central Highlands firefight, and was considered a Biloxi hero. He had received the Congressional Medal of Honor, a token given to him by President Johnson he managed to lose in a poker game. He was never the same after that Asian war.

Roy told his daughter she was special on his death bed. He said   don't let anyone tell you differently. He confessed to her he had been the world's worst daddy—" the fucking' bottom of the barrel" as he put it— but that he loved her and he had loved her momma, even though the little lady ran off one night with the town's most successful funeral director, Sam Hosteler. Roy didn't blame his wife. He was a mess.

A funeral director in Biloxi is prestigious, especially if you are also President of the Rotary Club and a deacon in the First Baptist Church. What kept it from being a scandal was the collective certainty in the community that Roy Blige was beyond redemption, and the fact a good many town folks still considered him a hero. Oddly enough and sadly, Ms. Clementine Blige was the victim of a hit-and-run driver just a year later on Bayview Avenue, and her crumpled body was pieced back together by that same successful funeral director, Mr. Hosteler.

Since they never found the car or the driver, Roy was a prime suspect, but he couldn't have done it. He was sleeping soundly in jail three counties distant on that particular night. Through it all, Cherokee was a daddy's girl and had absolutely none of her mama's pretensions. She never moved out of the family homestead, telling Clementine before she split—and that was what she called her, Clementine—that "daddy has no one. He has to have me." Her mother had embarked on a new life, and didn't mind in the slightest.

For certain, that night on the lake with Jeremy was not a pity coupling for Cherokee. Far from it. She wanted badly to connect on all levels, and intimacy was not necessarily even on the high end of the scale. It was just an element in the complete package of care. The crazy kid abstractly loved this fellow she hardly knew.

Early on, Cherokee had followed the stories that carried Jeremy's byline in the Sentinel and had been intrigued by the narrative flow, as if the words could be put to slow dancing cheek-to-cheek music. He was no Billy Faulkner, but then Faulkner wouldn't be Faulkner today. He probably couldn't even land an agent. On a professional level, she liked the way Jeremy pursued a news lead into a black hole and somehow managed to come out the other side. He seemed to get to the core of each topic and then painted all around it bright colors to complete the picture. She also knew his newspaper admired his tenacity but not necessarily his style. He wrapped every article in more literary language, and the Sentinel, in general, was written for a seven-year-old. The editor thought he was putting on airs when, in fact, he was merely an original.

Cherokee, like everyone, had followed the story of Jeremy and Sarah's missing four-year-old and how the child had been kidnapped from daycare at The Mall at Millenia.

She wasn't at all sure why she was obsessively drawn to this particular story, other than the fact she had read each installment of Britnell's feature series on a slum area of the community known ironically as "Lucky Lane." The writer took his readers into the shacks where women cooked on makeshift stoves on the floor, and the landlord came weekly to collect $50, which amounted to a princely sum for the day laborers.

Then, one day Jeremy appeared out of the blue as a guest on her own station's noontime slot, a time meant for bored homemakers and out-of-work husbands. It was neither a grand production nor an extremely profitable bonanza for the station. It was more a broadcast requirement because every station the land over had a yak-yak thirty minutes at the hour. A silver-haired soul almost always hosted it with a bowtie and a creepy but wide-as-the-Atlantic smile. WOLF's version was no better, no worse.

Jeremy appeared sincere in wanting to help other parents who found themselves in similar circumstances as did he and Sarah. His eyes gave away a naivety while at the same time being excessively hopeful that one more television program would somehow, someway lead to the return of his daughter. He reminded Cherokee of movies with the folksy but still erudite Jimmy Stewart that visited whatever home she occupied each Christmas with "It's a Wonderful Life." He wasn't as tall as Stewart, but he had that "aw shucks" demeanor that would endear him to viewers.

The gears shifted, and the wheels turned in her head.

She could show her Uncle Wilkie that she could contribute to the family treasure in a way he understood. All that stood in the way was the station manager, who, she was nearly certain, would be a pushover. Jeremy Butler Britnell would be her discovery.

She nudged Jeremy, who was sleeping soundly with one leg off the side of the trundle bed and who demurely had managed to slip back into his shorts. He stirred, yawned, but then went back to only semi-consciousness. His morning dreams went beyond pleasant.

"Not sure you hear me, alligator guy, but I have to tell you last night—well, really this morning in the wee hours—I rode bareback across a rhinestone prairie on a stallion named Jeremy. Wow, what a lovely ride," she whispered in the ear she had hours earlier attacked with her tongue.

"Uh, really?" he responded and shook his head to clear the sleep from his recovering cerebellum. It was as if she were referring to someone else. It took him a moment to wipe the groggy from his eyes and recollect,

"Hey, I don't lie about matters of the heart," she said, pulling on her jeans that had languished bedside on the floor. "But now, I need to get to work. It's almost noon. While my uncle is a kind soul, he has this crazy idea about employees showing up. Go figure. Guess that's how he got so rich."

Jeremy reconnoitered the situation. His first fear was that she would walk out the door, down the ramp, and poof, dissipate into fairy bubbles as if he had dreamed the entire 24-hour devolvement, which, he thought without rationality, just might be the gospel truth. He considered pinching himself as he watched her comb her hair in the reflection of the glass doors. After convincing himself Cherokee was not a mirage, he asked the headline question:

"Uh, Cherokee," he hesitated. "Will I see you again?"

"Holy Moses, Little Beaver, what do you think? Of course, you will. You think you can ravage me and then forget about me. Typical of a guy, don't you think?"

"I don't know. Maybe I am just a neophyte when it comes to tripping the light fantastic with someone I hardly know," he replied.

"Well Buster Brown, you seem to know me up close in at least five different carnal ways. Hell, I didn't even think a triple Salchow while making love was even a remote possibility," she laughed, backing away as he reached for her slender waist and only came up with air.

Embarrassed, Jeremy replied, "Come on, lady, you're just fuel-injected my ego. But that's okay."

"So, you asked coyly. 'Will you see me again?' I need you to report to work at WOLF at 9 a.m. tomorrow and to make sure you arrive on time; I'm going to go home, pack a small suitcase, and move in this evening."

"You're...?

You do have plugins for a hairdryer without causing a fire, right? What about a full-length mirror? A girl needs these things, you know. Also, and I don't mean to be pushy. But can I do a little redecorating? I can do the lower Bowery ghetto, but I'd like to add a little Biloxi panache."

"Would you like a canopy bed with frilly curtains? What about a makeup vanity in hot pink?" he asked sarcastically.

She put her finger to her lips and turned her head, as if she were considering any and every option available. It was all happening too quickly for Britnell. In his wildest dreams, he had only pictured a slow-moving stroll into a new relationship. He had never considered an outright charge of the Light Brigade toward domestication. He had not even fathomed a new entanglement ever, and certainly not so soon. He had been in like with Sarah years before he was in love. With this Cherokee, he felt he had fallen into a romantic purgatory between heaven and hell.

"I sense a slight timidness on my Swamp Boy's part," she said. "Trust me. You will get over it. It is not about me declaring what Cherokee wants, Cherokee gets. No. That would make me someone I'm not. Fact is, Jeremy, we're fucking fated, though it might take you a little longer to realize it. I'm a sweet kid, a better than average lay, and in a lineup of babes, I might not come in first as a looker, but no one would bet against me as first runner-up. It will happen between us if it hasn't already. And my intuition tells me this bus pulled out of the station hours ago."

"Cherokee, you're a little scary," said Britnell, sucking in a breath that would sink the Titanic if released. He wheezed between his pearly whites and shook his head slowly as if saying "no" when he was saying "absolutely yes."

Britnell wasn't at all prepared for what was happening. He had lived alone on the boat for three years. The old craft hardly had room for him. But then, with Cherokee, there wasn't much time to prepare for anything.

He said years later he wasn't thinking straight that night. However, two kids, a billy goat, a black and white rabbit, two dogs, and a gerbil later were proof positive there was no accounting for where lightning strikes. It was just before the seventh-inning stretch and the refrain "take me out to the ball game" of a Tampa Bay-Kansas City Royals contest when Cherokee nibbled Jeremy's ear, rolling her tongue inside.

His first impulse was to push her away, but he got over it.

On the battlefield, it's called initiating the match, an aggressive action to soften defenses. The same is true, one assumes, in romance, unless, of course, the attention is more Machiavellian and the motive is economically driven. That was exactly Britnell's first thought. He was a paycheck, but then, this lady was richer than a Rockefeller.

At this point, though, it was difficult for Jeremy to tell with Cherokee, who he had only met a few weeks earlier. Since that initial meeting, she visited him nightly, swooping onto his boat ghost-like, but only in his imagination. He couldn't, no matter how he tried, erase her from his consciousness. He chased away sleep, summoning her until the apparition crawled under covers beside him. The fact that she was, in living color, on his bed now, mostly undressed, and within hours of him having buried his wife, was monumentally confusing but not sufficiently disturbing to will her away.

"That tickles," Jeremy said. It was neither complaint nor irritation but more an understated passive comment.

The fact was, the tableau of early Christian upbringing was playing tug-of-war with his instinctive id on one side and his moralistic superego on the other. His id had the advantage by a long shot, which was pretty typical in such situations. He felt he was in control, though, and could call a halt at any time. He often fooled himself that way as a newsman and on such weighty topics as choosing plastic, boxes, or paper sacks at the Winn-Dixie market.

Cherokee had kept on her white briefs and a blue Polo shirt with a WOLF-TV logo. All in all, it was a fetching presentation for a guy celibate for nearly three years. He was lying nervous but comfortable in his olive-brown skivvies, and old Rumpelstiltskin — Sarah's pet name for his southern direction—was preening for glory. It was a blatant, uncontrolled show of the flag.

"Are you complaining?" She wiggled so close to him they were mating spoons. "Forgive me, Swamp Boy, but I want you. And not as a thirst quencher, but as an I want to wake up in the morning to sour whiskey breath and sweet sweat after the world's greatest shag. And then I want the same for dessert."

Jeremy was the type of fellow who allowed porno ads on the internet to tease but was sure if he were even to take a peek, the computer camera lens would light up like a klieg, klaxons would go off, and someone, somewhere would register him like a horny soul and, most likely, sex-crazed. A sex offender sign would be put next to his pickup in the sandy space under an orange tree.

"I know, you want to make money for your uncle off me," said Britnell, abstractly, keeping away from the main topic. He did what people often do in such embarrassing situations. He coughed in his hand and looked out through the sliding glass door to some distant object across the lake. He thought he saw a pelican, but it could just have easily been a vulture in the moonlit distance.

The truth was Jeremy was in a teenage wet dream zone, and though now mostly sober, was not quite within his wits. His retort to Cherokee bordered on an insult. It lacked any normal male intuitiveness. An average person might scream obscenities and flee the scene. This Ms. Blige was anything but ordinary.

"Believe me, Cherokee, I understand that, and I'm beginning to accept the idea, even if I never saw myself as a pitchman, even if it is for a good cause. I'm more of a behind-the-scenes type."

"Don't be obtuse," she feigned exasperation. "Did you hear me right, Jeremy? I said I wanted you. I know that makes me a horrible person, particularly on this particular day, but the clock has slipped past midnight, and this is, in essence, your birthday of sorts. You are now investigative reporter Jeremy Britnell, out to defeat evil and right wrongs. You have a new job, a new semi-girlfriend though you haven't realized it yet, as well as the aforementioned personal manager. You, my fellow, were struck with pixie dust this evening. Don't blow it."

She had rarely called him by his actual name, merely by a collection of random proper nouns that paraded through her head and, in some way, reminded her of a silly appellation that never came close to the mark. He knew this as the gospel according to the Britnell history of exploded egos. He was just plain old Jeremy, nothing special, not a swamp creature, and, by the way—he would later say—"there's no swamp Cherokee within thirty miles of this lake."

"So Jeremy, are you going to give me a long, wet kiss and seduce me this early a.m., or are you going to waste that terrific boner, which, if it expires, could cause you to break out in hives and have serious mental complications,"

Jeremy looked into her eyes, and they exploded in the moonlight into golden amber shards. They were slightly recessed, and he, no student of great art for sure, imagined a face painted by a 17th Century master, Vermeer. But Cherokee was no babydoll with porcelain skin. She had ragamuffin edges even though she was on the periphery of blue blood pretensions. At times, she could be that truck-stop harlot, but one who had a soft heart. Jeremy was the prime example of that. He had been tapped and trapped and was on a superhighway to being smitten.

Cherokee was, of course, right. He sighed as if realizing that the grass is green and the sky is blue for the first time. His breath came from the pit of his lungs. He was no longer confused or conflicted with his lovely Sarah in a cemetery a half-hour away, a place he would never visit for a convenient reason: She was not there. Sarah was in Dallas.

"Well, Cherokee, when you put it that way..my options are apparent and limited.

———

They ended up having a lifetime of nose bleed highs and sweet chariot lows, of catfights and mongrel dog dust-ups. It was apparent to others—if not them-- they were like peanut butter and jelly with a ripe half banana mushed in between. It was a damn near-perfect mixture of total opposites.

What she saw in him from the get-go was an unadulterated mystery of the scary kind. At first, it was intriguing, then damn near compulsion. Being brought up by the black sheep of the Blige family, the incredibly miscast Roy Blige, there were diminished expectations for her as the progeny of a ne'er do well. Roy could tackle at least a quart of vodka a day and still stand in line to collect winnings at the ponies.

When Roy's throat exploded from drink and his liver was eviscerated like mash potatoes, a 14-year-old Cherokee

— still Mary Blige at the time —paid her last respects to her daddy at the Gulf Coast Veterans Health Care System. Roy had been a combat veteran in Vietnam and had Post Traumatic Stress Disorder, something awful. He had managed, perhaps through accident or happenstance, to save the lives of most of his platoon in a Central Highlands firefight, and was considered a Biloxi hero. He had received the Congressional Medal of Honor, a token given to him by President Johnson he managed to lose in a poker game. He was never the same after that Asian war.

Roy told his daughter she was special on his death bed. He said don't let anyone tell you differently. He confessed to her he had been the world's worst daddy—" the fucking' bottom of the barrel" as he put it— but that he loved her and he had loved her momma, even though the little lady ran off one night with the town's most successful funeral director, Sam Hosteler. Roy didn't blame his wife. He was a mess.

A funeral director in Biloxi is prestigious, especially if you are also President of the Rotary Club and a deacon in the First Baptist Church. What kept it from being a scandal was the collective certainty in the community that Roy Blige was beyond redemption, and the fact a good many town folks still considered him a hero.   Oddly enough and sadly, Ms. Clementine Blige was the victim of a hit-and-run driver just a year later on Bayview Avenue, and her crumpled body was pieced back together by that same successful funeral director, Mr. Hosteler.

Since they never found the car or the driver, Roy was a prime suspect, but he couldn't have done it. He was sleeping soundly in jail three counties distant on that particular night. Through it all, Cherokee was a daddy's girl and had absolutely none of her mama's pretensions. She never moved out of the family homestead, telling Clementine before she split—and that was what she called her, Clementine—that "daddy has no one. He has to have me." Her mother had embarked on a new life, and didn't mind in the slightest.

For certain, that night on the lake with Jeremy was not a pity coupling for Cherokee. Far from it. She wanted badly to connect on all levels, and intimacy was not necessarily even on the high end of the scale. It was just an element in the complete package of care. The crazy kid abstractly loved this fellow she hardly knew.

Early on, Cherokee had followed the stories that carried Jeremy's byline in the Sentinel and had been intrigued by the narrative flow, as if the words could be put to slow dancing cheek-to-cheek music. He was no Billy Faulkner, but then Faulkner wouldn't be Faulkner today. He probably couldn't even land an agent. On a professional level, she liked the way Jeremy pursued a news lead into a black hole and somehow managed to come out the other side. He seemed to get to the core of each topic and then painted all around it bright colors to complete the picture. She also knew his newspaper admired his tenacity but not necessarily his style. He wrapped every article in more literary language, and the Sentinel, in general, was written for a seven-year-old. The editor thought he was putting on airs when, in fact, he was merely an original.

Cherokee, like everyone, had followed the story of

Jeremy and Sarah's missing four-year-old and how the child had been kidnapped from daycare at The Mall at Millenia. She wasn't at all sure why she was obsessively drawn to this particular story, other than the fact she had read each installment of Britnell's feature series on a slum area of the community known ironically as "Lucky Lane." The writer took his readers into the shacks where women cooked on makeshift stoves on the floor, and the landlord came weekly to collect $50, which amounted to a princely sum for the day laborers.

Then, one day Jeremy appeared out of the blue as a guest on her own station's noontime slot, a time meant for bored homemakers and out-of-work husbands. It was neither a grand production nor an extremely profitable bonanza for the station. It was more a broadcast requirement because every station the land over had a yak-yak thirty minutes at the hour. A silver-haired soul almost always hosted it with a bowtie and a creepy but wide-as-the-Atlantic smile. WOLF's version was no better, no worse.

Jeremy appeared sincere in wanting to help other parents who found themselves in similar circumstances as did he and Sarah. His eyes gave away a naivety while at the same time being excessively hopeful that one more television program would somehow, someway lead to the return of his daughter. He reminded Cherokee of movies with the folksy but still erudite Jimmy Stewart that visited whatever home she occupied each Christmas with "It's a Wonderful Life." He wasn't as tall as Stewart, but he had that "aw shucks" demeanor that would endear him to viewers.

117

The gears shifted, and the wheels turned in her head. She could show her Uncle Wilkie that she could contribute to the family treasure in a way he understood. All that stood in the way was the station manager, who, she was nearly certain, would be a pushover. Jeremy Butler Britnell would be her discovery.

She nudged Jeremy, who was sleeping soundly with one leg off the side of the trundle bed and who demurely had managed to slip back into his shorts. He stirred, yawned, but then went back to only semi-consciousness. His morning dreams went beyond pleasant.

"Not sure you hear me, alligator guy, but I have to tell you last night—well, really this morning in the wee hours—I rode bareback across a rhinestone prairie on a stallion named Jeremy. Wow, what a lovely ride," she whispered in the ear she had hours earlier attacked with her tongue.

"Uh, really?" he responded and shook his head to clear the sleep from his recovering cerebellum. It was as if she were referring to someone else. It took him a moment to wipe the groggy from his eyes and recollect,

"Hey, I don't lie about matters of the heart," she said, pulling on her jeans that had languished bedside on the floor. "But now, I need to get to work. It's almost noon. While my uncle is a kind soul, he has this crazy idea about employees showing up. Go figure. Guess that's how he got so rich."

Jeremy reconnoitered the situation. His first fear was that she would walk out the door, down the ramp, and poof, dissipate into fairy bubbles as if he had dreamed the entire 24-hour devolvement, which, he thought without rationality, just might be the gospel truth. He considered pinching himself as he watched her comb her hair in the reflection of the glass doors. After convincing himself Cherokee was not a mirage, he asked the headline question:

"Uh, Cherokee," he hesitated. "Will I see you again?"

"Holy Moses, Little Beaver, what do you think? Of course, you will. You think you can ravage me and then forget about me. Typical of a guy, don't you think?"

"I don't know. Maybe I am just a neophyte when it comes to tripping the light fantastic with someone I hardly know," he replied.

"Well Buster Brown, you seem to know me up close in at least five different carnal ways. Hell, I didn't even think a triple Salchow while making love was even a remote possibility," she laughed, backing away as he reached for her slender waist and only came up with air.

Embarrassed, Jeremy replied, "Come on, lady, you're just fuel-injected my ego. But that's okay."

"So, you asked coyly. 'Will you see me again?' I need you to report to work at WOLF at 9 a.m. tomorrow and to make sure you arrive on time; I'm going to go home, pack a small suitcase, and move in this evening."

"You're…?

You do have plugins for a hairdryer without causing a fire, right? What about a full-length mirror? A girl needs these things, you know. Also, and I don't mean to be pushy. But can I do a little redecorating? I can do the lower Bowery ghetto, but I'd like to add a little Biloxi panache."

"Would you like a canopy bed with frilly curtains? What about a makeup vanity in hot pink?" he asked sarcastically.

She put her finger to her lips and turned her head, as if she were considering any and every option available. It was all happening too quickly for Britnell. In his wildest dreams, he had only pictured a slow-moving stroll into a new relationship. He had never considered an outright charge of the Light Brigade toward domestication. He had not even fathomed a new entanglement ever, and certainly not so soon. He had been in like with Sarah years before he was in love. With this Cherokee, he felt he had fallen into a romantic purgatory between heaven and hell.

"I sense a slight timidness on my Swamp Boy's part," she said. "Trust me. You will get over it. It is not about me declaring what Cherokee wants, Cherokee gets. No. That would make me someone I'm not. Fact is, Jeremy, we're fucking fated, though it might take you a little longer to realize it. I'm a sweet kid, a better than average lay, and in a lineup of babes, I might not come in first as a looker, but no one would bet against me as first runner-up. It will happen between us if it hasn't already. And my intuition tells me this bus pulled out of the station hours ago."

"Cherokee, you're a little scary," said Britnell, sucking in a breath that would sink the Titanic if released. He wheezed between his pearly whites and shook his head slowly as if saying "no" when he was saying "absolutely yes."

Britnell wasn't at all prepared for what was happening. He had lived alone on the boat for three years. The old craft hardly had room for him. But then, with Cherokee, there wasn't much time to prepare for anything.

He said years later he wasn't thinking straight that night. However, two kids, a billy goat, a black and white rabbit, two dogs, and a gerbil later were proof positive there was no accounting for where lightning strikes.

CHAPTER 11
THE BOOK OF FAIRLEIGH REBORN

Somewhere in time and space, in this parallel universe of Jeremy Britnell and the various ups, downs, and all-arounds that greeted him with the turn of the minute hand, there was a book manuscript gathering dust in a storage facility in West Orlando.

It was simply black type on fading copy paper. One could assume that somewhere there were probably computer records of the book lying in the bowels of an ancient Apple laptop of a fellow who no longer gave a damn. His literary aspiration was floating balloons in a fool's parade. He had given up.

A reputable publisher picking up his first novel was no longer a knight's quest. His dragons and his demons loomed much greater. When it came to writing, he felt he could no longer put a sentence in its proper order, and that, as much as anything, was the reason he quit his day job at the local newspaper.

They were shocked. Jeremy seemed on an upward

career path in his chosen field.

Britnell at this time had no other visible means of support, and his wife was, in essence, a ward of the state, vegetating in a facility for the seriously impaired. The rumor was she was too far gone to return. She had checked into la-la land, Room 249.

Chronicling that first draft of history was no longer relevant to someone buried in his own story. He readily admitted it was a selfish act, but he could not help himself. Until Cherokee made an abrupt appearance, his only contact had been with the one-time mall security guard Purvis Periwinkle. His colleagues from work would call from time to time, but they had other more important things to do with their own lives of quiet desperation. Jeremy was thankful for that.

He had not forgotten about the book. It had taken two years of his life, and, as a famous novelist had said about writing, he had "opened up a vein and just let it pour out." The book was not top-of-the-mind awareness. After all, tragedy had taken a double-dip in his life, first Fairleigh and then Sarah. There wasn't much else to lose. He was living on cash he had received from the sale of his modest home and a scattering of freelance gigs.

He had, presumptuously perhaps, previously chosen characters for the novel's sure to be made movie. Ironically, the girl he decided to be, four-year-old Fairleigh, was getting older by the day. If he thought about it, given the fits of depression, he would cruelly joke to himself that by the time he is reunited with his daughter, if ever, little, Cali

DiCapo, an up-and-coming Disney actress, would have children of her own.

There was a time — it seemed so long ago—Britnell would write at least a thousand words a day, every day. He called writing a book a forced march through swamp water wearing combat boots with critters yapping at your heels and mosquitoes dive-bombing. It was a holy campaign, and he always charged on with enthusiasm up the mountain, though sometimes the progress was so slow it appeared he was wearing roller skates.

Fairleigh was not his first effort, but it was the only one he had finished, and felt satisfied with the result. Every sentenced in Fairleigh was a purposeful adventure, carefully studied and structured. But there was also joy in his daily journeys. The characters talked to him, and scenes developed before his eyes. They became neighbors in his hood.

Writers who claimed they only wrote for themselves were fakirs and pretenders to the craft. Britnell also believed one couldn't be a writer without first being a good reader, and he consumed good fiction that has stood the test of time, as well as biographies of both the famous and the obscure.

Before his dream of being a celebrated author exploded into tiny memory fragments, he had visions of appearances on the yak-yak circuit, exchanging witty rapport with the likes of Leno and Letterman. In each episode, his self-accounting now absent of shyness. He dressed in casual cool—a black sports coat, Levi's, and white, low-topped tennis shoes—an individual statement of a personality that had hitherto eluded him. Where before glibness always abandoned him unless he punched them into his computer, now he was a fountain of exciting tales and obscure tidbits the viewing audience found fascinating. These were the coughed-up mirages with which Jeremy went to sleep each night.

Who was this young wunderkind? Not him. For now, that steroid-laced personality, that effusive re-made literary doyen, was locked in a cat's cradle of hopes and wishes, languishing in an eight-by-ten bin at Harry's Storage. One supposes Jeremy could have pulled an electronic version from the depths of a laptop's innards, but that interest was no longer there.

The rent for the storage compartment, which was only the monthly cost of a modest dinner for two with cheap wine at a strip mall restaurant, had gone unpaid for months.

The proprietor had a home phone number for Britnell, but it was no longer operable, disconnected months ago. Since decamping to his houseboat, Britnell only used his mobile, a relatively unsophisticated Nokia. The storage space owner, Harry Stiles, who had alimony and gambling debts to pay, sent Britnell a certified letter, but it was returned to sender. It became an orphan rental space without recourse, and the contents legally could be— would be— sold to the highest bidder. Though several people came by and showed interest in the roll-top writing desk that Jeremy had inherited from a long-dead aunt, only one person made a bona fide bid.

His name was William Wendell.

Wendell, a bug-eyed fellow with no serious literary pursuits, eyed the pieces of relatively new furniture purchased on credit from Sears, and the washer and dryer, bought off a family in similar circumstances as Britnell: They needed money. He wondered if the roll-top desk possibly could be an antique. He pictured it as coming from a 1920s mansion in Newport, R.I. Being a broker of pre-used furniture, however, didn't suggest he had any talent when it came to appraising an old desk. His research was perfunctory. He did spy on top of the desk the two large manila envelopes designated with a magic marker, The Book of Fairleigh I and The Book of Fairleigh II.

He was slightly curious, but his heart was on turning a pretty penny on the roll top. He thought it would show just fine in the window of Wendell's Used Furniture and Disney Souvenir Sales, a binary offering that defied logic. But then, Orlando, once a sleepy Central Florida town, was awash in showy excesses and extremes since Disney brought his talking rodents to the community in the 1960s. How else could one explain the relative success of Holy Land World, Gator World, and SeaWorld nuzzled up so close to Walt's kingdom.

The book itself, combining the two envelopes, was rather significant, nearly 800 pages of double spaced type, much too large for Wendell to tackle if he were to embark on a reading excursion. His curiosity about its contents didn't invite further inspection. However, since there were no other bidders, he low-balled the contents at $149 and immediately felt he could have had it for less. Also, on returning home, his wife suggested he was an idiot, which was not far off the mark.

She had been on the lookout for art deco and not fake Ethan Allen that was not even in the same solar system when it came to her more refined tastes. She griped at him. She could have used the money paid to Harry's Storage to bolster their weekly grocery budget. She had also been eyeing a nearly genuine oriental rug for the living room, which, she felt, an interesting narrative could be developed.

However, the manuscript, "The Book of Fairleigh", did intrigue Wendell after he read the first paragraphs while dickering with Harry over the payment. He was a sucker for a good Christmas yarn, whether it started "the night before Christmas" or "there was a child named Fairleigh." He explored several more pages while Harry determined if the $149 check would bounce. It was then he hit on what he felt would be a utopian idea, for Wendell did, indeed, have an ego that soared over the moon on days he didn't take his bipolar pills.

Being an odd bird didn't exempt Wendell from being an enterprising one. It had never made him even modestly rich, but it was such blue-sky thinking that led him to combine the used furniture trade with selling copycat Disney merchandise to folks who couldn't afford the real McCoy. In this regard, Wendell was a bargain-basement dreamer chasing polka dot rainbows. Before even reading the book to its conclusion, he took a flyer on a publishing house in Atlanta advertised in Penthouse Magazine. Lo and behold, they accepted this novel by the first-time author. William Wendell.

The company this newly minted author approached went by the corporate handle, McGraw and Sons. The leading corporate executive, Michael McGraw, decided to represent Wendell's novel, though he didn't actually read it. The company was twice as sly as the intrepid Mr. Wendell, who sold his counterfeit Disney tchotchkes out of a pickup truck parked off the main artery leading into the theme park. It was also doubtful the twice-convicted felon McGraw ever had progeny he claimed as sons, but the name suggested some respectability and substance.

On the other side of this league of larcenists was Wendell. He, in a nod to civic duty and economic survival, off-loaded his merchandise at bargain prices because after paying $115 for a single ticket to Disney World, many couldn't so much as buy a snow cone once inside the complex, much less Mickey Mouse ears at $20 a throw for the cheap version. Using the imagination, one could call William Wendell a social entrepreneur. The fact was Wendell's Mickey ears cost six bucks, but he could, while the customer stood by his truck, embroidery little Susie or Frank's name on the skull cap for another four. His handy sewing apparatus was a good investment, and he next planned to go into inexpensive tee-shirts.

While Wendell was hoping for a windfall from authorship, he ended up with a mere pittance, settling on a few grand from this old fellow out in Hollywood named Cletus Reed. Reed seemed intent on buying the rights to the creation Wendell was now claiming as his. Out of fear of being discovered by the rightful author, McGraw changed the name and character in the book from Fairleigh to Frances Leigh.

McGraw and Sons didn't have the resources to market the book beyond a catalog listing which cost an extra $50. This item was listed as "various promotional services" in the contract. In reality, the company was your basic phony book mill. McGraw had high hopes the mark —the one who called himself an author—would order more copies for distribution to friends and relatives. These folks also would never read the book, but it might look presentable in a bookcase of other paperback books or, perhaps, prominently displayed on a coffee table.

At first, Wendell pretended to be the agent for the author, a fellow named Jeremy Butler Britnell, but when it came time to sign the contract, he confessed the book was actually his work and would now prefer his actual name, not a nom de plume. This Britnell fellow just might see the book and once again appropriate it as his work.

"Mr. Wendell, I don't care if you call yourself Zorro as long as your check doesn't bounce," said McGraw, who quickly had a cover designed for a few bucks by an artist in Bangladesh.

McGraw accomplished formatting the book through one of many services that offered such through the internet. In total, it cost him the princely sum of nearly $500, but he was able to triple that amount by charging Wendell $1,500. The entire transaction was kept off both his and McGraw & Sons books and away from the prying eyes of Ms. Lucy Wendell. She felt her husband's record of hare-brained schemes had about as much chance of succeeding as him winning the Florida Powerball Lottery. He did buy five scratch-off tickets each week.

While Wendell imagined he had a superior level of literary talents, they didn't extend beyond perusing his wife's bodice-ripping novelettes, Penthouse magazines kept near the porcelain throne, and a collection of vintage comic books, a habit he had acquired as a 10-year-old and continued through what passed for adulthood.

In other words, his literary inclination dead-ended after reading My Friends on Cherry Street in the second grade. However, he never gave up attempting to find what P.T. Barnum supposedly called "a sucker born every minute." He was a pretender to an intellectual realm. He even had a copy of James Joyce's "Ulysses" and had completed reading the first two paragraphs. However, should he die in his sleep, he instructed his wife to put a copy of the book in his hands. He felt it necessary for his image.

When Hollywood agent Cletus Reed came along and just happened to find The Book of Frances Leigh in a discount book bin, Wendell felt his ship had come in, though for sure it was more a canoe and not the Queen Mary. He retrieved his investment, which was a victory of sorts given his entrepreneurial track record.

The Book of Fairleigh, now called The Book of Frances Leigh, was about to be reborn. Britnell had never intended it to be more than a working title.

CHAPTER 12
THE BEST LAID PLANS

Cletus Reed would have preferred to get the skinny from the horse's mouth, Lee Atkinson III, reigning God of Panther Studios, who held the title by reason of marginal competence and birthright.

But Reed scared the bejesus out of Atkinson, who, at 50, had inherited the reins from his daddy, Lee Sr., who, in turn, was bequeathed majority stock by the long-dead founder, Roman Numeral One, Big Robert, a legend in the movie business.

Reed had nothing against the last of the Lee linage other than the man was frightened by his own shadow. In the presence of Cletus, he tended to mumble and stutter. Otherwise, he seemed a decent fellow, but probably not someone with the nerves to lead a major motion picture studio.

He certainly wasn't someone you would invite to have suds with you and shoot eight-ball-call-pocket in a pool room in Logan, WV. In the film business, a bad gamble on a flick could cost a bundle. The third one down the line simply didn't have the cojones to pass an occasional Hail Mary, but neither did Lee No. 2, his daddy.

In essence, it was the theory of diminishing guts. Reed well understood this phenomenon and managed to navigate the politics of hereditary ineptitude the best he could, which was skillfully.

Roman Numeral One, the great-granddaddy of the business, was rumored to have had a silent partner of questionable repute, and such talk was as true as most Hollywood tales are false. This particular man was one of the original prisoners when Alcatraz was opened in 1934 and was known by the romanticized name of Machine Gun Kelly, or the more plebeian George Barnes.

Founder Atkinson also had considerable holdings in Las Vegas and Palm Springs and was, if not a political kingmaker in some circles, an established pawn-maker, which, one might infer, was a savvy move for future standing, coming up in the rough and tumble 1930s.

He was rumored to be close to Machine Gun Kelly, and that didn't harm his business negotiations. However, Atkinson didn't wear the connection on his sleeve and went by the dictate that power is best used when left on the shelf. In other words, perceived strength often works better than bluster and threats. Everyone simply seemed to know about it, or at least they thought they did. However, the mystical power of perception could be deceiving; Barnes/ Kelly was serving a life sentence on a kidnapping charge.

Why the Lee brood that came after Roman Numeral One was intimidated by Cletus was a mystery? The writer/producer/agent was a mild-mannered sort who tended to say "yes sir, no sir," even to people decades younger and not as powerful. When Reed entered anyone's office, he did so with hat in hand, placed around his lower midsection. Reed was, after all, coalfield West Virginia born. Roman Numeral One, on the other hand, was brought up with servants around the home. They accomplish everyday tasks of laundry, dishes, cooking, and general housekeeping, opening the door for guests and serving coffee, tea, or, on occasion, more lethal refreshment.

The original Atkinson was not called Lee but Robert Buford Atkinson, who picked Lee for his son out of reverence for the Confederate general, Robert E. Lee. He was a farmer, but a farmer in a big way, with thousands of acres of Mississippi cotton, planted mainly through sharecroppers. Robert was a favorite among the help. They all agreed, he was a nice boy and a good boy, which was about the highest compliment one could receive in southern culture. He was also a smart boy. His route to Hollywood, not necessarily in the express lane, was helped along by these connections and his ability o take advantage of the smallest of opportunities. Some saw a lump of coal; he saw a diamond in the rough and seemed to have the Midas touch.

As for Cletus Reed, a casual observer would swear a summer breeze would send him taking flight like a desert tumbleweed. Where Roman Numeral One had played football for the University of Mississippi during the 1940s, Reed was captain of the debate team and a cheerleader at West Virginia University, before entering law school at the University of Mississippi. He had the same 31-inch waist he sported when he boxed Golden Gloves at 18 and a limp handshake that belied his solid as-nails character.

His daddy, Clarence Reed, felt for sure the son would become a lawyer and that he did. That led to his chance encounter with Atkinson. While Reed was rather good at law, it didn't interest him. He ho-hummed his way through three years. When a member of the Ole Miss football team was having trouble negotiating a contract with the Baltimore Colts as a first-round draft choice, Reed stepped in to broker the deal. It ended up being the first of the blue ribbon contracts in the sport.

Having walked off with a 20 percent commission, Reed believed he had found a calling. It was a long, twisting journey, but the agent role eventually led to Hollywood when his friend, Billy Faulkner, asked if he could accompany him to the city of tinsel to edit his novel for the big screen, called "Inherit the Wind". It didn't hurt that Roman Number One and Reed were both alumni at Ole Miss, though in different decades. That, in itself, helped bind a relationship.

The black wooden cane Reed used in his mid-80s wasn't for show. He traversed at a pace that left others behind. Even before cigar smoke and red lesions made it a low growl, his voice was baby soft and melodic, like a tenor whose cords gave out on the high notes of "Silent Night" at caroling time. There was absolutely nothing intimidating about Cletus Reed other than his intellect, which was considerable.

But, the respect—one might even say fear of Cletus Reed--was enjoined many years earlier when the founder of Panther found himself in awe of the much younger man. He was, romancing it only slightly, star-struck.

Cletus Reed played poker with Gregory Peck, a regular at the Reed table; he gave clarity to Faulkner's often clumsy dialogue. He was rumored to have had an affair with Rita Hayworth, He was never boastful about any conquests, and there were a few. Besides, Rita was Howard Hughes's girl, and Howard and Reed were drinking buddies until the agent found the love of his life and decided skirt-chasing, and tippling to extremes, was neither his forte nor his desire.

So, for the granddaddy of Panther Studio, Atkinson Roman Numeral one, Reed was on a pedestal, and he polished the white granite and gave that perch the greatest attention with generous salary boosts and bonuses. He was almost like the son Junior would never be, or the grandchild that Roman Number III could only aspire to be.

The older man never denied his admiration for Cletus, which made other family members jealous. Reed had been a godsend for the studio in the early days as it teetered toward bankruptcy due to a near sudden exodus of its stable of stars who attributed their dissatisfaction to the studio's parsimonious nature. Most all who stayed behind credited the unassuming Reed as the reason for their loyalty to Panther and not to the boss man. However, they generally paid him proper allegiance in person. However, while Atkinson was a shrewd businessman, he sometimes lacked the necessary people skills to communicate with his star lineup. He often treated them as backlot extras or benevolently as sharecroppers back on his Mississippi farm.

So, this family timidness around Cletus was an inherited virus. The problem was, as so often happens with the sons and daughters of sperm-fortunate chosen ones, the acorn did, indeed, fell very far from the tree. This was why the latest incarnation of Panther Studio hierarchy, Junior-Junior as he was sometimes called, decided not to have a conflict with agent Reed but to browbeat young Natalie Current with a little-noticed sentence in her Panther contract. Natalie, while not naive given her streetwise, waif upbringing, was respectful of her elders. This was not something any semblance of parents taught her, but possibly a grain embedded in her DNA.

This particular sentence in the contract read, in totality, "If the film production of 'Outer Worldly' should return its investment of $25 million, the party of the first part—being Natalie Currant —would agree to a sequel within 18 months of Outer Worldly's release." It seemed a natural and even expected amendment to the agreement on the surface and one rather common in film contracts.

No one had any idea "Outer Worldly" would be the breakout role for the young actress, much less a box office end-of-the-year hit during a rather disastrous year for a film crop of mostly melodramatic disaster flicks. Natalie, who wasn't expected to concentrate on such minutia, overlooked this aspect of the contract. Reed was the one who signed such agreements for his client with the studio. This one, however, appeared to be a standard amendment added later and was dutifully signed by Natalie. One could tell by the sloppy cursive; it was signed in a flash, perhaps amid other papers.

Reed and Natalie's meeting at Pinks Hotdog Emporium was supposed to be more of a social gathering than a business session on this particular Saturday morning. Reed was well into the pre-production machinations of his "Frances Leigh" project, looking to begin filming later in the spring. Not much of one for sentimentalities, Reed had brought along a second-hand gift, a small pearl neckless he unwrapped from a sheet of plain tissue paper.

As they sat down in a booth, Reed qualified the gift. "Don't take this as more than it is, but I wanted you to have this token of our collaboration over the last two years. It's been good, Natalie, very good, and you have given an old man a second wind. Also, please don't think I'm overly sappy, but I will tell you upfront that this neckless once was worn by my daughter when she was about your age. We gave it to her to wear to her high school prom. It's not expensive—just something that means a lot to me."

Natalie was flabbergasted as she hugged her cheeks with her hands. It suddenly occurred to her she had been extremely selfish by not having ever inquired about her agent's family. Natalie had never once visited his beach trailer, though she had heard talk at the studio he lived an ascetic life. She had heard mention of a dog but didn't know his name was Sammy, and in dog years, the mutt was as old as her agent, who, himself, had long-ago passed into the noble rot stage. Natalie, however, was as close to Reed as any daughter could be to him, but then he had never before offered information about his family. She had assumed he was a widower. She knew of no children.

In this regard, they were two peas in the proverbial pod. Reed knew very little about his talented client. Before a certain age, actually pre-school, her mind was blank. However, certain smells and snatches of life did bring hints of deja vu. The memories evaporated once she trained her mind, attempting to recall an event or place.

Unlike stories of babies being left on doorsteps, Natalie was a four-year-old child who was abandoned. She was left huddled in a wooden booth at the Purple Onion Lounge; a bar located a dozen blocks from downtown Charleston, WV. In the bar's darkness, the tiny kid could hardly be seen. She hugged the far end of the booth as if in hiding from the world. She was frightened.

After several hours of sitting alone, it became obvious the girl's parents were not returning. No one had seen them come in. Waitresses had paraded past but thought her parents were merely in the restroom or perhaps outside having a smoke. After two hours, the owner of the bar, Charlie Jones, took an interest. The child looked as if she had not had a change of clothes in weeks. She looked emaciated. Asked the basics, like her name and where she lived, the little girl went catatonic, the result, one could suppose, of being kidnapped by total strangers from the bosom of her parent's care.

"Oh, Cletus, I didn't even know you had a daughter. This is a lovely necklace. I can't believe your daughter would give up such a wonderful token of love from her papa. I can't take this. It's a very special gift, and she will miss it."

Reed wheezed, held his hand to his heart, and looked down at the pearls in Natalie's hands. "No, she won't," he said, closing his eyes. "She died many, many years ago. You would have liked her. She had green eyes, just like you. And how those eyes danced, just like yours. Sadly, she was struck down by a hit-and-run driver just about a block from where we are now. It was 35 years ago."

"Oh, Cletus, I didn't know."

Tears slowly swelled in her eyes, plopping to her blouse. They were not movie scene tears, but the real soggy, salty ones. She sniffled and tried to say something but couldn't. Their relationship had suddenly become more clear to her, and she now figured she knew the reason. Reed reached over the table and put two fingers over her lips as if it would snuff her tears while at the same time avoiding further emotional conversation.

"No, darling Nat," he said. "I wasn't thinking of Caroline when I discovered you in Annie Get Your Gun in that Charleston Light Opera Guild production. I was thinking, 'My, what an amazing talent. The voice of an angel'. You were so expressive and an accidental surprise that night. I was doing a favor for a friend just being in the audience. So, do something for me now, and wear this necklace if the occasion calls for it. When I see it, I won't be thinking just of Caroline but of our friendship. Now, this, my friend, is about as blubbery as I get."

"Cletus Reed, do you know I love you," Natalie sniffled. "I just do."

She could tell by the tenor of his cracking voice he was fighting back an emotional flood. He turned away, looking at a point far outside Pink's frosty windows and the traffic congestion on N. La Brea Avenue. He eventually spied the manila envelope she brought with her. It was a welcome diversion from memories come full circle.

"What do you have there?" he asked.

"I'm not sure," she said and added. "Cletus, I thought we were filming 'Frances Leigh' before starting into any other project, such as a sequel to 'Outer Worldly'.' I was excited about the script and working with that young Disney actress, Cali DiCapo. She's cool and will make a great Frances Leigh as a child. You have a magic technique to give her green eyes?"

"Easy solution. Contacts my dear Natalie. Contacts."

Reed perused the document as if he were memorizing it for posterity. When finished, he slapped it on the table, nearly upsetting the cherry coke Natalie had just received from Flo, a long-time waitress. He took a deep breath and dove into his inside breast coat pocket for his normal accompaniment, a silver flask with a mite of whiskey.

"This is going to take some fortification, despite that doctor's advice," he said. "This is not the contract I signed, and it is a document I would never have signed. We start shooting Frances Leigh in a couple of months come hell, high water, or me being put in prison for murdering some ass at Panther Studio. This never would have happened with the old man there."

Then, Natalie explained. "It's all my fault. This fellow from Panther came by and described himself as an executive assistant to Mr. Atkinson and said he has some papers to sign, including the lease on the studio apartment where I live. There was a whole stack of them, with an 'X' on the lines that required my signature. It was only this morning that I read the copy and knew right away this is not something to which we agreed."

"Well, Nat, you're right as rain there," said Reed, verbalizing his pique. "This document would have The Book of Frances Leigh filmed after the sci-fi flick, and that's not happening. Besides, I saw the script for the sequel, and it's an embarrassment. It looked as if it were written by a monkey high on peyote seeds."

"What do you think we can do about it. I'm so sorry. I really screwed up this time," she said.

"First off, I have a conversation with Roman Number Three, apparently the last of the genetic food chain and by far the highest-ranking nincompoop of them all," said Reed, a thin smile on his face. "And no, you didn't screw up. We merely have a slight diversion, and as Billy Shakespeare wrote, 'All's well that ends well, and believe me, darling, this will end well."

Then, the agent did something he rarely did at Pinks Hotdog Emporium.

"Flo, bring me one of those foot-long chili dogs, and I'll take the combination platter with coleslaw and large fries," he said to the waitress as she breezed by. "Oh, and onions, by all means, sweet Vidalia onions."

"But, Mr. Reed, your heart condition?" Flo admonished her long-time customer, who rarely had more than a coffee and two slices of unbuttered toast, along with the joy juice he kept in the flask. It was the first time Natalie had heard her agent had a problem with his ticker.

"Cletus, what's this about a heart condition? Why didn't you let me know," she said, creating deep furrows in her brow as she launched into a lecture about him taking care of himself.

"It's all relative, my child," said Reed.

CHAPTER 13
THE LITTLE GIRL AT THE BAR

Charlie Jones didn't know what to do with the pint-sized kid huddled in the far back booth of his bar. When he walked over to her, he was drying a highball glass and wondering what was causing the commotion.

The strange presence of a small tyke had drawn a crowd. Some were curious, some judgmental. Some ladies, the mothering kind, were mouthing the appropriate "oh dears" but not, by any means, taking charge.

After all, the Purple Onion was a bar, not a daycare center, and it was the shank of the night. Revelers were in high gear. Charlie had just said free shots for the ladies and a round of complimentary Rolling Rock beer for the guys. It wasn't a big deal: His Rolling Rock wasn't selling, and a distributor had given him several cases of lessor quality pear schnapps.

Still, Jones was annoyed at even minor disruptions. He had a lot on his mind, trying to keep the doors open under the weight of another economic wet blanket thrown over what was called "the Mountain State." The entire country was in a recession, but such a designation would have been a luxury for the region, which was more attuned to constant depression.

West Virginia had the hyperbolic motto, "Mountaineers Are Always Free," which leaned toward exaggeration with a good many owing their soul to the company store, or maybe to J.C. Penneys or, for sure, the Kroger and Big Bear supermarkets. Unemployment was hovering at 20 percent, and federal food stamps were the currency of the moment. Since you couldn't buy liquor with food stamps, Charlie gamed the system slightly by calling it corn or barley. He fudged, but, in essence, it was true. He knew it was wrong, but his customers needed a respite from everyday misery.

Folks hardly had enough cash to keep the kids in shoes and cornbread on the table. Most of the coal mines had dried up. The most traveled highway was the turnpike to North Carolina, which was not the promised land, but a sight better than West Virginia. Still, given all the hardships, his customers generally could come up with 75-cents for a beer, and Charlie had this habit of arbitrarily giving a house discount to everyone.

There generally was no such thing as one beer with the Purple Onion crowd, but maybe five or six with a whiskey chaser in between. The economic rule was for a barkeep to make 25 cents off each beer. If he took the time to calculate, Charlie's largess put that number at less than 15 cents.

A late evening crowd had gathered around, most curious and rather lubricated. The band, the Ting Tang Walla Walla Bing Bang Mountain Boys, prepared for a second Friday night set. They were not very good, but they were loud, and they were cheap. Charlie, however, was glad to see the end of their two-week contract and had booked members or the local Mountain Stage band for the rest of the month. He would pay Walla Walla their due plus an extra few bucks. He was a soft touch, which meant he was a piss poor businessman.

The child was whimpering. When Charlie stood over the wood-scared booth, she covered her face with her hands, as if she expected to be cold-clobbered, sliding so far down to the floor just a tiny head could be seen. In the near darkness, it looked like a pair of cats eyes. They seemed to dare a confrontation with her head cocked to the side, and her lips jutted out. Charlie had confronted friendlier rattlesnakes on Malden Mountain.

He attempted levity, which was not his strong suit. "What? Don't you like the band? Well, I don't blame you. They belong on Lawrence Welk and not at the Purple Onion."

His comment was, of course, totally out of the little girl's context. He might just as well have been speaking Swahili. His guttural redneck was, at first, scary to her. More than anything, after days of being cooped up in a sack and being shifted from one side of a near-empty van to the other, she was confused that any utterance would bring God's punishment. That was the term the kidnapping couple, the Johns, had used—God's punishment. It was always followed by a heavy slap with the backside of a hand. Ruth Johns had protested, but not mightily, "She's our kid now, Joshua, be careful. We want her to love us."

That message never really caught on with Joshua even after traveling several thousand miles of backroads to avoid authorities, either for a stolen vehicle or a purloined little girl. In retrospect, Joshua having a small child was an afterthought, and he never really bought into the idea. It was, however, Christmas season, and it seemed only marginally troubling to satisfy Ruthie. Neither had bonded with the child, which was rather normal given the circumstances. Joshua would burst out with a string of schoolyard curse words and exclaim, "The damn kid's a crybaby. Whatever happened to sugar and spice and everything nice. We should have taken a boy kid."

It was difficult to say why the Johns ultimately decided to skip out on paying for the steak dinner the two had consumed with relish like starving hyenas. Though Joshua, given the gaps between his teeth, had to take his in small bites, dutifully carved by his wife. The child was given an animal cracker to gnaw on. The escape seemed to be a family decision after the couple had a minor argument. They slithered out, pretending to visit the restroom. They exited the back door, leaving the child in the booth. They had decided parenting was over-rated.

Charlie was doing his best to connect with the little girl, but, frankly, he would have had more success conversing with an empty beer bottle. He had never had a way with kids, and didn't accept their societal place as anything special.

Never having had children — at least ones he actually met and acknowledged—Charlie was mismatched when it came to conversing with anything under four feet. He called them ragamuffins, crumb-snatchers, and rug-rats, and they, in general, scared the living daylights out of him in one-on-one encounters. He had been married three times, and some jokester printed the bumper sticker: "If you have been married to Charlie, honk." There was nary a baby issue from the official relationships.

Charlie naturally asked the girl her name in front of about a dozen Purple Onion regulars who had crowded around as if they expected the bar's owner to solve an unusual predicament. But Charlie's personality was not that of the heart of gold saloon keep. He was more a contributor to mayhem and not a peacemaker. Everyone knew he had spent several years in upstate Moundsville, a maximum-security prison, for manslaughter, though, of course, there were extenuating circumstances.

The child wiped her forefinger over her mouth as if to suggest locked lips, and she had nothing to say. In fact, she didn't respond to any of Charlie's multiple pleas, though that might have more to do with a tractor-growl voice that matched the man's gargantuan frame. Charlie was not a handsome man. He was, for sure, downright ugly.

In the abstract, he could be intimidating just by his physical presence. When asked about her mama and papa, the girl's eyes darted from side to side. They were big, glistening green ovals, part questioning but mostly frightened. It was a sore topic. For those travel days, the Johns had drilled into her that she was their kid, and her name was Mary.

On occasion, they passed a metal pan to the back. "There, kid, take a leak," shouted Johns. She couldn't. The poor kid held it in and thus was a mess when the Johns pulled up behind the Purple Onion.

CHAPTER 14
CHARLIE JONES' DUSTUP WITH BLUTO

Charlie had owned the Onion for the better part of a decade, and he ruled over his kingdom like a titled Duke, not in an aggressive way, but as a benevolent dictator.

He looked the part, not of an owner, but of the big burly barkeep who could also serve as the bouncer if the night crowd got out of hand, which it sometimes did.

He was born to the throne by way of a poker game and the loss of his 1955 MG-TF roadster. It was an even-steven trade with the previous owner whose luck had run out, and he needed wheels. Charlie held three of a kind, aces high, and his mark for the evening had two pair and relatively inconsequential cards at that. The game was witnessed on a Sunday afternoon by a half dozen patrons, so there was no sense in either side reneging. It would have killed their reputation, and Charleston was hardly more than a village, even if it were the State Capitol. A reputation in West Virginia is a big deal, second only in prize possessions to owning a   pickup with an extended crew cab.

Charlie had never previously had any entrepreneurial leanings but the Purple Onion was a bar, and he was fond of beer, as evidenced by a protruding tummy that looked as if it held two basketballs. The MG classic would have brought $22,000 on the market while the bar, which included a liquor license, and a brick, two-story building was appraised at close to $150,000. It was a fair deal for Charlie. After all, he had a hell of a time getting in and out of the sports car. Besides, his recent ex-wife had thrown him out of their modest West End home, and the bar's upstairs had a bathroom, shower, and small kitchen. His partner at the poker table was an honest man, but there was one surprise he kept to himself. There was a tax lien on the place which, before Charlie, was called the "Blue Parrot," a rip-off from the movie Casablanca. Charlie, for sure, wasn't a detail-type person. He merely envisioned himself holding court each night at the establishment.

"Are you hungry?" Charlie asked the little girl. There was a flicker of acceptance in her eyes.

"We make the best goddamn pepperoni rolls in West Virginia," said Charlie, and then coughed in his hand to muffle his ubiquitous, twice-a-sentence cuss word. The peanut gallery that crowded around him gave him encouragement and advice. "Ask her where she came from, Charlie? How old is she? We probably should call the cops."

"Listen, yahoos, stand back. Give us a little space," said Charlie, annoyed but at the same time having no idea how to handle the situation. He momentarily thought about calling his last ex-wife, but he quickly nixed the idea, realizing he had not paid alimony in several months. Besides, his previous encounter with her involved a cast iron frying pan, a bump on the head the size of Mount Everest, and a hasty retreat.

Over the years, the bar had become almost a clubhouse for lobbyists and legislators since it was only a stone's toss from the gold-domed capitol building where all sorts of skullduggery took place under the name of the People's Business. However, on weekends—most lawmakers, having departed Charleston for home—it was a hangout for regulars and nearby Eastenders who felt a certain parentage of the place. The establishment tried hard to be a honky-tonk, but didn't quite make the grade, perhaps because the music was way too eclectic, driven by Charlie's taste. That taste veered between the operatic Pavarotti, gutbucket blues, and Hank Williams Senior's old-time country. It wasn't unusual for the State's governor, on occasion, to slip out of his office a block over to have a cold PBR on occasion. Officialdom made the place almost respectable if one graded on the curve.

On occasion, the bar teetered on the edge of bankruptcy but magically, the precursor to "Go Fund Me" accounts came to the rescue with deadbeats catching up on their bar bills. The sheriff, who often stopped by the Purple Onion when off duty, somehow convinced the tax authorities to convert the seven (as in $7,356) to a one, which made it a manageable number for Charlie. In return, Charlie provided Sheriff Danny Jenkins with pepperoni rolls, all the beer he could drink and managed to let him win on the single, illegal slot machine on the premises. For a fact, though, Charlie was the king of corporate social responsibility long before it became a popular term, and blue-chip giants ballyhooed their generosity as community stalwarts. He somehow managed to come up with turkeys for the homeless on Thanksgiving and Christmas for the down-and-out, serving them on picnic tables in the parking lot. His ex-wives complained in unison about his kindness to others. His latest almost ex, Beverly, once remarked to the circuit court that "Good Old Charlie would give you the coat off of someone else's back."

The union with extra wife number three lasted longer than the others added together. It was not a marriage made in heaven, but at least it was slightly north of hell. Beverly found something good in Charlie, which she compared to finding a diamond in a lump of coal. Somewhere along the way, they lost the diamond, and all that was left was coal dust. That's when the frying pan became a near-lethal weapon. Charlie protected himself with a forearm and a Mohammed Ali rope-a-dope maneuver. Asked if he wanted to press charges against Beverly, Charlie said, "What for? I love the lady, and I deserved it."

This particular marriage assignment taught Charlie a lot about himself, other than self-defense. In the abstract, he learned he wasn't such a bad sort. Even his stint in Moundsville resulted from over-active fists in defense of a helpless street person who a cop was bullying. Most everyone in the East End had both a good and a bad word to say about the owner of the Purple Onion. He was that riddle wrapped in an enigma. He would never be selected the Valley's Man of the Year. He wouldn't even get a participation trophy. However, he was the area's ugliest and most interesting soul and rivaled the long-time street person named Aqua Lung for capturing the attention of neighborhood clothesline fascination.

As Charlie was attempting to shoo the spectators back, the child climbed from beneath the table without further coaxing and sat with her hands folded in her lap. She fixed her gaze on Charlie, and a partial smile appeared on her face. If she had to trust someone, why shouldn't it be this big bruiser? Then, with quivering lips and an unsteady voice, she uttered a name: "Bluto? You Bluto?" She pointed to his expansive belly and then to his black beard. She laughed.

"No, honey," I'm Charlie," he replied, mystified.

"No, you Bluto," she argued, then asked in a stern tone, "Bluto, what have you done to Olive Oyl?"

It took someone from the bar crowd, a lady who spent her days and nights at the Purple Onion, to rescue Charlie, who was out of his depth when it came to ancient cartoon lore. He hardly had a clue.

"Charlie, you dumb ass. Think Popeye. Think Olive Oyl. Think Bluto," said Hazel Meadows, as if she had just scored a trifecta on a quiz show. "Bluto is a bad dude on the old Popeye cartoons. And I thought you had an education, Charlie?"

"Well, now you know Haz. I fake all my smarts,"

Charlie laughed as he re-winded his memory to Saturdays at the West Virginia Theater on Summers Street when he was growing up. Then, to the little girl, "Oh, yeah, that guy. No, honey, any more guesses?" His voice was an octave higher and softer than his usual bar room continence.

"No, you Bluto, not Wimpy or Sweet Pea. Yep, Bluto." She pursed her lips together, confident she had pegged the barkeep as the heavy, cartoon character with staying power, dating back to the late 1930s.

Charlie waved to the waitress to hurry up with a pepperoni roll as if that were proper nourishment for a child who looked as if she could be the poster child for a Biafra refugee camp. The roll appeared momentarily, and the girl attacked it with vigor, pausing between bites to stare down her audience, which was starting to dwindle.

Charlie fumbled for his mobile phone to call his friend, Sheriff Jenkins. Danny was so acquainted with the saloon owner his number was on Charlie's speed dial. It was then, however, the Johns family had alternative plans as they burst through the front door of the Purple Onion. They had reconsidered running out on the child. After all, Joshua figured, the child just might belong to a wealthy couple. In for a penny, in for a pound. They had already kidnapped the child and taken her over the Florida state line.

"That's our little Mary you have there. Thank you for taking care of her for a wee bit while my wife and I slipped over across the street and had our van serviced for our trip to Dollywood in Tennessee," he said. Joshua reached for the girl. She threw the remains of her pepperoni roll at his face and then hugged the corner of the booth. "Now, little Mary, I know you dreamed of wanting to go to Dollywood. Be a good girl and come along."

Without further histrionics but with strategic intent, the child leaped into Charlie's arms and held his neck in a vice grip, snuggling up so closely one would have thought the two connected with super glue. "I don't want to go. I don't know who they are."

Since he had never previously displayed any parental affection around any child, Charlie was awash in contradictory emotions. He knew one thing: He wasn't prepared to release the girl they called Mary to this particular couple at this time come hell, high water, or a similar catastrophe.

"Mary, come to your mama," said Ruth Johns, and a tear flooded from an eye on cue. She brushed it away with the back of her hand. "You've never acted this way, child. What's gotten into you, child?"

The girl held even tighter to Charlie, who then asked the waitress to bring him the Johns' check. With one hand around the kid and another holding the bill in front of him, he read:

"Now, Mister, you and your Missus each ordered the Porter House Steak, which comes with two sides and a dessert, which you received. You, sir, ordered two doubles of Gentleman Jack whiskey, which, by the way, we keep on hand for special occasions since hardly any East Enders could afford it. It's the good stuff, though. Missus, you have expensive taste in wine. I'm amazed you even knew the name. We only keep that one on the menu for show. Since we don't carry it, Jack the barman told Jim, the go-fetch--it guy, to drive clear to the West End to find it. We like to take care of our customers at the Purple Onion. In total, if you add everything up, it comes to, would you believe, just shy of $125 without, of course, the tip. Would you like for us to add 20 percent or more for the gratuity? By the way, why didn't you order something for the child? Why is that, sir? It's obvious she was near starving."

Charlie was more than polite; he was solicitous.

"Just give us the goddamn girl, and I'll go out to my van and get the cash to pay the damn bill," said Johns, who was almost equal to Charlie in girth and height but whose squeaky voice didn't quite measure up to his size. "Come on, Mary, now you come with mother and me," said Joshua as he reached out and grabbed the girl by the forearm.

It was a mistake.

Her little teeth bit down more forcefully than a crocodile's chomp, and Joshua reflectively lashed out with the other. The open-faced slap, however, didn't have a prayer of connecting with its tiny target. Charlie grabbed the fist with the palm of his massive paw and twisted it back until a bone cracked, a report heard throughout the Purple Onion. Witnesses feared the worst. The story of Charlie's stint in Moundsville was a legend. Joshua backed up two paces, held his injured hand in the massive fold of his tummy, and charged with his one remaining arm while swinging roundhouses like a wind turbine.

Those present would later swear smoke was coming from Joshua's nostrils, and his eyes were cinnamon red, devil-like. The backwood aborigine was from so far up an East Tennessee hollow civilization never found the Johns' clan and he was a total cockup when it came to the art of fisticuffs. On the other hand, Charlie was base pugilist champion at Fort Campbell before being shipped to Iraq. He was ballerina graceful compared to his now one-armed opponent. He sidestepped the charge. At the same time, he unloaded with two short crushing jabs to his assailant's jaw that were as lethal as the one that felled an earlier opponent, giving the barkeep an express ticket to the state pen for manslaughter. As his opponent was going down in front of him, Charlie executed an entirely unnecessary coup d' grace, a chop to the back of his head. Joshua was a heap of flesh on the barroom floor, humbled in defeat.

One would have thought that would be the end of it, but Ruth charged at Charlie like a crazed banshee, kicking, flailing, and displaying a vocabulary church ladies generally avoid. She had claimed to be a God-fearing Christian, though that was normally part of the duo's con act. Several in the crowd, who had marvel and applauded Charlie's dexterity, grabbed the little lady. The only damage done was to the saloon owner's shins rendered black and blue with Gatling gun salvos from a pointed-toed, black shoe.

As for little Mary, she held tight to Charlie, virtually daring anyone to pry her loose. Totally out of character with what he called "those damn little rug-rats," Charlie had this out-of-the-blue mothering instinct. . It was unusual for Charlie, being a dyed-in-the-wool, he-man giant of the heterosexual persuasion. Even after the excitement, the child continued to cling to her new friend, grabbing his stubby fingers in a vice-like grip.

Joshua Johns got up from the floor, mumbled something about throwing up, and stumbled in the general direction of the men's room located near the back door of the bar. He was holding his stomach as if he were about to toss a gusher. As if on cue, Ruth made a bee-line for the front entrance, disappearing into the darkness. No one made a serious attempt to stop her. This was Saturday night; the patrons had had a tough work week and had little real interest in barroom soap operas.

When Sheriff Jenkins arrived at the behest of a Purple Onion dishwasher, the little girl still held on to Charlie as if he were a buoy. When anyone came close, she snuggled up even closer to her protector. When Jenkins tried to lure her away, even for a minute, she threw a fit and climbed on Charlie as if he were a tree.

"Charlie, I can't find anyone from child welfare. They've been closed for hours, and it's a weekend. Do you have any ideas?"

"Not really, Sheriff," said Charlie, but the fact was he had achieved a heavenly conversion as if a lightning bolt had struck him. He was smitten by the child hanging on his neck. "But...," and then he caught himself realizing he was about to do something rash, then continued, "But, Beverly's five-year-old niece visited us two summers ago, and there's an old cedar chest of outfits that might fit this little girl."

In essence, he wasn't offering temporary shelter for the child, only blue sky thinking on possible ideas. In the first place, he was a 65-year-old divorced man, a one-time jailbird, and a saloonkeeper who had no business having custody of a child for 10 minutes, much less an extended solution.

"Hell Charlie, I've known you since I was a kid. I think it would be okay if this child stayed with you through the weekend. I don't have any other options other than the jailhouse," Jenkins said. "I'll come over with child services first thing Monday morning."

Charlie stammered, "Wait, wait, I certainly didn't mean…my house is a trash dump of M&M wrappers, leftover pizza boxes, and enough empties to construct the aluminum Tower of Babel."

Sheriff Jenkins rubbed his chin and the stubble of a beard want-a-be. "Well, this certainly is a sticky wicket. Do you think Flo, your head waitress, could take her?" He already knew the answer to that, but manipulation was the stock and trade of lawmen.

"My gosh, Danny, Flo lives at the Holley Hotel. This is her night job. She has an early morning gig of turning tricks by the half-hour. An enterprising woman that Flo, but no guardian for little Mary," he said.

The little girl had joined the conversation with her head rotating between the uniformed sheriff and the apron bedecked saloonkeeper. She knew she had a stake in the conversation.

"Well, maybe she can stay until Monday morning, but I have to drive over to Huntington fairly early," he grudgingly said. However, when he looked at the girl who went by the name Mary, she smiled, and he not only accepted his decision, he momentarily embraced it.

"Great," said the sheriff. "I'll put out an all-points bulletin on your scofflaw dinner guests this evening and, at the same time, try and get a handle on where Mary came from, assuming she's not some alien from outer space."

Finding the Johns would not be difficult.

The sheriff had more work to do, recovering two bodies from the burning hulk of a Volkswagen van. Whether it was shots of whiskey or driving the van with one hand, Joshua failed to navigate a sharp curve on US 119 to Morgantown.

It rolled over a half dozen times down the embankment and then burst into flames.

CHAPTER 15
ALL'S WELL THAT ENDS WELL

To put it plain and simple, the sometimes irascible and bigger-than-life barkeep turned out to be a blue-ribbon dad, though a little rough at the edges.

Charlie came close to a reasonable community standard if one for fatherhood if one were to set aside the fact he was an ex-con and presided over a Charleston East End saloon.

Charlie's vocabulary even changed from the sometimes scatological vulgar to language that could be used in a church pew. Though, to local knowledge, he never darkened such a door.   Charlie spent half that first night tidying up his home and making sure there were no Penthouse magazines lying around, and that no mouse had been squeezed in the various traps he set for the vermin.

The kid journeyed to the couch like a somnolent toy soldier even as Charlie was outfitting it with linens. She was sound asleep the moment her head met the pillow. What fight there was in her was spent, and she now felt as comfortable as a kitten brought in from the freezing cold. Charlie stood over her and was puzzled. He couldn't understand his feelings.

Charlie had left the Purple Onion much earlier than usual, leaving it Hazel to lock up at 3 a.m. On the way home, with the child in the pickup's front cab minus a child's safety seat, the sign of an all-night Go-Mart convenience store caught his eye. He realized he wasn't nearly prepared for his little guest. He parked, locked the door, and went inside the convenience store where he bought a collection of snacks, a pint of milk, and cereal for breakfast, carefully selecting the one with the most colorful packaging. He glanced at the beer in the cooler but passed on it. He grabbed a couple of Coca-Colas.

The child waited patiently in the car until he returned. He did an about-face as he approached his truck, and went back inside the store. My gosh, he thought, she'll need a toothbrush, and he wondered mightily if he had sufficient toilet paper and any other toiletries a young lady might need. He was out of his depth and his element.

Charlie called her Mary, though there was no rhyme nor reason she should answer to that particular name, one assigned to her by two recently deceased kidnappers. The grim fact of their fiery demise wouldn't be known to the saloonkeeper until he got a call from his friend, Sheriff Danny, later on Sunday. They were obviously hightailing it out of West Virginia at a speed faster than the old van could reasonably manage. Navigating a curve on US 119 heading north was too great a feat for a fellow who had lost the use of an arm in a barroom fight. There was actually more to it than that: Ruthie kept insisting he go back and retrieve the little girl. Johns would much rather have slept with scorpions.

For sure, Charlie wasn't granted the title of dad. He both assumed it and then earned it, almost naturally, and there seemed a kinetic connection between the baldheaded giant and the child. It would be natural but too convenient to say this happened because Charlie rescued her from two tormentors, though that's where it started with him being called Bluto. Also, it was expected that the child's stay with this near-stranger would be brief. When Charlie called out Mary, she turned her head in his direction, but only because of recent history she experienced in a sack in the back of a van. When she turned her head, she closed her eyes and cowered, expecting the backside of a hand. It never came from Charlie.

When his last irreconcilable difference learned of Charlie's newfound status, she was mystified by the man she still referred to as "my Charlie." After all, Beverly had been the longest and conceivably the best of the ladies that took his name and filed for alimony.

In community conversation—and Charleston, though the state Capitol, was a shrinking berg—Beverly had been either too good for him or not good enough. The jury was equally divided between the regulars who frequented the Purple Onion and those who never had awakened with a hangover on Sunday morning to attended the First Baptist Church. Beverly was a church lady of some renown and sang in the choir. Even Charlie called her a saint, and this was both before and after she tossed him out and cold-cocked him with a frying pan.

News in Charleston, particularly the area encompassed by downtown up to the Elk River and bisected by Virginia Street, traveled faster than a flaming meteor. Beverly heard about Charlie's newly accumulated status as a instant parent between Sunday School and the morning church service. She didn't make it through the closing verse of "Just As I Am" before she bolted out the door and over to his house. She banged on his door before reasonable patrons of the Purple Onion had awakened for their first cup of coffee.

"I hear you have a little girl in there," she said through the screen door. "I don't have my frying pan with me this morning so you can relax, Charlie. "

"I wasn't worried, Bev," he replied as he opened the door. "I'm frying pan immune after fist-a-cuffs with a misbehaving patron last evening. What can I do for you? By the way, the check is in the mail."

"I didn't come for the goddamn check," said Beverly. She had never said so much as a "damn", relegating her verbal missives to Doris Day "gosh darn". But that was before she met Charlie. She brushed him aside and surveyed the three-room apartment with her eyes. "What a mess Charlie. You couldn't get one of those by-the-hour ladies at the Holley Hotel to also straighten up a bit."

Charlie started to protest that the place, while not spic and span, was good enough, but he knew it was useless to counter her declarative judgments. "What do you want, Bev, I've got a busy Sunday ahead of me?" Charlie knew exactly the reason she stopped by, but the back and forth guessing was a game they played, like shadows dancing the Minuet.

"Charlie, we both know you'd be somewhere behind the horror monster Freddy Kruger as a proper person to take care of a little kid," she said, making a beeline for the second bedroom and study where the child was still fast asleep on a couch.

"Quiet Bev, can't you see she's exhausted. She's been through quite an ordeal," said Charlie. He hushed his ex up with a finger to his lips.

"Oh, Charlie, she's so cute. We could have had one like this," she purred, "Only if you could have put me and a family before your precious Purple Fucking Onion."

"Shhh..," he repeated. "Watch your language."

Beverly was dreaming. Swapping DNA with his ex-wife, who was a looker while he was the ugliest fellow east of the Mississippi, would have resulted in a monstrosity rating a front-page blow up in the National Enquirer. The chemistry would not result in the cuddly treasure lying before them. Beverly had been Miss Firecracker of Kanawha County in the very distant past. Charlie looked like the hunchback of Notre Dame without the hunch.

The nightclub wasn't the only thing that stood between happily-ever-after and a lifetime hitching. Charlie had a few other bad habits. He had never been the most faithful of mates during his triple trips down the aisle to say "I do." In his mind, the promise was more an "I may or might" or, even a better qualifier, "perhaps, but who the hell knows." It was sort of a habit with him, even though he was madly in love with each his wives at the particular moment and his regrets were piled high like kindling stacked for a West Virginia winter.

"Well, don't get all gooey-eyed, Bev. She'll be turned over to Kanawha County child services in about..." He looked at his watch. "Early on Monday morning."

Both stood over the child, and in the clear light of day observed the purple bruises on her arm, and the bump on her forehead. The injuries were from being jostled around in the back of a van with a metal floor. However, neither Charlie nor Beverly was aware of the harsh courtesies extended to the child by the Johns family.

Sitting down in the kitchen, Charlie poured two cups of black coffee and offered his former wife an opportunity to have her say, which he knew would take a minimum hour of non-stop verbal bashing. He was surprised, though. It was a mix of hell with a dollop of sugar-coated praise for his handling of the Johns at the Purple Onion. The word had spread, and even caused the preacher, Reverend Billy Grimes, to insert a line in his sermon about being your brother's keeper. The incident wasn't really that relevant to the parson's message, but the parishioners knew he was referring to the former convict, saloonkeeper, and gentle giant Charlie Jones.

As Charlie and his former misses were talking, the child walked into the kitchen, half stumbling and wiping her eyes. She wondered where she was, and on what planet she had somehow landed. Could her whole recent existence be a bad dream? No, for a four-year-old, she was rather perceptive in the present. It was just the recent past that was a total blank to her.

"Hi Bluto," she said, and walked over and held his hand. Then, she looked at Beverly and was perplexed as another character had been introduced to her kid world.

Beverly had been married once before and had two grown boys. Without a lethal weapon in her hand, she could be gracious, and she had a smile that spanned the width of the Kanawha River running through the city. She had always wanted a little girl, but approaching her late 40s, her prospects of such had faded. Now she wanted little girl grandchildren, though, as luck would have it, the family was male gene dominant. Each of her sons had sons. After a half-dozen years with what she called her "practice first husband", it had been her fervent desire that Charlie would be the "till death do us part" partner. She was disappointed it had not worked out the way she planned.

"I'm Beverly," she said, holding out a hand, "And I understand you are Mary. That's a beautiful name."

The child pursed her lips and squinted but still offered a dainty finger. She was confused by being called Mary, but she didn't offer an alternative. She connected the name Mary only to the hellacious days she had spent wrapped in a sack and a nursery rhyme she had heard about

Mary having a little lamb, but it didn't make sense to her. If these folks wanted to call her Mary, then so be it. She could be Mary. She could be Suzy or plain old Jane. Mary was as good a name as any for a child nameless, as long as corporal punishment was not the punchline.

They spent the entire afternoon as if they were some kind of tight-knit nuclear family. They drove over to Coonskin Park and walked the path behind the clubhouse. They had lunch at the Tidewater Grill in the TownCenter Mall. They stopped in a toy store where Beverly bought a Barbie Doll for the child, which was her first. They traversed the lower pathway of Kanawha Boulevard next to the river and watched the coal barges navigate the waterway. The girl was exhausted but happy. Charlie had never missed a day without at least stopping by the Purple Onion on a Sunday, but on this day, he called in. Hazel wondered if he were ill.

Sometime during the afternoon, Charlie received a call from Sheriff Danny, who relayed the fate of the Johns. The van was a burnt hulk. The VIN number filed off, and it was impossible to determine its parentage. There was no identification on the Johns couple other than a charred billfold found on the ground, and that turned out to be a stolen driving license from a Traverse, Michigan man, long since deceased. His name had been Joshua Johns, and he had been a respectable senior citizen greeter at a Wal-Mart. There was no evidence in various police databases that the recently charred Johns had ever existed. Ruth Johns was also a complete blank.

Charlie saw no purpose—at this time—to tell the

child about the accident. The sheriff said he would need to talk to her but that it could wait a few days. Mary, or whatever her name, seemed to understand the call to Charlie was about her kidnappers. Her face formed a gloomy mask, and her eyes fluttered rapidly. The mere thought of seeing them sent shivers throughout her small, frail body.

"Don't worry, Mary, we're not going to let anything happen to you," said Beverly. The little girl believed her, and color came back to her face.

During the day, Charlie had engaged in more deep-down thinking than he had contemplated his entire life. Virtually no one had ever accused him of thinking beyond action and immediate reaction. Now, however, he mentally wondered where he had been and where he was going.

When it came down to it, no one depended on him except his employees at the Purple Onion. Absent Charlie, they would find other work. The loyal customers of the bar would find another watering hole within a day or so. Beer tastes the same most everywhere. He faced the fact: He was merely a five-minute bus stop for most of his customers, as well as his friends. If he were to die, there would be a perfunctory memorial service at the Purple Onion, and everyone would move on.

This little girl, however, was as real as the back of his hand. She was a pulsating being that looked up to him as her Bluto, her protector, in less than a day. It was an odd feeling. When he married Beverly, her boys were already college-bound. They never treated him as papa, but he was merely thought of as Charlie, the saloonkeeper, and the man their mother complained about to high heavens but seemed to love. Charlie wasn't just confused with this turn of his life. He was conflicted. What does he do now? There was no Socratic answer, and, then again, Charlie wouldn't know Socrates from Soupy Sales.

Interesting, his third extra wife had similar thoughts. She wanted definition in her life but felt she was simply like a piece of driftwood on the Kanawha River. Sure, people thought well of her, but the fact was she wasn't even the lead soprano in the church choir. The gears turned in her mind. It was not a manipulative process but one simply of future survival and placement. She began to wonder what could have been and not what was. It was a painful few minutes.

"What are you thinking, big guy," she asked in the presence of the child, who was still holding tight to Charlie?

"Bev, this little girl is from somewhere. Who knows where. Maybe she was abandoned at birth, and there is no telling who her mother is. She didn't belong to the folks that came into the bar last night. I have a thought—but it is a crazy one."

"I think I know what you're thinking, Charlie. I know you that well."

"It's not an impossibility—or, is it?"

"It won't be easy, Charlie. The girl needs a stable

home life. She needs someone who is there for her, both day and night."

The conversation's direction was apparent, but neither wanted to say out loud the most challenging part. It would require the child services folks and a local judge to recognize that which was not immediately apparent—that an ex-con saloonkeeper could bring up a child. It would require a female part of the equation. The last time a judge saw the couple together was to dissolve their marriage on the grounds of that billboarded two words, irreconcilable differences.

"I'm not against it," said Charlie, as if the unspoken part was obvious.

"Hell, Charlie, I'm not either, even though they'll I probably kick me out of the church choir, and the reverend will think I'm completely off my rocker," she said.

"Beverly Jones, are we talking about the same thing?"

"We're certainly heading that direction," she replied as she reached over and massaged his back and neck.

So ended the West End summit with irreconcilable differences leading to a conciliation, at least of sorts. As Charlie would later say, "the resolution was good enough for government work."

He had never been in government, though, other than the military.

CHAPTER 16
CENTRAL FLORIDA - THE DROWNING DUCK

Jeremy Britnell didn't take to television. Swamp boy was neither a swamp creature nor was he TV glamour. The lights played havoc with the weak muscle in his right eye, causing him to cock his head ever-so-slightly to one side.

He was what he was—a work-a-day scribe, a hell-bent-for-leather reporter with a touch of the poet. He did have a winning smile, sort of like the boyish actor Matt Damon. There seemed to be laughter behind usually serious continence,

If he had the touch of the blarney, it only manifested itself in front of a computer chronicling a murder, a heist, or a human interest yarn. He loved diving into the bramble bushes of the human condition. He could empathize with the downtrodden but be hard-nosed with the bureaucratic mayor. In this regard, he was fearless.

But, more than anything else, he could write a sentence that could be put to music, a funny story that caused a giggle interruption in the reader, and describe murder as if the reader were standing over the stone cold body.

However, and this was an Olympic hurdle, all this God-given talent faltered when he read cue cards from a distance to show WOLF-television he could, indeed, make it as a pitchman and host of a reality TV series. It was that damned eye again, causing rabid blinking, and then it went south from there.

Jeremy froze at his first audition and stuttered. He had that jackrabbit in the headlights look as if he knew he was horribly miscast. His stomach growled in body stereo, and he had this compulsion to excuse himself. As the old joke went: He had a face for radio and a voice for silent movies. He wanted to run, flee back to his boat, and on the way, replace the whiskey Cherokee had ceremoniously tossed overboard. What time does the ABC Package store open, he wondered.

But, in his nearly three decades, he had never let anyone down—not Sarah, not editors, not bosses, only himself. He had always achieved at least the lowest denominator on the success scale, whether as a journalist or 12-year-old selling donuts door-to-door. Failure to him was manageable, but he could not face failing for others. Even though he had lost Sarah under the most tragic of circumstances, he felt he must succeed, even though this new life role mystified him. More than that, it terrified him.

Then, there was this new lemon drop in his life, both sweet and sour. He felt he was on a rollercoaster that kept climbing. He knew it would reach a summit and head down around hairpin curves with a full head of steam. If prepared for the ride, he wasn't aware of it. The truth of the matter was he also didn't want to let Cherokee down. She had placed her bet, and though Britnell was confident the hand she held was not even bluff worthy, he would do his damnedest. Besides, he needed the dough to finance his search for Fairleigh; and, who knew, it was possible a television show would be the key.

The early reviews were not kind.

The first words Cherokee's uncle, William "Wilkie" Norton Blige IV, said to his niece were not at all encouraging. He had been shown a sub rosa audition tape by a jealous director at FrontPage Detective earlier in the day. The director, Henry Hyde, was a misogynist who felt threatened by the growing influence of this brash kid named Cherokee who appeared out of nowhere and just happened to be the boss's niece.

Hyde didn't know this fact early on, and his hostile attitude escalated when he discovered the big boss's pet had landed in his department. He had worked at the station for 15 years, even before Wilkie Blige had made it his southern flagship. He carried the authority of tenure but also of marginal success. His homegrown programs had made the cash registers sing. However, a more astute fellow would have sucked up big time. Hyde's antenna for subtleties was pigmy-sized. You don't overcome nepotism from the big boss by submarining his niece.

"Where in the goddamn Sam Hill did you find this rube," Blige, normally a mild-mannered sort, shouted. "I haven't seen anyone this awful in front of a camera since the fellow who became Clarabell the Clown on The Howdy Doody Show eons ago. He was so bad they put him in a buffoon suit, painted his face, and had him talk by honking a horn. Would this Britnell guy wear a clown suit?"

"I rather doubt it," said Cherokee without smiling. She was taken back but not daunted. "Besides, Clarabell was even before your time, so if you are going to give damning testimony, it has to be in the first person."

They were in the confines of Blige's private office, an island in an empire that spread over the media landscape of a half dozen states throughout the south and one station in Denver. Her uncle had chosen Orlando for the climate, his golf game, and what he thought would be edging into a comfortable retirement. It wasn't to be. He couldn't let himself out of the Monopoly game of business and capturing more properties. True to form, every time he rounded go, or, in this case, closed another deal, he was prone to shout: "Hot damn, this is just too much fun." He looked at retirement as a relatively recent 20th Century invention—which it was.

Blige's office was not voice tight, and the discussion slipped under the door and into the reception room where his private secretary of 20 years, Izzy Caldwell, ruled supreme. Within moments, the entire building would know the comeuppance given the new girl who arrived just six months earlier and had seemed poised for a meteoric rise.

Interestingly though, in those first few months, Cherokee, by dent of personality and persistence, had won over most every WOLF employee, including Izzy, who rumors suggested was Blige's one and only paramour and his primary adviser. Cherokee, though, had not made the slightest headway with daytime director Hyde. She was whip-smart and won respect by being Mississippi gracious, something her alcoholic daddy taught her during periods of lucidity. Even her uncle became a Cherokee fan, but he was determined not to give her too much rope. She had only recently graduated from Ole Miss, and he considered her a tenderfoot. Also, on the surface, Wilkie had never been close to his younger brother, who he considered frivolous in the extreme. He honored him, however, for his war hero status, as did most everyone.

"But uncle..." Cherokee attempted to continue.

"Mary, er Cherokee, or whatever you are calling yourself these days, how much have we invested in this Britnell fellow?" Her uncle asked a question to which he already knew the answer. It was the reason he was so rich. He was a bottom-line jockey in money matters and knew profit and loss statements by the month back 20 years.

"You're right, uncle, Jeremy needs work. Give him a chance," she said. She felt very small in front of her uncle's desk. It was big, like the deck of an aircraft carrier. Blige had inherited the desk when he bought the station lock, stock, and barrel. It seemed a waste not to utilize it. He generally did his business, though, standing up.

"And now you are going to give me a sob story about this guy's kidnapped daughter and the fact his wife recently died," said Blige. "And I am supposed to cry crocodile tears. Well, I can do that if it's what you really want."

Cherokee immediately identified the approach as a strategic gambit on her uncle's part. She was a Blige and could play the game, particularly knowing his primary interests: Keeping the peace and making money.

"Uncle Wilkie, that's not an argument I would make, though it's true. But, give me a little time with him. I'm going to make him into a star, and sponsors will be lining up for our program," she said and crossed her heart with her finger.

"Why are you so interested in this character. I can get that former police lieutenant in Miami who went up against the El Diablo drug gang and has bullet holes in him to prove it," said the uncle. "We already know Lt. Napoleon has television charisma out the wazoo. I don't want a rival —even if it is four hours away in Miami—to snatch him from under us."

There was a moment of silence, and then Cherokee renewed her defense which was more an assault up a fortified hill. She summoned her hard-nosed business tone, one that, perhaps, was inherited.

"Uncle Wilkie, you know damn well I signed Jeremy Britnell to a contract at ten big ones a month. I did it, of course, with the provision you give the final approval. The walls have ears in this place, and I am sure that sniffling snitch-bitch of a second-class director Hyde has already reported the sum and substance of my agreement with Jeremy. It's all contingent on his ability to do the job."

"Help me out a little here, Cherokee," he said, a sly smile coming over his face, one that was sufficiently wide for his gold-capped front teeth to shine. "Ten big ones. What's that, $1,000 bucks a month. Maybe we can experiment for a month or so?"

"Don't kid yourself, Uncle Wilkie, Oh Great One, you know as well as I it's $10,000 a month, and he will be worth every dollar if I have to go out and rope in sponsors by swiveling my caboose this way and that way down at Sam's Car Barn and the Piggly Wiggly," she said as she plopped down on the corner of his desk as if she were privileged to be so bodacious with the president, and board chairman of Blige media. Car Barn kept the lights on at the station with mega buys, and Piggly Wiggly had supported the Orlando station for years with weekly specials and a tie-in with the local Sentinel newspaper. They were both close to Blige's heart.

Then, as one can only do when their uncle owns the business and is at heart a kindly sort who happens to be indulgent with his only niece, she pushed the button—the one to blow the door off the argument. He knew what was coming. She was a Blige, straight from the loins of his drunken brother Roy who he hardly ever referenced but had loved dearly as youngsters. He had been his senior by three years.

"Dear Uncle, what can I say—you might be surprised—but Jeremy and I are kind of a couple. But don't think for a moment that clouded my judgment. We're almost engaged. In your old morality Southern Baptist way, you would consider me living with him to be a mortal sin. Unless, of course, we're betrothed."

She did expect such news to set him back on his heels and for him to wonder where he had let his little brother down with his renegade daughter's journey toward matrimony—or at least palimony. And this, right under his supposedly watchful eyes in the Victorian mansion they shared with a collie dog and an occasional sleepover with Izzy about whom Cherokee wasn't supposed to have a clue but did.

"What, you expected me to be shocked? Your daddy told me before he died you were the most high spirited of the clan," sputtered Blige. "The word he used was impetuous, just short of crazy. But he said for all the wildness, you also had a commonsense gene. I wondered, of course. But, with those last breaths, he told me to watch over you—but not too closely because, as he put it, 'Mary ain't no ordinary gal. She's bewitched, but in a good way.'"

Cherokee was under the impression the two hardly ever talked, one being an overachiever and the other a well-practiced boozehound. However, Roy was a drunk who also had bestowed on him hero status. That distinction, in itself—even liquored-up on pedestrian vodka —had given him special community status. The man was asked to participate in every Fourth of July parade in Biloxi. As long as he could stand on a float, city officials felt he could wear a uniform and toss candy favors to the little kids along the route. Roy had enjoyed the role immensely and had even laid off drinking the night before the event.

Biloxi had long deemed William Blige the brilliant businessman and Roy, the messed-up-in-the-mind war hero. The townspeople could forgive the aberrations of a genuine hero. As for Roy, he didn't consider himself a drunk—or even a hero—merely an excessive tippler at times.

He could live with that designation so long as people weren't overly preachy. He hated that. Overall, Roy Blige was comfortable with his lowered status and had long determined that indulging in legal beverages was preferable to a long life. In that, he got his wish. Roy's family always had sufficient money to get by, what with a disability pension from the war and the stock he had purchased early on in Blige Motor Company at the behest of his older brother.

"That was generous of daddy to say," Cherokee said, wondering what would come next, but then added, "You do know the story, don't you? My papa is my real papa, but my mama was far from being the loving mommy. Clementine was an imposter for the sake of decency and community standing."

Blige leaned back in his overstuffed green chair that matched the various desk accessories, including a tinted paperweight and an ancient Smith-Corona typewriter that he still used to type notes to himself. He let out a sigh that caused receptionist Izzy's ears to perk up just outside the door. She wondered what the hell was going on in this uncle-niece confab.

"I probably know as much about this episode that led to your being brought into this crazy world as you do. Your momma — or Clementine—certainly would not have told you," Blige said, grasping for words. "I always wondered how you survived in that house."

"Everything I know came filtered through cracks in the door as I grew older," said Cherokee. She moved to the straight-back chair at the side of his desk as if to reveal a family secret. "It wasn't easy, Uncle Wilkie. Clementine screaming at my poor dad. That was a daily happening. I can hear it now. 'Roy, your drunken binges have humiliated this family's good name. Why couldn't you be more like your brother William? And the child, Mary, when will you tell the little redskin she's the product of your roaming Willie and a Cherokee squaw who worked as a stock clerk at the A&P? I took care of that little indiscretion—well, me and Wilkie. I hustled her ass off to a home for unwed mothers and then raised the little girl as my own. As for the squaw, your brother made sure she had a job at one of his properties—somewhere in North Dakota, I think. I must be a saint to have put up with you for so long.'

"So, yeah, Uncle Wilkie, I've known the entire story for years. You know, I never called Clementine momma? My daddy was my daddy, and Mrs. Blige was auntie, even though she officially adopted me. I guess she thought she was doing the right thing."

By the time she had completed this megalith of a story, William Blige had his head resting in the palm of his hands. He truly had not known what Cherokee knew or didn't know. The fact she preferred answering to the name of an Indian tribe should have been a clue.

Izzy's ears were aching from being nearly welded to the door. She knew, however, Blige would reveal all over pillow talk eventually. At the station, Izzy's relationship with the boss was an open secret. It could have been out in the open, but Izzy had a husband who was the fleet salesman for Sam's Car Barn, and he traveled a lot. He was a gregarious sort. The husband, Luther Caldwell, also spent his weekends at area gun shows—sometimes traveling as far away as southern Alabama—or otherwise dressing up in green and olive camouflage fatigues and doing drills with Central Florida's very own unofficial militia outfit, "The Game Changers."

Caldwell claimed the group had to be prepared to keep the lefties from taking over the country, though there was no apparent threat at hand. However, other than those drawbacks, he had never put a hand on Izzy and kept his arsenal under lock and key except for an old-fashioned German Lugar he kept unloaded and displayed on a bookshelf under glass. It was an antique and more of a curiosity piece for visitors.

Luther had flashing billboard hints of Izzy's feckless devotion but never raised the matter. Izzy suspected he ignored the obvious because he got free tickets through the station to chow down in the VIP room for Orlando Magic basketball games. Izzy didn't seem too worried about it in any event, and the tradeoff made for an honest match, though one not certainly made in heaven. As for Blige, he loved the lady, and it was reciprocal.

"I don't know what to say," said Blige. "Your mother, uh, Clementine, had a strong will and a dominant personality. My brother was more a kid in a grown body. He didn't know what to do at the time. He thought he was in love with the A&P clerk. If you should ever try to reach out to her, her name is Enola—that means Magnolia. She's now the manager of our WOKL television in Denver. She never went to North Dakota. She started in a lowly assistant position in the company and worked her way up. I loaned her my name and a cover story, and she made the most of it, even getting a university degree. You have a lot of Enola in you."

The revelation was nearly more than Cherokee could bear. A massive gap in her life was added in the space of a 20-minute conversation meant to secure gainful employment for her new boyfriend, cum fiancee, cum, perhaps, life partner, the conclusion of which she hadn't a clue. It was merely a random thought carried forward into the etherial zone.

As to her birth mother, she filed away each confetti scrap of information. Meeting her had been a dream, though she had no idea whether the feeling would be mutual. She suspected it wouldn't. Lives diverge. The woman would be in her early fifties, probably settled into a comfortable Colorado life. Cherokee now recalled the 10-point type of Blige media executives and remembered seeing what to her was an unusual name, Enola Blige, as the general manager of one of her uncle's properties. She thought it must be her uncle's distant cousin.

"Well, now both you and I know everything, I guess," said Uncle Wilkie. "So where is that boyfriend of yours, and when am I going to meet him."

She looked into her uncle's piercing dark eyes. He looked severe. He was wearing a dark, three-piece suit, even though this was Florida and the temperature was hovering at 80. He squinted and wiggled his ears as if he were worried about what she was about to say. "Two questions Uncle Wilkie: First, do you trust me? And second, have you ever done something just because your heart said, 'Go for it, Wilkie?'"

Her uncle rocked back in his desk chair, and a smile broke up a frozen face.

"In the first place—if you want to keep me in a good mood—never use the name 'Wilkie', though Uncle William is perfectly acceptable. I even accept the moniker Willie. That's what my mama called me. I picked up that horrible nickname Wilkie in elementary school and haven't been able to shake it over a half-century."

"Hell, Uncle William, I'll call you the Grand Wizard of O-town if you wish. I just need Jeremy to have half-a-chance," she said. "I promise he's a hidden talent."

"Stop pleading Cherokee," he said. "It takes away from your tough-as-nails persona."

It was true. Cherokee's eyes and her droopy mouth suggested she was coming close to begging. It was as if she already had hat in hand at the corner of Orange and Pine, panhandling for a pint of booze.

"Now to your question: Cherokee, how in the hell do you think I built this sprawling media conglomerate? With some money in savings, I bought into this little cable station in Biloxi. I didn't know a damn thing either about business or television. Then, I got damned lucky and won an exclusive contract to broadcast the Ole Miss Rebels football games in south Mississippi. I just built on that foundation. I didn't have to bribe anyone or have anyone killed. What is it they say: Success is 90 percent showing up. I just showed up—though it helped to have been an All-American tailback under coach Johnny Vaught way back when. But you had a second question that I found even more intriguing. What was that first question again?"

"Do you trust me," she asked meekly?

"Honey, You are a Blige. We've had a lot of screwy genes coursing through this family over the years. Some of us couldn't find our behinds with both hands if we were wearing a blindfold. Some of us have been like your daddy, drunks, but kindly and courageous drunks. The world needs kind and courageous—even drunks.

"And me?"

"You honey, I trust you wholeheartedly, but it is a conditional trust. Don't fuck it up. You're my only relative of note, and the last thing I want to do is sell this corporation to some right-wing neanderthal in Australia. Follow your heart, but for god's sake, lead with that pretty noggin of yours."

Cherokee did have a plan, but then she always had a plan. She called it galaxy thinking, and it was based on a hunch. A hunch is even less reliable than intuition. It often lacks intellectual underpinning. It was a Hail Mary pass. It was betting the egg money at the roulette table in Las Vegas. It was Evel Knievel's Snake River Canyon motorcycle jump, but this time blindfolded, smoking high-test weed without the emergency parachute.

"Whatever you're thinking, Little Thundercloud, and I can almost see the wheels turning now, cough up the details," said her Uncle. "Perhaps I can put in my two cents."

Cherokee welcomed a partner who could backstop her run-away imagination when it came to Jeremy and his talent.

A few weeks ago, when Jeremy appeared on a Henry Hyde-produced program—one in which he seemed to shine—it was a tandem interview. However, she had prevailed on him to shoulder the entire FrontPage Detective talent load for his WOLF audition. His earlier appearance was interspersed with archival footage from true crime stories. In Cherokee's version, a single segment would be dedicated to finding missing children.

It was a logical approach and one favored by producer/director Hyde. However, it was too much for any one person to shoulder for a half hour.   A television audience during daytime hours has the attention span of a gypsy moth. A housewife simply has too many chores, and the deadbeat husband is popping another beer and waiting for a cops and robbers shoot-em-up on Turner Classics. Missing children, while compelling momentarily, would not hold an audience without a good dose of on-air personality. Jeremy rated high on the sincerity scale but came up short on television charisma, a necessary ingredient for game show hosts and docudrama jockeys.

There was one thing for sure: Cherokee and Jeremy had chemistry, driven by an intense, sweaty, sexual, between-the-sheets swapping of DNA. The type of collaboration leaves an audience wondering what went before and what was about to happen next. They played well off one another, mainly when it came to one-liners. They were George Burns and Gracie Allen, Sonny and Cher, Paul Newman and the Sundance Kid, alternating between straight man and wise-guy. Bringing missing children into this was dicy. However, there was no mistaking; the banter between them was cutting, often comical but never boring.

By Cherokee's musings, though, there was one boulder blocking the pathway.

"Uncle, I've got nothing against Hyde. He's a smart fellow and knows the business—but his forte is not what I call television of the moment. I have all these ideas in my head, and I don't know if they will work. But you have to give me a little rope—not because I'm your niece but because you are once again taking a chance like you did when you first launched Blige Media."

Blige stood up, walked from behind his desk, and then returned to his previous sitting position. He opened the desk drawer as if searching for something and then abruptly shut it again with a bang. He swiveled in his big man chair, staring out the window high over Lake Eola. His actions were of a man who was about to place all the chips on No. 23 red at the wheel. Cherokee studied his movements and his face. She knew before he made his decision.

"Hell, Hyde's been doing the daytime gig since dirt was invented. He's earned the lead-in to the evening news slot. It's a promotion, or at least he will see it that way," said Blige. Then, raising his voice: "Izzy, I know you've heard every word of my conversation with Cherokee. Tell Henry Hyde I want to see him in my office in an hour—and that I have news for him. No, raise that to 'I have awesome news' for him."

Cherokee rushed over to her uncle, trespassing with impunity on the no fraternizing commandment for a junior employee, almost knocking him out of his chair. She gushed her enthusiasm and planted a shaggy dog kiss somewhere in the vicinity of his mouth, which was wide open.

"Wilkie, uh, Uncle William, on my word as a part Cherokee native American, I promise that you will not regret this decision," she said, putting her hand over her heart. He laughed, clearly pleased with his niece's grit but also with a rare display of affection. As Roy's kid, she never was sure where she stood with Blige or Blige Media. It was her breakout moment.

"Well, first, little lady, you are not even part Cherokee," explained Blige. "You are part Seminole or rather Creek — Seminole was the name given to, in essence, Creek runaways from Alabama—and the other part, Mississippi mongrel, taking into account your daddy's propensity as a Tomcat kind of lover around Biloxi. As you can see, I've conducted a little research. Have I interfered with your role-playing? Upset your apple cart? You were so intent on being a Cherokee from the time you were a teen tyke, I didn't want to disappoint you. Besides, Blige seemed to go better with Cherokee—rather romantic —than Creek."

"So, I've been living a lie?"

"Not really Cherokee. You are who you say you are —and, quoting the lady writer George Elliot, 'It's never too late to be who you might have been.' Me? I still have dreams of being a pirate—and some people in business think of me as one, mainly when I am on the prowl for a new deal.

It was a fact. Cherokee had always seen her uncle as a staid businessman and thought only of her father as the family renegade. The morning was an eye-opener that allowed a little sun to shine in. Uncle William was a rambling wreck of a pretend pirate who had rainbow visions the same as she. Whether blue silk stocking businessman or drunken ragman, one could be happy following elusive pursuits into the horizon. The trick, of course, was not to encourage followers. In such case, you become a Pied Piper for, as Jonathan Swift would write, "A confederacy of dunces."

"Uncle, Jeremy is waiting in the studio to hear whether the verdict is capital punishment or merely banishment from the Blige media kingdom," said the Cherokee lady who had so suddenly become a Seminole princess.

"Well, what are you waiting for? Izzy, come in here. Let's get a few things on paper before I change my mind," he laughed, but his words had the hint of truth. Any other surprises, Cherokee?"

"Well.......what if I told you Jeremy comes with a 'come with'.

"'A come with? Now, what in Sam Hill does that mean?"

"He has an assistant, a Mr. Purvis Periwinkle," she said quickly, and as an understatement, as she drew in a breath. "He's an investigator Jeremy uses, and it all fits into the show's budget. He's an inexpensive hire, about the cost per week of one of your silk ties. Purvis assists in locating missing children. In fact, he would make a solid addition to the show. He has a certain comedic presence that balances the program's seriousness. It will be a great ensemble cast."

"So, what you're saying is I've agreed to hire your boyfriend, accepted your decision to change the program format, fired a long-time director and, finally, my new hire comes with a staff," Blige spit and stuttered, and then offered sarcastically:

"Do you think Jeremy would like a car and driver? What about a wardrobe and makeup team? A butler? What about a special dressing room. We could put jellybeans in a jar. Does he like cinnamon?"

Cherokee backed out of the office, and, as she did, Izzy gave her a thumbs up.

CHAPTER 17
PERIWINKLE IS ON THE CASE

Purvis Periwinkle's only training in the sleuthing business was as a very distant cousin to law enforcement. It was his couple of days as a rent-a-cop prowling The Mall at Millenia close to Disney World.

He wasn't that great at it. He was issued a billy club but not a gun. That was fine with him. Purvis didn't much care for guns, and when his granny gave him Roy Rogers' cap pistols for his fifth birthday, he traded with a neighbor kid for a ping-pong table set.

Some years later, he was distraught to learn that little Bobbie Baxter elevated that toy arsenal to a single .357 Magnum. After binge-watching Clint Eastwood's "Dirty Harry" movies, Baxter proceeded to depopulate a crowded theater, sending six people to meet whoever might be their preference as the often referred to maker.

But the world is run on serendipity, horse crap, and by well-meaning folks who don't know shit from Shinola, speaking, of course, of a dated shoe polish that outlived its advertising from the 1940s. This observation is as sure as day follows night, except in Iceland, primarily dark for three months.

The tossed rock glides across a lake's smooth surface, and it is purely happenstance what direction it heads after first splashing down. After a life of abrupt fits, Purvis's luck came when Jeremy Britnell intervened.

They were like Mutt and Jeff but worked together like fine whiskey and branch water. They seemed to understand one another, and when Cherokee came along, she was sufficiently bizarre for membership in this club. They didn't feed on one another's distinct aberrations, ignoring the odd ticks and the alchemy that, taken together, created a near brilliance.

Still, there was no one on earth physically more different than the gangly Periwinkle from the bullet-built former reporter who, for inexplicable reasons, Purvis felt he owed him a lifetime of servitude. It all had to do with his helping Purvis escape the overly-mothering clutches of his grandma, Gladys Hogan. Perhaps, though, the real reason for this allegiance was that Purvis was there for Britnell through two journeys into hell, the loss of Fairleigh and the never-to-return trip of Sarah to Dallas.

Britnell, however, had no use for serfs or servants, at least from the outset. He felt he had no use for friends after Sarah's death. It was the ultimate in Schadenfreude that this odd grandmama's boy would befriend him and that this bohemian-weird girl named Cherokee would also crash the membrane of his miserable existence. He wasn't sure he was ready for any of it. It just happened.

Purvis was thrilled to latch on as the Dr. Watson to Britnell's Sherlock, though he had absolutely no idea his role. Cherokee immediately saw him anchoring the far end of the couch on the TV studio set and interjecting occasional tidbits to move the dialogue along, as well as being a sidekick foil. She saw herself as the quid to Jeremy's pro; an alter ego-after ego to the star's shrinking violet personality. In other words, she would provide the spark that caused him to explode from his sometimes shell.

Anyway, that's the way the puzzle came together in Cherokee's mind, though she realized that the line from the Scotsman Robert Burns, that "The best-laid schemes o' mice an' men / often go astray" was undoubtedly at play. She would have to utilize all her magician talents.

Within a day, the research team at WOLF had identified several suitable topics and subjects within the station's viewership. It wasn't that difficult. The home of the Magic Kingdom was socially stratified. There was an abundance of runaways in ages ranging from 10 to 18. These were garden variety runners and nary a Fairleigh-style abduction among them. Still, there were compelling stories from weepy moms and dads and friends desperate to locate alienated youth who, one yarn had it, took flight because the miserly parents wouldn't shell out $1,000 for a prom dress at Macy's. Another took flight after not getting the latest iPhone on her 15th birthday.

Jeremy was not clairvoyant, and neither was he a

genius soothsayer. However, he did have a keen sense of where to search and could follow a clue to the ends of the earth. It was both an innate and a learned talent stemming from being a top-notch reporter. He was also a good listener, a trait he believed was his secret weapon. He had a bird dog sense and tenacity for following leads. His abilities complemented those of Periwinkle. Having been told by Granny Gladys he was a world-class loser so often, he was determined to succeed in his new role. The fiasco he had at Taco Bell, where he caused a near-riot due to his organizational ineptitude, haunted him.

From the very beginning, Purvis had a priority assignment.

While his friend Britnell spoke hardly a word over his days of grief, the poor fellow did rant and rave into a pillow at a certain point when all that remained in the whiskey bottle were dregs and 90-proof fumes.

"Periwinkle," he slurred. "Be a pal. The ABC store is less than a mile away, and on the middle shelf of the whiskey section, they have a bottle of Jack. I hear it calling me. It has my name on it."

"What is your name?" Purvis, who had babysat throughout the night, sleeping on the rug-less floor, asked.

"Are we playing games, Periwinkle? Twenty-Questions, perhaps? Pity a thirsty man, a recent widower, and a fellow who lost the two most precious things a man can have—his long-time love and precious child. By the way, my name is Jeremiah Butler Britnell. Now, can you make an ABC store run? I'll pay you back—a little short myself. Those fucking bandits at the funeral home took my last severance pay from the Sentinel."

"I'm aware of your lost child, Jeremy. Remember, I was the mall guard that tried to find her the day she went missing," Purvis reminded him.

"Did I ever tell you I wrote a book about how I thought her life might be as she grew up, and it started with a little girl on Santa's knee at that very mall? I've never been back there since that day. I can't. The book was life, imitating art, or should that be art imitating life. I'm a little confused, Purvis. Help me out here. Now, will you fetch me a replenished bottle of hooch? It has a black label, but if you have to get the green label, that's okay, too. Just stay away from the blue label—neither one of us can afford that stuff."

Purvis latched on to Britnell's detoured literary career as if it were a life preserver tossed to a drowning soul.

"Whatever happened to the book you wrote about your little girl? Do you have a copy of it? I'd love to read it," said Purvis, dispelling any doubts that the Taco Bell cockup and one-time mall cop couldn't read.

Britnell looked at him with a mixture of disbelief and wonderment. The last person to ask to read his book —other than his wife Sarah—had been a fellow named Bill Shakespeare, who claimed to be a successful literary agent. He wanted to charge Jeremy $5,000 to make commercial suggestions and recommend the book to a few publishers with excellent contacts. Having covered the Florida Land Sales Board, Britnell immediately recognized Shakespeare as a fraud and sent him packing. However, the truth of the matter was that the budding author didn't have five big ones to plop down at this particular roulette table and still contribute to the family's Christmas.

Purvis' query was basic curiosity but mixed with a little homespun psychology. The longer he could keep Britnell talking, the more sober he would become.

"Do you still have a copy of it?" Purvis asked.

"Copy of what?" Britnell had already journeyed on, leaving discussions of his literary dreams in the dust. His thoughts were only of returning to la-la land, and a thimble or twenty of whiskey just might do it. Yes, a bonafide liter would definitely be a game-changer. It might even put him out of his misery, and he could catch that same train to Dallas as Sarah.

"The book about Fairleigh. Stick with me, buddy. You are fading in and out," pleaded Purvis.

"Nah, I couldn't find a publisher, and so eventually I had it stored with some furniture at someplace on the west side of town. When Sarah became sick, and I moved on this boat, I gave up on the book. I had too many other worries, and chasing rainbows wasn't a priority," he muttered, closed his eyes, and was out cold.

Being a good and faithful Tonto to his Kemo Sabe,

the name the Indian gave to his masked pal, Purvis had every intention of bringing back liquid sustenance for his intoxicated friend. First, though, he embarked on a serious inspection of the boat. His mission had nothing to do with cleanliness. He wanted to find a receipt or any scrap of paper that might serve as a clue to where Jeremy had stashed the manuscript. Periwinkle wasn't the literary sort, though he was a compassionate pal. The book interested him strictly as a talisman to Britnell's current sorry state.

Eventually, he found a clue. It was in a bottom drawer in the kitchen taken up by an assortment of do-dads for cooking that Sarah had somehow found a use for but was a mystery to Jeremy. On a fragment of yellow paper, he discovered the name Harry's Storage Center and an address. Also on it was Britnell's nearly illegible signature, the exaggerated mark of someone more comfortable with a computer or typewriter than a pen. It wasn't that far away. He felt he could visit Harry's, pick up the whiskey, get back to the boat and nurse his patient sufficiently for him to stand erect and dutiful for Sarah's send-off, whether to Dallas or beneath the black dirt reinforced sand of the cemetery.

Periwinkle introduced himself to Harry Stiles, the proprietor, as representing one Jeremiah Butler Britnell. He revealed the tattered receipt and said he would like to pick up one particular item, a book manuscript. For good measure, Purvis flashed the tin badge he kept from his rent-a-cop vocation.

As for Harry, he looked skeptical and pulled out a cardboard box of files. After a long moment of rustling through paperwork, he had an eureka moment.

"I'm sorry to disappoint you and your Mr. Britnell, but that storage space was defaulted July 10, three years ago, and I've re-rented it twice since that time," he said, closing the makeshift file. "Yep. the paperwork says the contents were purchased by someone else. Your Mr. Britnell, my friend, was a scofflaw. I'm sure our administration people contacted him. He owed a lot of back rent on the space, and, under the law, we had the right to auction off the contents. That's exactly what we did."

Purvis pursued politely, though he had a lower gear of persuasion if necessary. "Well, would you happen to have the name and address of who bought the contents of Mr. Britnell's storage?"

"I'm sorry, but that's what they call privileged information under the laws of the State of Florida," Harry replied, though he had no idea what the legal ramifications were, if any. It also wasn't that he was too busy. He had been torn away from a Wheel of Fortune rerun on the office television,

"Damn," said Periwinkle, summoning his six-foot-four frame at least two inches taller. "I certainly thought we could do this the easy way."

"What do you mean?"

"I lied to you because I didn't want you involved in this up to your eyeballs," said Purvis as he pursed his lips and gave his best "make my day" Eastwood squint. "You saw my badge. I'm DEA. That, Harry, is the federal Drug Enforcement Agency. You've probably heard of it."

"Why didn't you say so upfront," said Harry, his voice as thin as a reed and his hands shaking. "I've got a little more information. What was in that storage bin? A body?"

"Not something quite so messy. It was about 50 kilos of pure cocaine. That's a little less than $3 million crack in street value," said Purvis, who wasn't an expert but reasonably reliable when it came to basic multiplication and taking in reality cop shows.

Suddenly, Harry's memory started to return. "Yeah, I sort of remember now. There was a roll-top desk in that storage. That's most likely where the drugs could of been. I'll be damn, right here at my own business."

Harry dove back into his scattered files, tossing papers this way and that way. After a few moments, he came up with the fellow's name who purchased the contents lock, stock, and apparently, cocaine.

"It was a fellow named William Wendell," said Harry, staring at the paper as if it were a buried treasure map. "Do you think......?"

"Harry, I don't think. I know. It could be this Wendell fellow killed Mr. Britnell, whose catfish chewed body we found in the Indian River just two weeks ago. That's why you couldn't reach the fellow. Wendell purchased the storage contents with the dope from you," said Purvis. "By the way, we think this entire caper is tied in with Pablo Escobar, the Columbian drug kingpin."

"Really?" Harry's eyes were like large, colorful Fiesta-ware plates. "I, I, thought Escobar was killed back in the 80s."

Purvis had overplayed his hand, but recovered quickly. "Yes, that's what we wanted you to believe. The son-of-a-bitched escaped and guessed what?"

"You mean William Wendell is Pablo Escobar?"

"That's what we surmised, but, as you can see, we're on his trail."

"But, I don't recall Mr. Wendell having a Hispanic-sounding accent? He seemed like your basic Ohio snowbird in Florida because of no state income tax, sun, and retirement."

Then, the key question. "I realize the chances are slim Pablo would have written down his address," queried Purvis. "Can you look through your papers again?"

Again, the rifling of papers. "It's right here. Pablo lives in east Orlando, but that's probably not Escobar's real address," said Harry. He handed the paper over to Purvis.

"Harry, we in law enforcement would like to thank you for your community service. You might be in line for a reward," said Purvis. "We'll be in contact."

Harry wondered, and wondered and wondered, but never heard from the Drug Enforcement Agency or Purvis ever again. But he had an interesting story to relate at his Saturday poker game.

CHAPTER 18
TAMING A PANTHER

Panther Studios was intent on playing hardball. The studio executives saw dollar signs in klieg lights and on Hollywood billboards with Natalie Courant revisiting her role in Other Worldly.

Flush with cash after their most recent box office hit, Lee Atkinson III was feeling his testosterone, and it was making him giddy. Besides, it was time the studio whittled that cantankerous Cletus Reed down to size.

It mattered not a whit that the script crafted for the sequel seemed to have been written by the Three Stooges. There was an attempt to make it less serious than the original and give Natalie a love interest millions of miles into outer space. In a nod to political wokeness, the scripted suitor was another young lady. The romantic juxtaposition offended neither Cletus Reed nor Natalie. But, it was just wrong, and, when it came to the young star, was that proverbial bridge too far.

When she kept delaying various appointments for initial script readings, the word was sent to studio boss Atkinson that his young star was kindly turning down invitations. She would smile at the various studio emissaries, and offer a hastily conjured excuse—my cat Fluffy is sick, I have a dentist appointment, or my horoscope says 'beware the ides of March' which really puzzled Panther. She was super creative as a neurotic, pampered star at the request of her agent. Natalie saw it as a game. She was not yet aware that she, with her agent's guidance, was threading the career needle by not immediately jumping aboard the new picture.

Reed felt a sequel for Natalie so soon would be the death knell of her career, and he thought the script was so phony it was a celluloid con on theatergoers. It would be the kind of flick that tested well with pre-puberty kids, but Rotten Tomatoes, the rating service, would not only give it low marks but would actually toss those stinking tomatoes at it. Reed could cite a litany of promising stars who plunged downward after an initial success, particularly if the return vehicle was garbage. He didn't want Natalie to be a one-hit-wonder.

In fact, Reed had no confidence in Outer Worldly II from the very beginning. It was the type of plotting he would trash can after the first couple of paragraphs. In the 1960s, he had advised Walt Disney star Annette Funicello against doing those pop-up tart movies. He thought they were microwavable before microwave was invented, referring to beach movies with Frankie Avalon for American International Pictures. A clause in her Disney contract allowed Funicello to do outside work. "Annette, I agree with Walt. This will end your shot at serious acting," Reed warned. It did. She remained bankable for the studio, but never considered a serious actress.

When Atkinson was informed of Natalie Courant's reluctance to even show up for an initial script reading, he was beside himself. "One good lucky picture and Natalie thinks she's Greta Garbo. What does she want—to be picked up in a pink Rolls Royce with Dom Perignon on ice and served by Brad Pitt. Sorry baby, Pitt's under another contract. But we own your pretty ass."

It was interesting that Atkinson didn't have the gumption to deliver such a message himself, but they were fluid words with which he could pump up his own machismo with a No. 2 assistant, Roane Best. He had several interchangeable No. 2s, but Best was the latest. For the most part, they were "yes men" (never women) dark suits around the studio.

"Remind her she has a contract to do a sequel prior to beginning any other project. We've covered her $2 million fee and are willing to give her a small percentage on receipts," added Atkinson to Best. "It's a sweet deal for a dame with only one film credit to her name. I want this sequel made, and I want it in the can before Fall. Who knows, we'll probably come up short this year at the Awards, but with Ms. Courant and the exposure this year, there's a shot for next."

Best shuffled his feet. Lee Atkinson No. 3 was a hard person with whom to converse. He yelled at a decibel higher than a Stone's concert, even when he wasn't mad at anyone. He also was a spitter when he got excited, and so his assistant attempted to keep a reasonable distance. This particular assistant, however, didn't act intimidated, though he also didn't protest. He merely rolled with the bombastic rhetoric.

"I will boss, but when I insist, she says all the details need to be worked out by Cletus Reed," said Best. "I tried to talk with Reed, but frankly, I am not at his level, and he won't answer my voice messages. I tried visiting his home. His Caddy was parked on the road, but he didn't answer my knock. I even checked the beach, nary a Reed sighting. I did leave a message on his trailer."

"Hell," said Atkinson, puffing up his chest. "He's a would-have-been-never-has-been with which my old man had to deal and the studio's founder put up with even earlier. I will crush the son-of-a-bitch like the ancient roach that he is."

Best didn't really believe the threat, but he replied, "That's right, boss." It was the safest pirouette he could manage in order to change the subject and only have minor collateral damage to his mental health. He backed out the door, leaving Atkinson alone with his thoughts. Atkinson was rather certain he held all the cards.

Atkinson contacted the studio's law firm, Betts, White, and Shine, and had them draw up an official letter requesting a meeting with Natalie Courant in the Panther board room on a specific date and time. The letter said she might want to bring legal representation. It was a strong hint the pow-pow was serious and had been escalated from a bargaining position to corporate warfare. Virtually every young actress in Hollywood envied—what they considered —Natalie's incredible beginner's luck. They would kill their momma with an ice pick for a chance to star in the Outer Worldly vehicle, which executives felt had the potential for a female Indiana Jones-style franchise. Also, to put it mildly, the studio felt they could enforce that classic line: "You'll never work in this town again" should the young star violate her contract.

On the appointed day of the meeting, Atkinson and three other Panther suits, with the exception of Best, were surprised when Natalie and her agent didn't fold prior to the meeting. Reed came through the door with his game face on, which actually had a crease of a smile. When they saw only Natalie and Reed. Atkinson immediately became nervous. He apparently had left his macho armor in the men's room. He did, however, take a seat at the head of a forty-foot long mahogany table, which, in itself, didn't suggest power but merely a false sense of inherited influence.

There was one thing Atkinson didn't realize.

Roane Best, the low man on the totem pole at this meeting, was hound dog loyal, but not necessarily to the fellow who signed his paycheck. To call Best a renegade would be an exaggeration. However, he grew to manhood with his granddaddy telling him about a theatrical agent named Cletus Reed. Reed had rescued gramps acting career when Congress's Committee on UnAmerican Activities zeroed in on him in the 1950s. He was called a suspected communist, which was true, but a shade sensationalized.

He had merely attended a mass meeting and was sufficiently naive to be photographed by FBI agents toting large single-lens reflex cameras. The pictures ended up in the hands of that now-discredited committee during what was called the Red Menace.

In other words, though he had never met Reed, the fellow was an honored figure in the Best household through a generation. Reed had eloquently spoken up for Jason Best at the Motion Picture Guild and had also put in a discreet call to the news personality Edward R. Murrow who was probably the one person most responsible for ending the witch hunt of disgraced Sen. Joe McCarthy.

But there was more. Roane Best, the grandson, had generated a mystic of his own as a tailback for the Florida Gators. In an important game, with the score tied, Best pulled in a long pass from quarterback Tim Tebow and was galloping for pay dirt and the winning touchdown. It wasn't to be. A tuba player in Florida's "Pride of the Sunshine" band couldn't quite control her giant instrument and stumbled onto the field. The collision was ferocious, the girl tumbled, and Best, still on his feet, doubled back to see if she had been demolished. He leaned down, grabbed her by the hand to lift her up. It was a scene witnessed by a nationally televised audience. Best was, of course, clobbered by two Ole Miss pursuing linebackers. While the coach never forgave him for the loss, the sophomore was anointed Prince Gallant by a federation of Florida's sororities. Best rarely played the remainder of the season.

So, in the Panther board room on this particular day, Cletus had an ally, though one would think a minor league one with virtually no influence over the outcome. After all, Roane Best was No. 2 to at least the third power down. At the Panther court, he was the one who only spoke when spoken to, and then in reverent tones. However, while he valued having a job, he wasn't a slave to it.

"Thank you Natalie and Cletus for joining us here today," said Atkinson in what promised to be —and started out to be—a polite but firm opening statement.

Reed coughed loudly into his hand and cleared his throat.

"Lee, we were summoned by your law firm, Misters Betts, White and Shine, who I assume are represented among the wall of gentlemen and one lady present—other than Ms. Courant— around this handsome table," said Reed, his voice now mellifluous and steady. "I remember when your granddaddy and I had these discussions around a rickety card table with two shot glasses and a bottle of sipping whiskey between us."

"That was a long…." Atkinson started to speak, but Reed interrupted him a second time.

"Hell, it wasn't that long ago Lee Number Three," responded Reed. "But you are right. Panther Studios has grown over the years and been rather successful. I'm happy to have had a little part in that success. Now, what were you about to say, Lee?"

Atkinson pulled out the contract, held it high, and then waved it for all to see as if it were a trophy.

"Cletus, let's make this as painless as possible. It's written here in black and white that Natalie is committed to the Other Worldly sequel. In the interest of Panther Studio and, actually, in Natalie's interest, we are insisting she fulfill this agreement. I understand you have some little dog-tailed project in which you would like her to participate. I understand that. I'm a reasonable man. We have no objections. But first, the sequel."

"Who's Natalie Courant?" It was Reed in a whispering growl. He surveyed the room as if he were looking for this particular Natalie.

At first, Atkinson wondered if the agent were having a stroke, or if dementia accompanied Reed's other health problems which, while not widely broadcast, were whispered in the industry.

"Cletus, she's sitting right next to you," Atkinson exclaimed with a look of bemused astonishment.

The agent looked to his left, then to his right. "I'm sorry Lee, for the life of me, I don't see Natalie Courant. I have seen her on various occasions on billboards. You possibly are speaking of Mary Jones, who certainly favors Ms. Courant in the movie posters."

Atkinson was not a person who enjoyed parlor games.

"I'm completely confused Cletus as is everyone else in this room, including Natalie sitting beside you. Are you merely having a bad day, or have you gone completely bonkers? I know we haven't always gotten along, but I am neither my dad nor my granddad, God rest his soul. I'm in charge of a studio that has fiduciary responsibilities to stockholders. That, my dear Mr. Reed, is why this studio is insisting on holding Ms. Courant to her contract."

"There you go again, Lee number three. I do have bad days, but I'm feeling perfectly fine this morning. The sun is shining, the grass has an emerald luster and you serve Colombia's finest coffee blend. I love those little cookie cakes. Can I ask where the studio buys them?"

Atkinson let his head fall to his chin, raised it back up, and when he did, rolled his eyes to the ceiling. "We're here for business Cletus, not the weather report or to discuss cake recipes. I've got another appointment in half an hour. Let's get on with it."

"Lee No. 3, please forgive me. Mary Jones is the lovely lady sitting next to me, and that has been her legal name since Charlie and Beverly Jones adopted her when she was four. Before that, we have no idea what she was called. She was figuratively left on the Jones' doorstep. The contract was signed by Natalie Courant, and while it wasn't under duress it was with sleight of hand—a bunch of papers put in front of Ms. Jones and misrepresented as a formality. But, since Ms. Jones had no authority to sign for this—what's her name again—oh, this Ms. Courant, it really isn't a valid agreement. I don't think we have anything else to discuss, but the company this morning has been grand, and we should do this again sometime. The coffee, however, could use a tad of Irish cream."

Atkinson leaned back in his chair, conjuring up what a previous version of Lee Atkinson might do in the situation. His frustration level was red-lining, and it showed in his everyday three-martini lunch-beet color. The original Atkinson, founder whose picture was on the conference room wall in a stern and staid pose, pin-striped blue suit. vermillion red tie and with a substantial brier pipe protruding from his mouth, would have guffawed so loud the coffee cups would chatter. However, this modern-day version of studio mogul had none of his granddaddy's savior-faire and retreated to his Maginot Line of legal eagles. Misters Betts, White, and Shine seemed anxious to take on this particular legal point and quickly dismiss it.

For his part, Reed was fairly certain a dime-store attorney would easily cut through his reasoning because half the world, even after one picture, knew Mary Jones as Natalie Courant and commonsense would prevail. Reed would lose the set, but he was having fun doing so, and the match was yet to be decided.

Mr. Betts, obviously the lead attorney by virtue of his name coming first, explained that any judge would rule in Panther Studio's favor, though perhaps admonish the studio for not dotting the "i's" and crossing the "t's". "We take responsibility for that little oversight," he said. The agent's gambit, though, was more a preliminary feint than a realistic legal maneuver. Reed's heavy artillery was waiting in the wings, yet to be summoned.

It all had to do with the letter Roane Best left one day on Cletus Reed's trailer door.

CHAPTER 19
BIG-FOOTING

Roane Best had typed the note. He attached it to Cletus Reed's trailer, took it down, and walked down the hill to his car. He then returned and timidly left it in the screen door.

It read:

"Mr. Reed, you knew my granddaddy, Jason Best, a journeyman character actor. I am an employee of Panther Studio, and I have to tell you--you are about to be sandbagged. I'm a fan of Natalie Courant, and I agree with you that making this idiotic sequel would harm her career. I would like to pay you back for the kindness you showed to my paw-paw back in the 1950s. I have a plan. Can we talk?"

At first, Reed was rather suspicious. Who was this young fellow? He was obviously someone enamored with Natalie, an adoring fan who felt this was the way he could accrue sufficient points to get close to the winsome actress. In the afternoon, Reed tore up the note and tossed it into the trash.

However, by evening, his empty attic mind that often remembered episodes from a previous century came back in cinemascope with the memories of Jason Best. He was lying in bed, listening to the pounding waves. My gosh, Jason was the creature in The Romantic Reptile of River Canyon. It flooded back to him like water from a nozzle cascaded over his head. Terrible movie, but Jason did a creditable job as a scaly monster with his only utterance being "ugh you" and sometimes "ugh, you, ugh you", which was apparently meant to be reptilian for "love you", hence the romantic lizard. It was so corny it became camp, kind of like the later parody, Attack of the Killer Tomatoes.

Amazingly, Jason Best went on to daytime soap operas and became a mainstay as the comical janitor on Hospital to Heaven, which featured nary a monster through its five-year run. Reed fondly remembered the versatile actor appearing in several feature-length pictures, one of which had Johnny Swift, his jack-leg associate on The Book of Frances Leigh, as director of lighting. Though he had influenced Jason Best's life and career, Reed lost contact with him, except for sporadic Christmas cards and a fruit basket sent once a year to Reed and his wife. He retrieved the letter from the trash and punched in the number.

"So, your granddad is Jason Best," said Reed, not sure what his second sentence would be. "How is he? I haven't heard from him in a long, long time. He was an amazing talent."

"Not so well, Mr. Reed," said Best. "He died 10

years ago. But I have to tell you—and it's because of you—he had a solid career for most of a half-century. Really, Mr. Reed, you were like a God in our household. My mom had three shrines with photos in our living room: Jesus, of course; Jackie Gleason, and Cletus Reed—and you were in the middle of this trinity. When I was a kid, I never really understood. Then my dad said, 'Son, what kind of tennis shoes are on your feet? They're Air Jordans. Well, Michael Jordan is not responsible for them, and neither is your daddy. They came to you through the largess of Cletus Reed. He was the reason I could afford them."

The old Hollywood hand was embarrassed when any effusive praise came his way. He was the humble sort, who tended to avoid the kiss-kiss receptions and phony accolades that served as everyday air-smack greetings. But, as if it were yesterday, Reed conjured the right words, though still trying to determine the context. "I'm so sorry to hear this about your granddad. I always liked Jason and thought he was getting a raw deal from that Congressional Committee. I didn't do anything special—just reached out to a few of my industry and news contacts. It was the early days. You could do that then."

Then, the penultimate question that was on Reed's mind. "How son, did you get mixed up with the Lee Atkinson crowd, knowing they tend to keep getting dumber the further down the genetic chain."

Best laughed. "No real mystery. I like movie making, and this was a way to break into it. My dad, Jack Best, also worked at Panther. I guess we were always company men—or at least I was until this week when I ratted out Mr.

Atkinson to you."

"Let me ask you something. Roane. What's your interest in Natalie Courant. Have the two of you ever met?" asked Reed, who was more than curious, as well as protective.   He realized Natalie had outgrown either bodyguard, caretaker, or chaperone, and he immediately had second thoughts that he had overstepped his boundaries. It certainly was none of his business.

"Nah, she wouldn't recognize me as Roane Best if I were in a lineup wearing a red nose and an oversized clown suit and ringing a cowbell.   I'm just that invisible to her," said Atkinson's soon-to-be unemployed No. 2 assistant.

He didn't say it with any disappointment, merely a fact of life. "But, I love those eyes.   Trust me, Mr. Reed, I'm not a stalker. My interest in Natalie is strictly of the bewitched variety.   In the movies, I'm not the guy who gets the gal. I'm the goofy jilted former boyfriend. You know, the good old soft touch."

Reed knew what the poor fellow meant. It was obvious he was a daydreamer, with visions somewhere south of reality. He probably didn't have a chance for a turn at bat with the movie star, much less amble on down to first base. Natalie was last seen at the Golden Globes out with British singing sensation Dalton Hill, the heartthrob of melting, gushing ladies age 13 to 103. Best felt his high-water mark was the adoration of coeds who admired his Sir Galahad gesture at Florida Field when he stopped his heroic run to attend to a hapless tuba player. All Roane Best had going for him was a good heart, which unbeknown to him at this time, was the first combination click to Natalie's padlocked heart.

There was a long moment of silence on the phone until Reed finally spoke. "Son, I appreciate your help, and I'm going to ask even more of you. Have you ever bet on a long shot?

"I am a long shot," Best answered. "What can I do on behalf of my family to repay a debt we owe you?"

"First, that's horse Pucky. Your granddad and your dad paid any supposed debt eons ago by simply living up to my recommendation. I might not have amounted for much through these many years, but you folks added a little gold dust to whatever reputation I might have in this business," said Reed. "Do you have a pen handy?"

"I'm sitting at a computer," Best replied.

"There are two people I want you to call, Mr. Martin Scorsese and Mr. Steven Spielberg, and tell them Cletus Reed needs a favor at about 11: 15 tomorrow. That's LA time," said Reed. "

"But, sir., there is no way in the world Scorsese or Spielberg would take my call," Best protested with a slight chuckle.

"Yeah, they will. I put Martin and Harvey Keitel together on their first feature film, Who's That Knocking at My Door back in '67, and, as for Steven, I'm godfather to his youngest daughter, Destry. Besides, the numbers I am giving you are super-secret so memorize, and forget in 24-hours."

"I can do that," Best said, haltingly, and still not sure of his assignment.

Reed explained: "I've been in contact with both regarding my Frances Leigh project, and they know the inside dope. Without asking, they wanted to be backseat investors, and they are aware of my gentlemanly tete-a-tete with Atkinson. I told them I was doing this film by my lonesome, but I needed their moral and persuasive support with a persistent Panther CEO, not to mention also needing Spielberg's distribution muscle. They feel the same as I do: A sequel at this time for Natalie would be a backward career move. You have Atkinson's mobile number. The phone will be in the hands of the one woman on his team, his executive assistant. She will hand it to him when Martin and Steven make a conference call. Atkinson will take it because the names Scorsese and Spielberg are golden. I could do this myself, but I would rather be able to say I was hands-off—no matter the outcome "

——-

In the rich, wood-paneled conference room of Panther Studio, the low vibrating buzz of a mobile phone on silence interrupted the tense atmosphere of the high-level pow-wow. Lee was already internally congratulating himself he had bested a Hollywood legend, one his daddy feared and his granddaddy revered. Cletus Reed sat quietly midway down the table on the side closest to the sun beaming through the window. He had a false dejected look on his face.

Lee squinted at Reed, trying to adjust his eyes as the mid-morning brightness filtered through. "Ethel, could you shut that damn phone off," he barked, and Ethel Max looked down at the screen and saw the caller.

"Mr. Atkinson, it's Steven," said Ethel.

"I don't care if it is Jesus Fucking Christ in his Birthday suit, woman. Can't you see I am trying to take care of important business," yelled Atkinson, bringing his fist down on the table, though not hard enough to hurt.

Then, in a meek voice, Ethel ventured forth. She was accustomed to her boss's frequent outbursts. She didn't take him all that seriously and was first hired when Lee Atkinson II ran the place. She was also due to retire soon.
"

"Uh, Mr. Atkinson, it's Steven Spielberg on the phone along with Martin Scorsese. Would you like for me to take a message?"

The studio chief sat up straight, corrected his tie that had gone astray over his ample belly, and attempted to act nonchalant in the face of his team of lawyers, as well as Reed and Natalie.

"Oh, I'll take it," he reversed. "They've heard about the Outer Worldly sequel and probably want a piece of the pie. Well, it's too late. That party is already underway.

"STEVEN, MARTIN, my old friends. What can I do for you?"

"Lee, it's about another of our friends, Cletus Reed. We understand you have a meeting with him today," said Spielberg. "We're very interested in his new project, Frances Leigh. We've both read his script. It reminds me of how we once wrote dialogue before we felt no film would work unless it had a body count of hundreds and buildings were blown up. We understand the two of you have a little disagreement. You've reached out to DreamWorks to work with Panther on your Other Worldly sequel. We've discussed it and Martin agrees. We can't collaborate until Reed's picture is a wrap."

"I had not anticipated this," said Atkinson, but in such a low tone, it could not be heard by others in the room.

Atkinson took the call off the speakerphone. All Reed and Natalie could hear were his hushed whispers. The studio executive would nod his head and say, "Uh, yes. Uh, I hear you. Uh, we'll reach an agreement with Mr. Reed I am sure."

It was presumed that Spielberg and Scorsese ended the conversation with pleasantries because Atkinson smiled faintly, rather shyly as the connection ended. He simply said, "We've had some new developments."

Then, he told a whopper to satisfy his eggshell ego.

"Steven wants to talk with me about another pet

project of his. Scorsese is in on it as well. I need to pull some information together for him. Oh, your issue, Cletus, it's polka dot baby shit compared to what else I have going with my friends Steven and Martin. I'm going to shelve 'Other Worldly' for now. Go ahead with that little picture of yours, but don't expect a penny from Panther for it. Your little poodle doesn't even have a bark, much less a bite."

Reed smiled. "I totally understand Lee. We all know about trains already pulling out of the station. By the way, it's a far piece back to Malibu, and I need to discuss with Natalie a few things. We start pre-production next week after a final script review by Scorsese."

His last remark was absolutely false. However, at this point, while he took ownership of the script, he didn't want it ballyhooed around Hollywood that it was totally his work. Besides, Scorsese would love to have a credit. If it bombed out of the test gate, he would take Scorsese's name from it. That was an aspect of the business Reed never understood. He went by instinct and knowing the nuts and bolts of a good story. He looked at test results, but felt to depend on them was like a drunk man holding on to a lamppost.

As the mystified legion of lawyers was filing out—and Atkinson had already exited for his non-existent next meeting—Reed grabbed Roane by the arm, asking him to hang back for a minute. Natalie was at the agent's side, having said nary a word during the 30-minute conference. Now, she felt like doing a victory dance.

"Why don't we all go over to Pinks for lunch," she offered.

"Oh, Roane, I don't believe you two have met. This is Natalie of the bright green eyes. Natalie, this is Roane, the new executive producer on The Book of Frances Leigh. That's if he should decide Panther is not up to his creative and intellectual level."

Best was in shock, but accepted the hand that was offered as he looked into her eyes. Ironically, she would go to sleep later that evening, grabbing a teddy bear given to her by her late papa, Charlie, and wonder why this fellow Roane so intrigued her.

"Yes, let's go to Pinks. I can use a little cherry Coke with fortification," said Reed. "After all, it is past the noon hour, and it's cocktail time in London."

CHAPTER 20
LITTLE MARY JONES (CHARLESTON, WV., 1998)

Mary Jones started her life with Charlie and Beverly with a giant hiccup. The Kanawha County Family Services Unit had a hard time reconciling what was to what should have been.

The officials — a prim-looking church lady accompanied by a uniformed agent with a badge—would prefer to see a Norman Rockwell scene of playful continence, tow-headed cuteness, and dancing freckles around a Thanksgiving table. But from credible witnesses, and what they had already learned through rumor on the street, they figured it to be more a Jackson Pollack paint-dripping amalgam of unanswerable questions concerning civic decency.

The round pegs didn't fit into the square holes and given another place and another time, there was no way on god's blue-green earth the trio would pass muster as a legitimate family unit. They simply didn't look like the prescription in the family service manual. It had been written decades earlier when Father Knows Best was the model of harmony and domestic decorum.

Besides, the backstory was haunting.

The little girl had been dropped off in a saloon, a honky-tonk. The couple believed to be her parents had taken off without her, as if dropping off laundry at the laundry. On that early Sunday morning—after stopping at a Go-Mart for two Nehi orange sodas, Red Man chewing tobacco, and ready-made sandwiches—they had met a fiery end on dead man's curve on Highway 119 near Clendenin. They had decided child rearing probably wasn't their thing. There had been some pushback from Ruth Johns, but Joshua, ever the practical one, said because of the fracas at the Purple Onion, and the fact they were in a stolen car, law enforcement probably wasn't far behind. Besides, his arm hurt like hell where Charlie Jones had crumpled it like a Dixie Cup.

So, family services felt for sure there would be issues with a child staying another night with a bar owner, and one it was well-known had an illegal poker slot machine in a backroom. This seemed to contradict common acknowledgment that Charlie was also careful to serve correct and ample measures of whiskey and keep the riff-raff out of his place. Hence, he was often visited by Sheriff Danny Jenkins for libations when the lawman was not on duty, as well as Governor Buford Wells, even when the state official was on the job. He was better than your average "Charlie" at community relations, though his past misdeeds often reared an ugly head. He simply couldn't live down the murder charge.

It was hard to get around the fact Charlie spent time in Moundsville for manslaughter, though even here, there were, of course, extenuating circumstances. His reputation within the community had a long tail, and he was able to transfer the Purple Onion's liquor license from the previous owner without significant trouble. The hearing drew only one complaint, this coming from the man who sold Charlie the place, who, after the fact, felt he got the short end of the deal. The license was transferred even though, being an ex-con, Charlie couldn't vote for either the sheriff or the governor.

Expecting an early morning visit from family services, Beverly had spent the evening reacquainting herself with Charlie after their new and instant daughter was sound asleep. It wasn't a half-bad reunion, with even a few new ruffles and flourishes. She, of course, wondered about the improved technique but brushed it off assuming her ex had gleaned them from the porno channel. Wherever her re-imagined ex's moves originated, it made her forget church choirs and the secret crush she had on the married preacher down at the Baptist Church.

When Annie Jarrett and the officer accompanying her, Jim Jeffers, knocked on the door, it took a few moments for Beverly to answer. Normally Annie, being a brave soul and on the job for two decades, would not see the need in bringing a chaperone. However, this was Charlie Jones' house and his reputation was divided between thinking him a dangerous and serial sinner, and those on the other side who merely considered him a lovable rogue. In truth, he was probably both.

Whatever vision conjured prior to the visit, they encountered a G-rated family in a relatively normal setting. Little Mary was deep into a bowl of Captain Crunch cereal while watching a Loony Toons on a small, kitchen television. On the other hand, Charlie was perusing paperwork on how much Red Stripe beer to order for the upcoming Charleston Regatta. Beverly opened the door for the pair wearing a checkered apron and giving her biggest West Virginia welcome to the visitors, a modified version of the Minnie Pearl HOW-DY. She introduced herself as Charlie's bride, which wasn't officially true at the moment, but getting damn close for a second time helping of matrimony with the fellow.

"I'm Charlie's wife, Beverly, welcome to our home," she gushed. "I'll put some more coffee on. Would you like some country-cured ham and some eggs with buttermilk biscuits? Won't take long."

They declined. Having been briefed by the sheriff, the family services contingent had not expected to meet the missus. They were there simply to extract the kid from the clutches of a man of questionable repute who ran a bar and was known for violent outbursts, though the accusation was exaggerated.

"You're Charlie Jones' wife?" asked Ms. Jarrett who seemed incredulous.

"It's a technicality, honey," replied Beverly. "But you're here to see that darling little girl." Then she called out, "Charlie love, come out and meet the folks from family services. They're here to see Mary."

Charlie came out to the front room as the screen door swung wide. With him was Mary, clinging to Charlie like she did the night at the Purple Onion. She had a horrified look on her narrowed face. She figured the strangers were there to abduct her from her peaceful cocoon, and she wasn't going to go without a fight. Besides, she was only midway through her big bowl of Captain Crunch and having been deprived of food by her former captors, she was storing up for any future uncertainties. She was into survival mode.

"Mary," said Ms. Jarrett. "How are you?" It was an obvious opening question, but in an oh-so obviously staged setting. The child didn't reply. "May I come in?" The question was directed to the child, but both Charlie and Beverly were gracious in waving them inside the modest home, directing them to the living room where there were pre-set coffee cups, and pastries hastily purchased at the Krogers down the street.

Ms. Jarrett surveyed the room and did a military inspection of the surroundings with her roaming eyes. She pretended to be disapproving in her silence, but, in fact, was rather surprised at the normalcy of it all. She had anticipated a disaster. There was not the expected layer of dust on the mantel of the fireplace.

The sheriff had told her by telephone not to be shocked. Charlie's a decent fellow, but he's been a bachelor for quite a while. So, if you come across sour milk and partially empty Chinese food cartons, that's the man's everyday habitat. But, for the most part, he's a tamed soul with a good heart. Sheriff Jenkins had no idea that from Saturday night to Sunday morning Charlie and Beverly were once again a couple, and decided that a four-year-old Les Miserable poster child could be a blessed gift without the mess and bother of potty training a wee tyke. They had fallen for the kid, and she seemed at least tolerant of them, though confused.

The child had been scrubbed of road dust from being in the back of a van, and Beverly had come up with a powder blue pinafore dress over a soft pink blouse and black patent leather shoes purchased from a discount store at the Town Center Mall. The girl's minor wounds from continuous back-of-the-hand knocks and being tossed from one side of the van to the other had been patched up and over. Beverly planted a deep blue ribbon in her hair.

Mary, or at least the girl they only knew as Mary, peeked from behind Charlie's massive frame. She had a resolute look of little brat determination and her voice mirrored her face. "I don't want to leave," she said, almost as if it had been rehearsed. The fact was, it wasn't so much a solid bonding with Charlie, but total fear of any other options. After the melee at the Purple Onion, she felt safe with him, and the presence of Beverly was growing on her. It didn't hurt she had a hamburger and all the fries she could eat at the Tidewater Grill. That was followed by two scoops of fudge ice cream. Charlie hung with them for a while, but then spent the afternoon at the Purple Onion. It was prime rib Sunday, and Charlie was the chef. Duty called. Beverly skipped her usual Sunday church routine.

"These things are always difficult," said Ms. Jarrett, words that were always a procurer of bad news dribbling out. "But young Mary has already been in your care for two days, and our rules are that emergency care can not be extended beyond 48 hours."

The child seemed to understand every word that was said. Tears came to her face, avalanching down to her just purchased pinafore. She stuck her fists to both eyes but did not cry. She whimpered. Ms. Jarrett was a hard-ass but was equally compassionate if an occasion deserved it. In other words, she was moved by the theory of unexplained expectations. She had checked earlier with her supervisor and was told that a ready-made foster family might not be an option on short notice.

The social worker went into another room and made three phone calls from her mobile, one to her supervisor, one to Sheriff Jenkins for support and a third to County Judge Harland Dredge. There were whispered conversations. After 20 minutes, she returned to the discussions.

"With Judge Dredge approval and the agreement of my supervisor and support of our sheriff, I have made a decision to allow Mary to stay in your household temporarily—with weekly check-ins by our office—until such time as a judge can officially make a decision," she said, and then paused, "Or we find a home more suitable for Mary."

She never did find that perfect home. She didn't try

all that hard.

Intuition is often a scary visitor to the here and now, and Annie Jarrett, having made that initial decision, moved on. She would later recall, when a nation adored the green-eyed Natalie Courant, there was simply a voice whispering in her ear to let well enough alone. That, of course, was hyperbole. Ms. Jarrett, a practical, no-nonsense spinster, was neither mystic nor maudlin. Over the years, she had grabbed dozens of youngsters from loving foster homes to place them with more suitable care. It was a wrenching experience, but she had grown immune to the process.

Mary Jones grew to ladyhood in Charleston's East End. She entered the first grade at Sacred Heart Catholic school, though Beverly was a Baptist and Charlie was an admitted heathen. Located on Quarrier Street, the school was simply the closest to where they lived and residents often saw Mary, her hand in Charlie's, being walked to her class. Later when Charlie and Beverly purchased a victorian home on a hillside in the city's South Hills District, she attended George Washington High, acted in Kanawha County Players productions, and sang as a regular on the Mountain Stage weekly radio program. She had wowed the show's host, Larry Gross, in an audition that left him and other regulars spellbound. She had started with Kris Kristofferson's Me and Bobby McGee and ended with Dolly Parton's lilting I Will Always Love You.

Evidently, the ties that bind between Charlie and Beverly was the mystery girl from nowhere, the one named Mary. They doted on her, and, in doing so, on one another. Already an East End institution, the Purple Onion became even more of a mecca, especially when the green-eyed girl happened to stop by—which was often to see Charlie—and when it was open mic night and she would perform a set of her songs. The Purple Onion was also her first job after high school, though she wasn't old enough to serve drinks.

Ironically, Mary didn't often question, at least to her parents, her lost childhood. As she grew older, the black hole of what happened when she was a toddler, became a place she rarely visited. Her life was filled with acting, music, and fleeting relationships with boys who always ended a date night in frustration, if not despair. The prettiest girl at George Washington High was an alluring and elusive lover. While Charlie was prepared to send her to a fancy music school, the one called Juilliard in New York, Mary was content to stay closer to home and had planned to enter the University of Charleston until an agent named Cletus Reed interrupted her life.

Then, within two months after graduation, Charlie up and died on her.

It was the most potent cup of sorrow she had ever experienced in an otherwise charmed life. People just weren't suppose to die on her. She had only known a cocoon of happiness. It caused her to re-evaluate everything. When Reed left a card with his number on it, she simply wasn't ignoring it, there was no place in her heart for good news. She couldn't comprehend what would be the break of her lifetime. So, the old agent persisted.

Early on, there was, of course, a nationwide search for the birth parents of this mystery child. It was not cursory, but the databases revealed a total of 460,000 missing children each year, though most were runaways and not kidnapped. The stars in the searches never lined up for a child once called Fairleigh.

During this time, Jeremy Britnell felt his life was snakebitten what with his daughter being kidnapped, his wife committed due to her mental complications, and later her sudden journey to her magical Dallas—which really wasn't that sudden, but in retrospect was a certainty. He was, in almost all respects, a mess.

But Jeremy's daughter, now called Mary, was only 800 miles to the north, and a slight dog-leg to the left on a Triple-A map, where she lived with a dog named Ruffles and Beverly, a damn good substitute mama.

Beverly was not an exacting disciplinarian but was wise. Mary was not a perfect daughter but was steeped in commonsense. As mother and daughter, the two made great sisters.

CHAPTER 21
(SPRING 2021) - REALITY-TV

Jeremy Britnell had never been to the Big Apple. It wasn't that he was a homebody, but circumstances simply had forever dictated his personal time and space. He was roped into limited geography.

It also wasn't that he was uninterested in the world around him. He dreamed of Kunming and Katmandu, of Calcutta and Cairo. He was, in fact, extraordinarily curious, but he felt everything in its time.

Now in his early 40s, he still had time for adventure and misadventure, though within limits. Money didn't seem to be the problem. He and Cherokee had been fortunate. Sponsors lined up to get a 30 or 60-second slot on their program, What's Happening Now, but they gave away broadcast space to what they termed "causes that matter." While Jeremy was anything but your basic do-gooder, he felt his contribution to society could be partially fulfilled by reuniting children with parents.

On the home front, Jeremy's eyeballs could roam within limits. Cherokee was a free spirit but she didn't brook any hint of dalliance. He was sometimes obtuse, but not dumb. He stayed within his lane, not just some of the time but all of the time. In his whole life, he had only scored with two women (not counting the slam-ma'am of youth), Cherokee and Sarah, and both times—with only limited engagement in heavy breathing, and sweaty entanglements, it resulted in three kids, two at one pop with Cherokee and Fairleigh with Sarah. His sperm was damned lethal.

This particular March day, from the back of a stretch limousine, Jeremy gawked at the skyscrapers and marveled at the strangeness of the denizens as the black car maneuvered through Times Square traffic. A fellow with a cowboy hat and boots, and in his whitey-tighties was strumming his Martin Dreadnaught and singing a Hank Williams Sr. song about cheating hearts. The guitar covered strategic parts. Jeremy wasn't so much surprised at the sight of a nearly naked gent—he had read about him— but more perplexed that the fellow had to be cold. A late-season chill still hovered over Gotham City.

"Funny people," he chuckled and tossed his head negatively from side to side. "You don't see this in downtown Orlando."

"You need to get out more honey," Cherokee stonily said.

The third member of the trio, Purvis Periwinkle, was

taking in the sights from a facing seat. He pondered what he could do to one-up The Naked Cowboy.

"Hell, that's all I wanted to see coming to New York —the singing Naked Cowboy. Now that's a gig I would like," he said.

NBC Studio had sent the car and uniformed driver for them to make sure they made it to 30 Rockefeller Plaza. They were being treated as if hayseeds. They weren't the headliners on what would be the 1,400th, 5 p.m. taping of Jimmy Fallon's Tonight Show.

"I don't know Purvis," said Cherokee, looking out the window as if bored by the conversation. "You have to have some semblance of a schlong to fit into those Fruit of the Looms and play the guitar. Do you even know how to play the guitar, Purvis?"

"Britnell, what's Cherokee talking about? What's a schlong?"

"Your Johnson, Purvis, your thing, your manhood," said Jeremy as if schooling a kindergartener.

"Oh, my wee-wee," said Purvis, suddenly enlightened. "Cherokee, to my knowledge you have never seen my, what was it, schlong. Don't pre-judge the schlong-meister."

"And I never want to see it," replied Cherokee, coaxing a nervous laugh out of both Jeremy and Purvis.

For sure, the little cabal wasn't your basic yahoos in the big city. They were low, high brow, coming from the fantasy world where tourists throughout the globe come to pay homage to a 92-year-old rodent called Mickey Mouse. They were television people, WOLF, The Voice of Wonder World, the branded appellation owner William Blige pinned on the station when virtually every dog-ass attraction had the appendage world as in Sea World, Gator World, Holy Land World, Circus World, Exotic Plant World, Shoe World, and, of course, the granddaddy of them all, Disney World, now at the half-century mark.

They had come to the big city with all the acclaim and baggage that their lowered status conjured and required. They were a tightly knit group and had been for more than a decade.   It was a strange amalgam, personalities tossed together by happenstance and the guiding hand of a Joker in painted face, but without the red nose.   In other words, you got what you saw, and it was a sure bet you rarely understood what you saw because it changed with the directions of the wind and Cherokee's intellectual whimsey.

A magazine writer for the Orlando Sentinel wrote they defied description, though the way they saw their capsuled environment, they were as normal as the suits that filed into the law and accounting firms each day on Easy Street and Main Street everywhere. They didn't consider themselves misfits, only rarities. Their plumage was oddly colored, and always memorable.

Jeremy was comforted that sitting beside him was his bride of nearly a dozen years, the one he loved after saying he would never love again. She was the one who allowed him to pet, even bridle her, but not break or attempt to tame. Cherokee was his muse, his teacher, his inspiration, and he hers. Together they were a creative explosion, something that generally doesn't work well in show business unless one is George Burns and the other Gracie Allen in black and white with snow from a rabbit ears antenna creating a fuzzy picture.

The couple's drama— and yes, she adopted his name without fuss or encouragement—was, however, played out in living, often raucous color. They did fight like caged cats on occasion—a sound that normally precedes mayhem—but it lasted mere moments. Then they made up for hours with jokes, tears and rounded it off with serious coupling. They walked this high wire of a relationship as confidently as the acrobat Wallenda, though they without a net. It should be noted that various of the Wallenda family didn't survive. Jeremy and Cherokee defied the odds.

Quite suddenly, or at least it seemed, there were children, a freckle-faced boy named Jon Thomas Britnell, and then a doe-eyed lass they called Enola Lynn, named after Cherokee's mama. The boy was the elder by 23 minutes. As they grew, they seemed carbon copies of their parents, gathering in critical traits of both, with the glow of bronze skin stemming from Cherokee's native American parentage. They were as normal as two kids could be in this a rather unorthodox family.

This life transition didn't stop Jeremy from thinking about and pursuing his quest to find Fairleigh. He often recalled in sadness the loss of Sarah, and Cherokee encouraged this, even placing a picture of his late wife in a prominent place on the boat. The boat itself was no longer the floating tub of old but had been replaced with a 43-foot Albin trawler and moved to an Indian River marina. It was a 50-minute trek along the Beachline highway into the Orlando television studio three days a week when they produced their program.

Life did, indeed, move on and the view in the rearview mirror became hazier by the day. Jeremy wondered, quite often, if there was something missing within his soul. After all, perhaps he should be devastated for the rest of his life. He wasn't. He couldn't be. It wouldn't be fair to Cherokee, or the memory of Sarah, or Jon and Enola. He kept his memories close but refused to let them suffocate him. Like the song he once wrote, he took any regrets "and hung them in a tree, where the Spanish moss is flowing, and whispering to me." He took comfort in the reality of the Omar Khayyam line "The Moving Finger writes; and, having writ, Moves on: nor all thy Piety nor Wit Shall lure it back to cancel half a Line, Nor all thy Tears wash out a Word of it.". He took it as a universal, timeless truth. Best not to question it.

It had been a slow build, but after several years, the show's influence was expanding. It became the most viewed local production in the station's viewing region and had caught the attention of larger markets. William Blige, the money man, liked it because it always came in within budget, and low and behold the margins after expenses topped 25 percent. He bicycled it to other stations in his expanding portfolio. Since it was a popular franchise, it got Wilkie—a nickname he couldn't shed—premium tickets to awards shows throughout the year, including the Academy Awards.

Early on, Cherokee determined that the show needed a wider focus, and changed the title to the more immediate What's Happening Now, deciding that her original idea of simply finding runaways was a one-trick pony. Most of the rascals showed up prior to the program having an opportunity to air. Jeremy was not only okay with this but relieved.

That's why they were cruising midtown with the destination being The Tonight Show, with Fallon. Blige had campaigned for the exposure. When the show finally reached out weeks ago, Jeremy, who seemed on the planet Mars on such matters, asked his wife whether Johnny Carson or Jay Leno was the show's funnyman and host. She expressed exasperation.

"Carson's dead. Leno's doing car shows," she said. "You need to watch more television, fellow. Otherwise, our audience is going to think your mind took leave of you back in the Howdy Doody age."

"Who's Howdy Doody?" quizzed Jeremy, though he was joking.

"I have no idea. Papa Roy told me about him, long ago," responded Cherokee.

They didn't come to the pre-recorded show with a rehearsal or even a thought as to what possible shtick might spark interest. They were warned that the singer Simply

Red was the featured guest, followed by a TV psychologist. They were casually dressed as if they had walked off their own set.

Britnell was in faded Levis, no belt, a black tee-shirt, cut-off sneakers sans socks, and a light leather jacket, for which his wife admonished him. She was an animal rights activist and a vegan now for many years. He liked hamburgers and Chili dogs, and for sure the jacket he had worn since high school was his comfort covering, even in Florida sunshine.

Cherokee, only half native American, had appropriated both halves as her culture. Her dark hair was in pigtails, and a red cloth band separated her forehead from short bangs. Her turquoise jewelry was understated by a single bracelet but still obvious with its splashes of bright blue. She wore a tan mini-skirt that ended just before shouting indecent. It was an affectation appropriate for her still young but maturing age. Even after double-babies, she was super-fit, working out an hour each day. On occasion, Jeremy would bag the gym. He preferred the swimming pool. Cherokee's white blouse was simple with an ever-so-slight branding touch, WOLF-TV on a small pin. Jeremy also showed the flag, a press-on adornment that carried the WOLF logo. He knew Wilkie would be pleased.

Purvis had spent the morning of the flight pondering his closet. He thought for a moment he might wear his old Taco Bell uniform or even the clothes as a guard for The Mall at Millenia. He chuckled at the irony and wondered what his departed granny would say about his odd fashionista tenancies. He actually had on a conservative blue suit he had had expressly tailored for his elongated and slender body. Due to the success of the program, his salary had been tripled, and he could afford both a life and a collection of silk ties. In a nod to convention and contrast with his two partners, he wore the freshly pressed suit and stuck a paper rose in the lapel.

They were, by most any account, an incongruent trio, but perhaps not to someone who was at Woodstock and still sheds tears over guitar genius Jimmie Hendrix. The Fallon audience skewed broad but not deep, sometimes the veritable franchise fell below a million viewers, but largely it was a middle-aged crowd. Fallons' antics, humor, and guests didn't play as well with youngsters who thought Justin Bieber was a talent. Simply Red and the TV doc didn't represent an improvement. One hadn't had a hit in eons and the doc put viewers to sleep. Fallon had berated the show's producers to mix up the talent, and bring in fresh faces. The tribe from Central Florida, lobbied by Wilkie, was a Hail Mary reach, and The Tonight Show suits felt they might be a bridge too far for the audience. That's why they were at the tail end of the show, more of an afterthought than any nod toward audience pleasers.

"We might not have sufficient time for your segment depending on the audience reaction to the previous guests," said a producer when they arrived at the studio. "Can you stay over tomorrow? We'll put you up in a suite we reserve at The Rock."

Cherokee stood up, and went nearly cheek to cheek with him, though she was four inches shorter. "Listen, (One could almost imagine the word "bozo" coming after,

241

but it was not voiced), I left my two babies 1,500 miles away at your request. We suspended a taping day, but still, my Uncle Wilkie will have to pay a studio staff who are union. Also, I'm not fond of traveling tourist class, and lunching on a bag of peanuts and a cola. That's simply not the way you treat the guest of an affiliate of the N-B-C. We pay your bills. It's doubtful this third-ranked late-night spot will do anything for Jeremy's career, not to mention mine and our friend Purvis. So, and I mean no disrespect here, we want air time. You will not be disappointed. Would you like me to speak with Mr. Fallon?"

The fact was Cherokee's babies were eight years and 29 minutes younger. The trio had upgraded at the airport to Business Class tickets and had a relatively comfortable two-and-a-half-hour Mimosa-drinking flight. But that wasn't the point. This was one Indian princess who had not changed an iota since Jeremy's first encounter with her. She bulldozed opponents. She made them think her petite body could lift them, take a gulp, and tossed the bones away for dog scraps. Once they realized this, they tended to shiver for their careers. They might have wondered if Cherokee was all bullshit and bluster, but no one wanted to test her resolve.

This particular producer, Manny Stewart was actually a many-year veteran of NBC and had previously worked with Jay Leno and before that Johnny Carson. He stood in silence for a full thirty seconds. He shifted his furry eyebrows this way and then that way, looked up to the ceiling, then down at the floor in a tense standoff. It was Matt Dillon drawing down on desperadoes in Dodge City. It was David sizing up Goliath. Then, wisdom prevailed, he smiled.

"You had me at having to leave your babies, Ms. Britnell," Stewart surrendered. "Obviously, I miscalculated. Having come all this way—coach class no less—you deserve to be treated by The Tonight Show not with just a modicum of insincere respect, but with the entire enchilada of a Big Apple welcome. We obviously misjudged your ensemble's importance. Forgive me, please." He bowed, and at the same time put a hand over his heart in contrition.

Cherokee eyed him warily, wondering whether this older gentleman was phonily slick, or, in essence, putting her on with saccharine flattery. Whatever, he was damn good at it. He had handled an irritable Bob Dylan who lost his pick inside his super jumbo Gibson SJ-200 just prior to going on with Carson. He had managed Cameron Diaz and Julie Roberts who ended up wearing virtually the same dress when they met on the Leno couch. To Stewart, this crew from Florida's problem was like a flea on the back of a tick on the back of a big old dog. Not much at all. Jeremy tugged at her arm, gently, a sure sign she could tone it down a notch. Not terribly diplomatic himself, compared to Cherokee he was an English butler in a Jane Austen novel.

"Apologies excepted, Mr. Stewart," Cherokee backed off, contritely. "There are times I can come on too strong. Just ask Jeremy. I forced him to marry me after only our second meeting. I wasn't even pregnant at the time. Can you believe that?"

Stewart blushed, not knowing what to say. After an awkward silence, "Well Cherokee, can I call you Cherokee, I'm sure I can stretch out your segment. I'll talk to Jimmy. So, if you three can relax in the Green Room for a while, I'll retrieve you when it's time to go on. Just be as natural as you are now."

Back in Orlando, their show had its own Green Room, only it was Rose-colored and not called the Rose Room, but simply a staging area. The Tonight Show room didn't have finger sandwiches and potato chips like back at WOLF but fresh shrimp, foie gras, and spice roasted pumpkin seeds that could be washed down with either sparkling water or sips of champagne. From the label, it looked expensive, even the water. Purvis took to the champagne as if it were Dr. Pepper, and complained that what was called foie gras tasted suspiciously like liver. He hated liver. His grandmother liked it, serving it up three days a week. She told him it was good for him.

"Okay," Jeremy said after the producer left. "You have bulldozed us one more time to relevance, but what are we going to do with the time. I left my guitar on the boat. Can't sing, anyway. He said he wanted us to just act naturally. That can be scary in a civilized culture."

"Relax Swamp man, it will be a piece of cake. If it starts to drag, I'll give a war-whoop and show my titties."

"Really?" exclaimed Purvis, the odd man out in the conversation.

"You wish, pervert," she replied and gave him a

playful nudge.

Having come of age in a significantly more conservative era and in a family with a table lamp of Jesus, Jeremy was anything but pious. His family, however, did have an assortment of Woolworth Five&Dime icons scattered about the house and were religious about going to church on specific days, such as Easter. Jeremy often winced at his wife's awkwardly off-color remarks, but he had become accustomed to them, and not only accepted them but coveted them as he did her other idiosyncrasies. If she were a little ditzy, it was in a cool and calculated way.

Cherokee always knew what she wanted, and the out-sized portion of her desires had a lot to do with her fellow. She had encouraged him to write, though he would simply remark that he needed to keep his day job. After Fairleigh's disappearance, he simply had no appetite for fiction. There was too much real life at hand to clobber him up the side of his head whenever he started getting dreamy. The Book of Fairleigh. a working title, was that bridge too far and too close at the same time. He had long since lost the whereabouts of the printed 500 pages and the computer disc went to a graveyard many moons ago.

Jeremy's 9 to 5 position—though generally, that eight hours ended up being at least 12—was spent crafting scripts these days for their television program. He had melded the work into a true-life narrative, and with his wife's keen showbiz ear, combined it with three distinct characters and a special guest. Jeremy was the straight George Burns to Cherokee's Gracie Allen—only it was in living color and not 1950s black and white. Purvis

Periwinkle was the goofball for the ages. You could call him Curly, or Moe, or Larry, or, if you stretched it a little, say he was Stringbean, the ill-fated banjo picker comedian from the Grand Ole Opry who was murdered in 1973.

The guests on What's Happening Now were nearly irrelevant extras. They were certainly not foils, but they were more like an added adjective tossed in to dress up a sentence. It was live-TV in front of an audience. Cherokee wanted the viewers to even see the fuck-up bats that often flew into the studio, and took the dialogue in strange and weird directions. If someone accidentally let a fart escape, it became part of the show. The audience tuned in largely to see and hear the banter between the ensemble which could stray into the galaxy. Few came away more enlightened, but they were entertained, and that was the object. In a nod to the program's serious intent—and on Jeremy's insistence— the program's middle segment was focused on missing youth, and what progress had been made through the week to find a child.

In the Tonight Show Green Room, they awaited their fate. This was national TV. They could either blow off the doors or simply blow it. Jeremy was betting on the latter, and hoping no one back in Florida would have eyes on the TV when it aired later in the evening. Cherokee was obviously confident. She was always confident. They had a brief chance to meet Simply Red and shake hands with a TV doc, Dr. Phil. Cherokee didn't appear nervous in the slightest while Jeremy and Purvis had chewed their nails to the quick, and were nibbling on gumdrop wrappers after having emptied the bowl. With 20 minutes left in the program, they were told they were going on in five.

Cherokee's advice to Jeremy was simply "listen to the question, and then come back with something terribly witty," as if he had a Gatling Gun response to generally mundane queries. After all, he thought, the audience has shrunk to a million and a half, and his dull appearance could send it spiraling so deep the bottom-feeding catfish wouldn't pay attention. He feared for the program's future. He could almost see the headline: "Troupe From Florida Causes Fallon Train Wreck."

They walked in single file, Cherokee in the lead, followed by Purvis and finally Jeremy lagging behind. Fallon walked to the edge of the platform and shook hands, giving air kisses to Cherokee, which Britnell took to be a Hollywood thing in New York. He wasn't into air kisses and hugs unless directed toward Cherokee.

"Ladies and gentlemen, please give a big round of applause for — (he had to look down at his cue card)— from Orlando, Florida, the hosts and cast of the fabulously successful TV program What's Happening Now. Jeremy, what IS happening now?"

It seemed an obvious lead-in to knock out of the park.

"Hell if I know, Jimmy. You tell me. No, wait, since you asked, I will tell you. They're rioting in Africa, They're starving in Spain. There's hurricanes in Florida, And Texas needs rain. The whole world is festering, With unhappy souls. The French hate the Germans, The Germans hate the Poles; Italians hate Yugoslavs, South Africans hate the

Dutch—And I don't like anybody very much! "

Fallon was taken back by the loquacious fellow in white tennis shoes. "Uh, haven't I heard that somewhere before?" he asked.

"Of course you have Jimmy, about sixty-plus years ago. I wasn't born yet and neither were you. It's a Kingston Trio song from 1959, and can I tell you something—it's not a secret—not a fucking thing has changed. We're still, as the old Barry McGuire song, "On the Eve of Destruction.""

"You know we're going to bleep out your F-bomb. Sorry, NBC rules," Fallon said with his impish smile.

"That's interesting, Jimmy," replied Britnell.

Cherokee thought Jeremy was having one of his out-of-body experiences. Her husband wasn't like this. He apologized on their show once when he used hell and damn.

"If Amy Winehouse or George Carlin said the same words, would they be bleeped?" It wasn't a challenging question, and Britnell had a sincere, curious mask across his face, his eyes narrowed. He also knew Winehouse and Carlin had slipped their earthly coils.

"Yep, my friend, same rules, but since both Amy and George have passed on, I doubt the question will come up," explained Fallon.

"Interesting to ponder," replied Britnell, looking out

beyond the studio lights, the applause sign, and the audience. "Jimmy, can I ask you something?"

At this point, Fallon was not sure what to expect. He was hoping Cherokee or even Purvis would jump in to steer the conversation to sanity. Since Cherokee was knockout gorgeous, she was a crowd favorite the moment she walked on stage.

"You know, Jimmy," interjected Cherokee, "my Swamp Man here is right. Nothing has changed since the 1960s except the hemline of skirts go up and down, a jumbo size peppermint chocolate mocha introduced at Starbucks, and tickets at Disney reached the stratosphere Really Jimmy, there was a mass shooting the other day at a school, little kids were slaughtered. But the fucking NRA — I know I am going to be bleeped — rules, man. Our country is quickly cooking itself to death with global warming and no one is in a hurry to do anything about it. Add to that, we had a total ignoramus as your President. Notice I didn't say 'my President'."

"Yeah man," said Periwinkle, who had remained silent.

"Uh, uh," stammered Fallon. "I agree with you. I'm all in when it comes to social commentary—but do you guys do anything else. Like maybe sing a song, or do a dance. Ever tried clogging? What about a comedy routine?"

Fallon turned his attention to Periwinkle. "Now, Mr. Periwinkle, what do you do on What's Happening Now?"

"I do what that guy does over there," he said and pointed to The Tonight Show announcer Steve Higgins. "I'm a sidekick. You know Jimmy, your foil. I'm sort of like Pancho, you know Jimmy, like 'Hey, Cisco, Hey Pancho'. Do you remember? Well, more like Gabby Hayes without the beard."

"Anything else, Mr. Periwinkle? ventured Fallon.

Purvis shrugged. "Not really, my cat Wonder Woman talks, but she's not here at the moment. Besides, she only talks in Moldavian. Oh, I also model men's underwear, and have a local brand call the "Periwinkles". That's why I am so impressed with your "Naked Cowboy" on Times Square. Would you like for me to show you my Periwinkles?"

Fallon seemed to think for a moment, and then said, "Nah, we'll pass on both the Moldavian cat and the Periwinkles. Maybe a future show, the one that will be called "4 a.m. in the Morning with Jimmy Fallon."

He then turned back to Britnell. "We've only a few minutes left. Any parting words for our viewers?"

"Yes," replied Britnell, "We have a cause we support. We try to locate missing children. Some are runaways, but occasionally there is a case—like with my daughter when she was four. She was kidnapped from a mall in Orlando. I'd appreciate any tips on missing children. We are sort of like a televised milk carton giving parents hope to find their kids."

"That's super nice," said Fallon. He seemed relieved the segment was almost over. He thanked them for being on and gave a final plug for What's Happening Now, "the latest breakout show from Central Florida."

As the credits were rolling, Purvis had stripped off his suit pants, dropped them to the floor, and showed the Jimmy Fallon world that his hot pink Periwinkles were, indeed, a fashion statement.

It was something they couldn't bleep, and the audience went wild. Purvis continued to strip his shirt off, and make several body-builder poses, an avocation for which he was not well suited.

Perhaps, it could be said Purvis had found his true calling.

—-

Why Cletus Reed was watching The Tonight Show on the evening of March 23, 2021, was purely accidental. He was channel surfing and just happened on the show when Jeremy Britnell was deep into his social rant.

The poor fellow struck Cletus as being damned naive, an ingenue but with a conscience and a good heart. Having lost his Caroline before she turned thirty, he felt the fellow's continuing pangs. For Reed, it was decades ago, but feelings are episodic and most anything could remind him of his long-ago loss.

He understood this Britnell fellow.

Often, at this hour, he was knee-deep in Turner Classic movies. Occasionally, a film would come on in which he not only knew the long-dead actors but had actually participated in writing the scripts. There was a time he was on the "A" list of people, he partied with them—or at least attended the soirées —and occasionally was invited by Bob Hope over to play poker. He was a lousy poker player but didn't mind losing his bankroll. There was more from where that 200 bucks came.

it was also the day of his victory over Panther studios and he was celebrating alone with Johnny Walker Blue, his old dog, Sammy, and the 12-inch, television. Earlier, he, Natalie, and that young fellow had celebrated at Pink's Hotdog Emporium. He noticed a spark between Natalie and Roane Best, and he was caught between excitement for her and—my gosh, at his age—jealousy. It was mere fatherly protection, nothing more.

He made absolutely no connection between the Francis Leigh movie script and the passionate Jeremy Britnell. There was no reason to even ponder. But, more than anything, Cletus was a storyteller, and when Britnell mentioned a missing daughter, it caught his attention.

What was the back story, he asked himself?

There could be an interesting human interest yarn here. He thought, summoning various genres. Though he conjured it in the abstract, it was simply one of several script ideas offered to him each week.

Then, he had second thoughts,

Nah, I'm on the downhill slide, my biorhythms need whiskey shots to gyrate and my bones are dust tired. The Book of Frances Leigh would be his last project. No more climbing mountains.

CHAPTER 22
PURVIS: AND HIS HOT PINK PERIWINKLES

The improbable occurs simply because it is improbable.

Why does a toddler playing with a python go viral, or a tiger taking a household kitten as one of its litter garners a million views on YouTube?

It's a little bit of a mystery, though it's not complicated. Dog bites man is commonplace, but man bites dog is considered news. Purvis Periwinkle would, if this installment of the Tonight Show were left intact, be seen by an estimated 1.7 million viewers of Jimmy Fallon's show. As it were, it was viewed by nearly three million, taking the late-night ratings from less venerable programs whose parentage was suspect. Those network programs didn't extend back to 1954 with the comic and ultimate host Steve Allen. Then, along came the king, Johnny Carson.

So, Purvis was, in essence, man biting dog. Only on this occasion, the man was wearing his pink Periwinkles in front of a slice of folks who would see the Fallon show only if the ending segment were to bypass network censors.

A studio executive monitoring the program immediately sent word to cut the offending clip, expecting to see a slew of complaints if aired. He also suggested the outlaw clan from the What's Happening Now show never be invited back. This particular NBC suit was high enough up on the peacock network food chain to have influence.

After all, the clip did show a bulging outline of Purvis' manhood which was super-sized and, to some, damned impressive. The fact that he did a Michael Jackson moonwalk, cupping his crotch with his hand, could be considered an extraordinary but unnecessary exclamation to a lewd act, should one's mind veer that direction. The visual depiction, however, didn't violate any of the network's six offending words which tended to get the late social comic Lenny Bruce in hot water. it was merely a graphic demonstration, and young eyes would mostly be in bed by this time.

Tradition, however, was It couldn't and shouldn't be shown, except as archival footage at the network's Christmas party where people could whoop and holler to their alcoholic content. It was a fact, though, the studio live audience couldn't exorcize the vision, and, in fact, clapped wildly without the benefit of a flashing applause sign when Periwinkle did his thing. Cherokee was proud of her and Jeremy's protege, though, the more conservative half, Mr. Britnell, wasn't quite sure.

Producer Manny Stewart corralled a flustered Fallon

immediately after the credits had run and the audience was filing out of the studio. Fallon had paid his dues and had put in his time to get the coveted prime Tonight Show. He didn't want to blow an opportunity. He had hosted the show for the last half dozen years, and his contract was up for renewal at a time ratings were flagging.

"Jimmy, the studio brass are going to ask you to take out the segment with that loopy Periwinkle character," Manny said. "Don't do it. Trust me on this one. I'll go to the very top on this if I have to."

"Come on Manny, the guy was outrageous, burlesques to the max. It's the sort of stunt that got the Smothers Brothers pulled," said Fallon. "And they disappeared for—hell, they still haven't come back."

It was an animated toe-to-toe, belly to belly discussion between producer and star. Fallon felt his career was at stake while the veteran producer didn't have that much to lose. He had been around NBC since God invented dirt, had a big house on Long Island Sound, and a bevy of grandkids who mostly liked him. His fourth wife was also partial to his usually quiet personality and she was an heiress. He continued producing because it still lit a candle inside him.

"I'm telling you Jimmy, it was only 20 minutes but the most interesting segment since Carson came on stage with a turban and his Carnac the Magnificent sketch," said Manny. "Yeah, sure. The network will whine. Those lily-livered cowards complained to Walt Disney that Tinker-bell's costume was too sexy. Trust me on this one. By the time this airs tomorrow night, I predict Periwinkle will he all over the Internet. There won't be anyone who hasn't seen it—even before it airs on the Fallon program."

"But how?"

"Leave it to me," said Manny. "I might be a tad old, but I know what buttons to push when it comes to generating publicity. Periwinkle will be a hashtag for the ages."

In television language, Fallon would later call his decision that immaculate reception emitting from 30 Rock. By the time the program aired, Periwinkle's pink undies were trending in viral happiness, dominating Facebook, Twitter, Instagram, and even Porn Hub. The video seemed to spread faster than the deadly Corona virus which was on its third New York wave. In essence, Purvis Periwinkle was an overnight Honey Boo Boo, the goofy kid from Georgia who was so corny she was camp.

For the first time in a long while, The Tonight Show didn't just lead the ratings but dominated them. Studio hierarchy realized the phenomenon when other late-night hosts began using Periwinkle jokes in their monologues. By the time Jeremy and Cherokee's plane landed at Orlando International Airport, Manny was on the phone asking about a return appearance. This time, he said, they would be the headliners, and yes, the network could pay double scale. Also, and this clinched the deal, Jeremy would get a chunk of time to discuss the plight of missing kids, and talk about his daughter Fairleigh.

As for Purvis, he already had a licensing deal with a Chinese garment company in Hong Kong to produce Periwinkle briefs in a variety of electric colors. He hit on the brilliant idea of attaching a condom pocket to the briefs for easy access, especially when the lights were out. That was actually Cherokee's idea, but in an interview with Advertising Age, she insisted it was a Purvis' brainstorm.

"Hell, Purvis the Pervert, I don't need the notoriety. I'm already billed as the brains of this outfit while Jeremy is the sensitive creative type," Cherokee told him. "Any more acclaim and it will go to my head, and I will have to diet because my noggin's too heavy. Besides, you need the credentials—not me. Because of you, we're all going to be able to retire to a tropical paradise on pink panty money. Glad I invested early. It's like getting Buffett's Berkshire Hathaway stock at $20 a pop."

For the record, less one thinks hostilities were rampant among the three characters from What's Happening Now, Purvis often called Cherokee Bossy Squaw Woman, and both branded Jeremy the Blind Blood Hound because he did, indeed, see only a little out of his left eye, and his head tilted to one side. Still, through hook or crook, he managed to sniff out great storylines for the program.

Cherokee wasn't surprised when she received a call from the folks at Victoria Secret wondering if Periwinkle could design a style similar to men's briefs, but for the ladies, including the condom pocket. It would be equal opportunity lingerie. Women should have just as much right of access to handy condoms as a man. The order

Victoria Secret conjured would have Chinese ladies in Guangdong turning out copious amounts of garments round the clock. At first, Cherokee demurred. She wasn't sure in the age of aggressive feminism it is a great idea or an absolute turnoff. The conditions in the factory also bothered her. It was only after she negotiated a decent wage, an eight-hour day with lunch and tea breaks and air conditioning, did she finally agree.

If only Granny Gladys Hogan could see Purvis now. She would do a double backflip in her grave. Periwinkle, however, realized his shortcomings on the business side and with advice from Wilkie Blige located fulfillment and marketing teams. He tried to get The Naked Cowboy to endorse his underwear line, but the fellow said he was sticking to his whitey-tighties. There were no hard feelings, but Purvis felt the fellow missed out on a golden opportunity.

Purvis, though, had a larger mission in life, quite aside from modeling Periwinkle briefs. It had to do with his slavish devotion to Jeremy Britnell, and by extension, to his bride Cherokee and brood, the youngsters, Jon and Enola. He was attached to them like a barnacle on the bottom of their Albin trawler. Jeremy had rescued a 30-year-old from being treated like a five-year-old under the smothering care of Granny Hogan. She would have preferred he remained in a playpen.

Periwinkle began his search for the missing Book of Fairleigh as if he were a Round Table knight looking for the lost silver chalice. If finding and recapturing Pablo Escobar came with it, he was game for that as well. It took him a while to remember he had made up the Escobar story. His mind often took flight that way, call it brain fog or a slight list toward harmless insanity. He could walk, talk, chew gum, and recall the words to obscure Hank Williams songs at the same time, but for the life of him, remembering the daily requirements of life often escaped him. A doctor once told granny Hogan that Purvis was just a shade shy of having savant autism. Having a heart of larceny—and after seeing the Rain Man movie with DustinHoffman and Tom Cruise—she took him to a Las Vegas casino. If it were true, he could ace the blackjack table. She lost $1,000 in less than an hour. That's when she took Purvis to sign up for work at Taco Bell, a position that required elementary mental dexterity. It was beyond his talents.

Periwinkle had grown to love adventures and most every day with Jeremy and Cherokee had been wilder than any attraction at Disney. He also was an oversized pal for the Britnell kids. They treated him kindly, but almost as if he were a shaggy Saint Bernard. If there were a ghost of a chance of retrieving Jeremy's lost novel, Purvis was intent on being the fellow to do it.

It had been said by some that Purvis' elevator stopped at mezzanine level and went no further. That wasn't true. For all of his abstractness, he had managed to formulate a business plan for Periwinkle's briefs (with the assistance of Cherokee) and had added the necessary value proposition with a discreet condom pocket. This particular accruement was made with fluorescent so it could be seen in the dark. In the beginning, Purvis could not figure out the purpose or practicality of the insert, though as he became more popular after the Jimmy Fallon show, so did his opportunities for female companionship. It suddenly dawned on him.

On the Escobar chase, it was, of course, more mythological for Purvis than real. Before pursuing the address given him at Harry's Storage, Periwinkle did a deep dive on Pablo. He saw pictures of his bullet-riddled body, and a contingent of Colombian National Police celebrating over it. He saw where his body had been dug up to establish evidence in a paternity case. Any reasonable person would figure the man called the South American Robin Hood would have long since taken his own journey to Sarah's Dallas. But, who knows? Then, reminded himself, "Oh hell, I made that part up. Didn't I?"

Purvis's dance card had become rather crowded. After his Periwinkle undies became famous (he modeled them himself at Macy's) he appeared on the popular TV program Shark Tank and there ensued a bidding war among the five billionaires to provide him backing and promotion. He soon had to hire an assistant just to keep up with the demands on his time. Though some channels at first refused to allow Periwinkles to be advertised, all eventually fell in line, and even allowed a demonstration of the condom cache, as Purvis called it. By this time, of course, all kinds of previously sensitive things, such as magic pills for erectile dysfunction and women's "heavy flow" days were being advertised in prime time. The Naked Cowboy called, but it took a while for him to get through. He was now interested, though Cherokee shut the door on that rapprochement. "He needs you Purvis, but you don't need him, either naked or in a see-through tuxedo."

The budding undies king kept putting off his intention to show up on Pablo Escobar's doorstep which was a mere 45 minutes away from Purvis's West Orlando abode where he lived with a big greyhound in what was once called a garden apartment. The dog had refused to chase Sparky, the mechanical rabbit at the track, and was destined for oblivion when Purvis stepped in.

With his conscience nagging him over his lifelong responsibility to Jeremy, one fine day he hopped in his cinnamon red Porsche 911 Targa with its S carburetor and journeyed to East Orlando. The address given to him was in an older, rather rundown neighborhood of Azalea Park. There were suburban stamped-out cinderblock homes on quarter-acre lots. They hardly had sufficient room between them to have sex with the window open, and in the mid-1950s sold for $11,000. Now they were being advertised by realtors at $225,000 and more.

It wasn't that Purvis had grown snooty with his newfound wealth from pink Periwinkles and continuing fame on What's Happening Now, he just felt the area was sad and cheerless. He remembered growing up with granny in such a neighborhood where the most excitement came when the mosquito-spraying truck journeyed down the potholed streets on Tuesdays and Fridays. Then there was that neighborhood tough guy, Nicky Morales, rumored to have spent a stint in reform school at Marianna in Florida's Northern Panhandle. Every housing area had one. You had to make sure the coast was clear before scampering past his house. For Periwinkle, the scene brought back a flood of dark memories; but, perhaps, contributed to his late-blooming flamboyance.

He came upon a corner lot prescribed by the address. There was a sign on a truck in the front yard, bigger than life, Wendell's Used Furniture and Disney Souvenirs. The truck was sitting up on concrete blocks and had outdated license tags from yesteryear. The hood was up, and a naked distributor cap was sitting on the running board. My, how far the mighty Pablo has fallen, Purvis thought.

As he approached the front door, he saw candlelight in the house and an outline of someone through a large picture window. An unlit Christmas tree was still up, though it was mid-Spring. He knocked, but there was no answer. Then someone in the darkened house tripped, and apparently dropped whatever it was they were holding.

"God Damn," was the shout, a man's voice. "There goes my fucking whiskey. Can you call an Uber for me, Janell? And if you cleaned up once in a while I wouldn't stumble."

"Well, you ass, if you brought home a little money so we could have the electricity turned back on, you would be able to see," came a woman's voice.

It obviously was an unplanned response. The secretive occupants were given away, and, in the interest of practicality, gave up their subterfuge of not being home. A haggardly-looking woman of advanced middle-age opened the door, brushing back her grey, stringy hair which contained streaks of faded yellow. She put on a manufactured smile.

"If you're with the damned Internal Revenue Service we don't owe a Goddamn cent, and if we did, we don't have it," she said before Purvis introduced himself. Periwinkle was dressed in his Jimmy Fallon studio suit and looked not just decent but mostly official.

He lowered his voice an octave, getting into character.

"No, lady, you have the wrong branch of government," said Purvis. "You ever heard of the FDEA?" The ruse had worked before so why not go for gold. "We received word you might have been on the receiving end of more cocaine than one person could utilize in a lifetime. Is your husband home, madam? I think I heard him misplacing his whiskey bottle when I knocked on the door. Is your husband William Wendell?"

Janell Wendell was nervous and cocked her head to the side. Still, she had an attitude. "Of course I've heard of the FDEA. It's the Florida Department of Elephant Asses," she smirked. "Nah, I know the drug cops. No dopers in this house."

Her voice was reedy like a witch's echo. Her eyes darted one way, then the other. She looked beyond Periwinkle thinking a posse was probably nigh, about to swoop in, surrounding the home they were six months behind in making bank payments, electricity off and they got water furtively from the neighbor's outdoor faucet.

"You asked about Wendell, and his first name is what? Oh, William. Oh him, that William Wendell," she followed as if she wasn't at first sure. "I can assure you my William has done a lot of things in his life but has never been involved in drugs." Then she shouted to the gray figure in the background, "William, get your ass out here. Some officer has misinformation about us and is asking if you have any of that angel dust."

Wendell came to the door. His appearance was that of what a mess would look like if a garbage truck slammed into an ice cream vendor of tutti-fruity. His eyes were so bloodshot they screamed death, and his ruddy skin could be used to strike matches. He had sprigs of hair, but in thatches and near the forefront of his head. If was evident, his best days were in the rearview mirror.

"I heard you say you were from the IRS. Hell, I haven't made enough money to pay taxes since 1973, but if you're here to repossess stuff, the truck's a wreck, the house is mortgaged to the hilt, and the most valuable possession I had was my old dog, and he died last week. So, state what you want and get the hell off my property."

To Purvis, it was one of the most depressing monologues he had ever heard. He had a fleeting thought of writing him a check, something Periwinkle did quite often having made sufficient money to, as they say in country music, put on the dog a little.

"Calm down, Mr. Wendell. I'm from the Federal Drug Enforcement Agency. The fact is you purchased a locker from Harry's Storage a few years back, and we have reason to believe that the contents contained a shit load of blow," said Periwinkle, coming up with terms he had heard on television"s Law and Order franchise. "We had been told that the contents might belong to the late drug kingpin, Pablo Escobar. You, sir, are obviously not Pablo, but I have to inquire about the loot you made off with as a result of that purchase. Do you have a roll-top desk?"

"That's Janell's," said Wendell, growing slightly bellicose. "And there wasn't anything in it when I bought it except termites. I can sell the desk to you—including the termites—for $20.45." Wendell calculated just how much a fresh liter bottle of Sam's Club bargain hooch would cost.

Purvis cut to the chase. "It is quite possible Mr. Wendell, you could be an accessory after the fact to one of the largest narco heists in history. We have on good authority, after much investigation, that the storage facility was rented by the drug kingpin Escobar. You, in essence, were the apparent middleman—perhaps unwittingly, but who knows? We'll see how a jury sees that. Did there happen to be a book-length manuscript in the contents you purchased from Harry's storage?'

Wendell didn't know quite what to say without seriously incriminating himself. After all, he was the felonious one. He had changed the name on the manuscript to The Book of Frances Leigh and pawned it off on a printing company as if it were his genuine artistic work. He had become the equivalent of an instant author. Presto. It was a wholesale misappropriation of the literary effort and not simply a minor league infraction. At the time, he had thought nothing of it. It had been small potatoes and in Wendell's lexicon, hardly a serious offense, sort of like jaywalking. Wendell had been a small-time con for a lifetime.

Even the Mickey ears he sold within sight of Disney World tended to fall apart before the end of the day. Much of the used furniture he sold he discovered sitting beside garbage bins waiting for the trash heap. He surveyed the richest neighborhoods for his loot, sometimes adding a little paint or polish here and there. His biggest paycheck had come when the fellow from LA, Cletus Reed, wrote him a check for the rights to his fraudulent claim that became The Book of Frances Leigh. He didn't even remember the original name of it. He didn't even read the book. He skimmed it. Jeremy had tapped into his own life, his hopes and dreams for his daughter to capture the heart and soul of the manuscript. He had to open a drawer that contained his feminine side to address issues with sensitivity. Wendell was well aware that was a leap he could never make.

"No, there was nothing of the sort," Wendell lied. "I don't know nothing about any manuscript. I'm not a big reader, mainly watched television when we had electricity."

"No William," Janell interrupted. "Don't you remember? You sold that manuscript to some fellow who came through and inquired about it—after you made a book out of it. Don't you remember?"

Busted, Wendell stammered, and had a sudden bolt of recollection, but only after he gave his wife a look that most often precedes mayhem. She faded into the background, realizing it was a major faux pas of an aging mol of an aging small-time crook. She whimpered in silence.

"Oh, uh, that book. It wasn't very good so I made considerable changes to it," said Wendell, who then tumbled into one lie after another. "It was just a raw manuscript—not good enough for publishing so I took the basic theme and improved it. Pretty much re-wrote the entire book and took it to a publisher in Atlanta. They recognized its potential and published it."

"Did it sell?" Purvis wondered just how far this William Wendell would go in spinning his tall tale.

"Oh yeah, it sold very well, but this fellow — I forget his name —showed up one day and wanted to buy the rights. I wanted to purchase Janell here a nice diamond for our 40th anniversary so I agreed," he said.

Janell rolled her eyes to the sky and breathed in as if it were her last sarcastic breath. She held it there. She felt the footsteps of impending doom, whether it was the cops, the newspapers, or the Holy Ghost in which she fervently believed.

"Mr. Wendell, you wouldn't happen to have a copy of the book you published lying around would you?" asked Periwinkle.

The fact was, the man had about 340 copies in a closest, as part of the deal he had made with the McGraw

Publishing Company. He thought he would sell them from his truck, setting up a table in Orlando's Eola Park. However, there was no great demand from folks walking by on a Sunday stroll. He even lowered the price to $2 and still no takers. He eventually was chased off by Orlando police for not having a vendor license.

Wendell continued, the smooth palaver of deceit: "Copies of that book. Nah, but I thought you were interested in missing cocaine that supposedly belonged to Pablo Escobar. By the way, wasn't Escobar killed long ago."

"Supposedly," said Purvis, who retreated to his taciturn dialogue. "But we in drug enforcement have to check out every lead. I am interested in who bought the rights to the book you say you improved. You say he was from Los Angles? What was his interest in buying out your rights?

"Well, officer, I'm a little confused," said a puzzled Wendell. "Are you interested in cocaine, that damn desk, or someone out in LA? As for the desk, we still have it. Couldn't sell the damn thing with termites holes."

"Take your pick," offered Purvis. "Any information you have could be helpful. Do you have the name of the person who bought the rights to the book? That would be helpful. I feel the cocaine, and this book are inexplicably connected. Maybe it'll lead us to Pablo."

It was obvious Wendell was going to be miserly in offering up more information. In fact, always cagey but generally conman smooth, Janell's husband suddenly buttoned up. She pretended to sweep the front porch around them.

"To tell the truth, I don't remember, and my record-keeping is nil," said Wendell, not wanting to give up any more information less he all but signed a confession admitting he had published a book that wasn't his to publish. "Nah, it was a common name, maybe Brown or White or Smith...

"Or John Doe or Ronnie Rumpelstiltskin or Tom Thumb," smiled Purvis. He was sure Wendell was hedging. His sarcasm, though, was too obtuse for the con.

Then, Wendell suddenly offered up a clue. "You know, the fellow being from Los Angeles, wanting to buy the rights to the book—he just might be in the movie business."

As soon as the words fell from his mouth, Wendell regretted them. He quickly moved on. "Could you use some really fine used furniture? Do you have kids? I have genuine Mickey Mouse ears to sell."

Periwinkle stared into Wendell's bloodshot eyes until Wendell surrendered and fixed a gaze on a snail making its way across his driveway. "What the hell," he said. "I think his name was Reed."

"Thank you Mr. Wendell. The law enforcement community is grateful to you," said Purvis.

Purvis bid goodbye to William and Janell and headed to the nearest Starbucks, a fine retreat if one wants a quiet table in the corner. There are times a mobile phone and Google can be man's best friend.

Within thirty seconds he found The Book of Frances Leigh on Amazon. William Wendell was listed as the author. It wasn't a best seller, and in fact, was listed somewhere below three million other books in sales. In other words, it had sold an estimated seven books, most likely to buyers who stumbled on it by mistake. There were no reviews listed for it.

Amazon had featured a sample chapter. Ironically, Wendell's editing—what little he did—was not top drawer. While the book was titled Frances Leigh, it was listed as Frances Lee throughout the initial pages.

Purvis ordered a half dozen copies. Maybe it would help Wendell and his Janell get the electricity back on, he said to no one in particular.

CHAPTER 23
THE BOOK OF FAIRLEIGH

Jeremy Britnell had long ago left his Fairleigh book on the other side of his conscious mind, a memory abandoned in the rain, the sleet, and atop the piles of dirty snow, though his home was sunny Florida.

He thought about it on occasion, but that occasion was rare. After Cherokee came into his life, he thought of it not at all which is not to say the little girl wasn't constantly on his mind, as were thoughts of his late wife, Sarah, the great times together, and the sadness later.

It caused him to traverse dark canyons. Was he forgetting his daughter? Was he forgetting Sarah? Does there come a time he can no longer remember the smell of Fairleigh or of Sarah's dated but intoxicating Shalimar perfume?

And, he wondered, how in the hell did he and Sarah come up with the name Fairleigh? In those days, before all life's hell broke loose, he only had an occasional beer. What were they thinking? Across the literary landscape, there were no poems, songs, or Shakespearean references to anyone or anything owning up to the name. It was as if they had pulled it from the clouds.

Cherokee and he were no longer strangers, together now nearly 15 years. He knew every turn of her brown body. He had explored the nether reaches, sucked her sweet breasts, and had reached mind-bending highs that brought whimpers, groans, and primeval, guttural noises echoing through the boat. They seemed never to fall into a casual rhythm or be bored with delicious anticipation. It was a new day, every day, and it had been through the birthing of two children and beyond. There were arguments, of course, bloody animated arguments. They both could be volatile. But they always ended before their heads hit the pillows, and their bodies rocked gently with the waves the river.

But was he cheating on Cherokee when his mind wandered into nostalgia? She poured him a drink, stroked his hair, and said "I don't mind another in your head. We are, in fact, friends."

"We? Who?" he asked.

"Sarah," she replied, then smiled and added, "Don't ask Swamp Man, it's a woman thing." He wanted to ask but dared not. It's sometimes better to leave mysteries in the closet.

Perhaps it was also that way with Fairleigh's odd name. In truth—though he didn't often revisit possibilities —he was aware it came from his own hand, lodged in deep space. He hadn't forgotten, just misremembered.

It came from the songs his late father sung as they traveled late at night, returning from a cookware party held in clapboard farmhouses planted amidst orange groves. There were usually three couples around the table. His old man cooked everyone a meal, and then, when they were full of roast beef, gravy-soaked rice, sweet carrots, and buttermilk biscuits, he sold them stainless steel pots and pans. Everyone should know, he was convinced, how to cook food the waterless way.

At some point during his spiel, he would pick up two aluminum pans and bang them together. Metal particles would fly. "See," he would say, "Causes cancer." They would ooh and aah.

It was a parlor trick. However, his old man's sincerity sold heaps of pots and pans, and, from him, it was heartfelt. He never saw himself the carney. Then, driving home, he would have a song in his head, maybe in his heart. He made them up as the car rolled over the washboard backroads of Central Florida. With the windows down, the orange blossom fragrance more powerful than was his pop's brier pipe with a Captain Black load. Fairly, barely, merrily, rarely—a jumble of words, he would string them together and sing to this 12-year-old and a hound dog called True Boy panting away in the back seat. It was fairly late last night, the wife was barely sleeping, I was merrily creeping in, though she was rarely without the rolling pin. Oh, fairly, fairly, merrily what should I do....fairly, fairly, merely, I'm in a fine stew. Of course, they made less sense than a Dr. Seuss verse, but he would belt them out in notes for which there was no musical scale known to man. Yes, that was where the name Fairleigh came from.

When prodded by Purvis Periwinkle, Jeremy casually revisited the storyline of his book, but never in an active way. He, in fact, had very little time what with a television program to host; and, in his spare time, meeting with parents whose children had disappeared for whatever reason. He insisted on personally meeting each one. He wore his empathy on his sleeve, and they were appreciative in their longing. He didn't limit it to missing children, but also to husbands, wives, or the dementia-suffering elderly who might have wandered away. Actually, some weeks this was the largest category in a state where aged skewed toward the stratosphere and addled old men walked away from the shuffleboard courts.

Britnell often seemed annoyed that Purvis would even bring it up, shooing him away. However, he did it gently, as was his way. As a fiction writer, he had not approached a typewriter or computer to compose another line in years. The pecking away at keys was devoted to the commercial exercise of coming up with good editions of What's Happening Now, where he put his narrative skills to good use. He and Cherokee often collaborated, but framing the show was almost always in Jeremy's wheelhouse. His main thought was providing a good future for Jon and Enola, and protecting them at all costs.

Over the years, he made no effort to reach out to other publishing houses. Agents didn't accept first-time authors unless they had a lurid story to tell or had slept with somebody famous and were hell-bent on gabbing about it. A serial killer book could get published if it were written in the first person—and by the serial killer. Britnell struck out on all these counts, though he joked that Cherokee was getting quite a name for herself in the local television world as his co-host. He thought, maybe he could write under her byline and have an instant bestseller. He was not jealous. He was proud.

A Nielsen rating put Cherokee at the top of female hosts in Florida, though there were only a half dozen others. Her popularity was also rivaled by Periwinkle who offered up witty Shakespearean asides—some even with unintended wisdom. His talents had been hidden for so many years that they just exploded when watered and given sun. Jeremy also worked on improving his hosting game, not to be outdone by his cohorts. He was better at it than he thought he would be; and, given his nature, he cheated somewhat by judging on the curve. His demeanor, though, won the day. The character Cherokee had picked for him was the character he was, and, after time, it fit more securely than a wet leather glove.

The Fairleigh book was dead, just as, apparently, the girl for whom it was named was also logically gone with a ghostly breeze. She had disappeared without a trace. It was as if a ferocious hurricane had come ashore, and when it departed, hardly a leaf was stirred. It left only heartbreak. Even missing children pictured on milk cartons are eventually retired or rotated. They become irrelevant, particularly if a four-year-old now would be in her budding 20s. She remained simply an unsolved case down at the Orlando Police Department. The FBI kept it, somewhere, in the bowels of its DC headquarters.

Ironically, what Jeremy came to view as The Book of Fairleigh was never intended to carry that title. Because he had patterned the book on his daughter, he had slipped her real name in throughout, meaning to change it as the book went to print. He felt it guided his writing, and his dreaming of what could be. He realized it needed a more colorful title.

Purvis, though, wouldn't let up. He had this odd compulsion to please his boss, whether Jeremy wanted to be pleased or not. What Jeremy wanted was interesting but beside the point. Periwinkle was Don Quixote on a mission. He had saddled Rocinante and was charging forth with lance in hand. He, in fact, had secured a copy of The Book of Fairleigh, now named Frances Leigh, and was digesting and bisecting it. He felt it would give him a clue into the essential Jeremy Britnell, as well as help him track down the eventual nesting place of the book. Was meager sales on some discount shelf at some small bookstore its fate? Currently, it had an Amazon ranking somewhat below Isabel Smith's How To Teach Your Dog To Sing in Harmony.

As Periwinkle delved into the novel, he became misty, almost balling.

It was the story of a girl's life as the author dreamed it would be. It was a sweeping landscape of dreams, disappointments, adventures, and misadventures. The opening curtain was of a first Christmas memory, and how the little girl befriended a department store Santa, a seemingly incorrigible fellow known for his curmudgeonly manner and his less than dependable ways. In novelistic life, this seasonal hire of Jordan's Department Store was a drunk, a thief, and an addict. He went by the name Happy Goodman. He had been in and out of the Orange County jail multiple times. He called it his Motel 6 home. The fact was, Happy was based on a character that Britnell often ran into given his various reportorial jobs at the Orlando Sentinel, from covering the city courts to what was known by newsmen as the cop shop. Jordan's Department Store was desperate when Goodman's parole officer talked the manager into taking him on, saying he "wasn't a bad sort." He fit the description, sufficiently overweight and more so with padding, and a come-with flowing white beard. While not having the resume of a jolly old man, he made up for it in physical resemblance. He could certainly go through the motions of being a mirthful, good-hearted character.

In the novel, it was the beginning of a beautiful friendship, a close relationship that served both the little girl through her early life and the Santa who was figuratively pulled from the gutter by the smallest of hands.

He, this Happy Goodman, became the iconic symbol that steered Fairleigh away from the dark alleys of early life and gave her lessons she would hold throughout her years. He was, in essence, the wise godfather, the totemic figure for the little girl. It was with the girl's father that Britnell used literary license, making him a character very much unlike that of the author. To say the least, he was absent without leave from his parental duties.

When he had literally consumed the 250-page book,

Purvis leaned back, took a swig of beer, burped, and proclaimed to his empty apartment he was going to bring the little girl home.

CHAPTER 24
THE GOOD, THE GALLANT, AND THE GRATEFUL

For whatever reason, Natalie Courant felt she had to get Cletus Reed's permission when Roane Best called her a couple of ticks before midnight and, haltingly asked her for a date.

For him, it was a moon shot. He figured, perhaps wrongly, he was a reserve for the Toledo Mud Hens and she a genuine star with mega-potential and bigger than life billboards across the land.

His hand grasping the cell phone was sweating. His voice was pitched much higher than necessary for a casual request for a coffee klatch. He cleared his throat to hide his nervousness.

Roane had elevated the difficulty of his action to Hannibal's crossing the Alps on elephants. A student of history, he had read that most of the elephants died. He figured he needed Hannibal's publicity guy, both in his literary endeavors and his love life.

Inflating the product was not exactly his forte—at least in real life. As a storyteller on paper, he could be masterful. In actual dialogue with a pretty girl, however, his tongue became twisted, and the words piled up like a five-car wreck.

Realizing the clock was running down, he thought about waiting until morning to call her. He paced the floor of his Wilshire Boulevard flat above a swanky women's dress shop. He could manage the higher-priced rental, but barely. At 31, he was still paying back his student loans after his football scholarship was withdrawn for reasons of unnecessary gallantry his sophomore season. At least that was the coach's thinking.

Unlike Jeremy Britnell—the mystery papa of his dreamscape intention — his first book about a mythical country in the throes of a violent revolution had edged into the lower end of the novel-selling charts. He had lived the story Hemmingway-style, volunteering to shuttle medical supplies and food for the Central American cause. He was given a heavy-duty Jeep and a sidearm he did not know how to load or shoot.

It had not been his intention to get emotionally involved in the revolution. But close only counts in love affairs and horseshoes. He had gone to Central America as a freelance reporter, but — somewhere along the line—he crossed the line and became a participant. He traced it to witnessing a Guatemalan major popping off rebellious farmworkers like mechanical ducks at a fairgrounds shooting gallery. Roane was helpless. His pistol was not loaded. Reliving the incident, he wondered if could have killed the soldier. Probably yes, but maybe no.

When the landowners become oligarchs, the peasants become revolutionaries. Best sided with the peasants both in life and in his fiction. He was all in for the cause, and the US government jerked his Defense Department accreditation. Since he flunked out as a dispassionate journalist, he used his notes to write his first book. The royalties from his effort were meager but steady. Oprah Winfrey's book club was yet to call and absolutely no one had optioned the movie rights.

"No," he lectured himself, phone at the ready. "It's now or never. I'm going to call her."

Best over-dramatized. The dopamine jitterbugged into high gear, kicking in a neurotransmitter that would move him to action. It was a process he often utilized, such as having the gumption to walk away from a well-paying Panther Studio for an offer from the noted agent Cletus Reed, a fellow who, according to street talk, already had one foot in the grave. Roane was low on the totem pole at Panther, but they paid rather well so long as he said "yes" with deference.

The budding author and now Reed co-producer had felt chemistry with Natalie and it was damn near causing him to have a puppy love meltdown. It was exhausting. He knew if he called it a night without phoning her, he would toss and turn, and rerun possibilities. His mind would be on a continuous video loop. He had never been forward with women; and, for an odd reason, this was a strength, like Popeye's spinach. They adored his shyness, his cowlick, and his dancing blue eyes.

Otherwise, Roane was rather ordinary. He was neither tall nor short, slim nor chunky. His dress was casual, certainly not flashy in an industry known for excesses. He was Mister Every Man, a dusty-brown-haired fellow who looked and handled himself a little like the late Beatle, George, certainly not the heartthrob Paul or the overly outgoing Ringo. He looked like a fellow who would drive a boring gray Ford sedan, which he did, and not a muscle or sports car.

However, he was heart-attack serious about his writing craft. Tinseltown, to him, was a lunch break and piss stop. He saw himself on a winding road toward a New York Times bestseller. Though he and Britnell's worlds had never collided, both were passengers on the same slow train with its yonder destination.

Roane, though, for reasons he was not totally aware, was being given a boost by an unseen hand, a fellow he had never previously met, though about whom he had heard often. His name was Reed.

"Why, Mr. Best, do you always wait until midnight to call lady friends from the studio? Or, dear sir, were you simply going through your speed dial and came up with Natalie Courant? By the way, call me Mary if you wish. My real name, Mary Jones, but I answer to either—even a 'hey, you" will do."

She relaxed him with her casual banter.

"I learned this morning at Panther Studios your name was Mary," said Best. "As for your unlisted phone number, I hijacked the help of Mr. Atkinson's secretary, Ethel, to purloin it from your file. Oh, and I like both Natalie and Mary. When it comes to old movies, no one can top Mary Pickford."

"That's interesting," she enjoined. "I don't know a Mary Pickford. What's she been in?"

Roane realized he was heading into territory where even a 10-year age gap could make a difference. He watched Turner Classics while she obviously feasted on more modern fare.

"Sneak peaked my Panther file, huh. What an inventive mind you have. When it comes to names, well, you know Hollywood. Is Roane your real name or is it something like Horace Honeysuckle?"

"Actually, I think my parents meant to name me Rowan as in the English actor in the Mr. Bean sketches, but my pop was celebrating a little too much and it came out Roane, like the color of a horse," confessed Best. "He just wrote down on a form what he thought was the proper spelling of Rowan."

"My, aren't we chatty in the wee hours," said Natalie. "I've become accustomed to Natalie. It definitely sounds more interesting. Cletus came up with it. He worked with Natalie Wood years ago. He might have had a thing for her.

Anyway, I don't question Cletus' motives. The man works in wondrous and mysterious ways, as you found out today with that smarmy Lee Atkinson. As for names, Cletus is old school."

Best had been around Panther Studios long enough to know very few actors and actresses kept their given names from when they first came down the chute. Exceptions were both his late grandfather and his father, though neither had become someone who would be called a star. It was a Hollywood given. Marilyn Monroe came from Norma Jeane Mortenson, Kurt Douglass was born Issur Danielovitch, and Hedy Lamarr was transformed from Hedwig Kiesler. He was happy with Roane. It fit nicely on the cover of a book and was unusual enough to perhaps spark interest.

Natalie's situation was more complicated. She had no idea her real name. The name given her by hayseed kidnappers and made official as Mary by Charlie and Beverly Jones was comfortable. She was now settling in, however, to Natalie Courant, especially since she saw it on a 30-foot high billboard at the corner of Wilshire Boulevard and Western Avenue.

She was in her Other Worldly spacesuit for the photoshoot. Her space helmet off, and her hair blowing in a red planet wind. Her perky but not overly dramatic breasts were exaggerated beyond anatomically correct proportions, and she had this I'll save the world heroic expression on her face. Her tiny brown cheek mole, of which she was proud, was wiped clean. The image had been photoshopped to sexy extremes to put butts in theater seats and cause male hormones to high jump. It had accomplished its purposes. This was Hollywood. Of course, she would have been dead in two minutes without her helmet in Martian elements, but thank goodness for suspensions of disbelief.

The outlandish and sometimes cartoonish exposure didn't go to her head, even though Panther Studios had plastered it in strategic venues in cities across America in anticipation of the Academy Awards. She just thought of Natalie as that other person. She refused to adapt a Natalie personality. She faced everyday life as a plain and simple Mary Jones, both in appearance and personality.

In movie-land lore, she admired few, with the exception of the previously noted Hedy Lamarr of yesteryear. It wasn't because of Ms. Lamarr's beauty or even her acting ability. She wanted to be a Hedy Lamarr because the woman was multi-dimensional, even to the point of co-inventing a torpedo guidance system during World War Two. No, Natalie's interest didn't go toward engineering, but she knew she wanted to be more than a flavor-of-the-moment actress. In truth, she didn't have a Marilyn Monroe-style body. She was just damned cute.

While Natalie was not expecting Roane's call the night of their Pinks Emporium celebration, she felt it would come. It was just a matter of time. During the evening gathering, their eyes seemed to meet and lock in ways that didn't suggest accidental happenings. On several occasions, sitting next to one another, their legs brushed. They said "excuse me" in unison. Then she smiled coquettishly. He blushed. This didn't mean they were engaged, merely engaging. It was a customary tribal dance of two people interested in one another, if only slightly at this point.

Leaving Pinks, Natalie shared a taxi with Reed who dropped her off at her small apartment near the studio. She had not yet seen the fame or dough that would suggest a Beverly Hills mansion. She didn't even dream of one—it wasn't her—but she did have thoughts of one day building a home for her and her to-be two kids in West Virginia's Canaan Valley. She pictured the kids, but the husband part was fuzzy. It was a boy and a girl.

"What do you think of this fellow Roane?" she asked her friend, mentor, and—though it wasn't official—guardian. She was looking out the Caddy window as she inquired, making it seem an afterthought. Reed wasn't at all surprised at the out-of-the-blue query.

He replied with a smile. "Oh, you mean the fellow you were sparking with tonight at Pinks. He's okay, I guess." Cletus was being coy.

"Sparking with? What an archaic term. I think I heard that phrase in a Jimmy Stewart late, late, late-night showing of golden oldies from the early 1920s." She was being sarcastic about Reed's time-warp.

"I doubt it girl," said Reed. "Talkies didn't arrive on the scene until 'The Jazz Singer' in 1927—even before my time—and my good friend Jimmy's career didn't take off until 1935.

"You knew Jimmy Stewart?"

"Yeah, he and his wife Gloria played bridge with my wife, Abigail and I," said Reed, matter of factly. "But, speaking of Stewart, this Roane fellow reminds me a little of him—though a half foot shorter."

"Really?" She was more than curious. "Tell me why. I hardly see the resemblance. Maybe I should take a closer look. What do you think, boss?"

"First, don't call me boss. I'm your agent. You hired me. Your only obligation to me is to help us make the best damn picture since Citizen Kane."

"Okay, boss," she ignored.

"There's no reason you should see a resemblance," said Reed. "You weren't born when Stewart passed. But it's not about physical characteristics, Natalie, It has to do with demeanor, attitude, gumption, and not taking one's self too seriously. It has to do with a lot of undefinable human tics that make up who we are or hope to be. It mostly has to do with the heart. Stewart had heart. I know more about your new friend than he does. His father Jack was a friend. His grandfather Jason was a friend. I was glad to help his granddad get out of a political jam that could have killed his career, and I have, in ways he will never know, watched over his dad's career from a distance.

"And so now Roane Best enters Mr. Reed's magic window?" she said.

"Yeah, Roane is the third in the line. He's kind of a pet project. He doesn't know it and don't you tell him, but I got Vidalia House to read that second novel he was shopping around. It's a good yarn. If I wasn't mostly retired, I'd take a look at its script possibilities."

"Hmmm," acknowledged Natalie, leaning back in the seat. "I was just sort of wondering. So, you are like the fairy godfather to the Best family."

"That's taking a little too far. I'm just a friend of the family" he replied, modestly. "Frankly, the Best's had dropped from my radar. When Roane got in touch with me, I had to search this empty attic brain to recall our close association."

Then, Reed filled her in on the skinny. "Roane is working with us now. He broke ties with Panther after going over to our side on the Other Worldly sequel issue. I've asked him to come on board as an assistant producer. He'll be working closely with our director, Johnny Swift."

"Really, I must be dense. All this happened today," she said. "I'll be damn. And this director, Swift. I've never heard of him. What's he done?"

Reed laughed. "You'd be surprised. Not much of anything. You probably never heard of Here Comes Bloody Santa Claus. It went straight to video in a Hollywood minute."

"Uh, can't say that I have," she replied, confused.

It never crossed her mind she had walked away from Panther, a major studio, and was taking a gamble. It didn't concern her Reed was an octogenarian with a heart problem, or that he lived in a trailer with a hound dog and memories of a green-eyed daughter named Caroline. Natalie, whether a Courant or a Jones, was basically that girl from West "By God" Virginia who had made an overnight splash in Hollywood. She could either be a one-hit-wonder or another Nicolle Kidman who had her first big hit, a $10 million budget Dead Calm and has won accolades and $22 million paydays for much of three decades.

She put her trust in Reed. He had kind eyes, a soft voice, and though the total opposite in size and mannerism from her papa, Charlie Jones, was torn from the same cloth.

Arriving at her apartment, Cletus jumped sprightly out of the "Hud" caddy as if he were a teen, and skipped around to the other side to open the door for a lady. "Get a good night's sleep. Have a great weekend. We've got big days ahead."

It was more an admonishment than evening salutations.

"Cletus," she asked, "Can I kiss you goodnight? Just a little peck on the cheek? "

"No," he replied, then smiled and grabbed her head in his hands, and gave her a grandfatherly kiss on the forehead.

She left the car wondering, what if…not about the movie she was about to make, or any skepticism about a director whose only claim to fame was a horror "B" flick, but about Roane Best. She was wide awake when her phone rang. It still startled her.

--

"You're right," Roane added, cradling his mobile. "It's way too late for a phone call. I took a chance. I'll ring back tomorrow. I'm really sorry to disturb you, Natalie. I just needed to go over a few pages of script for a run-through next week." Best was blabbering.

He had just been hired as an associate producer and was taking the position seriously. Two days earlier, he had placed a call to his father, Jack Best, semi-retired now in Tennessee. He had bought a farm just outside Nashville. He beat around the bush for a few moments and finally asked him if he knew Cletus Reed, knowing his father had bounced around Hollywood circles for years and knew most everyone. There was a gulp of silence on the line. "Son, if it's Cletus Reed you want to know about, I can tell you this. Whatever the man says, you can take to the bank."

While the job at Panther Studios was not Roane's life's ambition, it was a wave in that general direction, and it would also allow close encounters with Natalie. He had not yet informed the studio he was on his way out the door. Atkinson, however, didn't really give a fig whether he left or stayed. He knew his first name, only because it was unusual, but in a crowd of assistants, it was doubtful he could pick out Best in a lineup without a name tag. Employees were interchangeable. Besides, he was upset he had been big-footed by Scorsese and Spielberg on some dog-ass project that Cletus Reed was muscling in front of the Outer Worldly sequel—and Panther didn't have a piece of the action. It was independently financed and produced.

"Mr. Best, you have to know that's a gigantic fib you're saying. Because no, I am sure, you won't call me back tomorrow," she replied flatly. It took him by surprise.

Roane felt he had wrecked his chances with Natalie at the corner of over-eagerness and misunderstood intentions. His ego, as far as Natalie was concerned, was as fragile as Waterford crystal. It was a rookie mistake. Never one considered suave, he was more Mickey Rooney than Mick Jagger. If he had a flair about him, one couldn't detect it under a microscope.

"You mean you don't want me to call tomorrow? You mean you're going out with me is out of the question? You mean I need to slow down a little because Brad Pitt is probably on hold?" Roane was trying to be comical in a sad way.

"Wow, Roane, you do have a wild imagination, and you also ask a lot of questions. Boy, you have it wrong. What I mean is I would like to continue this conversation until you get tired of talking to me or I hear a rooster crow," she giggled.

"Really?" He was incredulous. He had prepared himself for a fall. He didn't have a Plan "B". "I've never seen a rooster in Hollywood. Really, Natalie, there's absolutely no competition from Brad?"

"You're goofy. Brad is a very conflicted fellow these days. Besides, I still haven't gotten over his jilting of Jennifer," she said. "Anyway, He's way too old for me. "

"And, I'm not?" There was a decade between them. She graduated from a high school in West Virginia only two years earlier.

"Yes, probably. Just don't pull any false teeth out and drop them in a jar, and I think we will be okay," she said. He thought she was kidding but wasn't sure. "Roane, I'm fucking with you. Relax."

"It's not easy Natalie," he said

"Roane, I'm a West Virginia girl. You know, wild, wonderful West Virginia. I grew up fast. You're talking to a kid who was abandoned in a honky-tonk when she was a toddler. I grew up singing Patsy Cline's Crazy on top of the bar at the Purple Onion saloon. The daddy that adopted me, Charlie, spent time in prison for manslaughter. But he's the man I most admired. My adopted mom, Beverly, was salt of the earth, but — as long as it is not the sabbath —her cursing would cause Quentin Tarantino to blush. And guess what, I'm neither a virgin nor virginal, but I am very, very particular."

"Are you saying yes to coffee—maybe a beer date, perhaps breakfast at some greasy spoon— and in the light of day, with both my arms tied behind me?" he asked, bargaining.

The cell phone was heavy with her sigh. "Maybe. I think I am sliding in that direction. Slowly, especially since you've geared that nervous falsetto voice of yours to the semi-sexy groan."

Was she teasing? Was it playful flirting, or more? With an actress, it's difficult to tell when the acting has kicked in and the truth will out. Natalie had never taken an acting lesson in her life, yet she was all method, a natural state for her. It presented a quandary for Roane, but, for sure a pleasant one. The conversation seemed on a curvy though homebound course.

"By the way, in my few moments of idle time tonight, I looked up your name on YouTube and came up with a fascinating video," she said. "You had your 15 minutes of fame while still in college. It was inspiring. It almost brought tears."

"Oh shit," Roane moaned. Best, who generally used Doris Day curses such as "oh shucks" or "oh fudge" could easily guess his most embarrassing television snapshot. "I hate to ask, but the most viewed clip was when I played football for Florida. I was a knucklehead. it has been viewed a half-million times. I broke the tuba player's collar bone. She sued the school, and it cost Florida something like a quarter-million dollars for it to go away."

"Shhh, I'm watching it again on my iPad," she said. "I don't think I have ever seen anything so chivalrous. You were like Sir Walter Raleigh reaching out a hand to help that poor girl up. You stopped play. You were tackled. You lost the game. You mean that bitch sued you?"

"Yes, the video probably doesn't show that the coach benched me after the episode. I hardly had a minute of playing time the rest of the season," he said. "Hell, I wasn't that good anyway. I would have probably tripped before I reached the goal line."

Best's first thought was this Hollywood chick thought him a sap. Who the hell throws an important game because a tuba player gets in his way—only a world-class loser. She, however, was thinking just the opposite. Natalie had already watched the video a half dozen times prior to the dinner at Pinks. She had an interest beyond casual. It had to do with a fatal curiosity of the nearly unconscious kind.

"Yeah, after graduating I never returned to the Florida campus. I think they now sell bobblehead voodoo dolls in the book store with Roane Best written on it. It has a soft tummy so students can stick pins in it," explained Best. "I feel the sharp prick about a dozen times each day. They haven't forgotten."

He was, for certain, exaggerating, but his self-deprecating humor was a comforting balm for the young actress who was getting to know and judge him by the millisecond. She liked his smile, which probably should never be a game-changer, but weighed heavily on the scale. She reminded herself that a previous near-boyfriend had an ear-to-ear grin but bananas for brains and a wild monkey's manners.

"Sorry Roane, now I know you're full of blarney. I'm

sure you became an instant hit with every coed who was at the game, saw it on television, or has seen the viral clip," said Natalie. "It reminds me of what Brad did to producer Howard Weinstein when the sleazy old fucker hit on Gwyneth Paltrow. He spoke truth to power. Said he would deck him if he propositioned her again."

"That story, Natalie, is somewhat endearing. Mine, I'm afraid, is more a Keystone Cops charade. It was happenstance and, perhaps, to be sure, misfortune," he said.

Though he initiated the call, Best was anxious to leave the topic. It was a painful reminder of missing near greatness. It was the only game Florida lost that year. The quarterback, Tim Tebow, had the option to toss to three others who were more fleet of foot. From Tebow's very harried point of view, it was an afterthought, an "oh, what the hell, Roane's open." Best thought the disaster just might be a sign of what was in store for him throughout life, near misses. He wondered if his novel would be more of the same.

"Well, how about a late coffee tomorrow—uh, to discuss the script," said Roane, screwing up courage, and charging forth with eyes wide shut.

"But Roane, we're sort of like colleagues. You sure a date would be approved by the professional etiquette gendarmes? I mean, we're working for the same guy, the very honorable and slightly prudish Mr. Reed. This old guy I love. I don't want to disappoint him."

It almost sounded like a show stopper. But, he countered:

"Natalie, it's okay. Relax. My interest here is purely business. It's only coffee at the Dialog Cafe. It's not an official date. We'll even call it business brainstorming. On Monday morning you can tell Cletus we worked on the weekend, and I worked with you on your lines."

He was thinking in supersonic speed, though by this time he was prone on the floor with his head propped against a chair and a puppy dog named Jingles slurping at his face. "Getaway, Jingles, scram."

"Roane, that's not nice, and while Jingles is a perfectly good name, it's probably not one I would prefer prior to a half dozen Limoncellos, and having my ears caressed," she chuckled.

"Yes, Natalie, I have an LA dog pound mutt," said Best. "We get along very well except when I am resting on the floor with my cell propped up against my ear, and I am floundering in conversation with a starlet."

"Starlit," she countered. "You and Cletus are just full of anachronisms. I realize I've only had one movie, but I would appreciate you calling me an actor."

"Properly admonished," he apologized.

"Really, I didn't mean it that way. I'm just happy we're having this conversation. Really now, Mr. Best. What was your reason d'être for pursuing our very, very fledgling relationship? To tell you the truth, I'm damned disappointed. Cletus told me you were shy—but really. You do like girls, don't you? If you're the other way, that's okay too. I'm very liberal-minded for a West Virginia girl."

"All my life I have liked girls, from the time I was in kindergarten, but you intimidate me," he admitted.

"What? Me? Little 5 foot, three inches me, a girl who could easily be blown over if a stiff wind powder-puffed its way across Malibu," she laughed, again it was more of a giggle.

"Yes," he replied, matter of factly.

"Roane, my telephone GPS suggests you are only 10 minutes away from me. This might seem terribly forward, but tomorrow is Saturday and in most of the civilized world we inhabit, it's not a workday."

"Yes, I suppose," said Roane, "What are you suggesting Natalie?"

"I'm suggesting something totally out of character for me. Because, I am, in most instances, a good girl—and I promise I will be a good girl," she said, hesitantly.

"Yes." He couldn't anticipate what was to follow.

"I'm going to knock on your door within the next 20 minutes. Hell, Roane, it's the only way either of us will get any sleep. Just give me time to grab a toothbrush and a few things. Oh, and this doesn't mean I'm going to sleep with you before we have that coffee date."

Roane should have been gobsmacked over the moon. Instead, he was terrified. Fantasy life is full of Jeremy-Cherokee re-runs. It can happen in the abstract. It's all in the DNA.

She knocked in eight minutes. He met her at the door with a bottle of champagne he had leftover from an after-party for the Golden Globes two years ago. He had not been invited to the event, but anyone can have an after-party. His was with Jingles.

They shook hands as if strangers as she crossed the threshold. Then, they curled up on his sofa and talked through the remainder of the morning. The puppy-eyed them suspiciously. They slept.

At 10 a.m. Roane and Natalie went out for that coffee. The official part over, they returned and journeyed from sofa to bed.

CHAPTER 25
PURVIS TAKES A ROAD TRIP

Cletus Reed knew all along shooting a movie based on a fictional character named Frances Leigh would be a difficult sell to any investor in his or her right mind.

The title was more boring than polka music. It had a Christmas theme but two other movies from major studios were planned for the season. There was nothing to commend it, except the anticipation of Natalie's second role.

Would she be a flash in the pan, a direct-to-video afterthought, or would she light the sky so brightly it established her as the lady-in-waiting to the famous doyennes of the silver screen?

Reed felt the book was nothing short of brilliant. To him, it hit all the emotional buttons of a National Velvet or a Philadelphia Story. It had you tearing up prior to a plateau and then smiling on the downslide. In between, Natalie showed her versatility. She could deliver comedic lines in purposeful ad-libs.

In his heart, he was convinced William Wendell, who signed away the book to him for a screenplay, could not have written it. It had to be written by someone who had in the back of the mind a Puccini soundtrack. It had the dramatic wallop of a Madam Butterfly but with a dollop of first-class humor.

If anything, writing it as a screen drama was a challenge. Reed hated to drop a line. He had read better books, but not one that grabbed him so completely as Frances Leigh. He was certain Natalie would make a wonderful Frances.

However, there wasn't one shoot 'em up in the 150-page script. Nary a single building was blown to smithereens. There wasn't even a decent love triangle, though Reed considered adding a sweet sex scene sans total nudity.

In Outer Worldly, Natalie had stripped to her panties and a provocative tee-shirt. The then director had shamelessly stolen it from Sigourney Weaver and the first movie in the Alien franchise. Reed approved the scene which didn't endanger its PG rating, only making the flat comment that his client was not nearly as tall as Ms. Weaver.

But in The Book of Frances Lynn, any squeamish moments evolved into a daily slice of life scenes and a soft resolve. Where was the serial killer on the loose? The underworld characters? Who would play the old man, the

Santa, who befriended the girl?

Other than being a nice yarn, there was no there, there. There was only suspense and a huge measure of dynamic tension that was resolved conveniently, unexpectedly, and happily by curtain time. It was a nice package but was it sellable to a theater audience?

Both Spielberg and Scorsese thought it was a beautiful screenplay but neither was sufficiently excited to bankroll it in its entirety. Both liked the Natalie girl. She was a bankable newcomer. But the vehicle was a questionable long shot.

It was neither fish nor fowl, and the only way it could pretend to be both and entertaining at the same nexus would be to thread the needle. The most popular current flick in pre-production was a Kong versus Godzilla extravaganza. The public simply wasn't into drawing-room dramas, even if Santa Claus was a central character. But, who knows, they thought, miracles can happen. Few thought It's a Wonderful Life would become the most iconic holiday story of all time, but even it had a slow start and was at first thought a bust.

For a good friend, Scorsese said he would find what he called a suitable director for the project. His own dance card was full, but he had someone in mind that could "massage the hell out of it." Reed didn't want it massaged. He wanted it told—as it was. That's okay, replied Reed, I have Johnny Swift and his crew.

In a phone call, Spielberg had asked Reed, "What if you added zombies to the script?" He wasn't kidding. He thought it could be turned into a horror spoof. Reed shook his head and pulled the phone away from his ear. Then said, "Steven, dear friend, you are a master at what you do. This film possibly will be a disaster, but it will be on me— all on me. There will be no collateral financial damage. But I do appreciate your thoughts."

They were puzzled by his choice of Johnny Swift as the director. They looked up his IMDB and discovered a listing for an award for a breakfast cereal commercial, a stint doing cookie-cutter spots for cooking oil, and, of course, Here Comes Bloody Santa Claus. They also saw Swift had produced shows for the great comedian, Bob Hope. There was absolutely nothing of significance that would lend itself to a sensitive film. His Wikipedia page was three paragraphs and indicated he currently lived in Nashville where he was filming public service announcements for various causes and the Tennessee Public Broadcasting Corporation.

The two famous directors were concerned. They wondered if it necessitated an intervention, after all, Reed was up in age. While he appeared intact with his snappy attire, perhaps his marbles were mush. The last thing they wanted was for their old friend rollerskating to the poor house.

However, friendship being friendship, they took time from busy schedules to visit the agent at his Malibu trailer. They found him hard at work organizing a shoot that was to begin in two weeks. It was scheduled for a Christmas launch date which was natural given the theme. He was dressed casually, and it seemed out of character.

"Cletus, old friend, you don't have time to release by Christmas. It's six months away," said Spielberg. "And about this director, Johnny Swift, he's hasn't completed a major project. His track record looks like a demolition derby."

Scorsese piped in as they sat on Reed's deck overlooking the Pacific Ocean below. "Cletus, it will take you three months just to get the permits. The script has a dog in it. You need approval from the Orange County Humane Society. You're using a child, Cali DiCapo—you will need a fistful of waivers. A movie with a kid is a whole different ballgame."

Cletus leaned back in a green-mesh deck chair and held forth in the breeze. He could hear beach revelers below. Darkness has fallen and a herd of youngsters was partying around a campfire as Reed listened to these two industry giants. He smiled.

"Guys, I appreciate your concern, but I've worked with Swift. I passed over others to drag him out of retirement. His eye, his demeanor, his sensitivities—they are all perfect for this picture. As for permits, Swift has been working on them for the last three months. We've scouted locations. Script read-through and rehearsals begin next week and shooting in three. We've got it down to a three-month wrap. We're using a dog-leg crew Johnny put together, and I have Jack Best's son, Roane, wrangling the production. They are all union, but not necessarily the union you might have in mind. They're teamsters. Early in my career, I worked with most of them."

Spielberg asked about the budget. His first major film "Jaws" was considered low budget at $40 million, and that was nearly 50 years ago. "Today, you hardly shoot a Pepsi commercial for that," he said.

Reed demurred on actual cost since both men had kicked in to support a friend and he liked playing financial matters close to the vest. "Hell, Steven, compared to Jaws my movie is about what you would pay for a haircut on Hollywood Boulevard."

Though the receipts were still rolling in, Outer Worldly had already topped $120 million, and it starred an unknown Natalie Courant who signed on for a million and change. Contrary to agent norm, Cletus took pocket change from the deal. He told Natalie he just needed sufficient funds to provide Sammy with Alpo, his favorite dog food, and, of course, he said, "I do like single malt scotch."

Reed had budgeted $6 million for his film—most of it his own money—and the two directors had written checks for a million each from their rainy day funds. Cletus had promised both they would be rewarded if the film went over breakeven. They both ponied up quickly. It must have been help out an ancient agent week.

The directors realized their visit to save Cletus Reed from his own folly had come to naught. They muttered that he was a stubborn cuss, but wished him luck. "Let me know if you find that Swift guy is not up to your expectations," said Scorsese.

They called for their drivers who were parked near Zuma Beach on the coast highway. While waiting, Reed's mobile rang with the "1812 Overture". He figured it was a robocall. His number was unlisted, which was unusual for an agent. Normally, the phone is the lifeline of the agent business, folks who survived by what they could accomplish with multiple contacts. For the aged agent, the damn thing was an annoyance.

Reed answered, and then wished he hadn't. He didn't say much and Scorsese and Spielberg were curious. Cletus's face had darkened as if a thunderstorm had suddenly rolled in and he was caught without an umbrella. He gave a couple of taciturn nods toward understanding, "yeah, uh-huh, interesting. You have my address obviously since you have my unlisted telephone. I'll see you when I see you. I'm working from my house trailer."

"Any problem?" Spielberg thought the one-sided conversation he heard was as if Reed were being blackmailed or bribed.

"Oh, no, just someone wanting to sell me an extended warranty on my pink Caddy," he tried to joke. "They have no idea the car's 60 years old, or that, before he died, Mr. Newman offered me a quarter million for it."

It was not a plausible story.

"You sure, Cletus?" said Scorsese. "You suddenly became heart-attack serious."

Reed waved away the question as he narrowed his eyes, and wrinkled his face to suggest the call had been merely a routine disturbance. They left, but it was the topic of conversation between them as they walked a hundred paces to their limo rides home.

CHAPTER 26
A STRANGER CAME TO MALIBU HILLS

It was more than a nuisance call.

Purvis Periwinkle wanted to make inquiries about a movie script based on a novel called The Book of Frances Leigh by first-time author William Wendell of Orlando, Florida.

The stranger questioned whether Mr. Wendell had a legal right to sell any aspect of the book for commercial purposes because it wasn't his to sell. Purvis felt strongly that it should be a face-to-face meeting, and he would be catching a plane West the next day from Florida.

As soon as Reed stepped back into his trailer, he gave Sammy a pat on the head, fed him a dog biscuit, and slowly made his way to his computer where his good friend Siri could answer almost all of his questions.

"Hi Siri, darling, do you have any information on a Purvis Periwinkle?" It was an unusual name.

"Here is what I found for Purvis Periwinkle," she came back shortly.

Cletus, always the gentleman, replied, "Thank you, sweetheart. You're terrific. Can you fix me a martini, a smidgen of Vermouth, with three large olives?"

"I'm sorry, I didn't understand," Siri replied. "Would you like to reword your question?"

"That's okay, Siri, I knew I was pushing my luck."

The Wikipedia page on Periwinkle had both pictures and brief information about the Taco Bell employee turned security guard turned talk show foil and funnyman for What's Happening Now, a local afternoon TV program broadcast from Orlando. There was also a picture of Periwinkle demonstrating his pink Periwinkle undies on the Jimmy Fallon show. In spite of himself, Reed laughed out loud. This guy can't be real, he thought.

Many things went through Reed's mind. In 85 years you encounter strange characters by the dozen, perhaps this one was harmless. He didn't sound threatening on the telephone, merely determined.

Perhaps this Periwinkle character was looking for an agent. Reed wasn't about to be bullied into representing the fellow; and, if it had to do with Wendell's book and the authorship, it was a minor wrinkle that could be worked out. Reed never trusted the Wendell used furniture and Mickey Mouse ears entrepreneur. The fellow had been reluctant to discuss the origin of The Book of Frances Leigh, and on his second visit to see him, was downright hostile.

On YouTube, Cletus watched parts of several episodes of What's Happening Now, starring Jeremy and Cherokee Britnell. If one could pull off a comedic hour with a serious social purpose, they appeared to have accomplished it. He perused information about both Jeremy and Cherokee, learning that Jeremy had become involved in helping create the program after his own daughter went missing fifteen years ago. While not mentioning his late wife, Sarah, a deep dive in Google suggested Cherokee was the niece of a fellow who ran the flagship station and also had an empire that stretched throughout Florida and beyond. Reed surmised the public evidence laid waste his initial thought that he was being set up for a con. Even this Purvis sidekick seemed legitimate, though colorful.

Reed reminded himself not to worry about things before they happen and that when they do happen, there were always options. He was a firm believer in having a backup plan in his back pocket.

The next morning, Periwinkle was on the six-hour, non-stop flight from Orlando International to LAX. Given the time difference, he would arrive early afternoon. Before leaving, he told Cherokee he needed a couple of days of R&R to visit an ailing relative on the West Coast. No problem, she said, we don't shoot again until midweek. She was curious, but not overly concerned. She was fairly certain Purvis had no living relatives. He had once mentioned having a momma, but the last time he saw her he was hardly a month old and doesn't even recall what she smelled like.

Purvis was wearing his Jimmy Fallon Tonight Show suit, but he managed to stuff his suitcase with Periwinkle briefs just in case he ran into a business opportunity. He had rented an executive limo service to meet him at the airport. As an ad hoc gumshoe detective on a case, he looked more like a model for Pierre Cardin. He did have on a $350 Kaden Beret because, for sure, this was Hollywood.

It was a glorious Sunday, and Reed was spending it sunning on his deck, smoking a Cohiba cigar and petting Sammy who was slobbering in the warm weather. Cletus had a feeling he would have a visitor, and sure enough, Purvis ambled down his driveway. He had taken off his beret, perhaps feeling it was too much of an affectation. Besides, it was hot. The sprigs on top of his mostly defoliated head glistened.

"I didn't expect you so soon," shouted Cletus, who spied him as he departed the limo in the distance. "You must be Purvis Periwinkle."

The driver waited for him. He was obviously not anticipating a long meeting. He ambled up the walkway, as if the session with the agent was a routine palaver, and not threatening combat.

"Well, Mr. Reed, I'm a working man, and I have to get back to Orlando in two days," Purvis hollered back, using a white handkerchief to wipe sweat from his brow.

"You don't need to shout, son. I'm old, but I'm neither feeble nor deaf," replied Reed. "Maybe we can get your business decided in short order, and you can get back to Mickey Mouse land in time for a late nightcap."

"That would be grand. I feel dizzy on the left coast," he replied, still shouting. "I've never understood you people out here. You are very complicated in a simplified way."

"How so?"

"Well, a lot of you wear cowboy boots," replied Purvis. "And the only horses I see are in the movies."

"I could take you to Santa Anita race track, down the freeway a piece," replied Reed.

"No thanks, I'm a combatant for animal rights. Horses should give kiddy rides for people weighing no more than 45 pounds, and spend the remainder of the time doing what they do to produce more horses," replied Purvis.

Once on the trailer's deck, Cletus offered him to pull up a chair. "Well, we might not agree on why you are here, but I've never favored horse racing, making beasts of burden carry too much burden is cruel."

"I like that Mr. Periwinkle," said Cletus. Since it was Sunday, the agent had a bucket of ice handy and a picture of Tequila Sunrises, already a quarter empty. He was indulging himself more than usual.

"Care for an afternoon refreshment, Mr. Periwinkle," Reed inquired.

"Don't drink," replied Purvis, sounding more righteous than intended. "I mean, maybe a beer on occasion, but I'm mainly a Dr. Pepper fellow. You wouldn't have a Dr. Pepper, would you? Hell, I don't think Florida is this hot."

Reed disappeared inside the trailer and emerged with a cold Dr. Pepper, along with a silver platter of smoked salmon, slices of prosciutto, a selection of cheeses, and Carr's water biscuit crackers.

"As you can see, I actually was expecting you," said Reed. "If we're going to have an unpleasant conversation, I wanted you fed and happy."

"Mr. Reed, it doesn't have to be a difficult conversation. I had that with William Wendell a few days ago back in Florida. The man took some convincing to confess a book he palmed off as his own work was, in fact, one written by my boss nearly 20 years ago."

"And you are claiming that book was written by — I'm guessing here—Jeremy Britnell," he ventured.

"Well, it's a fact the main character was changed to Frances Leigh, but, yes, it was penned by Jeremy. In other words, your planned motion picture is based on my boss's work," Purvis explained.

"And this Mr. Wendell coughed up this

information," said Cletus.

"Well, not exactly, I had to use methods of persuasion that did not entail violence, but it certainly could have," said Purvis. "When he learned, rather falsely, the book belonged to a Columbian drug lord, he had second thoughts and became—I guess you could say—loquacious. Do you understand loquacious? I just learned it."

"I do believe I do," said Cletus, understating his vocabulary. Reed was circumspect in all his business dealings. His questions had questions, but he held his counsel. "So, Mr. Britnell sent you out here to confront me, knowing I have already committed substantial resources to produce this movie."

"Heaven's no," replied Purvis, acting insulted. "I did this on my own accord. Jeremy long ago gave up any interest in the book, though he had written it for his daughter. She went missing when she was four. Let me ask you: What made you read the book and then want to make a movie out of it."

Reed was puzzled. If Periwinkle planned to fleece him or bully him, he had an odd way of getting into it.

"I read about it Mr. Britnell's misfortune on the internet last night," said Cletus, sipping slowly his drink. "Very touching. But, Mr. Periwinkle if you are not representing Mr. Britnell, what is your interest? Money? Or, are you looking for representation? I'm not taking on any new clients."

"Representation? For what? My Periwinkle undies? My theatrical career as a foil on a television show? As a stumblebum who owes Britnell a life-saving favor. Nah, Mr. Reed, I just want my boss to get his literary due. I want him credited for writing the book. That's all. Simple as that."

Purvis had downed his Dr. Pepper and had grazed through a plate of snacks. "Sorry I ate all your food. I'm not fond of plane food." He continued, "Here's all I want —and when I say I want I'm really saying, I insist. My game is not blackmail—only justice for Jeremy."

Cletus was waiting for the other shoe to drop. It fell, but gently.

"I'd like for you to blaze across the silver screen that the screenplay was based on a novel by Jeremy Butler Britnell. That would bring a smile to his face. Writers are like that you know. They say they only write for themselves, but that's pure bullshit. They want to draw a crowd. Also, I'd like to see you use your vast influence to re-publish the book in its original form under Jeremy's name."

"Is that all?" Reed was incredulous. "Mr. Periwinkle, I really, really don't understand you. You travel all the way across the country. You hold all the cards. You could ask for a percentage based on revenue. You could have asked for the moon for Mr. Britnell. Consider your request done. Anything else?"

"Of course there is, Mr. Reed."

Here it comes, thought the long-time agent. "Yes,

I'm listening."

"It would be really nice if you could invite Jeremy and his wife, Cherokee, to the premiere. While you're at it, I'd love an invite as well. We could do an issue of What's Happening Now from Hollywood.

Reed laughed. In the twilight of a fascinating career, this scene would be the cherry on top.

"Would you like for me to have the attorneys draw up a contract that Mr. Britnell would receive top billing for script based on his novel? I am more than pleased to put his name as co-scriptwriter," said Reed. "I'd like for you, Jeremy, and his wife to be my guests at the premiere. and I am more than happy for you to come to the premiere at Grauman's Chinese Theatre. It has a capacity of 932, but I will make sure your contingent has a dozen seats in the best section. Does that take care of everyone? What about your wife? What about kids? What about Mr. Blige?"

Purvis was embarrassed by the agent's generosity. Just a few years ago he was eating at the employee table at Taco Bell.

" A handshake is fine, Mr. Reed. If I hurry I can make the red-eye back East."

As Purvis walked toward the waiting limo, Cletus shouted out to him: "The original title of the book wasn't Frances Leigh, was it?"

"Naw, Mr. Reed, it was Fairleigh, his missing

daughter's name," Periwinkle replied but kept walking.

"That's what the movie will be called then,' said Cletus, The Book of Fairleigh.

With that, Purvis had fulfilled his mission. Sitting in Delta's VIP lounge, he thought about calling Jeremy with the news, but his second thought was that he would like to deliver it in person.

As the jet gained altitude through the dark sky, he was satisfied he had accomplished his purpose. He couldn't wait to tell Jeremy that his long-ago book would live through the silver screen.

Relaxing in First Class —a million miles from the memory of Granny Hogan—he asked the flight attendant, "Do you have any Dr. Pepper?"

Then, he added, "Forget that. It's a long trip. Can you bring me five of those little bottles of whiskey? The good stuff if you have it."

CHAPTER 27
TO THOSE WHO WAIT

Jeremy and Cherokee were surprised when Purvis showed up at the studio bright and early for him, around 10 a.m., and was anxious to go over storylines for the coming programs.

He was ebullient, with a grin on his face quite often described in slang as shit-eating. In his hand was a package from the Cheesecake Factory, containing multiple slices of chocolate caramel cakes topped with Snickers.

"Periwinkle, you know I have been on a diet since I was 16 and that Jeremy was told by doctors to keep sugar intake to a minimum," said Cherokee, though she then expressed gratitude for his thoughtfulness.

It was an overstatement. Cherokee could easily fit into junior-sized dresses from Macy's, and her husband, who doctors suggested might be a borderline diabetic, worked out daily by swimming laps at the YMCA.

"What's the occasion?" asked Jeremy. "You getting married or something? The Orlando Magic finally won a game? Did you win $20 on a Florida Lottery scratch-off ticket? Maybe you need a raise? Hell, you're already more well-heeled than we are. Periwinkle's Panties are making you the underwear king of haute couture."

Cherokee chimed in, "Purvis, are you having a dopamine attack or something. Need a Xanax for the old nerves."

Periwinkle's face looked smug like he had swallowed a lemon and was trying hard not to show a reaction. He was busting a gut with his news but trying to act cool. He was not succeeding. His poker face was about as deadpanned as Batman's nemesis, the Joker.

"You probably, guessed I was not visiting a sick relative this weekend," he said with his jaw jutted skyward. "I confess I don't have—to my knowledge—an aunt or uncle sick or healthy. I flat-out lied. Before yours truly, Granny was the last of the line, though my prospects for propagation have increased, though not to the point of celebration. No, my giddiness originates elsewhere."

"We were curious," said Cherokee. "You've acted rather strange lately. We just assumed —well, I'm not sure what we assumed. You seemed very intense like you were a cat stalking a mouse."

Cherokee was not far off. Britnell had given him his big break as a partner with the What's Happening Now show, and Periwinkle was laser-focused on returning the favor to the Britnell's. He apparently had watched too many Indian blood brother scenes at the movies. However, Jeremy and Purvis, fairly similar in age, treated one another more like siblings than corporate partners.

"Let me ask you a couple of questions: Number One, is it possible for the show to be taken on the road?"

Cherokee advanced an answer having to do with location, cost, and other logistics, but Purvis put a finger to his lips to suggest questions came after his reveal. He hinted at a logical outcome.

"What about as far away as the other coast?" he inquired.

"Tampa-St. Pete, it's feasible," said Cherokee. "We have a sister station in Tampa. It all depends on the reason."

Periwinkle again put his pointing finger over his lips. She was out of line again. "Wrong coast. I'm speaking of the left coast, crazy California. What if we did a story on the premiere of a Hollywood movie with an Orlando angle?"

"Do you know of one? What's the Orlando angle?" There was obviously a landing strip for further questions at this point.

"Yes, a local author wrote a book two decades ago, and it's finally getting some attention," said Periwinkle, a mask and blank eyes now covering his usually wide-googled and expressive face. "A movie is being made out of it. The premiere is Christmas season."

They were skeptical. To take a crew 2,500 miles across the country to shoot a single segment would never be approved by Wilkie Blige's green-eyeshade financial militia. Occasionally he would toss a Hell Mary as he did with What's Happening Now, but, as a general rule, he was tight-fisted. The result was a medium-sized media empire.

"I'm usually the one who is carefree with my uncle's dough, but he would never approve of this. He'd say do a local interview. If the writer is in California, we could fly him out here for the segment. It would be cheaper."

Then, Purvis gave the pre-punch line. "Wilkie has already given his okay. He told me not more than 30 minutes ago he would like to even join the entire crew in LA."

"YOU WHAT?" Cherokee shouted. "Periwinkle you might be a favored son of half of Orange County, Florida these days, but you have no right to go behind our backs and explore aspects of our program with my uncle."

If she were a cartoon, steam would be rolling from her ears.

"Doggone it Cherokee. Calm down, please. You'll crack your war paint. I spoke to him because I wanted to surprise Jeremy with what I feel will be very good news. Britnell's book is being made into a Hollywood movie."

"My book? What in Sam Hill are you talking about, Purvis. I don't have a book, much less a movie script," he said, rising out of his chair. He had been watching the verbal ping-pong between his wife and friend with minimal interest. Now, it had turned into concern.

"Tell that to a Mr. Cletus Reed, a famous Hollywood agent. Scriptwriter, along with you, of course," said Purvis, pulling up a chair and casually mounting it backward. "Have you ever heard of a book that had in the title, Fairleigh?"

Even the name brought sadness to Jeremy and roiled a cloud of dark memories from a distant past. It was a name and vision on his mind as his face hit the pillow each night. He had a defensive reaction.

"Purvis, you idiot, you've been scammed royally," Jeremy smirked. "The book I wrote was deep-six-ed an eternity ago. I hope you didn't spend a ton of personal money on your whimsical journey to L.A. I can't believe you brought this matter up with Blige. I can't believe you bought the line some huckster told you."

Cherokee had her head in her hands, raising it only enough to try and make peace between her two best buddies. "Okay, my reconcilable differences, let's be rational. Purvis, what on earth gave you this idea."

"Guys, it was never an afterthought. I've been pursuing the whereabouts of that manuscript for years, ever since I babysat Mr. Offended over there on that old tub of his. He was drunk out of his mind and was carrying on a soliloquy with the devil. His little girl had been kidnapped two years earlier and Sarah's funeral was two days away. It was a rather tense time."

Cherokee remembered it well. It was also her curtain call to tread none-to-gentle into Jeremy's miseries, and she did it like a possessed bumper car driver at the fairgrounds.

"If you remember Jeremy, I spent the night on the boat with you, and instead of getting into my cups with booze, I search for some evidence of your earlier healthy existence. There had to be a lifeline, somewhere. I found it in your junk drawer, a single scrap of paper with the name of the storage facility. They had long before legally sold the contents as having been abandoned. You stopped paying for the storage."

"Yes, I vaguely remember—not that evening—but depositing much of my life into one of those storage bins. My life actually didn't take up that much room. There was an antique roll-top desk. That useless manuscript was in it. And yes, I'm, a scofflaw, I didn't keep up with the $30 a month rent. So...Periwinkle, get to the point."

"Well, Jeremy, Cherokee, nothing is simple. I talked the storage manager into giving me the name of the person who bought the contents, William Wendell. Wendell is to literature what Kermit the Frog is to music. Nada. He lives right here in O-town and is somewhat of a shyster. He sells Mickey Mouse ears out of the back of his van."

Cherokee interrupted. "This is getting complicated Purvis. Should I take notes? Maybe you need to leave bread crumbs so we can follow."

"I'm getting there. Wendell found the unpublished book in the roll-top and thought he could be an instant author. He removed Jeremy's name and gave the book a different title, The Book of Frances Leigh. I think you know where I am going from here."

Britnell was thinking ahead. "Let me guess. He took it to a low-rent vanity publisher and got stuck for the cost of printing 300 books, plus a fee for sprinkling a few press releases which would never see the light of day. I've come across this before—and walked away. But where does this fellow Reed come in."

"I'm getting to it," said Periwinkle. "But during this interrogation, could I have a slice of cheesecake I so graciously brought to this pow-wow? I'm famished."

Cherokee brought the box over and curtsied before him. It was her way of apologizing. He pulled a plastic fork from his shirt pockets and dug in for a Periwinkle-sized bite.

"Not bad," Purvis said. "Really, you ought to try it. The big fellow upstairs had several slices."

"Yes, we already know," said Cherokee. "My uncle was the first to know whatever it is you are so damned reluctant to tell us that you have to have a mid-morning snack to continue."

"Sorry," said Purvis, as if he actually were. He put

his hand over his heart in contrition, exaggerating for impact and sympathy. He continued:

"I eventually managed to get Wendell to confess his sins. He thought the roll-top desk had belonged to the Columbian drug dealer Pablo Escobar and that it was full of cocaine. It helped that I told him I was from the US Drug Enforcement Agency, and we thought Pablo might still be alive and looking for his many millions of dollars of pure, cut white powder."

"Oh God, Purvis, this is getting curiouser and curiouser," said Jeremy. "Did you do anything illegal—other than impersonating a federal cop? We're probably all going to jail."

"Nah, Wendell became very, very cooperative," said Periwinkle.

Cherokee was thinking the whole scenario would be a good installment of What's Happening Now. Britnell, on the other hand, was wondering how much bail and legal defense money it would take to keep Purvis out of the pokey.

"Anyway, as they say in the Captain Blood classic, 'fate intervened'. Somehow a copy of the book wound up in the two-dollar sale bin at a used bookstore in Carmel. Your new best friend, Cletus Reed—a voracious reader—happened to glance through it and plopped down the two bucks. That night, he read it, and before the week was out was convinced his latest client, Natalie Courant, would be perfect for the main role of Frances Leigh."

Britnell perked up but was still not convinced. When you have double-barreled disappointments, you tend to look at everyone peddling an opportunity as Harold Hill, the con man in The Music Man production. He didn't know Natalie Courant from Dolly Parton. He watched an occasional movie on a streaming service with Cherokee but wasn't a dedicated stargazer. He liked Paul Newman, but informed he died a decade ago, he quipped, "I was not so informed."

Cherokee, however, was up and beaming. She loved the fantasy of movies. Give her a bucket of popcorn, without butter, and she could sit through a triple feature. As a child, she loved the feeling of being in a theater, enveloped in the velvety curtains, and even watching commercials for the snack bar. There was a time, growing up, Jeremy wouldn't miss a Saturday matinee, but not in years.

"Natalie Courant. She was in Other Worldly, and she's up for an Oscar. She's being described as a young Meryl Streep. She's a kid, barely 20, from West Virginia. I've read about her, a fascinating story," she said.

"Let's not get too excited," said Jeremy. "These types of projects are difficult to get off the ground. You say this Reed is a powerhouse in Hollywood. I've never heard of him."

Purvis had done his homework. In staccato fashion, he reeled off movies, actors, and actresses, a resume that would impress even a skeptical former journalist, as he gave

Reed's bonafides.

"Jeremy, he's the real deal," said Periwinkle. "Look him up on the internet. He's got more references to him than...than Abe Lincoln. He's old but still hustling. Your book got to him. He's financing the picture almost entirely himself, with a little help from Steven and Martin."

"Uh, who in hell is Steven and Martin," quizzed Jeremy. Purvis had apparently gone Hollywood.

"You know, bosses, Spielberg and Scorsese," he responded.

"Oh, them," said Jeremy, sarcastically, as if he were intimately acquainted with the industry titans and the group would probably meet them for lunch in an hour or so. He had seen a couple of their movies, many years ago.

Purvis' mouth was in overdrive. "We've all been invited to the movie's premiere. Isn't this great news? And isn't it a great idea to do a full hour of What's Happening Now from Hollywood on your movie Jeremy?"

"Periwinkle, calm down. It's not my movie. I wrote a book a long time ago. It was sentimental dog mush with a few gumdrops stuck in the goo. I came to terms with that long ago. I'm a journalist—not a Faulkner, Hemingway, or a Steinbeck. I can tell a 300-word story in a wink and shout hi-you Silver, but I'm not a novelist. Did you say he really liked my book? I took the book to a half dozen publishers. They all turned it down. They said it lacked a suspension of disbelief. I'm a wordsmith, but not an author."

"Obviously you are, otherwise Reed would not have gambled a fortune and put forth his latest discovery, Natalie Courant, to make this particular movie," argued Purvis. "Do you guys agree to do an installment of our program from Hollywood in December?"

Britnell was getting exasperated with the conversation. He didn't want to revisit a topic that had caused him so much pain. Just thinking about it brought back the horrors of that day in the mall. His book was about a little girl named Fairleigh who lived a rather normal but adventure-filled life. It had nothing to do with her being kidnapped and her mother dying of heartbreak. He had written, in essence, a fairytale with no expectation of its eventual nightmarish ending. Fairleigh—even with a name change to Frances Leigh — was a beautiful four-year chapter of his life, and then it very suddenly ended one day in the middle of the Christmas season.

"I'm not agreeing to anything," said Britnell, and went back pretending to rework the current week's programming.

Then, Cherokee interrupted. "I assume I have a vote here. Are you crazy Jeremy?"

Both Britnell and Periwinkle were startled by her animated reaction. Her face looked like she had declared war on the whole white man nation, and was out for scalps.

"This is a silver bullet opportunity blasting through the Florida sunshine. It is fucking fate. The storyline is novelistic in itself. A lost book, a tragedy, the doggedness of Periwinkle here, and the discovery of what, by all accounts, is buried treasure. I don't want to be too commercial here, Jeremy, but I am closely related to Uncle Wilkie, and I smell a huge success for What's Happening Now. Can't you see it?"

"What?" said Jeremy shooting an angry glance at his bride. They were known for near-daily tit-for-tat dustups that lasted all of 30-second. They almost always ended accompanied by an imaginary Brahms lullaby. "My God, Cherokee, I should make money out of a family tragedy? Forget it."

"Jesus, I don't want to be maudlin here, but the fact is both Fairleigh—wherever she is—and Sarah— somewhere in Dallas, would want you to take advantage of good fortune," she said and waited for a certain pushback.

Britnell glared at her. His expression, though, was one more of sadness. She almost started to cry, and Cherokee rarely shed a tear in public. She continued:

"Jeremy, you've spoken to me about that day at the mall. You and Sarah took Fairleigh to see Santa Claus. You told me the only thing she asked of him. Remember."

"I remember," he whispered.

"All she wanted was for her daddy's book to be published. She didn't ask for a Barbie doll, or anything little girls normally want, Even at her age, she knew how important that first novel was to you," she said, walking over and putting her hand on his shoulder.

He looked up at Purvis, and said, "I'm afraid I will not see Fairleigh in this actress. I've stopped trying to imagine her after so long. I once had a mental picture of how I thought she would look growing up."

"I can't say," replied his friend. "I've never met her. I do know from pictures she has green eyes, and I know your Fairleigh had green eyes."

"What do you want to do, swamp man? asked Cherokee.

"Road trip," he replied and held up his hands to surrender.

CHAPTER 28
MAKING A MOVIE

Pulling a movie together and herding Vampire Bats have a lot in common. There are a thousand and one disparate parts that have to fit together, and a modicum of civility is the order of the day.

If not organized with military precision, it becomes what is described in the vernacular as a cluster fuck, or a shit storm of fender-benders at every intersection.

Managing personalities is the essence of the art. The director can't be bothered with minutia. It takes a foreman, a wrangler. It takes a psychologist, a diplomat, and a ballbuster.

In reality, Roane Best was none of those. He was a gentle soul.

He had never been in the military and somehow had managed to avoid all the stepping stones of youth—cub scouts, boy scouts, school ROTC. Anything that suggested a strict regimen was an anathema to him. He was a free spirit, though with an inner calmness.

What he was was an idea man. Along with that came a healthy combination of the proper ingredients that make for a pretty decent movie wrangler, including an easy-going personality and an unusual capacity for taking and managing risks.

Perhaps it was in the genes, after all, he was sired by movie veterans—his mama had been an assistant to costume designer Edith Head—and learned the business early on at the family dinner table. He knew how to stop fights before they begin and soothe hurt feelings. As a lawyer, he was adept at negotiating with unions and making sure the producer, in this case, Cletus Reed, was aware that the budget was so tight it squeaked. Despite his seemingly modest living arrangements, Reed tended to be rather frivolous in movie making.

For sure, this particular job wasn't Best's calling in life. He was, by the narrowest of margins, more a barrister than a lawyer, and more a writer than a barrister. While he managed to pass the California and Tennessee bar exams, he had never appeared in court, and—having left Vanderbilt law school on distant memory clouds, he couldn't possibly handle wills, divorces, and property contracts.

His mind, though, leap-frogged complicated issues. He didn't so much wade through the problem as cast it aside. They were immaterial to him. He kept his eyes on the prize. In this case, it was to make a good movie in the service of Cletus Reed and to elevate Natalie's prominence as the new "it" girl of cinema.

The initial introduction to Johnny Swift's version of movie-making wasn't all fluff and cotton candy. Swift genuinely felt the carefully crafted script was a gift to humankind. Properly executed, he believed it could be embraced for the ages. It didn't hurt that it was, in essence, a Christmas story, insuring seasonal box office returns. This was ironic in that Reed believed as much in Peter Cottontail and the Tooth Fairy as he did in Christmas.

However, the book that became Frances Leigh and Reed changed back to Fairleigh was a story of compassion and triumph. It was both a sad tale and a gloriously happy one. It was based on the type of book Reed liked to read, one where the good guys not only survive but walked away from life's rubble a little scarred but with heads held high. He always pulled for the underdog. His favorite movies featured the strong, but silent types. He was all Shane and Alan Ladd and High Noon and Gary Cooper.

Roane had technicolor dreams of being a successful writer, not unlike an early Jeremy Britnell living on the starboard side of America, a man Best heretofore had no reason to meet or even know of his existence. Reed had briefed him on the legitimate author of the Frances Leigh novel by shyster William Wendell. He had fallen in love with the book and the central character, in this case, the actress named Natalie.

As for himself, Best had reached a literary plateau, but at a level expansively described as modest. There were no star-spangled achievements, just modest sales, and hopes that dangled like icicles snapping in a frozen wind.

However, the truth will out. Best had an overriding motive for agreeing to accept a job with an old agent who not a single millennial could recognize. They, most likely, would still scratch their heads and pretend to be acquainted with the Hollywood giant, even if they were faking it simply to be friendly. Hollywood was both fiction and fake, opening itself up to Moliere-like ridicule to veteran insiders such as Cletus. Roane, though, was from birth swaddled in Hollywood's history, having both his grandfather and father veterans of the business. Perhaps, he thought, there was a chance Reed would decide on one more project.

In fact, a recent conversation at Reed's Malibu trailer went like this:

"Yes, son, I read your book. You're no O'Henry but I was surprised at the surprises," he said. "That's important. It's got most of the elements to write a serviceable screenplay. You need to learn not to just wave and say howdy-doody to your characters. You need to embrace them with a hug—even if the central character is, in fact, you. The book is probably not for me, but I can recommend it to others. Anything is possible. This is By-Golly, Gosh O'Mighty Holly-golly Wood."

Encouragement for a writer often comes with faint praise. Best immediately went back to his computer and began sketching out another novel. This one was also vaguely autobiographical, about a professional football player who threw a championship game due to some silly, chivalrous act.   Reed and Best met every morning to discuss production schedules, and Roane took the opportunity to go over the book outline with his new mentor.

"Ok son, I was generous with your initial effort," Reed critiqued. "A few course corrections and character adjustments and that effort has potential. On this latest book synopsis, I'll be frank, and use here words of Dorothy Parker to aspiring writers, Shoot them now while they're still happy.

"The idea was horrible wasn't it," Best asked.

"The idea wasn't horrible. You lived it. The execution was embarrassing. Rewrite it, but this time address your central character as a stranger. You're too close to him.   But young man, I admire your enthusiasm and your willingness to grab hold of a historic vignette that apparently scarred you. I'm an agent and a few other things, but not a psychologist. On the whole, the treatment is over-indulgent, and I found myself wanting to watch television, and damnit, I rarely watch television."

Roane understood. It was like a lesson from a movie land Socrates.

All along, Reed knew Best had ulterior motives for leaving Panther Studio. Why would anyone leave a good-paying job to team up with an old guy who was like a truck in low gear trying to once again reach the crest of a mountain? Most of the agent's friends had retired and were playing daily rounds of golf in Palm Springs. Many were dead.

"I appreciate your help," said Reed. "I thank you for siding with me against Panther Studios. It's also true we have a quid pro quo at work here. I can coach you on how to get to where it is you think you want to be. It's certainly not an express highway. By the way, so can Johnny Swift. What I really want to know is why in the hell did you take this job? We're on a skinny budget—you're in charge of it so you certainly know we're pinching the copper out of pennies. I told you to set your salary, and I would try to agree to it. But the figure you penciled in didn't come close to your Panther Studio contract. Are you the idiot son of Jack Best or are you playing me?"

"I'm playing you, Mr. Reed, pure and simple. It's mostly about Natalie, sir. I realize my ballpark is a Little League field and her's is Yankee Stadium, but she walked into my mind and I've locked the door behind her. You ever have that feeling, Mr. Reed?"

"That's interesting," said Reed, with a friendly smirk under his breath. "But damnit son, quit mixing metaphors. You don't need purplish prose, you need language awash in the alluvial soil of the human soul. You need a little bit of Faulkner's reverence to the problems of the human heart in conflict with itself. That alone, with agony and sweat, make for good writing. Oh, I'm sorry, did you mentioned Natalie?"

He had an impish smile, and his eyes were owlish, his brows thick and flared. "Well, what you're experiencing happens sometimes. When I was younger it happened with each full moon, and then my Abigail came along and that old moon just stood still in the sky for decades. What does Natalie think about all this?"

"She says she feels the same way. It's a little scary," said Best. "Fact is, I said yes to working with you hoping to get close to Natalie."

"So, Roane, you used me," replied Cletus, screwing up his face into a basset hound-frown. "You've probably already deflowered this young lady, huh? And you have no shame in this? What this could do to her career? America's sweetheart swept away by a film industry hack, erstwhile lawyer, and potboiler author? I can't wait to see what Variety writes. I'm not sure the two of you are prepared for it. My god."

He cupped his face with his hands. It was more an act than a feeling. He was smiling into his aged and gnarled fingers.

Roane shuffled his feet. He looked down at his scuffed brown loafers. He started to reply but halted. He couldn't recall being this uncomfortable since the coach's news conference after the football game in which he had taken defeat from the jaws of victory. Then, though, he marched forth, eyes-wide-open, bravely for a fellow on the precipice.

"She wanted to get your blessing," said Best. "But she insisted I approach you. You know, like in the movies where the boyfriend asks the girl's father. Natalie has no idea who her real father is and Mr. Jones, her adopted father, died several years back. You're nominated. She says she doesn't do anything without asking you first. You're the designated papa."

"I appreciate that—I think," said Cletus. "But I am not the girl's father. I should be so lucky. You know I had a daughter. She was killed by a hit-and-run driver around the corner from Pinks Emporium.   She looked a lot like Natalie. She also had green eyes. It's why I named our little movie a Caroline Production."

Reed paused for a moment to take in the historic sweep of life, most of it good, some of it tragic. His eyes became moist, masking the twinkle that magnified his personality. He lost his daughter in her prime, he lost Abagail in midlife, but both still spoke to him in whispered tones. Calamity often stalks the good and the humble, and there is no way on God's blue-green earth they can totally bury the sudden flashes of nostalgic memory.

The old gent inhaled deeply.

"Well, hells bells son, if you're asking my permission to do what I would imagine you've already done, I'm fine. You do know Natalie isn't even old enough to legally drink in California for a few more months. She's not allowed a glass of champagne at Fairleigh's premier. Don't you think she's a little too young to stumble into matrimony? I realize Sandra Dee was only 16 when she married Bobby Darin, but we know how that worked out."

"I'm no Bobby Darin. I can't even carry a tune," replied Roane.

Reed was actually ahead of Roane on this. Best mainly wanted to find out if Cletus was okay with him dating his No. 1 client and de facto charge. While Best was a decade older than Natalie, both were wizened by life experience and neither had actually assumed marriage or forthcoming baby carriages. It was Cletus who was the hopeless romantic. He pictured himself in his remaining days with a grandchild and was already writing the fairytale script in his mind. He hoped she—and of course it would be she—would have clear green eyes.

Then, Reed abruptly switched topics. At this stage of life, he felt an urgent need to multi-task. He had invested virtually everything he had in Fairleigh being a success, even a modest one would do as the capstone on his career.

"How do you think our movie is coming. I apologize for not being there each day, but the doctor is a damn Nazi. He's insisting my ticker needs relaxation. I trust you and Johnny Swift," he said. "Just don't let Johnny improvise with the script—not a word."

It was a difficult assignment. Swift had an overwhelming personality. He was, however, respectful of Reed's wishes.

Best had leased an abandoned warehouse from Panther Studios and then cobbled together a suitable movie set by pulling in chits Reed had collected over the years. The script was basically a three-act play that could be shot on a sound stage with second unit filming taking place in suburban Los Angeles, including on the agent's picturesque Malibu spread. Spielberg's Amblim Entertainment had stepped forward to offer his Bungalow 477 on the Universal Studios backlot as production headquarters.

The good news was that Roane and Swift hit it off from the beginning and worked together like Fred Astaire doing the waltz with Ginger Rogers, including a repartee that ranged from comedic asides to Swift's outlandish stories, most of which were actually true. Best not only listened to them but laughed at the punchlines. At the end of a day's shoot, they gathered in the production tent and downed Red Stripe beer, congratulating themselves on a good 12 hours. They were usually joined by Natalie who rarely wore her actress's face and was comfortable simply kicking back with the crew. One could tell she had spent many hours at the Purple Onion..

"Well, " Roane said tentatively, "Atkinson dropped by the set the other day in the middle of the first Santa encounter with Natalie," replied Best. "He said it was a shame she didn't have the Panther muscle behind her at this juncture of her career. He hinted you had hijacked her future for a whimsical last hurrah. He had no idea who was playing the old man, Santa."

"And....

"Nat didn't miss a beat. She was in the zone with the scene. Swift was happy. I know because he gave off that war-whoop he does. Natalie? She just said, 'Mr. Atkinson, I realize you're disappointed, and when we do the Outer Worldly sequel, all your exes can splurge on new Porsches.'

Atkinson left, but seemed annoyed."

"He had no idea that the old man playing Santa was Dan Duval?" asked Reed.

"Not a clue. I heard him tell an assistant to check on it," said Best.

Reed chuckled. "Roane, you would be surprised what talent can be had in the ranks of the homeless. I chased down Dan several years ago pushing a grocery cart along the Pacific Coast Highway. It was loaded with junk, including an Indian wool blanket taken from my porch. He admitted he stole it when I caught up with him. I liked him as a character long before I came across the Fairleigh book. Come to find out he had appeared in a number of 'B' westerns as the bad guy. He's been sober now for 20 years, and a friend of mine for half that. When I read the book, his face and voice jumped out at me."

"And there I have the backstory," said Best.

"I have to tell you, Roane, we haven't heard the last of Lee Atkinson," said Reed, pulling a crumpled letter from his jacket. "It's from his lawyers. He's seeking a percentage of what the movie makes. So much for capitulation. The bastard changed his mind."

"Let me take care of it, Cletus," said Best. "This is a detail you shouldn't have to worry about."

"You're the legal eagle. What's our play, son?"

"Knowing Atkinson, he's probably figuring our movie will go straight to video and subscription services. Give him a good percentage of video, nothing from subscription, and certainly nothing from theaters. Then, withhold it to the last possible moment from video. That business is dying, anyway."

"Damned interesting, Roane," said Cletus, rubbing his chin. "I knew there was some reason I brought you on. What about a counterattack. I don't want to just beat him. I want to make him have a few regrets. Not that I'm mean-spirited. I worked with his papa and grand papa. I just want him to learn a lesson. He should know when I bring him a gift like Natalie, someone with staying power, it behooves him to realize I have a strategy, and that I have worked on it with Natalie."

"Believe me, Mr. Reed, he will have regrets—not because of his pocketbook, but because of his pride," said Roane.

Reed rubbed his chin, the way older people do when they don't quite know what to answer, but was trying to figure it out. "Today, it's all about public relations and perception, son. That's never been my game and certainly isn't my forte."

"I have another thought," Roane ventured.

"I'm all ears, son," replied Reed. "I can lose money. That's okay. I've done it before. What I can't lose is a jousting match with Panther Studios. My ego is minuscule, but what there is like crystal—a little fragile."

"Confession time, Mr. Reed. The first time I saw Natalie she wasn't prancing around in her underwear in Outer Worldly causing preteens to burst out of puberty," said Roane, being slightly the smart-aleck but realizing, at the same time, how close his boss was to the actress. He didn't cross that line.

"No," he continued, "I saw her first in the National Geographic magazine, page 44, May 2018 edition. "She was fully clothed in her trademark Atlanta Braves baseball cap, jeans, and boots. Her face was smudged with grime and sweat such that she looked like Katherine Hepburn in African Queen."

"My head is swimming, Roane. Make a little sense," said Reed. "I'm probably an addled old man, but I'm discombobulated here. Focus on a point."

"You would have had to spend hours with Natalie making a little sense out of her life," Best explained. "I did. Her adopted mom, Beverly Jones became obsessively religious after Charlie Jones died."

"The truth was I was more focused on her future than her past, though I was vaguely aware of the story," said Reed.

"Mrs. Jones became a missionary in Bangladesh. Nat, not being that committed to the Holy Ghost went along with her to administer to the indigenous Rohingya tribe after Charlie died. These are refugees who fled Myanmar. They were being persecuted because they were

Muslims."

The hourglass was seeping sand like an avalanche. Reed was impatient. "What does this have to do with Atkinson and the likelihood our Ms. Courant will be sued for breach of contract."

"Mr. Reed, I'm a lawyer who has never practiced the profession, but I am pretty sure at this juncture, we have not breached anything, but that's not the point. He could tie us up in legal documents for months, setting back Fairleigh, even years."

"Well, I don't think I have the luxury of years. Go right ahead son," the agent said with exaggerated politeness, waving his arm in a loop-de-loop to emphasize he didn't have all day. "At my age son, I don't even buy green bananas hoping they will ripen before my expiration date."

"Mrs. Beverly Jones quickly found out it was dangerous to preach her Southern Baptist lingo to Muslims. They had fled Myanmar when attacked by nationalist Buddhists. The religious crusade simply didn't add up. Ms. Jones returned to West Virginia, but Natalie stayed on in the refugee camp helping them grow little patches of food around makeshift homes. She pitched in with medical workers, becoming attached to a British aid group. The pictures in the National Geographic tell the story."

Reed laughed. "Is this is what you lawyers call a long story, short. I still have no idea how this helps us, though I get the drift to where you are heading."

"Of course you do. It was your idea, Mr. Reed. 'Public Relations', you said. What a bellringer of a story it would be. This 18-year-old on the cusp of stardom traveling halfway around the world to aid unfortunate refugees. Violence has again broken out in Myanmar and the refugee problem in the Cox's Bazaar region of Bangladesh is critical," said Best. No one takes on a social icon. You ever hear a bad word about Mother Teresa?"

"You mean like the late Princes Di or maybe even the actress Angelina Jolie," said Reed. "How does Natalie feel about this?"

"She will tell you flatly she's against using her charity work with the Rohingya as leverage against Panther Studios, but at the same time she believes the picture has an important message," said Roane. "She's for it, but using it in a subtle way."

Reed's eyes lit up like a Vegas slot machine. In the early days, he would dream up various public relations activities to get his unknown clients a break. It was an aspect of the business he actually did like. He didn't call it public relations—simply being a good agent.

Roane was ahead of the conversation. He pulled out the National Geographic edition from his backpack and laid it out on the table. "I've already negotiated with the freelance photographer. It cost $500 bucks and tickets for him and his wife to the premiere of Fairleigh."

The pictures were dramatic. They showed Natalie

hauling water up a hill. It had her with a hammer in hand patching up a hole in a Rohingya shack. In one picture, she was holding an emaciated child. A tear could be seen rolling down Natalie's cheek. The child had already died.

Reed could do subtle. Best, a quiet fellow, even a little shy, however, thought and acted in Dolby Sound and Technicolor.

This required something more. He was thinking giant billboards at the corner of Hollywood and Vine and surrounding the Panther Studio backlot. He was thinking of a good two-minute report on Entertainment Tonight, and an interview with Erin Burnett on CNN giving an update on the Rohingya plight and Natalie's involvement.

"So, I've got your permission to spend a little money?"

"Yes, I'll take it out of my cut for the movie—oh, I've already divided that so many times its non-existent," said Reed. "Take it out of petty cash or a miscellaneous fund."

They both laughed. Every time a new expenditure put them over budget, they reached into an imaginary rainy day fund. It had become a running joke. Reed had even considered selling his trailer. However, it was a crucial part of the movie set.

"Don't worry," said Reed. "We had a windfall today. A fellow in the clothing business contacted me and said he was in for $3 million. We can afford the billboards."

CHAPTER 29
THE UNDERWEAR KING

Roane Best was suspicious when the angular fellow with a goofy grin first darkened the door of the on-loan Steven Spielberg bungalow. The movie maestro was away shooting a war epic in Normandy.

It was not a good time for visitors. The Book of Fairleigh, the movie, was well into its third month of a tight 90-day project. Every moment of every day counted.

Roane was arbitrating a scene Johnny Swift insisted was necessary to the script but Dan Duvall, the Happy Goodman Santa character, was trying to suggest his "B" movie experience in Westerns entitled him to a forceful objection and creative license.

"That fucking Santa cap is hotter than Hades," said the kindly Mr. Claus. "Besides, I have a nice head of hair. My curly locks stole the scene when I was hung in High Noon at Killer Gulch.

"That was back before our Roane here was born," responded Swift. "Now you look like a homeless vagrant."

"Well, I've been there, too," smiled Duvall. "It wasn't a bad life. I always knew the soup kitchen where my next hot meal would be served. I had a comfy down sleeping bag, and street friends galore. Now, I take orders from a man who produced Crisco commercials."

"Yeah, we know the story, Duvall. You were somebody back in the prehistoric days. Tell us again how you scored with the ladies on the Mickey Mouse Club. That's a good one," replied Swift.

The entertainment press had written several blurbs about how a street person had a co-starring role in Reed's new movie. It was the backroom talk of Hollywood and was one of several fascinating Fairleigh film tidbits that were creating low level noise around the project.

The fact that the name of the project was suddenly changed from Frances Leigh to Fairleigh was curious for sure and rated a few lines in Variety, and a 20-second clip on Entertainment Tonight with Roane giving the briefest of explanations. He had been coached by Reed to save the reveal until just prior to the films release.

The inside battle with Panther Studio had not gone unnoticed, especially with Natalie Courant's Cox Bazaar posters—in cooperation with the United Nations—popping up bigger than life not just around Hollywood and LA, but also in New York, Chicago, and Atlanta. This attention was mainly due to the behind-the-scenes work of

Cletus who had re-discovered his previous role in press agentry. The word was out that the film was being produced at less cost than Fonda's 1969 Easy Rider. That was an exaggeration. Fonda's classic was made for $400,000 and Fairleigh was at $3 million and skyrocketing. An average production, however, could easily top $100 million.

Panther Studio's board of directors had called a special meeting to inquire how this particular production had somehow slipped through their grasp, along with newcomer Natalie Courant. Lee Atkinson stammered and stuttered but grabbed on to the crumb to which Best had agreed: A 25 percent cut on the video release. However, there was no specific time certain for the release. The board was anything but satisfied, and Atkinson had long ago frittered away his majority share in the studio. While not on life support, the studio was living on its previous laurels, a period in which Cletus Reed had been a driving but behind-the-scenes force.

Roane, who was one of several assistants to Atkinson in a recent previous life, was contacted daily by the Panther Studio head. He offered financial assistance and the Panther distribution network. Best, though, informed him Spielberg's Amblim Entertainment was already locked into distribution. Really, Lee, we have it covered, he said, forgoing the usual Mr. Atkinson honorific.

"Let's call a truce with Panther," said Best in a call to Reed. He had read Napoleon who supposedly had read Plutarch. "You must not fight too often with one enemy, or you will teach him all your art of war."

"That makes sense to me," replied Reed. "Besides, it was getting too easy and too boring. What do you suggest?"

"If Spielberg agrees, and that's a big 'if', let's give Panther a slice of Netflix, along with a future certain date for video release—and, oh, a co-producer mention on the credits," said Best. "When those billboards of Natalie cropped up and the story of her relief efforts appeared in industry publications, Atkinson hoisted the white flag."

There was silence on the phone. Roane could tell Reed was contemplating the possibilities. "But what do we get, other than the pleasure of not being harassed by Panther," he finally said. "And, as you well know, an associate producer tag is the equivalent of what a former President called 'a warm bucket of spit'."

"Yeah, you're right, but we're talking Lee Atkinson, and his knowledge of the industry was left outside his massive ego door," said Roane, and then added a sports analogy. "What do we get? We get a future draft choice that will help restore the coffers of your Caroline Productions. I would suggest a healthy piece of the pie for Natalie's Other Worldly sequel, and, if I might be so bold, a $10 million lock for our gal."

"Son, I like the way you think," said Cletus. "You're hard as nails, but you have the face and demeanor of a choir boy. Maybe you can take a shot at that Other Worldly No. 2 script. As it is, it sucks."

—-

Like all the hiccups during the filming—and there were dozens of minor eruptions each day— the one between Swift and Duvall ended amicably. Roane did his impression of a referee on a Friday night fight card, keeping the sides apart while being Solomon-like in adjudication.

On occasion, Natalie would wander into these discussions: "You guys!" she would exclaim. "We're all going to be proud of this little flick. So, let's get at it."

For some reason, the bickering would cease, as if a flame extinguished. She had an unfair advantage in any melee. She had been an unofficial bouncer with an unlimited portfolio at the Purple Onion and never had to call in re-enforcements.

Best, manning a tall chair next to Swift, suddenly looked up from the notes he was taking at the stranger. "And who are you?" he asked. He would prefer, with the movie behind schedule, not being interrupted by civilians when game-planning a crucial scene.

"Oh, man, I'm sorry. I just stumbled in here," said Purvis Periwinkle. "I got off the sightseeing bus at the corner and it seemed all roads led here. Is this Spielberg's complex. Wow."

Best treated the stranger like he knew a visitor to Hollywood should be treated. "Fellow, you seemed to have gotten lost. Let me give you directions back downtown. Did you wish to visit Grumman's Theater and see the handprints of stars?"

"That would be nice," replied Purvis about the tourist stop. "But I was there earlier today. Fascinating. Everything is Mr. Best—that's your name, right. Roane Best? Since I am here, I would love to get a briefing on how our movie is coming."

"OUR picture?" asked Roane. Swift and former vagrant Duvall had become interested in the conversation and moved closer.

Natalie, who had been in her dressing room preparing for a close-up, walked in but did not at first interrupt the palaver between Best and the stranger. He looked vaguely familiar to her. She was intently listening when Periwinkle turned to her, gasping.

"My God, you're Natalie Courant, aren't you? It is such an honor to finally meet you. Would it be possible to get a picture with you, maybe an autograph? I'm a huge admirer. I have the UNESCO poster hanging in my apartment back east."

"Yes, but..." she trailed off.

The interloper had pulled out a small camera from his pocket and gently pulled Natalie to him. She pulled back. After her panties scene in Outer Worldly, she figured every wholesome male with unwholesome interest pictured her in the near buff.

Natalie was immediately engulfed by a squad of

amateur body men. Roane stepped forward, ready to protect if need be, as did Swift and Duvall. They knew of several instances where obsessed and loony fans had terrorized studio stars. Most all were harmless, but a couple had turned into deadly stalking incidents.

Periwinkle quickly put the camera back in his pocket, pulled out a white handkerchief, and stuck his hands in the air in surrender. "Hey, I'm one of you guys," he protested. His voice was squeaky high, but mirth, not mayhem was in his blue eyes.

Swift was an inch taller than the Purvis, the six-foot-three intruder, and Duvall was more menacing than any bad outlaw villain who ever graced the silver screen in a cookie-cutter "B" movie. Best was not intimidating, but one got the distinct impression he would strike like a scorpion if Natalie were in danger. His lip was curled and he had devil eyes like something awful.

"Step away from Ms. Courant," said Best, a formal declaration.

Periwinkle did as instructed, but started talking a mile a millisecond. "You fellows have it wrong. I'm not here to interfere. I wanted simply to meet Ms. Courant (now he was being formal) and look in on my investment."

"What investment?" said Swift, convinced the oddball was more dangerous than he first appeared.

Then, Natalie recalled. "I know you from somewhere."

Best joined the chorus. "How did you get my name."

Then Natalie: "My God, are you Purvis Periwinkle of Periwinkles Pink Panties. I saw you on television two nights ago. It was a demonstration I could have done without, but it was very illustrative—if not informative. Relax guys, this is our friend Purvis, the fellow who funded the billboards for us and the reason we're not on bread lines."

Roane then recognized the name and not just from his discussions with Reed. The influx of Periwinkle cash had appeared suddenly on the balance sheet, giving the production some breathing room. Purvis was, in fact, the picture's holy savior. Arrangements had already been made for the production's premiere and Periwinkle had a VIP perch from which to enjoy it, along with the Britnell clan and Wilkie Beige.

There were extended apologies all around, including from the quarrelsome Duvall who admitted he had a complete set of five Periwinkle Panties of different colors. "Sadly," he said, "at my age, I haven't had the opportunity to use the condom pocket. I did buy stock in your company, though."

They were all curious. Why did this character open his considerable wallet? Was he the reason the name of the production was suddenly changed from The Book of Frances Leigh to The Book of Fairleigh? It came about early in the production, and Cletus Reed had given an interview to Variety explaining the book's authentic author was this television host in Central Florida named Jeremy Britnell. It only rated three paragraphs in the publication and two lines on NBC's Entertainment Tonight.

"Well, since the guns have been holstered, I'd like to have a seat and tell you the story of Fairleigh," said Purvis. "The book was left in a commercial storage bin which was purchased by a rather unscrupulous fellow. He changed the name on the manuscript and published it as his own. I was able to track down the book, and Cletus, being the kind soul he is, agreed to change the title and give authorship rights to my boss, the author Jeremy Britnell. Just a little elementary detective work on my part."

Periwinkle finished his monologue with a satisfied smile. They had several questions, but Purvis was completely out of answers. He just followed his nose, a few clues, and solved the puzzle.

"Was the novel based on a real girl named Fairleigh?" The question came from Natalie, who'd leaned so far forward in her chair it was about to topple over. She loved a mystery.

"It definitely was, but that's the second part of the story. Fairleigh vanished almost in thin air," said Periwinkle. "By the way, Natalie, that's a lovely emerald pendant you have around your neck. It matches your eyes perfectly."

The remark was more than a casual aside, a non sequitur. Natalie felt it deserved acknowledgment and even an explanation.

"Mr. Periwinkle, it was a 'come with'. I was adopted at the age of four. I came to my new home with this shiny bauble and the clothes I was wearing at the time."

"I see," said Purvis.

His eyes clouded over. He suddenly didn't want to pursue the discussion further. Such a journey could be dangerous, a dark canyon of conjecture. It wouldn't be fair to Jeremy who had run down dozens and dozens of such leads. He would continue his private quest, but not involve his boss at this juncture. It was too improbable.

Periwinkle's mobile rang. He welcomed the interruption.

"Folks, this has been fascinating. Thanks so much for your time. I know our movie is in good hands. But, that's my limo pickup and due to head back to Florida. See you at the premiere."

Roane Best was suspicious when the angular fellow with a goofy grin first darkened the door of the on-loan Steven Spielberg bungalow. The movie maestro was away shooting a war epic in Normandy.

It was not a good time for visitors. The Book of Fairleigh, the movie, was well into its third month of a tight 90-day project. Every moment of every day counted.

Roane was arbitrating a scene Johnny Swift insisted was necessary to the script but Dan Duvall, the Happy Goodman Santa character, was trying to suggest his "B" movie experience in Westerns entitled him to a forceful objection and creative license.

"That fucking Santa cap is hotter than Hades," said the kindly Mr. Claus. "Besides, I have a nice head of hair. My curly locks stole the scene when I was hung in High Noon at Killer Gulch.

"That was back before our Roane here was born," responded Swift. "Now you look like a homeless vagrant."

"Well, I've been there, too," smiled Duvall. "It wasn't a bad life. I always knew the soup kitchen where my next hot meal would be served. I had a comfy down sleeping bag, and street friends galore. Now, I take orders from a man who produced Crisco commercials."

"Yeah, we know the story, Duvall. You were somebody back in the prehistoric days. Tell us again how you scored with the ladies on the Mickey Mouse Club. That's a good one," replied Swift.

The entertainment press had written several blurbs about how a street person had a co-starring role in Reed's new movie. It was the backroom talk of Hollywood and was one of several fascinating Fairleigh film tidbits that were creating low level noise around the project.

The fact that the name of the project was suddenly changed from Frances Leigh to Fairleigh was curious for sure and rated a few lines in Variety, and a 20-second clip on Entertainment Tonight with Roane giving the briefest of explanations. He had been coached by Reed to save the reveal until just prior to the films release.

The inside battle with Panther Studio had not gone unnoticed, especially with Natalie Courant's Cox Bazaar posters—in cooperation with the United Nations—popping up bigger than life not just around Hollywood and LA, but also in New York, Chicago, and Atlanta. This attention was mainly due to the behind-the-scenes work of Cletus who had re-discovered his previous role in press agentry. The word was out that the film was being produced at less cost than Fonda's 1969 Easy Rider. That was an exaggeration. Fonda's classic was made for $400,000 and Fairleigh was at $3 million and skyrocketing. An average production, however, could easily top $100 million.

Panther Studio's board of directors had called a special meeting to inquire how this particular production had somehow slipped through their grasp, along with newcomer Natalie Courant. Lee Atkinson stammered and stuttered but grabbed on to the crumb to which Best had agreed: A 25 percent cut on the video release. However, there was no specific time certain for the release. The board was anything but satisfied, and Atkinson had long ago frittered away his majority share in the studio. While not on life support, the studio was living on its previous laurels, a period in which Cletus Reed had been a driving but behind-the-scenes force.

Roane, who was one of several assistants to Atkinson in a recent previous life, was contacted daily by the Panther Studio head. He offered financial assistance and the Panther distribution network. Best, though, informed him Spielberg's Amblim Entertainment was already locked into distribution. Really, Lee, we have it covered, he said, forgoing the usual Mr. Atkinson honorific.

"Let's call a truce with Panther," said Best in a call to Reed. He had read Napoleon who supposedly had read Plutarch. "You must not fight too often with one enemy, or you will teach him all your art of war."

"That makes sense to me," replied Reed. "Besides, it was getting too easy and too boring. What do you suggest?"

"If Spielberg agrees, and that's a big 'if', let's give Panther a slice of Netflix, along with a future certain date for video release—and, oh, a co-producer mention on the credits," said Best. "When those billboards of Natalie cropped up and the story of her relief efforts appeared in industry publications, Atkinson hoisted the white flag."

There was silence on the phone. Roane could tell Reed was contemplating the possibilities. "But what do we get, other than the pleasure of not being harassed by Panther," he finally said. "And, as you well know, an associate producer tag is the equivalent of what a former President called 'a warm bucket of spit'."

"Yeah, you're right, but we're talking Lee Atkinson, and his knowledge of the industry was left outside his massive ego door," said Roane, and then added a sports analogy. "What do we get? We get a future draft choice that will help restore the coffers of your Caroline Productions. I would suggest a healthy piece of the pie for Natalie's Other Worldly sequel, and, if I might be so bold, a $10 million lock for our gal."

"Son, I like the way you think," said Cletus. "You're hard as nails, but you have the face and demeanor of a choir boy. Maybe you can take a shot at that Other Worldly No. 2 script. As it is, it sucks."

Like all the hiccups during the filming—and there were dozens of minor eruptions each day— the one between Swift and Duvall ended amicably. Roane did his impression of a referee on a Friday night fight card, keeping the sides apart while being Solomon-like in adjudication.

On occasion, Natalie would wander into these discussions: "You guys!" she would exclaim. "We're all going to be proud of this little flick. So, let's get at it."

For some reason, the bickering would cease, as if a flame extinguished. She had an unfair advantage in any melee. She had been an unofficial bouncer with an unlimited portfolio at the Purple Onion and never had to call in re-enforcements.

Best, manning a tall chair next to Swift, suddenly looked up from the notes he was taking at the stranger. "And who are you?" he asked. He would prefer, with the movie behind schedule, not being interrupted by civilians when game-planning a crucial scene.

"Oh, man, I'm sorry. I just stumbled in here," said Purvis Periwinkle. "I got off the sightseeing bus at the corner and it seemed all roads led here. Is this Spielberg's complex. Wow."

Best treated the stranger like he knew a visitor to Hollywood should be treated. "Fellow, you seemed to have gotten lost. Let me give you directions back downtown. Did you wish to visit Grumman's Theater and see the handprints of stars?"

"That would be nice," replied Purvis about the tourist stop. "But I was there earlier today. Fascinating. Everything is Mr. Best—that's your name, right. Roane Best? Since I am here, I would love to get a briefing on how our movie is coming."

"OUR picture?" asked Roane. Swift and former vagrant Duvall had become interested in the conversation and moved closer.

Natalie, who had been in her dressing room preparing for a close-up, walked in but did not at first interrupt the palaver between Best and the stranger. He looked vaguely familiar to her. She was intently listening when Periwinkle turned to her, gasping.

"My God, you're Natalie Courant, aren't you? It is such an honor to finally meet you. Would it be possible to get a picture with you, maybe an autograph? I'm a huge admirer. I have the UNESCO poster hanging in my apartment back east."

"Yes, but…" she trailed off.

The interloper had pulled out a small camera from his pocket and gently pulled Natalie to him. She pulled back. After her panties scene in Outer Worldly, she figured every wholesome male with unwholesome interest pictured her in the near buff.

Natalie was immediately engulfed by a squad of amateur body men. Roane stepped forward, ready to protect if need be, as did Swift and Duvall. They knew of several instances where obsessed and loony fans had terrorized studio stars. Most all were harmless, but a couple had turned into deadly stalking incidents.

Periwinkle quickly put the camera back in his pocket, pulled out a white handkerchief, and stuck his hands in the air in surrender. "Hey, I'm one of you guys," he protested. His voice was squeaky high, but mirth, not mayhem was in his blue eyes.

Swift was an inch taller than the Purvis, the six-foot-three intruder, and Duvall was more menacing than any bad outlaw villain who ever graced the silver screen in a cookie-cutter "B" movie. Best was not intimidating, but one got the distinct impression he would strike like a scorpion if Natalie were in danger. His lip was curled and he had devil eyes like something awful.

"Step away from Ms. Courant," said Best, a formal declaration.

Periwinkle did as instructed, but started talking a mile a millisecond. "You fellows have it wrong. I'm not here to interfere. I wanted simply to meet Ms. Courant (now he was being formal) and look in on my investment."

"What investment?" said Swift, convinced the oddball was more dangerous than he first appeared.

Then, Natalie recalled. "I know you from somewhere."

Best joined the chorus. "How did you get my name."

Then Natalie: "My God, are you Purvis Periwinkle of Periwinkles Pink Panties. I saw you on television two nights ago. It was a demonstration I could have done without, but it was very illustrative—if not informative. Relax guys, this is our friend Purvis, the fellow who funded the billboards for us and the reason we're not on bread lines."

Roane then recognized the name and not just from his discussions with Reed. The influx of Periwinkle cash had appeared suddenly on the balance sheet, giving the production some breathing room. Purvis was, in fact, the picture's holy savior. Arrangements had already been made for the production's premiere and Periwinkle had a VIP perch from which to enjoy it, along with the Britnell clan and Wilkie Beige.

There were extended apologies all around, including from the quarrelsome Duvall who admitted he had a complete set of five Periwinkle Panties of different colors. "Sadly," he said, "at my age, I haven't had the opportunity to use the condom pocket. I did buy stock in your company, though."

They were all curious. Why did this character open his considerable wallet? Was he the reason the name of the production was suddenly changed from The Book of Frances Leigh to The Book of Fairleigh? It came about early in the production, and Cletus Reed had given an interview to Variety explaining the book's authentic author was this television host in Central Florida named Jeremy Britnell. It only rated three paragraphs in the publication and two lines on NBC's Entertainment Tonight.

"Well, since the guns have been holstered, I'd like to have a seat and tell you the story of Fairleigh," said Purvis. "The book was left in a commercial storage bin which was purchased by a rather unscrupulous fellow. He changed the name on the manuscript and published it as his own. I was able to track down the book, and Cletus, being the kind soul he is, agreed to change the title and give authorship rights to my boss, the author Jeremy Britnell. Just a little elementary detective work on my part."

Periwinkle finished his monologue with a satisfied smile. They had several questions, but Purvis was completely out of answers. He just followed his nose, a few clues, and solved the puzzle.

"Was the novel based on a real girl named Fairleigh?" The question came from Natalie, who'd leaned so far forward in her chair it was about to topple over. She loved a mystery.

"It definitely was, but that's the second part of the story. Fairleigh vanished almost in thin air," said Periwinkle.

"By the way, Natalie, that's a lovely emerald pendant you have around your neck. It matches your eyes perfectly."

The remark was more than a casual aside, a non sequitur. Natalie felt it deserved acknowledgment and even an explanation.

"Mr. Periwinkle, it was a 'come with'. I was adopted at the age of four. I came to my new home with this shiny bauble and the clothes I was wearing at the time. "

"I see," said Purvis.

His eyes clouded over. He suddenly didn't want to pursue the discussion further. Such a journey could be dangerous, a dark canyon of conjecture. It wouldn't be fair to Jeremy who had run down dozens and dozens of such leads. He would continue his private quest, but not involve his boss at this juncture. It was too improbable.

Periwinkle's mobile rang. He welcomed the interruption.

"Folks, this has been fascinating. Thanks so much for your time. I know our movie is in good hands. But, that's my limo pickup and due to head back to Florida. See you at the premiere."

CHAPTER 30
AN ALLIGATOR ON A BUTT
(ONE MONTH LATER)

Purvis' experience with women was limited, though as a multimillionaire founder of Periwinkle's Pink Panties Enterprises the boundaries of his emerging personality could hardly be contained.

Still, how could he ask Natalie Courant, a movie star who was garnering more ink these days than Lady Gaga, whether she, did, indeed, have a birthmark in the shape of an alligator on her butt.

It wasn't that difficult to convince the Orlando Police Department to open up the long-dead file of Fairleigh Anne Britnell. It was thick, but with minimal information.

There was a handwritten notation from the then chief that, in all likelihood, they were looking for a corpse and not a living, breathing girl. The usual pedophile directory was mined. Even though it was evident the girl had been kidnapped, one detective felt sure the Britnell's had something to do with the girl's disappearance. They actually chased that red herring.

In the file, it was noted that the child was wearing navy blue shorts, a white blouse with red embroidery, and canvas shoes. She had a small child's neckless with an emerald pendant that matched her eyes.

However, the motherlode was in the medical report. While she had no other obvious physical characteristics, she did have a birthmark that, if studied close up, was in the shape of a small alligator with a wide-open mouth. When he returned to his apartment, Periwinkle took his Other Worldly video off the shelf and fast-forwarded it to the bikini panties scene where Natalie was doing battle with a very ugly creature on board the spaceship. He was disappointed. Though it wasn't the best possible video copy, there apparently wasn't even a hint of an alligator where Natalie's sculptured back heads into her shapely bottom.

Not to be deterred by a grainy video, Purvis put in a call to Cletus Reed.

"I have to know, Cletus. Does Natalie have a birthmark in the shape of a yawning alligator on her butt," he asked?

At first, there was silence.

"Purvis, now why in God's name would you interrupt my siesta to ask a question regarding Natalie's bum? How the hell should I know? I'm an old man, and my thoughts these days don't venture to belly button level much less further."

"Well, If she did," said Periwinkle, "it might be a clue as to who she really is. It's important—for me, you, and for Natalie—and for the Britnell's."

"What in Sam's Hill do the Britnell's have to do with Natalie Courant?" Cletus mumbled into the telephone.

Reed yawned and stretched. He had not been prepared for the afternoon call. He tried to maneuver the hammock such that his feet reached the ground and he could steady himself. He felt a little dizzy. Currently, he was rather happy with his little world. Everything was in its place. Natalie was happy with a new fellow. Roane said the movie was going swimmingly, and Swift and Duvall, often at each other's throats, had once again smoked a peace pipe with a huge load of Acapulco Gold weed.

"Damn, Purvis, I respect you to high heaven—my gosh, I'm told that you went from a general screwup at the Taco Bell to ruling over an underwear empire. That takes gumption, gonads, and a big gulp of intelligence, but that this poor girl lost her parents in a horrible traffic accident is the honest-to-God story. Her adopted father who she loved dearly then died rather suddenly from clogged arteries brought on most likely by the Paul Bunyan Breakfast specials he served at his bar. So, she's been raised by hillbillies and an ex-con. Natalie spent her formative years working at a bar in West Virginia. Her struggles have had to overcome struggles. She has a relatively peaceful life now, and I'd like to do my part to see that it stays that way."

"Well, it's probably nothing," said Purvis. "I looked at the video of Outer Worldly this morning and in her nearly nude scene, I didn't see a birthmark of any kind," said Cletus, who blushed that he had paid so much attention to that particular part of Natalie Courant anatomy.

"Of course you wouldn't have seen it," said Reed. "Anything that doesn't add to the scene is airbrushed out, and I am sure if Natalie happened to have a —what was it —oh, alligator birthmark, it would have been zapped."

"Oh, so it is possible?" question Periwinkle.

"Purvis, this is Hollywood, anything is possible. Rabbits sing and dance. Donkey's talk. Ogre's are heroes and queens are black-hearted villains—and an old guy like me still has a chance," said Cletus, laughing into the phone at Periwinkle's naivety.

Then, he added, "In that advanced age and the twilight of a mediocre career, I confess to being a little jealous and protective of Natalie. The fact she reminds me so much of my Caroline hurts a little. If you have any clue as to who her real parents are, I want you to go for it. She deserves to know. But, for now, it's the hillbillies."

"I'm glad to have your blessings," Mr. Reed. "Your career has been extraordinary. Don't you ever read your own clippings?"

"Not really, Sammy does sometimes," Cletus said, referring to his dog. "Oh, the one person who can tell you about that butt birthmark—unless he's completely clueless —is Roane Best."

"Roane?"

"Yes, he has a special relationship with Natalie, if you know what I mean," explained Cletus. "But when you make that inquiry, you might want to maintain a cautious social distance."

"Why?"

"Purvis, are you sure you ever graduated from Taco Bell," chuckled Reed. "I'm told Best has a wicked left hook."

CHAPTER 31
IT'S A WRAP

Moving a television program clear across the country for a single program is a feat similar to the Carthaginian Hannibal crossing the Alps with 37 African elephants to conquer the Roman army.

The easiest part was getting the people in place, but given personalities, that can sometimes be difficult. However, it's generally just a plane ride, hotel rooms, and figuring in a livable per diem. What's Happening Now, however, had grown into a major production. It was being looked on by NBC as a possible mid-season replacement for a Sunday slot heading into prime time.

While Hannibal lost most of his elephants through starvation and disease, that particular public relations gimmick got him a special mention in history books for the next 2,200 years. He was called a brilliant tactical commander. No one, to our knowledge, called him crazy, and he; in fact, cold-clobbered the Romans in his initial battles. Success was not to last. He was later defeated and had to retreat, thus ending the Second Punic War, but that defeat never really made it to the highlights reel.

Neither did this move from the land of the talking

rodents in Central Florida to Hollywood. Fast Forward to 2021 from BC time to—in the vernacular—Miller Time.

The logistics of the What's Happening Now move were left to Henry Hyde, the cashiered former director of the program that was previously known as FrontPage Detective. One would think after these many years Hyde would let bygones be bygones. He was now older than dirt, and the place in memory where hate is kept should have healed.   Hyde still held a simmering grudge against Cherokee who orchestrated his previous program to a TV land Siberia. He was not a fan of nepotism—which this clearly was. He held his breath, waiting to get even.   Fifteen years is a long time to hold one's breath without turning blue and dying.

Over the years, Cherokee had tried to sweet-talk him and bring him back into the fold.   The Britnell's even had him over for dinner on the Fairleigh at a Indian River Marina on two occasions. Each event, however, ended with him having too much to drink. The result was his mouth was engaged and he let his feelings spew forth.   Jeremy ended up having to drive him back to his Orlando home, stopping alongside the highway for him to upchuck

Hyde, though, was more than adequate at what he did, sort of a corn beef hash version of television. He simply was not the personality for the Britnell's program. Cherokee was both a star and a co-director of the program, along with an apprentice youngster named Jimmy Sheets who was new but competent. Jeremy was comfortable with him. Hyde was so jealous you could see the green tint.

Hyde never came to terms with a demotion, though it was presented to him as a promotion and more money was added into his bi-weekly pay. For several years, he licked his wounds and plotted a comeback. Everyone at the station felt he had succeeded. His crime program had decent ratings, though rarely did it match the production or budget of Jeremy and Cherokee's What's Happening Now. It hurt even more that his old program, one that had morphed into a hit, was now considered network ready, one of the few programs ever to be drafted from local to national. The Blige network tended to focus on local programming and put resources behind them.

When asked to honcho the move of Britnell's program for one week and a single edition, Hyde sulked, but eventually got with the program. It came as a personal request from the big boss, Wilkie Blige, who always got along with Hyde but still looked forward to his retirement which was set for the end of the year. He had been at the Orlando station for a quarter-century, and in the Blige network family for five more years.

This new assignment was Hyde's first major attempt at butterfly wrangling. It wasn't his forte, and his heart wasn't in it. It was somewhere in East Bongo-Bongo land. The easiest part was getting the crew in gear. The veteran director had been promised a big bonus following this Hollywood assignment. He had just wrapped up a hectic three-month sprint to get a summer's worth of FrontPage Detective in the can. The whole crew, including Hyde, were given a week's R&R in Southern California after the week's effort.

The program was to move lock, stock, and barrel—most of it on a FedEx wide-bodied 747 jet, along with many members of the production crew tagging along. The rest of the crew were taking various flights with the hope that they would arrive at the same place at generally the same time, LA's International Airport.

In reality, it wasn't that difficult of an assignment for Hyde. He could have easily delegated it to a capable assistant and should have. He, however, attacked it as if a Rubik's cube puzzle. He made it more complicated than it was.

Hyde managed to mix up the airline reservations of the crew and somehow landed the What's Happening Now set and production crew in Nome, Alaska. It's a far piece from Nome (OME) to LA's (LAX).

The director thought of it as a big joke, and with retirement in sight and locked in, firing would only add more pay to his final check. It was, in his view, the ultimate payback after years of watching the golden darlings eclipse him.

Hyde never made it to Hollywood where a nice hotel suite had been booked in his name. However, half the crew landed in Nome and found not a single hotel room that had not already been booked. It was Nome Frontier Days week. To make matters worse, the charter plane had developed a landing gear problem and couldn't depart for Los Angles until repairmen and parts were flown in. Several crucial crew chartered a single-engine plane and hopped-and-skipped until they made it to LA.

These calamities happened 24 hours prior to the Fairleigh movie premiere which was to be preceded from the same stage by the Hollywood version of What's Happening Now. The assistant director Jimmy Sheets wondered aloud if swarms of locust would now descend on them. He was ready to cancel.

"The hell you will," said Cherokee.

On the phone, Henry Hyde, containing his giggle, explained to Cherokee he possibly could have mixed up the airports. "I'm old, and sometimes I get confused. My eyesight is not that great."

He acted befuddled, like a cartoon character, so much so she felt sorry for the old fellow.

"That's all right, Henry. I'll figure something out," she said. "Don't worry. Your blood pressure will blow a gasket, and this is a fixable issue—not a crisis."

Hyde was puzzled. It was the opposite reaction he would have had. He would have marched into Wilkie's office like a 10-year-old tattletale, exaggerated the dilemma, and placing the blame squarely on Cherokee's minuscule organizational talents.

Cherokee, though, would remain calm even if her house were being airlifted by a tornado. She would wait for the microwave popcorn to run its course and the last kernel popped. She looked at every issue as merely a problem to be solved, never an apocalypse. When told by Hyde of the mixup, she asked a few questions, and then suggested he not inform Wilkie, knowing heads would roll, mainly his. Wilkie, along with Cherokee's mother, Enola; and Blige's main squeeze, Izzy Caldwell, had suites at the upscale Beverly Hills Hotel, a mere eight minute walk to Rodeo Drive.

"Don't worry about it. We always have a backup plan or three," she said, non-plussed.

Indeed, she did.

Cherokee knew something to which only she and Purvis Periwinkle were privy, and Purvis, at this moment, was doing research at a Hollywood Hills apartment where he had been invited to spend an afternoon relaxing at the pool with Roane and Natalie. He hoped to discover what he suspected to be true; but, thus far, had been shut out in his investigation. The two kept Purvis's sleuthing to themselves. Cherokee didn't even reveal his plans in nightly pillow talk with Jeremy.

"Henry, have you ever heard of the play 'Our Town" by Thornton Wilder?

Hyde replied with an arrogant snicker. Every self-respecting director had read and seen the Wilder play. Most likely, they would have directed it at some point in their careers, maybe in high school.

She continued: "Well, you probably know that whether it's Shakespeare, Thornton, or Tennessee Williams, it's the initial idea that carries the story. We have the idea, and the personalities to carry it forward."

"I'm confused, where does Thornton Wilder come in?" said Hyde.

"Well, my friend," replied Cherokee. "The play is performed without a set on a mostly bare stage. With a few exceptions, the actors mime actions without the use of props. We'll just have to stretch our imaginations and talents, Henry. We can do it. Don't worry. Sure, you fucked up royally but the show goes on."

Plan "B" was beyond Hyde's ability to comprehend. He was not an improviser. He painted by numbers, and to think outside the box to him was a territory he couldn't envision. It was a dark forest with lions and tigers. On the other hand, Cherokee tended to invent new boxes. Hyde scratched his head, put the phone down, and walked into a new life.

Meanwhile, Purvis Periwinkle went swimming.

His mission was rather specific. Look for an opportunity to survey Natalie's fanny but in the least invasive way possible. Purvis was wearing his own Periwinkle Swimming Briefs for guys. Speedos had picked up the license in a transaction that easily paid for his multimillion investment in Fairleigh.

When Roane and Natalie approached him, Purvis was already lounging by invitation on a deck chair with a gin and tonic in his hand. Though Natalie was wearing the briefest of bikinis, the frontal view was not the optimum one for observation.

Time was running out.

If worse came to worse, Purvis was prepared to ask her outright. Natalie, do you have an alligator on your butt? In extremis, he would brazenly pull the suit down to the approximate geographic territory where he thought a birth mark might be. Embarrassment for Periwinkle wasn't the same as an embarrassment for your basic John Doe. It wasn't even in the same solar system. He grew to manhood with a batty grandmother. Shame in the pursuit of a noble purpose was no vice.

"I don't want to be rude Purvis," said Roane, suddenly, "but you seem to be staring intently at my girlfriend. Is there a reason for this? I do it all the time, but you, my friend, are a step away from being a stranger."

"Yeah, I know Roane," blustered Purvis. "But damn, I have to know. Does Natalie have an alligator on her butt? It's a simple, straightforward question."

"You want what?" A what, where?" responded Roane, rising out of his chair.

"A damn alligator, that's all," replied Purvis.

Natalie turned sideways toward both Purvis and Roane. "You mean this little thing. Cute, isn't it?"

It was there in all its glory, a yawning or laughing alligator. Take your pick. However, for Purvis to relate the genesis of his curiosity, he would, for all practical purposes, ruin the premise of the What's Happening Now program from Hollywood.

"Purvis, I know you are weird. I was told about you," said Roane. "That's okay. I understand weird. But, for sake of comity, could you keep your wondering eyes holstered?"

CHAPTER 32
A CHANGE OF PLANS

Jeremy Britnell was not in the best of moods. He was fuming. There were two reasons for this: One, he had just heard Henry Hyde had tossed a huge plate of spaghetti on their Hollywood plans.

He had hoped to breeze in, do their show, change into his monkey suit, and after the premiere of Fairleigh rent a snazzy convertible and head up the Pacific Coast highway with Cherokee to San Francisco.

Cherokee had agreed to the plan without the slightest hesitation. She just smiled, which was a little unusual. Obviously, she had second sight or had received a preview of the logistical cockups.

He wondered for a moment if his Indian princess was possessed. He began worrying about the two tykes at home who were no longer tykes, Enola was 13 and much like her mother, while Jon, a few minutes younger, was rather disappointed he wasn't traveling with his parents. He had seen "Outer Worldly" and had fallen for Natalie, who he called "a babe." They had been left with the harbor master's wife for the week.

The question remained: How in the world could they pull a show together with part of the crew stuck in Nome, Alaska, along with the simple but delightfully colorful What's Happening Now sets? Designed by Cherokee, they helped the cast and crew step up their game, providing emotional impact. The visual montage of Milk carton kids in various stages of life, tasteful done, added a little oomph. It was a reminder of what the show was all about. Jeremy referred to it as "my reason for being."

Stripped down the show was basically a sophisticated version of the old Beverly Hillbillies half-hour re-created as a 60-minute talk show. Jeremy was the ring leader, though not necessarily the ringmaster. With his wry, often sardonic remarks, he kept an intellectually humorous balance throughout the show. He had never lost that youthful shyness, and he wore it like a favorite sweater. He patterned himself after the one-time host Dick Cavett.

Purvis, though, was Clarabell the Clown from the 1950s Howdy Doody Show, but without makeup or seltzer water. He was the unpredictable sidekick who gave the program its edge, and nearly at times, taking it over the edge. Cherokee was that halfbreed with a saucy tongue, bordering on what was not allowed to be said over America's airwaves. She knew the line she could not cross and straddled it like a high wire act.

From day one the show had been a collaboration.

Jeremy, however, had always had the say-so when it came to invited guests. Rarely had he hosted a dud, which is not to say every show was star-studded. They were all, though, interesting and had a theme and an angle, just like he would construct a feature story as a reporter. The ensemble cast read over his very loose script a couple of times and had grown accustomed to the art of ad-lib. It seemed a seamless production.

On this day Cherokee had handed him a list of guests which included a lady with whom he had no familiarity, Natalie Courant, the actress starring in the Fairleigh movie; Cletus Reed, the money muscle behind the movie; Johnny Swift, a director without portfolio other than a couple of horror movies; and, oddly enough, a retired West Virginia sheriff by the name of Danny Jenkins. The last one was a puzzle to Jeremy. He scratched his head trying to make a connection with the West Virginia lawman.

"Hell, the only one interesting is that old sheriff guy," said Jeremy, and kicked an imaginary object so hard he almost toppled over. "Why are we here, Cherokee, this Hollywood stuff isn't our style. Our program has a theme, a reason for existence. It has a surprise ending in virtually every episode. This is just about goddamn celluloid pulp flickering across a screen. It's Crackerjacks without the toy at the bottom."

"Are you finished…" said Cherokee?

"No, I'm not. Frankly, I can't envision some actress playing my daughter. It seems so surreal. I've even hesitated to look this Natalie up on the internet," he droned. "I guarantee you she is not someone I would have chosen. Who is she? Some flighty California chick?"

Cherokee attempted as best she could to soothe the caged panther. He was wearing down a path in the hotel room carpet.

"Actually, she's a very talented kid from West Virginia. She grew up waiting tables and tending bar in a honky-tonk. She has the voice of an angel," said Cherokee, thinking the backstory might bring him around. "She's no airy Valley girl. For god's sake, she's the adopted daughter of an ex-con who owned a saloon. She's the type person about whom you once wrote feature stories."

"Might I ask how you know all this?"

"From Periwinkle," said Cherokee.

"That figures," Jeremy dismissed.

"And might I remind you, swamp boy (she had not called him that in years), it's, in essence, your movie. It's your story. That long-lost book of yours has been re-released and the buzz is already happening. You always wanted to be a writer and now, by golly, you've made it. So quick sulking."

"Yeah, sure, an instant grits author. Slam, bam, thank you, ma'am. Sis-boom-bah. It was simply a break—it remains to be seen if it was a lucky break."

"Lucky break? Before you make a billboard-sized ass

of yourself out here in Hollywood, think of all the people who have been in your corner since day one," countered Cherokee. "And I count day one as the day I walked into your life, and we shagged good and crazy until daylight. I consider day one as when that misfit Periwinkle walked into your life—and mine—and we both prevented you from drowning in alcohol. I consider day one as when my uncle gave you a chance to pull together What's Happening Now. Day one is a metaphor of our 15 years, starting out on that old tub on a lake with alligators and water moccasins. I have not only lived with you through ups and downs and all-around, but also with the ghostly presence of a wife named Sarah and the memory of a daughter named Fairleigh. This movie never stops running."

Jeremy looked up at the ceiling. "I never asked the goddamn book to be released. Why should I be reminded of that pain? Why do I need to be reminded my little girl was kidnapped? It was difficult, but I closed out that chapter of life a while back. I no longer have nightmares. I have you, Cherokee, and Jon, and Enola. That's all this heart and mind can hold at this time of my life."

"Oh pity fucking you," she shot back at him with an energy that scared him into silence. "So many people have worked hard to do something for you. At least have the decency to play along."

"But our program…". It was almost a whimper

Britnell often obsessed over the program. He wanted each installment to be better than the last. If it wasn't, he figured it would reduce audience share. In truth, he had little competition in local programming and was the No. 1 program in Central Florida week after week. He was a local personality, though he seemed to care little for the honor. He was simply competitive.

"Cherokee, what kind of a program can we put on without our What's Happening Now set, and a list of guests that sound about as exciting as white bread. Is it possible to cancel?"

"Don't be difficult Jeremy or I will un-marry you," taunted Cherokee, forcing an evil smile.

She was very good at this. It was as if she practiced it in front of her makeup mirror. But, the fact was, he loved her to Pluto and beyond, and her daily worry was that some dread disease, car wreck, or imaginary hitman from who knows where would cause him harm. She worried a common cold would turn into the Bubonic plague, or that a stubbed toe would send lethal germs to his brain. It was amazing that two people from different planets would be so perfect for one another.

"Well, go ahead half breed. I dare you," he shot back. "Without Uncle Wilkie, you couldn't purchase a stick of bubble gum."

"Jeremy, if I left you. you wouldn't be able to find your shoes, much less your way back home," she laughed. It was a she-devil's laugh, and he loved it.

This is the way it always went often with Jeremy and Cherokee. The big explosion, the back and forth jousting, and finally the makeup where they would fall into a bed if one were handy—though a soft landing wasn't a requirement.

She once said that fighting with Jeremy was like saddling up on a white steed, guns blazing, to attack a strawberry shortcake. There was no fight in the fight, and the making up was a very nice experience. Sometimes they fought just to get to the making-up part. After years of togetherness, the book had the same cover, but each page was different. It made life more exciting. It was like rollerblading naked on the deck of their trawler at midnight, which they had done on occasion.

Their tete-a-tete was interrupted by a call to Cherokee's phone.

"Hi Purvis, what's the good news? And my fingers are crossed for that good news?" She appeared nervous and then broke into a smile that stretched into tomorrow.

"What is it, Cherokee," Jeremy asked.

"Just a little detail about our show," she replied, matter of factly. "I'm on top of it."

"You're so damned relaxed about our big chance. You sure you haven't been popping Prozac with your Corn Flakes," said Jeremy who knew for certain his wife had sworn off anything more than a single glass of red wine at night to keep in shape.

She set a good example for him—though he failed to follow it to the tee. He wasn't even close. He ad-libbed, switch-hitting at times between a smooth Tennessee whiskey and an even smoother Ukrainian vodka. However, he limited his indulgences. As for dalliances, neither had to worry. They felt they had achieved nirvana. Other roads were barren prairies to nowhere.

Cherokee asked him to have a seat. This was always a sign of cloudy skies and an issue he would have to address. A shiver tap danced up his spine. Jeremy generally fled from confrontation, much preferring the comfort of his guitar and being alone within his thoughts. He would go away and work on a storyline for the next show. He would compose a song. He was within himself in those moments. With Cherokee, though, there always seemed no way out. Whatever it was, it had to be confronted.

"Hit me with it," said Jeremy. "I've had a bucket of bad news already. One more of the same can't hurt that much. Snails taste much the same after you rename them Escargot, sautéed them, and gotten use to the smell and texture."

Cherokee unveiled her plan, which only seemed to him a minor diversion of their show.

While they were co-hosts, he was considered the central focus. Even in jeans and often a day-old worn sweatshirt, he carried the gravitas for what the program stood. Cherokee said she wanted to take the lead in this particular edition. Besides, she argued and he acknowledged, he really wasn't up on these show biz folks. It took a weight off him. He could follow, as well as lead. He could sit back, almost enjoy the hour as an observer, tossing in a few dramatic add-ons and questions from time to time.

"I'll try to stay awake," he said.

"Oh, there's one other wrinkle, the network executives decided to move the show up a wee bit. We're filming live at 4 p.m. to catch Sunday early prime on the East Coast," she said. "It also had something to do with the networks' obligations to air a football game.

"Oh, is that all. I like football," he replied, realizing this jalopy of production was held together with hemp and masking tape. It was now totally out of his control. He had to enjoy the ride. "Is there anything I need to do to contribute tonight? Do you have any jokes for me? Magic tricks? I could cook my famous Western omelet on stage? "

"Nah, as the late Buck Owens sang, just 'Act Naturally", she said. "Oh, and remember you have an audience of maybe 20 million but don't be nervous."

"Just think," Jeremy replied. "When I wrote for the Orlando Sentinel I had a fan base estimated at, maybe, five, and you couldn't be sure about them."

CHAPTER 33
WHAT'S HAPPENING NOW

There were only seven chairs on the stage. They were the metal folding type, like one might find at an outdoor revival service. The lights were low when Jeremy Britnell arrived. He squinted.

Coming in from the noon sun, he could hardly adjust to the darkness. It was a purple haze with a sea of gold and red curtains and matching seats.

He was three hours early. Jeremy was, by nature, a worrier. The details of life were happenstance. He connected the dots elsewhere, rather precisely. It was one reason the What's Happening Now show had gained a local foothold and now was on the verge of a national tryout. Britnell viewed most of life as a competition but with no participation trophies handed out. There were win, and there were loses, but nothing in between.

Sometimes he was cautiously anal. It was not a factor with which he was not aware. He kidded himself about it, though only after whatever issue prompted it had melted away. Then he could relax, kick back, and just be Cherokee's manufactured swamp man. He didn't even attempt to live up to her fictionalized version of him, though he could play the role for the camera's eye. While no one would consider him glib, he had a philosopher-king, aw-shucks, aura that served him well.

There had been talk about him running for Congress, but not from him. He wouldn't hear of it and turned aside multiple emissaries from the GOP who somehow had the idea he was a Republican. He was steadfastly independent. There wasn't room in his life for both his family and a 10th Congressional District of more than 800,000. Besides, he supported the current Democratic Congresswoman, and, when it came down to it, was painfully shy unless a camera was pointed at him. Then, he could have an out-of-body experience and turn on his cracker charm.

Believing he was alone, he took a seat on the front row of the expansive auditorium. and stared up at the gigantic IMAX floor-to-ceiling screen. Within a matter of hours, his book would be portrayed in living color and Dolby Sound. But it was really no longer his story. He had buried it ages ago when he abandoned the manuscript in a storage facility. Fairleigh, that girl with the whiskey-sounding name was no longer a little girl but a memory in freeze-frame. In his mind, she was still only four. In the book, he had projected wistfully into the future. It was not a perfect future, but a good one, full of adventures, a few heartaches, but also sunny days of joy and hopefulness.

He visited the past occasionally, but only to remind him that there had once been a bright human being with green eyes and light auburn hair. That damned Periwinkle. Why did he have to dig up these memories he hid so deep in his gut, his planetary being? It wasn't just unfair. It was cruel, and now here he was reliving it for a television program for millions of people. They cared not one whit, he reasoned. To them, it was just another fantastical story. Fairleigh was a fiction, a celluloid figment walking ghost-like over the screen while patrons at Saturday matinees ate jujubes and crammed buttered popcorn into their mouths.

But he surely knew why.

Cherokee had told him. She and only she could see the totemic of his struggles, so complicated it appeared as if dozens of slithering, poisonous snakes were clustered together with no end. Cherokee could, however, step back. She knew the reality. She knew Purvis had gone to the ends of the earth to construct plausible theories.

He had tracked the clues, what numerous others had failed to put together. It wasn't because they didn't try, they simply didn't have the mental wiring with which Purvis, a borderline savant, was born. As of this late hour, she even knew more. She knew the simple but elaborate morality play that was developing moment to moment. She knew for sure. Only Jeremy was left in the dark, and there was a reason for this. Call it show business. Call it kindness. Most of all, call it a gamble.

Britnell collected his thoughts. It had been a long winding road that led him to this particular theater on this

391

particular day. For a while, in the pale darkness, he felt deep space isolation. In the shadow of the red velvet curtains with images of flowing palms, he thought back to his childhood, growing up in Orlando and taking a city bus to Orange Avenue and the Rialto Theater. From an early age, he like being wrapped in the solitary cocoon of an afternoon matinee. Those were good memories convoluted with the here and now, which was, at best, confusing to him.

Somehow, a sparrow had managed to sneak into the cavernous theater. It flapped its wings, tweeting ferociously, nervously flying from one perch to another. To Jeremy, it was a metaphor for the What's Happening Now program just hours away. Why did Cherokee insist on a live program on the same day as a movie premiere? It didn't make sense. But, most of all, he dreaded meeting Natalie Courant, the girl who would play his daughter. If he couldn't picture her now, how could anyone else possibly cast her? It was such fiction.

Jesus, all we need is bird shit dive bombings during the show, Jeremy thought.

Several hundred invitations had been sent, and the curious had responded. If worse came to worse, they could hustle a few people off the street. There were always crowds and tourist groups ogling the forecourt pavement with the palms and feet of some 200 stars. Some of the concrete slabs were retired from time to time to make room for more personalities to put their mark in the concrete.

About half the people attending the live What'sHappening Now program were coming at the invitation of Cletus Reed, whose mega influence had eased the way for the nationally televised program at the prestigious venue. Cherokee had tapped into her West Coast friends for a few attendees. It was a free show, but the program's name without a pre-ad blitz would never have generated the excitement.

Cherokee had assured Jeremy all would be ready for showtime. She would have his tux and for her an evening gown for the later premiere. Even though an extra in this particular production, the program was still his baby. After all, this was an audition for the big time.

A black man with an unlit pipe came out of the shadows. He was the only one around. The name on his shirt read, "Hal."

Hal was in charge of setting the stage at the Grauman theater, a place where in 1927 Mary Pickford and Douglass Fairbanks attended the inaugural event. It had been the site of many premieres and The Book of Fairleigh would draw interest and a Red Carpet gaggle. The entertainment press would all be present. This was primarily because Variety teased it in a feature article the prior week. The question on everyone's mind was whether the film could possibly match the success of Natalie Courant's Outer Worldly. The writers, without seeing the film, were skeptical. In a week, it would be fanned out to several thousand screens across the nation.

"Hal, Is this all there is?" Jeremy kept looking

around for a curtain to go up and a smidgin of razzle-dazzle to grace the magnificent showplace. He walked up on the stage.

"That's what it says on the paper I have here," said Hal. His voice was craggy and deep. "I have to tell you, this is probably the least work I have done to prepare for a program in my 30 years here. Mostly I'm here to help set up for the premiere tonight. Are you connected to the premiere?

"Yeah, sort of. I guess you could say," Jeremy said, a toss-away line.

Britnell took out his mobile. Cherokee picked up after one ring, knowing she had a nervous husband. She managed her most soothing voice, one just as appropriate to someone on a psychiatric couch.

"Cherokee, I'm at the theater. It's rather lonely. Are you sure I'm in the right place? Nothing has really been done."

"Jeremy, you were going to leave everything to me. I thought you went to get a haircut."

There was only a slight hint of pestilence. He was following her instructions but was in danger of veering over the center line and crashing into a tree. He had gotten the hair trim.

"Yes, but…"

"Swamp boy, get yourself together. Think back to that first night on your boat. You took a leap of faith. You put all your chips on going for broke, and by God, it ain't been half bad, has it, hon?"

"It's been magic," he replied, softly. "But Hal here says..."

"Trust me, swamp boy. I'll be there within the hour to greet our guests. I have your tux for that red carpet stroll later tonight. I'm wearing the black sleeveless number where the back disappears into my behind and makes me say things that embarrass you. We're going to knock them dead. Our crew should arrive at any moment. Love you. Gotta go. I have to lose a couple of wrinkles and put on my Wonder Woman face. Bye."

She called him back within 30-seconds. "Oh, Jeremy, one other thing. I know you're not thrilled to do this program around your book and the green-eyed kid, but do be gracious to her. For me, please."

Britnell was curious. Cherokee wasn't always so solicitous about other women, particularly one as attractive as Natalie Courant. His wife had edged into her mid-40s, but she knew she could hold her own against most any 20-something-year-old. She seemed to be promoting this Natalie girl, such was the Twilight Zone enigma.

When Cherokee hung up, Jeremy was again all alone with Hal. He had arranged the chairs in a near-perfect circle.

"What do you think my friend," Jeremy asked him. "Perhaps we're going to have a seance, or play that song and the music stops everyone dives for the chair. You know, eight people for seven chairs."

"Beats me, not my rodeo," the old man said. "I'm just a hired hand."

Purvis Periwinkle was the first from the Orlando contingent to arrive for the program. He walked in looking amazed and had a goofy Gomer Pyle look on his face as he surveyed the theater.

"If grandma Gladys could see me now," he said. Then, "You nervous, Jeremy? Cherokee sent me over to babysit you."

"No, not really," Britnell dismissed. It was a lie.

"In that case, I'll consider my mission has been accomplished," said Purvis who was already dressed in his Tonight Show suit, and, as usual, would add comic class to the program. "I'll call her back and tell her you're cool— that you are not quivering jelly and you don't yet need a change of underwear. Anyway, I want to explore the neighborhood a bit. I'll be back before showtime."

"Be careful," Britnell replied. "You don't know this neighborhood. It's easy to get lost."

Jeremy often treated Purvis with kid gloves, worrying needlessly. It had taken years, but Periwinkle, after being treated like an oddity by his grandmother and others, had managed to navigate life as well or much better than most anyone. He still kept his quirks, but they just added to his complex personality. He was, as his grandmother often said, "peculiar. That's what Purvis is. I gave him a 50-dollar name, but he still has a 50-cent brain. I believe his mom did drugs."

"Don't worry, boss," replied Periwinkle, who actually had a more impressive bank account than did Britnell. "I'm bulletproof, and I learned karate from watching old Kung Fu movies."

When he had left, a light filtered into the theater from the front of the auditorium. Jeremy saw the outline of a woman in a baseball cap and white jeans. She tentatively walked down the aisle.

"Mr. Britnell? She called out, but It was more of a question than an acknowledgment. She seemed unsure of herself.

Jeremy hoped the figure walking cautiously toward the stage was not Natalie Courant, the one whose poster was bigger than life on a billboard across the street. He wanted reinforcements around him, for Cherokee to be a buffer between them. He started to not even answer but realized a reckoning was coming regardless.

"Yes, that's who I am," he replied. "You are...?"

She answered the inevitable. "I'm the Fairleigh from your movie," she said when about halfway down the center aisle. She was hardly visible in the middle of a sea of empty seats. She was so small. It was as if a child was coming toward him.

Britnell had the urge to hold up his hand and say, No lady, you're not Fairleigh, and frankly, it's not really my movie. Then, he remembered his wife's admonishment to be on his best behavior. He was generally polite to nearly everyone so it wasn't difficult.

"Glad to meet you Natalie." he held out his hand as she maneuvered the stairs to the stage. She stumped her toe on the third one, falling to her knees. A small case with a change of clothes went flying.

"Oh, fuck-it," she said, and then apologized for her language. "Sorry, Mr. Britnell, I'm near-sighted and sometimes venture out without my glasses. Vanity, I guess."

Well, at least she is human, Jeremy thought as he retrieved her case which landed a few feet away. He helped her up.

"Did you hurt yourself?" he asked, genuinely concerned.

'Nah, I grew up doing pratfalls," she laughed. "I worked in my dad's bar. I broke fights up. I'm hurt proof."

It was hard for him to imagine this pint-sized lass breaking up a chess match, much less a barroom brawl. He figured this must simply be part of the story package that public relations people had invented around her. He admired a good public relations touch.

After the initial entreaties and introductions, he motioned her to have a seat and took one himself in the semi-circle of folding chairs. He apologized for the sparse setting, but she brushed it off with the wave of a hand and a smile.

"I enjoyed your book. I read the script some months ago, but I just got hold of the book when it went on sale at the Larry Edmunds Bookshop just a few blocks from here," she said. "I brought a copy with me for you to sign. Would you?"

This was new for him. He had never been asked to sign anything he had written, and this was the first book that was actually published with his name on the cover. Britnell was curious. He had never seen the movie script and only had a vague recollection of the book he wrote. At the time he wrote and re-wrote it, he could quote back passages from it.

"Was the script faithful to the book? I haven't seen it," he said.

"Cletus did an excellent job. I've tried my best to fit into the Fairleigh character as you imagined her growing up," said Natalie.

Jeremy found himself attempting to imagine Natalie and the grownup Fairleigh, someone even he had never met except through his fictionalized account of who she might be and who he wanted her to be. He closed his eyes and superimposed this actress before him over how he would imagine Fairleigh today. It wasn't a perfect fit, but it was close.

"It's my understanding from Mr. Periwinkle that your wife—Cherokee, I believe—will be the host for the program, and she will lead a conversation about the book and movie and how it came about. That's cool. I would like to know more about it myself."

"You know Purvis?"

"Yes, he was over at my apartment earlier today swimming with my fiancé, Roane Best, and me. He's a really funny guy. After a couple of hours, I feel like I have known him forever," she said.

"Yeah, well Purvis has that effect on people," said Jeremy. "Some people think he's a little weird. Perhaps he is. That's why he fits so well into the What's Happening Now family. We're all a little off."

"That's an interesting observation," she said. "Perhaps that's why I was meant to have a role in this movie. I'm not a model of normalcy. My God, Mr. Britnell, my life has been like one of those silver spheres in a pinball machine at the Purple Onion, my late pop's bar. No one knows where in the hell that little ball will land. I like it that way. I don't do planning well. If it wasn't for Cletus, my agent, I'd be like a girl high on locoweed, bouncing off the walls."

Under his breath, Jeremy replied, "You remind me

of my wife, Cherokee. She's totally unscripted. I've grown accustomed to it. More than that, I've grown to like it."

"I had a telephone chat with Cherokee the other day," responded Natalie. She's what you guys call a 'cool chick' and we 'wannabes' are green with envy. She gave me a rough idea of what to expect this afternoon. Then, she said to expect the unexpected."

Britnell laughed. "Natalie, at this point I think you know more about the show than do I. I'm sort of the extra pilot riding along in the jump seat. But, don't worry, if it's a disaster, we'll all find work—somewhere. You think I'm too old to be a stunt man?"

She quickly countered, "Do you think I am too young to be a hatcheck girl or maybe sell popcorn at the concession stand? If you find a job after this, will you remember your buddy here?"

Jeremy was becoming more comfortable. His visions of Fairleigh always led into a dark tunnel. As ridiculous as it seemed, he was now filling in the contours of who she was or might have been. Of course, it was fiction, but it was his personal fiction. It wasn't just the green eyes though, but that was where the visions collided.

He joked, "Whatever we do Ms. Courant—Natalie— we'll do it as a team. I might have to get Ms. Britnell's permission first. We've grown accustomed to having food on the table."

CHAPTER 34
LIFE'S BUT A WALKING SHADOW

At the appointed hour, all were seated. The red "On the Air" sign flashed on, and an audience of, perhaps, 300 in an auditorium that sat three times that many, politely applauded as a curtain came up.

It was a curious collection of souls, both on the stage and sprinkled throughout the theater. The most perplexed person was the erstwhile star of What's Happening Now, Jeremy Britnell.

He was seated next to Cherokee Britnell, who leaned over just prior to the raised curtain and whispered, "Don't worry swamp boy, I've got this one covered," She squeezed his hand.

As it was oftentimes in life, he was unsure what she meant, though he knew, whatever the outcome, that the intent was purposeful and honest. It was like a blindman's journey. Who knew what was beyond the next bend.

The raised curtain revealed the eight metal chairs, and in each was a person who would portray a vital role over the next 60 minutes, minus commercial breaks for the Fairleigh movie, and Periwinkle's now-famous underwear and a short visual retrospective on Natalie's limited career, filmed and edited by Johnny Swift.

As for the others, the Britnell's, Natalie Courant (seated opposite from Jeremy), Cletus Reed, who had a wizened but perplexed look; Purvis, who seemed comfortable gazing at the theater's ceiling and a cheerful sparrow; Roane Best, next to Natalie; and Swift, a director with nothing to direct in this odd slice of cinema verite. Finally, there was the odd man out, the retired sheriff Danny Jenkins, who Cherokee called on to fill in the crucial background.

The puppet master was the half-breed, daughter of Roy Blige and the Indian woman, Enola Blige, a suspect union of mostly respectable people who, in essence, left the reservation. In this case, it was a damn good thing. Enola Blige had flown in from Denver at her daughter's invitation. Cherokee and Enola had become quite close over the years. Her romance between Roy had, indeed, been star-crossed but had flickered brightly for that moment in time. She had attended Roy's funeral, making no announcement. Only Wilkie Blige, her patron saint, knew she was there, and this afternoon, seated side-by-side, they were in the audience, as anxious as anyone to see what Cherokee had created.

Television dead time, with no action, is like the stillness of a church funeral as the body is being viewed by a line of tearful mourners. There was cold white noise. There was the hushed whispering of an anxious audience, the shifting legs of a seated but eye-wandering audience. There was that chirp from the sparrow who was still present and gathering in the unusual scene. He, or maybe she, seemed to have become rather comfortable on its various perches, flitting here and there high above this collection of diverse interests.

All eight participants, the actors one might say, kept eyes on Cherokee, waiting and wondering her cue for something to happen-- anything. Air time is expensive. Purvis's ad team had paid $250,000 for four 60 second spots. Roane had squeezed an equal amount out of the Fairleigh budget while NBC chipped in a cool half-million on its What's Happening Now gamble.

Then, the awkward silence was broken. It startled the audience.

There was a piercing burst of a melodic electric guitar, a haunting riff, a song Jeremy realized he had composed 15 years earlier. It was called "Rolling On" and the ultimate line went "pay no attention to the signs ahead, roll me to the end of the road I said, rolling on." The solo was being performed by the shaggy-haired Brian May, Queen's lead guitarist. The music reverberated through the cavernous theater with May blasting out the soulful ballad from one of the private balconies in the theater.

The music went on for sixty seconds with May taking a bow at the end. This orchestration didn't happen by accident. May had agreed to be a more mature spokesman for Periwinkle's Pink undershorts for men. May, well into his 70s, was a long-time Purvis idol. He was not a Freddie Mercury fan, but he admired May's intellect and his journey into astrophysics. Periwinkle moved in strange and mysterious ways.

When the music concluded with a single, sustained burst of suspended chords mixed with minor notes, Cherokee stood` up and walked to the center of the circle of chairs. She spoke in her rich voice. It sounded like what molasses would be like flowing from a bottle if a soundtrack were applied.

"Welcome," she said, The audience grew quiet.

Cherokee smiled a demure, playful smile. Her dark eyes danced around the auditorium, from the first row to the last. There was not a trace of nervousness in her face and her svelte frame flowed with the modulating sounds of her voice.

"Welcome to this Hollywood edition of What's Happening Now. For those of you who have seen the program hosted by Jeremy Britnell, and his everyday side-chick, and often a thorn in his side, moi, I'm Cherokee. Yeah, what the hell, we sleep together, and I got to tell you, even after 15 years it's not a bad ride. Wow. El Diablo. But I have to be careful tonight. I've been warned by our god spirits at NBC there are certain things you can't say—those dirty words that got Lenny Bruce in trouble. Does anyone remember Lenny? After Jeremy here, Lenny's my fantasy lay, and he's been dead for my gosh, 60 years. You got nothing to worry about, Swamp Boy. I have teenagers at home in Florida tuned in. Hey, kids, we blocked the porno channel. There's either Disney or us. The beer in the refrigerator is not for you."

That was Cherokee, inching up to the boundaries of what was not proper, but only crossing it a smidgin. Britnell buried his face in his hands. Her characterization of family life was not an exaggeration. Jeremy had learned long ago to tumble with the waves and hopefully reach shore, shake the sand and move on. Mortification was not allowed.

There was a round of applause and laughter which seemed louder than the mere few hundred people in the building. In the first few seconds, she had opened the door to their lives. It was her way of saying, This is who the fuck we are and we don't have any plans to change." In television's wasteland, children were shooed to their rooms, but parental eyeballs motioned for their significant others from the kitchen to see this bizarre, live play. On the East Coast, the program had hefty competition from Entertainment Tonight, and, for news junkies, CNN's Erin Burnett was getting warmed up against the Republicans. The internet spread the new news of this freaky What's Happening Now program faster than clothesline gossip.

Cherokee introduced the seven other people on the stage. Periwinkle gave a huge wave and tossed air kisses. He turned to the audience and slipped his trousers down in the back just enough to show the product and a logo of Periwinkle Pinks, though this time they were rainbow-colored. Hell, he thought, I used my bubble gum money for five years to buy ad time. Cletus merely smiled at Cherokee and nodded his head, wondering, perhaps, what foolishness had overcome him this late in his life. Most of his colleagues from back in the day were already propping up cemetery headstones.

Johnny Swift tipped his director's cap and gave a friendly wink to the camera. Roane had an expression as if the cat had swallowed the sparrow that roamed the building. He had given a vow of secrecy to Cherokee not to reveal the denouement of the program. He held Natalie's hand, not as a sign of possession, but support. He knew what was coming before the sixty minutes expired. Sheriff Jenkins simply had a lost expression. He knew his purpose, but it was a small part of this pageant play. When his turn came, Jeremy looked perplexed, lost, and it was apparent he thought the program had already gone off the rails. Maybe they wouldn't find work—anywhere. He once bagged groceries at Krogers, and, to his knowledge, they didn't have an upper age limit. Wal-Mart could always use greeters.

Cherokee continued her expression-ladened monologue, varying her voice as if a conductor directing a symphony of woodwinds and a cello, with an occasion flute mixed in.

"Those of you who have previously watched our program know that—especially with Purvis here—it is not ordinary. It is eclectic with a dose of 1960s early psychedelic tossed in. It can be slightly profane, which is damn hard to do from our base in Central Florida—Neanderthal-villa, I call it. We specialize in surprise, though not shock. At the same time, we try to have a socially redeeming theme. Tonight is no exception, and I believe you will see we have succeeded.

" Of the eight people, including me, on the stage, four will be completely shocked, I believe, and an equal number by necessity are in on what is happening. Other than myself, this play has been constructed by my pal Purvis, my new friend Roane Best and Sheriff Jenkins without whose help this show would be a total bust. One thing we have done especially well on What's Happening Now is re-unite missing children and relatives. It has been, for a very personal reason, swamp boy here's holy mission."

Britnell was confused. This obviously had nothing to do with reuniting the Joe Hodgkins family with their little boy who has been missing for three years. Jeremy had been working overtime on that one. It had reminded him of his own tragic circumstances with Fairleigh. In this case, it was over on Florida's West Coast, and the kid had simply vanished at Tampa International Airport while the family was waiting to board a flight to New York. All that was found of the four-year-old was a stuffed animal. Each of the parents thought the other was watching him.

Britnell had invested many hours and considerable resources, both his and the station's in finding little Joe, but to no avail. If Cherokee had managed this, it would, indeed, make for an interesting episode of What's Happening Now. However, none of the guests on the show seemed to have any connection to the Hodgkins case. Britnell hid his disappointment. By the process of elimination, he figured the young actress was in for a surprise.

Natalie looked at Roane, pulled her head back in

friendly surprise, "So, mystery man, you're holding out on me. Could it be you have a wife and three kids somewhere, and this program is about to disclose it? Why would you cooperate with something like that?"

The audience laughed.

As Cherokee spoke, the spotlight captured her every move. She danced slowly in the near silence. The guitarist May played a simple melody. The one-piece corset sleeveless dress she wore was a $2,000 extravagance from Bergdorf Goodman. She often shopped at Sam's Club, for she looked just as great in a home dress. This, however, was a coming-out party, and she was dressed to the nines—especially in comparison to Jeremy in his faded jeans, black turtleneck, and low-topped white tennis shoes without socks.

"Tonight our very special guest is none other than the star of Outer Worldly, that intergalactic feature that is up for an academy award for Ms. Natalie Courant as the intrepid command module pilot."

Natalie interrupted, "Let's not go overboard, Cherokee. I never left terra firma except to squeeze into a simulator on Stage 4B at Panther Studio. The most danger I faced was being claustrophobic. Actually, I'm afraid of heights and this was Pluto and beyond high in movie-speak. As for an academy award for best actress, my gosh, I've yet to pay my dues. I'm honored to be in the same breath with Roberts, Streep, Portman, and Kidman, but the fact is I'm a tinhorn among this group, and, don't tell the studio, but I'm pulling for my friend Streep."

Cherokee carried on with Natalie in a conversational tone, almost as if they were the only two persons involved in the show.

"But, I think that's what makes you special, Natalie. You are so unassuming. You take people by surprise. You have this nice quality in what I understand is a dog-eat-dog business. Isn't that true Cletus Reed."

Reed's mind was on the developing mystery and the surprise of one's life. The cranium gears were in low. "Uh, yeah, I've been in this business before 98.8 percent of the folks in this studio was born, and I've never met a personality like Natalie. But that's why most of Hollywood will hate her. They don't understand nice. It's a foreign language. Like something in Swahili."

"Don't let me fool you. It's all fake, Cherokee," Natalie laughed. "You know my story. I'm an orphan kid who grew up in a bar in West Virginia. Even my name, Natalie Courant is an invention by my agent, right Cletus? But, please, my boyfriend Roane Best is sitting beside me and, so far, I have him fooled. Though he seems to know secrets about me that I don't."

She winked at Cherokee and showed off a hand with an engagement ring. It was not ostentatious.

"Okay, ain't that the truth," interjected Reed. "I don't know who the hell this lady is, but, for some reason, I bankrolled the Fairleigh movie. I'm too old to lose my shirt —again—so I'm counting on Natalie to sell tickets, popcorn, and those Tootsie Rolls. Okay, little miss? We have a to put butts in those seats."

"I can do that," Natalie replied. "I can also operate a popcorn machine,"

Cherokee took back control. She liked the continued repartee but felt in an hour show she had to keep it on point. "I think we have established that you two are more than agent and star. You seem great friends."

"Him? Natalie said, incredulously. "Cletus? Yeah, he's my best bud, my mentor, my North Star, my hero. I'd do porno if it would help Cletus recoup the bundle he put in The Book of Fairleigh."

"Aw shucks," Reed demurred.

The theater audience laughed. Jeremy wondered if this conversation were leading anywhere, and figured at any moment the Hodgkins family might still come on stage, as his wife announce the happy uniting with long-lost little Joe. There had to be more to the program than a mere chat between a starlet, Cherokee, and the old agent who seemed almost disinterested.

"Okay, we have a mutual admiration society," said Cherokee. "But tell me, Mr. Reed, how did you discover Natalie Courant."

"Quite by accident," replied Reed in his gravelly voice that could sound like a semi-truck. "I saw her in a local production in West Virginia of Annie Get Your Gun.

I felt she had it all. She was a dynamo on stage. So, I lobbied and got her a tryout for "Outer Worldly."

"So that was the beginning," said Cherokee, as a montage from the movie in which she was nominated for Best Actress was shown on a theater screen and to televisions around the nation.

Britnell was thinking, Oh my gosh, this program is a re-enactment of the ancient and musty, pre-color "This Is Your Life" show from the 1950s. He had seen reruns where host Ralph Edwards surprised the week's guest by opening up a big red book of his or her life. He wondered if Cherokee would pull out the red album. He had the desire to slink off the stage and go shoot pool somewhere. The only person steeped in nostalgia and old enough to remember early television was Reed. He must have had something to do with this, thought Britnell.

"But Natalie Courant has come a long way since those days back in West Virginia busing tables, singing with her band and keeping the peace at her dad's bar, the Purple Onion," droned Cherokee, then bubbled, "But as you noted Cletus, Natalie didn't start out as a Natalie. Her name at the time was, frankly, was the same as my first given name— Mary. Right?"

The question required a simple answer, but Natalie looked momentarily confused. "The truth is I don't have the any idea what my real name is," said Natalie. "I was only four, and that is what I was called by my parents. But I don't have any recollection of them. They evidently tired of me. I was abandoned, fortunately, at the Purple Onion.

From what I understand they were really weird."

Cherokee turned to Danny Jenkins, the former Kanawha County sheriff, "And what happened then-Sheriff Jenkins?"

The retired sheriff picked up the story. He had an authoritative voice. "Sadly, we don't know anything about Natalie's parents. Their van ran off the Interstate not more than 20 miles outside Charleston and burst into flames. There was nothing left of the parents or the van. It was a horrific fire. There wasn't even a vehicle identification number."

Cherokee turned once again to Natalie. "It was so fortunate this couple, whoever they were, didn't take you with them. I understand the man who later adopted you, Charlie Jones, had something to do with that."

"Yes, I've been told the story many times, but, in truth, I know nothing of it first hand," said Natalie. "I am told I have repressed memories, and that it might someday come to me—but not now."

"Natalie, What's Happening Now is a program about surprises, hope, and dreams for a reunion. It doesn't always work out that way. Sometimes, the truth hurts. However, we can be certain the couple who left you at the Purple Onion that night were not your parents."

Turning to Natalie, "Natalie, would you like to find out who your parents are? Would you like to know they didn't abandon you?"

Natalie was hesitant. "I, I don't know…I didn't come here today with this in mind. If you have some idea, do I really want to know at this late date, after more than 15 years? I honor Charles and Beverly Jones as my parents and I am sure I always will."

Cherokee lowered her voice, playing both to the television audience and to those in the theater. "This is understandable. With the aid of Mr. Best, we were able—without your knowledge—to obtain a DNA test from you. But, again, do you really want to know?"

Natalie's eyes were popped wide. She shook her head yes and no all in the same moment. "I guess I am curious," she said softly. However, she was not ready for the curtain to be pulled and a stranger to step out and expect a hug.

Jeremy vacated his rather lackadaisical pose and sat up straight in his chair. Cherokee had stirred him from his doldrums. Had his wife, indeed, pulled off a coup with Natalie Courant. Ratings would skyrocket for the show. He wondered, why hadn't she let him in on this? They had no secrets when it came to the show's production over these many years. Well, I guess, the little Joe Hodgkin's story will have to wait. He would have been upset if he wasn't now thoroughly engrossed in the unfolding tale.

For a moment, Cherokee left Natalie dangling, purposefully. She was summoning her theatric heft to milk the right emotions from the story. She turned to Cletus Reed.

"Cletus, what was it about The Story of Fairleigh that made you think this was a movie where Natalie would be a perfect fit," she asked. Reed was on the edge of his chair. He had questioned whether a television show prior to the film's premiere was even a good idea. Now, he was interested in where this was going.

"I was captured by Mr. Britnell's dialogue, though I didn't know it was his writing at the time," said Reed. "It had a magic, but truthful quality to it. I knew exactly what he wanted for this little girl, and how he hoped she would maneuver through life. It wasn't a selection on a whim. I knew Natalie would be perfect for the part of Fairleigh."

Reed suddenly stopped talking. He took a deep breath. A tear formed in the corner of his left eye. He took a handkerchief from his pocket and dabbed both of them. It was an unusual experience for him. He was not an overly emotional man. He executed movie deals for clients as if he were a stone-faced croupier at a Vegas blackjack table. Inside, he was a chick flick weeper, but on the outside his steely blues were icy.

"I'm only being partially honest. The little girl, Fairleigh, had green eyes. My Caroline also had green eyes. She was killed years ago at a street crossing not far from here by a hit-and-run driver. She would be about 20 years older than Natalie now. I realize that's no reason to bet the farm on movie production. But, what the hell, believe or not, I can be a sentimental cuss."

Natalie knew the story. She wore a pearl necklace Cletus had given her, one that his daughter had worn to her high school prom. She knew how Caroline died at an intersection near Pinks Hotdog Emporium. She left her chair, and walked over, and knelt beside her agent. She whispered the same words she did the day he gave her the jewelry. "I love you, Cletus," she said.

Though it seemed improper at the time, the audience felt compelled to applaud and to sniffle. It was a television moment that would have made Oprah smile.

Cherokee continued: "So now we know the backstory, and that not all stories on What's Happening Now have happy endings. But many can and do. I believe this one will.

"No, Natalie. The man and wife who fled the Purple Onion after leaving you there—and, by the way—they didn't pay the bill, were named Joshua and Ruth Johns. They were an itinerant couple who made a living off cons and scams. Their fate was the accident that night, veering off the highway into a tree. You were so fortunate not to be with them when they left the bar. How do we know this? Excellent question, uh Mr. Purvis Periwinkle?"

Purvis came alive. "In another day, another hour, a time when law enforcement had better computers without so many glitches and electrical currents weren't being taxed, it would have been a relatively simple solution and the ill-fated Johns would be in federal prison and not burnt to a crisp on a stretch of West Virginia highway."

The underwear king's penchant for drama had kicked in.

"It started, strangely enough, when I began looking into the whereabouts of Jeremy's missing manuscript The Book of Fairleigh. The book had been found in an abandoned storage facility by someone who pawned it off as their own work. Mr. Reed saw the book in the two-dollar sale bin of a bookstore and became interested in it. I was able to track it to my friend Cletus and get Jeremy's name properly installed as the rightful author. But that's just part of the story."

Purvis halted his explanation long enough to have his words sink in, not so much to a television or theater audience, but to certain individuals in the stage circle. Jeremy had cocked his head to the side, listening intently. The cobwebs from times long ago were being swept away, held by singular strands. Natalie wondered where the story was going. It was like the opening Britnell song by Brian May, Rolling On. There appeared to be little notice of warning signs ahead.

In the theater audience, there was total silence. Someone dropped a paper cup, and only it caused a stir. Even the sparrow had stopped chirping, having found a perch of its satisfaction. Who's to tell of the television audience? One can only assume they anxiously awaited a resolve, gnawing fingernails.

"Please Purvis, go on. You have millions on the edge of their seats," said Cherokee, beckoning with her arms.

"What can I say Cherokee, you and Jeremy are my best friends and I came into Jeremy's life at a particularly tragic time for him and his late wife, Sarah. He had helped me out when I was figuratively lost, and I felt I owed him big-time," he said. "His child had been kidnapped. His wife died, in reality, of heartbreak. But, I have to tell you, it was Cherokee who really was his lifesaver. I simply wanted to help plug that big hole in his heart."

He had stopped to take a breath. The audience held theirs. Jeremy's eyes were saucers.

"Fact is, 460,000 children, go missing each year in the United States. Most are minor incidents, family members kidnapping another family member. Most, even runaways, eventually return—and, of course, Fairleigh was only four years old. Fairleigh became a statistic, and through a consequence of bad luck, a measure of incompetence, and simply poor law enforcement tracking, she was not found. I simply retraced the steps. It's all part of the What's Happening Now service. And I want to thank Sheriff Jenkins for his work with me on this."

Jeremy had risen from his seat. He wasn't believing what he was hearing. He looked over at Natalie, and she at him. It was mostly a scared, uncertain glare.

"What the hell are you saying, Purvis. That this actress playing Fairleigh in a movie is actually Fairleigh, my daughter?"

Natalie had gone limp. She once had parents she never really knew. She had kidnappers for her parents for several weeks. Charlie and Beverly Jones were her most solid connection to having a family. Then, there was Cletus

Reed, who she thought of as a loving grandparent or Uncle. She was confused, but at the same time felt a connection with Jeremy Britnell meeting him alone on the stage earlier, and when she had read The Book of Fairleigh.

Cherokee took back over the program which was bumping up to its one hour.

"Jeremy, love, swamp boy who stole my heart if not my virginity on your sorry excuse for a floating tub 15 years ago, the one who gave us two great kids, to go with your wonderful Fairleigh. It is all true, proven by DNA tests, and something you might recognize if you ever changed Fairleigh's diaper as a child, a birthmark on her butt in the shape of a big alligator. As they say in court, 'indisputable evidence'. Oh, and then there's the emerald bracelet you and Sarah gave her as a child. She's wearing it now as a pendant."

Jeremy remembered. He choked up and turned away from the cameras.

Then, Natalie Courant did something no one expected. The relatively modest Ms. Courant pulled a Purvis. She pulled down her jeans in front of the audience, revealing Pink Periwinkles.

And then, she pulled them down to her lower thigh and that old alligator was yawning big and wide. She pulled them back up and walked over to Cletus Reed. She took him by the hand and walked him over to Jeremy.

"Cletus, my great friend," she said softly. "Meet my

daddy. He goes by the name Jeremy Britnell.

CHAPTER 35
AND IN CONCLUSION:
ALL'S WELL THAT ENDS WELL

Cletus Reed

Cletus Reed didn't die, at least not until he was 97. His old dog, Sammy predeceased him. It made him sad, but Natalie made him a present of Sam II, a frisky Brittany Spaniel puppy.

His death certificate cited "natural causes" as the reason for his demise since old age was not an official medical term for departure. Cletus would have been disappointed. It wasn't an interesting exclamation to a well-lived life. He would have preferred a memorable, exotic disease.

However, with his late-in-life success, Cletus suddenly had a new project on his hands, and that kept him churning his legs and his mind. It was pre-production on a sequel to The Book of Fairleigh, which, in essence, was the next chapter and not truly a sequel.

It was both truth and maybe a little fiction, a mite Hollywood-ized for commercial consumption, though the elements were all pre-ordained.

Reed convinced Jeremy Britnell it would only work if both a book and the screenplay were written by the same person, Jeremy. Britnell pretended disinterest for an hour but talked to Cherokee.

"Jeremy, you are a writer. As a TV host, you're okay, but then if you painted fences for the city of Orlando, you would be okay. Fate gave you this break you dreamed about. Do it," she said.

That's all the encouragement he needed. Within the hour, Jeremy called Cletus back. His words were, "Mr. Reed, I will try not to disappoint you. Sign me up."

The Natalie Courant story as unveiled on the What's Happening Now Hollywood version quickly became a national and worldwide sensation. Every news outlet from CBS's 60 Minutes to Al Jazeera clamored for interviews.

Reed's movie, The Book of Fairleigh, was a game-changer for the movie industry. Many studios wanted Reed for his subtle visual plays, as opposed to disaster flicks and detective shoot-em-ups. Drawing room dramas with a touch of pizzaz were the most coveted scripts. Sure, they were a little dated but the movie-going crowd was ready for a little schmaltz,

The Fairleigh movie made a lot of money. Panther

Studios even did well with negotiated rights when given a date certain for cable distribution. They didn't need the dough, but Spielberg and Scorsese earned playing-around money.

Panther studio's Lee Atkinson III asked Reed to become chairman emeritus of the studio at the request of his board. The studio was eyeing the upcoming Fairleigh sequel and seeing another hit. They didn't want it going to a competing studio.

Before he would accept the title—which was largely ceremonial—Reed told Atkinson he had to have total creative control with absolutely no interference from Panther on the Fairleigh second act. There were a couple of other criteria: Johnny Swift, his career revived, would be the director, Natalie would play herself and Purvis Periwinkle would make a great Purvis Periwinkle. Finally, he asked the studio to shelve Outer Worldly II. His client had out-grown it.

Atkinson swallowed his pride, and the studio readily agreed to his requests.

One day, shortly after the premiere of The Book of Fairleigh, Reed jumped into his 1958 Caddy and drove to Hollywood Memorial Park Cemetery. He wanted to have a private conversation with his late wife, Abigail, and their daughter, Caroline, who rested side-by-side.

"I'm going to be a little bit longer in joining you. But I know you both like a good yarn. Let me tell you about a girl named Fairleigh. She has green eyes just like you,

Caroline."

Purvis Periwinkle

Purvis had outgrown his cocoon, but it had not outgrown him. He was becoming a celebrity in his own right, even more famous than the naked cowboy in Times Square.

He had made more money than his Grandmother Gladys would dream possible. He certainly outshone his namesake, the long-dead vaudevillian Purvis Periwinkle.

His mother, if she knew he existed, would re-own him.

But Purvis wanted to remain in the What's Happening Now fold. Everything else was a side gig. Eventually, he realized, Periwinkle's Pink briefs would be yesterday's fashion, sort of like 1950s calypso pants. He had a home with the TV program.

The program was going national. Its one-shot debut impressed the NBC brass, and sponsors for the official launch were lining up for those 30-second slices of commercial confetti. The question was could the program pull rabbits out of the hat every week? It was doubtful they could birth blockbusters such as the Fairleigh story at will.

However, leads flooded in. Periwinkle, already a

partner in the program, was given the title of executive producer to pull storylines together. He had a knack for it. One day, he got a telephone call from Little Joey Hodgkins, missing for more than a year.

The boy, now seven, managed to telephone Purvis who listed his semi-personal number in chyron on each program. He didn't handle all the inquiries himself, but they were filtered through an assistant. If they looked promising, she put them directly through to Periwinkle.

Little Joey had slipped away from the woman who had insisted he call her mommy. He had seen the Hollywood edition of What's Happening Now and wanted desperately to be back with his parents. He was at a 7-11 store off Orlando's Orange Blossom Trail.

"Stay put son. Purvis Periwinkle is coming after you," he said.

Then, he called the Hodgkins' family.

"Your boy is coming home," He loved saying that line.

Fairleigh Britnell-Best

Natalie Courant didn't win Best Actress for "Outer Worldly".

She wasn't disappointed. She was honored that Meryl Streep, who did win, made a special mention of the young actress at the awards ceremony.

In her speech, Ms. Streep looked into the future. "My guess is that young Natalie Courant will be holding this magnificent statue twelve months from now," she said.

She was right.

A year later The Book of Fairleigh—based on Jeremy's book and Cletus Reed's screenplay—won best picture and Natalie won best actress. Johnny Swift was honored as best director.

Not long after the Fairleigh premier, Natalie, along with Roane Best, appeared on the boat dock leading to what was now a 91 foot Hatteras Motor Yacht, the pride of the Indian River on Merritt Island.

She didn't call him dad, or papa, merely Jeremy, or sometimes in jest, Swamp Boy. But then, she never addressed Charlie Jones as papa, and the saloon owner was happy with simply Charlie.

She had had a complicated, topsy-turvy 21 years. Who knew what was in store for her future. She didn't want in any way to leave her past behind, but circumstances suggested she not dwell on what had been.

Natalie would always wonder if something unexpected would interrupt happiness. She clung close to Roane, who was her anchor.

She and Cherokee hit it off, more like sisters, erasing a twenty-year-plus age difference. They all drove into Orlando one weekend to visit theme parks with Jon and Enola, who both protested that they had outgrown Disney entertainment.

Natalie spent the next few weeks hanging out on the boat's bow with Jeremy, waiting for the sunset. They discussed many things, including Sarah and what she was like.

"I wish she knew you now Natalie," said Jeremy.

She reached over to him. "My name is Fairleigh Britnell-Best. I am so happy to meet you."

Jeremy and Cherokee

Cherokee was right as rain. Jeremy was not meant to be a television host on his wandering way through a rather interesting life. He was a writer: A damn good one.

The Book of Fairleigh was his first hit, but more were to follow, including the next chapter in the Fairleigh saga. Jeremy's edition of The Book of Fairleigh became a No. 1 New York Times Best Seller with the release of the movie.

Jeremy stepped aside as co-host of the program he

founded with his wife, only making occasional guest appearances. He devoted himself to writing the sequel to his first Book of Fairleigh. Predictably it was called What's Happening Now, the True Story

On the other hand, Cherokee was a natural for the program. No one knew what thought would come from her curious mind or what words would flow from her mouth. It kept an audience on edge. Though the conservative radio talking heads complained mightily, she always responded with a short retort: Fuck-em.

Tee-shirts were printed. They read, "Cherokee says Fuck-em." She had become a national personality and must-watched television.

Things were not always lily fields and buttered popcorn at the Jeremy household. Given the nature of the two inhabitants, there were firecracker explosions from time to time and an occasional nuclear blast.

But, the storyline was real and continued. It was considered one of the most successful of celebrity marriages—sort of like Paul Newman and Joanne Woodward's had been.

Jeremy, who worked from the couple's boat on the Indian River, came into the salon area one day to find a picture of his late wife, Sarah. His wife had put it in a prominent place.

"Swamp boy, I love that woman. She brought us together. We're all going to Dallas someday. I'd love to meet her in person," said Cherokee. "But later. Right now we're having too much fun."

The End

Made in the USA
Middletown, DE
30 January 2022

59977026R10245